PERFECT TOGETHER

OTHER BOOKS BY NORA JOHNSON

FICTION

The World of Henry Orient
A Step Beyond Innocence
Love Letter in the Dead-Letter Office
The Two of Us
Tender Offer
Uncharted Places

NON-FICTION

Pat Loud: A Woman's Story
Flashback: Nora Johnson on Nunnally Johnson
You Can Go Home Again

NORA JOHNSON

P·E·R·F·E·C·T
T·O·G·E·T·H·E·R

A WILLIAM ABRAHAMS BOOK

DUTTON

DUTTON

Published by the Penguin Group
Penguin Books USA Inc., 375 Hudson Street,
New York, New York 10014, U.S.A.
Penguin Books Ltd, 27 Wrights Lane,
London W8 5TZ, England
Penguin Books Australia Ltd, Ringwood,
Victoria, Australia
Penguin Books Canada Ltd, 2801 John Street,
Markham, Ontario, Canada L3R 1B4
Penguin Books (N.Z.) Ltd, 182-190 Wairau Road,
Auckland 10, New Zealand

Penguin Books Ltd, Registered Offices:
Harmondsworth, Middlesex, England

First published by Dutton, an imprint of New American Library,
a division of Penguin Books USA Inc.
Distributed in Canada by McClelland & Stewart Inc.

First Printing, July, 1991
1   3   5   7   9   10   8   6   4   2

 REGISTERED TRADEMARK—MARCA REGISTRADA

LIBRARY OF CONGRESS CATALOGING-IN-PUBLICATION DATA:

Johnson, Nora.
    Perfect together / Nora Johnson.
        p.   cm.
    "A William Abrahams book."
    ISBN 0-525-93316-6
    I. Title.
PS3519.O2833P47   1991
813'.54—dc20   90-25929
                                                   CIP

Printed in the United States of America
Set in Goudy Old Style

Designed by Steven N. Stathakis

PUBLISHER'S NOTE

■

To my grandsons,
Nick and Ian

■

PERFECT
TOGETHER

O·N·E

· 1 ·

ONCE I HAD IT ALL: ENERGY, HOPE, ENTHUSIASM. I KNEW ALL the answers. My hair was a dark and shining cap, like the shoes on my narrow feet, the dress like a satin slip I wore the night I met Charlie. I worked all day, danced all night, drank wine, ate hearty, and never gained an ounce. It seemed whatever I wanted I got, till the day the gold ran out.

Charlie was new to New York. A physicist, he'd left his job in DC for a private corporation here, which gave him more freedom for his research. It didn't take him long to decide he wasn't going back—with a little help from me. Our backgrounds were very different; he'd grown up in an Ohio town. But I think it was that very difference, and the tension we shared, that drew us together.

I'm restless, nervous, throwing off pointless sparks, pawing the ground impatiently. Charlie was, then, quiet, deliberate, very concentrated, with piercing eyes—"Scorpio eyes," my mother called them. I sensed something deep as a well and thought, He'll never leave me—though that might have been a wish or a prayer. What I really felt was his focus, his ability to hang on and not let go. That, I knew, was what I wanted.

It was when the city still glittered: the mica in the side-walks, the careless shine of everything on wet nights. It was all

3

for Charlie and me—and we were perfect together. Walking those wet streets, clinging to each other, running the last block toward home, I'd never felt so free and supple, so confident. First we lived together, very romantic and daring then, and quite soon decided it would be crazy, or sinful, or even unintelligent not to marry. So we did, at City Hall, with a gang of friends cheering us on, then celebrated afterward at Maxwell's Plum.

I'd taken charge of him, showing him around and introducing him to my friends. I pulled him out of himself; he quieted me down. He entered parties cautiously, usually talking to one or two people the whole time; I toured the room, prattling and bitching. But he would have made a new friend, while I clung to the old crowd; he came home with something new he'd learned, while I complained of boredom, saying I'd be hung, drawn, and quartered before ever going to another cocktail party. At the same time I knew, perhaps more than he did, how important our friends were, for we had no family around—no loving aunt to invite us to the country for Thanksgiving; parents who were, most of the time, voices on the phone. Charlie and I needed each other a lot, and for years we knew, without really talking about it, that a third person would throw our perfect balance off in ways we couldn't even predict.

I rationed my time carefully. I kept my priorities straight. I wasted no energy on unimportant things, always aimed for perfection. But my attention was scattered as I tried to cover all the bases. In a curious way I even considered inattention a desirable modus operandi, though I would have denied it, as would my friends. "Oh, I don't have time, I don't have a minute," we were always saying. Our lives were contests in obsessive busyness. It was almost a sickness. On a Sunday visit to the Frick, that isle of solemn peace, Charlie looked at paintings while I mentally argued an approaching case; then, on the way home, I made myself think about what I told myself I'd seen at the Frick. Everything was subject to this triage of attention, and the less important things, like the small balls, ended up at the bottom.

Arthur Zeus, my brilliant, terrible ex-boss, once said, "Nobody who works for me gets pregnant. I've considered requiring sterilization of all my female employees." It wasn't clear

4

whether he was joking. I'd been warned of the job's heavy obligations when he hired me. "You work twenty-four hours of the day, Ms. Letterman. Even when you're asleep your mind will be working on the day's unsolved problems." I was thrilled! Zeus & Wenberg was one of the top firms in the city. I would have done anything he told me to, including not get pregnant. We all laughed when he said it. I didn't think about it—I don't think.

Later, Charlie reminded me: "You were never crazy about the idea, Fran, especially after an evening with the Hellers," whose apartment smelled of curdled milk and rang with infant cries. "And I wasn't either; you'd charmed me with your stylish doings. You'd made my life an adventure. I never wanted it to end. I knew a baby would stop it all dead."

But the idea haunted all of us. The women had hushed-voice lunches. Terry was afraid a baby would turn her into her own neurotic mother, Pam and Julio couldn't afford it. I said I'd consider it if we had the social programs they had in Sweden—flextime, maternity leave, on-site day care. Or a full-time nanny wouldn't be so bad. Jill, her voice trembling, confessed that Alex did want one, but, "I'm so afraid of losing myself after all the struggle, I don't know what we're going to do."

To be fair, the mothers at Baby Heller's first birthday party did not seem as miserable as might be expected. Harassed, yes. Tired. A little dowdy in their blue jeans and nursing bras. But cheerful and shockingly unenvious of my fine free life. One even recommended a certain downtown fertility clinic, assuming the choice was not mine. I laughed as I went back down the stairs, parenthood having reduced the Hellers to a walk-up in a West Side brownstone. How long ago it seems!

Charlie and I settled into my rent-controlled apartment in the East Fifties. Four good-sized rooms, fireplace, beautiful ceiling moldings, and brass doorknobs—two hundred a month. There had been a marital collapse and hasty exit in 9B and I'd walked into the building at the right moment. I did it all in pale gray and navy blue, very cool, very city. How I loved that apartment! I took my time, didn't rush, waited till I could get exactly what I wanted for the first time ever. I wanted a few perfect things, and my taste was precise and finite. Expensive, yes. The carved church door I had shipped back from Venice, where my mother lives, cost a fortune. But each time I walked into my living room, it gave me just a hint of the deep and solemn peace of Italian churches, as close to religion as I ever got.

Later, I'd walk in the door as though entering a tomb. The study: the polished desk; the teak shelves where the books, the television, and the stereo fitted so nicely; the framed prints—soon they would all be stuffed around in other places to make room for a crib and a bunch of teddy bears. Well, this was what we wanted. But there would go my perfection, my solemn calm—just what *I* wanted. Never again! How strange it was that just as I had established myself, I elected to give it away to a strange, small, disruptive person. (But if I hadn't, then what? What would be the point of anything?)

As it turned out, the room was never made into a nursery because we moved to Rivertown.

"I've never gotten over that apartment," I told Dr. Bread. "I will always love it. The whole trouble started when we left there, I know"—which was what I thought that week.

"Ah! Every session a new moment when the trouble started! And each time a little earlier. And when will we be back to when the trouble really started?"

I knew what real start Bread was after. Five minutes after I was born, when I was rolled in a blanket instead of being enfolded in my mother's arms. When she failed to put me to her breast, out of vanity, but handed me over to a nurse who dispensed bottles. When she failed to comfort me enough at my father's funeral . . . when she packed me off to school in the country . . . moved in a lover, carelessly allowed him to steal all her money. I know the list Bread loves, the list of hopelessness.

"Of course you were conflicted about having children. You did not have one single example of positive mother love. What does your Lulu admire? Fun! Kicks! Astrology magic! The aggressive qualities you try to supply since she has none of her own." (Bread's theory.) "As a woman she's a washout: hysterical, unrealistic, pointless. What has she ever achieved?"

"She lives in a palazzo."

"A palazzo! This is to be admired? Anything else?"

6

"Well, she had me. That's not so useless. Not so bad."

"Oh, no? From what I hear it is not to be counted. I am only quoting you. She should have been rich too. And all-suffering."

I knew his game. Throw the worst things I said back in my face. "I was talking about the apartment. *You* brought Lulu into it."

"She is already in it, which you know very well. This is not court."

Court. That was where I could speak, tease out the truth, move people to where I wanted them to be. There I wrapped myself in a silver veil no one could penetrate. I'd worked hard to become a good divorce lawyer, my specialty at the time.

"In the apartment everything was calm. The light was silvery when it slanted in the French windows onto the rug and the carved door. It was on the back and not noisy. There I was happy. I don't know why we ever left."

"You know."

More tears, which had brought me to his door. On and on they went. "I did it for Charlie. I did everything for Charlie."

Somebody had told me about Bread. I chose him over the sleek cobra psychopharmacologist, the bright chipper behavior modification therapist, and the damp-eyed hypnotist in maroon whom I weepingly interviewed. Something about this morose anachronism in nubby brown tweed, cold pipe, and nameless accent won me. His office is in someone's converted stable out near Morgan's Hill Cemetery. I go there three times a week and the insurance covers it.

· 2 ·

I REMEMBER THE EVENING CLEARLY. PALAZZO GRIGIO, WHERE Lulu my mother lives, is not on the Grand Canal but on a small one in Cannaregio, over near the Ghetto Nuovo. Nor is it really a palazzo but an antique Venetian house, part of which is let to a tenant. It rises up sheer and mossy over the dark lapping waters below, facing a narrow street on the other side. A wrought-iron balcony with pots of geraniums abuts my mother's bedroom; by the kitchen window is a little niche containing a mosaic of Jesus and the Virgin Mary. The neighborhood is quiet, frequented mainly by longtime inhabitants whose needs are largely taken care of by the local shops and restaurants and the undistinguished church in the simple square. One night, in that square, sat a young mother nursing her baby and . . . our eyes met. I'd found someone who had something I didn't.

I was thirty-six then, Charlie thirty-four. He, Lulu, and I were coming home from a dinner whose price would probably have fed the mother and her child for a month. Full of scampi and pasta, as well as a couple of bottles of Gavi, we capered along singing "Funiculi Funicula," which is the sort of thing my mother enjoys, though not too loudly for this is a quiet neighborhood. Into the square, past the church, toward the *caffè*—and there was the young olive-skinned madonna, her white dress pulled down over one breast, sitting in the shadow by the old fountain. Her deep eyes watched us as the baby's small head moved in its rhythmic, primal pulse. She might have come right out of a Raphael except for the can of soda in her hand, a kind of orange squash you saw everywhere, whose noxious color shone iridescently in the darkness. In another mood I would have been disapproving of the stuff she was pouring into her body and that of her child. But that evening I knew it was somehow transformed to nectar.

Lulu's maid, Giulia, was serving our coffee and rolls the next morning as I stared thoughtfully at Charlie. Always handsome, he got better-looking with the years—and at that time I considered us to be approaching middle age. Lulu was peeling an orange with her long double-jointed fingers, the peel hanging down in a spiral as instructed by some waiter.

"You're so pensive, Francesca." I smiled. "You used to have the same expression in front of the toy store. The little girl who can't wait for Christmas."

The little girl, never *her* little girl! In her multicolored silky bathrobe, Lulu hunched on her elbows, her long streaked hair tied back with a ribbon. One of the cats, Marcello, purred against her still-handsome bare leg.

"You were never around at Christmas, Lulu."

"Oh! Where was I, then?"

"Out dancing or something. Anywhere but with me."

Lulu froze, and Charlie lowered the book he'd been reading.

"Want to go back to bed, Fran?" he asked. "Get up and start again?"

"No. Sorry, it just popped out." I glanced at her. Why did I do it? The film couldn't be rewound or replayed. A fight might have helped, but Lulu refused to do it, and I always ended up with a nagging pain in my gut. She looked at me for a minute, then picked up the cat.

"You were a dark, mysterious child, Fran. And now you're becoming a bitter unhappy woman, and over nothing." And she walked out of the dining room, which in the palazzo took a long time, with much clicking of clogs across the marble floor and more from the hall, till she reached the tattered rug on the stairs. Through the open shutters I heard the *slush-slush* of the oily green water as a boat went by. Charlie turned a page.

"I love her," I said to the coffeepot. "Why do I say these things?"

"Because you don't ever *not* say things." He closed the book. "I'm going over to the piazza and buy a paper."

He stood up, scraping the chair on the stone floor. I closed my eyes as he left the room. If I had everything, why did I feel, sometimes, as though everybody else had something I didn't, something I desperately wanted but couldn't put my finger on? I took a deep breath.

"I'll go with you, Charlie," I called, running after him. "There's something I want to talk to you about."

Bread never even asked me about suddenly wanting, after years of *not* wanting, a baby. Simply the tick of the clock! Weren't a million women in my position? So we want it all, what's wrong with that? This is America! There must be a way to have everything, it's just a question of finding out how. And don't we deserve it, after all those years of being mistreated by men?

Bread never asked the really hard questions; I doubt if he even thought of them. When you say you want to have a baby, Miss Jones, Miss Letterman, Mrs. Morse, is the emphasis on

9

have or *baby*? For you don't really *have* it, you know. Consider the words of Kahlil Gibran, who called a baby an honored guest in the house. It's all give and not much take, and it goes on for the rest of your life. So really you want to *give selflessly* to a *borrowed* baby—not quite as appealing!—and one that might return your generosity by growing up into a charmless person or by leaving you quite coldly . . . returning only (if you are lucky) for guilt-ridden visits or managing to be halfway around the world the day you draw your last breath.

But I didn't know that. A few perfectly chosen things now included a baby.

This happy decision also delivered me from guilt for hurting Lulu's feelings. How the Palazzo Grigio lit up! Hugs, kisses, a bottle of champagne, then a celebratory dinner on the roof of the Hotel Danieli where we thought of names, discussed schools, planned birthday parties and visits to Grandma as though I were already pregnant. We lurched drunkenly back through San Marco, stopping for a brandy, and then on home, where I threw my diaphragm out the window into the canal and we made love for the first time with nothing between us.

Something changed for us, though I can hardly say what. We'd never been so close or so loving. There was a kind of sanctity to our lovemaking now that it embraced the future. We looked deeper than ever into each other's shining eyes. Maybe this time, this egg, this triumphant sperm!

When we told our friends back in New York, something went between the men. They shifted their weight from one leg to the other, smiled down at their wineglasses, caught each other's eyes. Paul Heller put his hand on Charlie's shoulder and said to hurry up, his son needed a friend. And Alex Lehmann said, "It'll be good for Fran." I remember standing at a bar one summer evening, late-afternoon sun pouring in as we contemplated parenthood: six of us out to dinner together, the suntanned women in pale linen, the men in summer jackets and bare necks, the icy drinks on the massive oak bar, iris and snapdragons in big white vases. It was a familiar scene; we went out for dinner all the time.

But the evening we announced that we were "trying" . . .

something flowed between the three men, something mellow and amber and sexy, an authority, a secret fraternal knowledge, a specialness and difference between them and us that had never been there before. Usually we were all chums, all on the same plane, living the same lives, like a bunch of kids playing in the sandbox. But now, parents. . . . Parents? No, it wasn't even that. It was this dramatic thing we were about to do that divided us up, fenced the women off into an unfamiliar category. What strange waters!

What happened to Charlie was still hidden, so subtle I didn't see it at the time. I became self-conscious, almost shy, in love all over again—though for years our gestalt had been one of easy best friends. Now I missed him during the day, even sending him a red rose or singing to him over the phone. I bought lingerie in navy blue lace, creamy satin sheets, and Rigaud candles. I greeted him in soft light, jazz on the stereo, wine in the bucket. If one of us couldn't get home, we made love at dawn. Had any woman ever been as in love as I was, or as lucky? Certainly not Lulu, I thought, with her string of lovers, her lonely old age with only the stars for company.

"You were happy with the prospect of at last being a voo-man," said Bread.

But wrong! I was already a voo-man—because I had a voom! I was happy with Charlie's and my new romance, our new difference. My best friend and close companion had taken on a new sheen of depth and mystery or—forgive me—dominance. And so glorious was this, so unexpected, that I was startled when Charlie wondered, after a year or so had passed, why I wasn't pregnant. I'd almost forgotten!

First there was the sperm count. Then the postcoital test. The basal body temperature chart. The X rays, the laparoscopy, the endometrial biopsy. Dr. Lamborghini looked at the results and shrugged.

"There's nothing wrong with either of you, Fran. But—you both work hard, get stressed. I tell my patients to go on a vacation. Try to turn your heads off."

So we went to Bermuda and spent most of the time in bed. We went to Stowe but hardly skiied; we borrowed a friend's house on the Cape and only sailed once. Then we stopped because we were getting tense about missing work.

In the doctor's office, I waited in the stirrups while Charlie went into the bathroom to "fantasize," with the help of the nudie magazines in the rack, and thereby "produce the specimen" which was then injected into my waiting vagina. After several months of this (Charlie had started bringing his own nudie magazines, having read the old ones cover to cover) they tried ovulating agents, which produced a couple of doomed pregnancies, dark odorous wastes I was supposed to collect and return to the doctor's office. Inspecting one with a beating heart, I saw four curled little fish, or did I dream it? I know I had a dream about four Charlie-faced, Fran-faced fish swimming in a fish tank in the study.

I got on it the way I did on a case. I put my head down and ran with it, obsessively, single-mindedly, for I'd found that was how things got done. I started in the library, moved on to the phone and a bulging file. I talked to doctors and other infertile women. When I found an especially well-rated clinic, I signed us up for more tests. I was good at such steely concentration.

But the rusty spots of blood kept appearing. I coldly scrutinized my body in the full-length mirror. Any differences? Breasts changed? Was the belly I'd kept so flat starting to soften? I might not be menstruating; I could be pregnant and bleeding. It had been known to happen. I gave up my aerobics class, stopped smoking and drinking. When I turned forty my determination doubled. I truly believed I could do anything I set my mind to, that hard work and persistence paid off—my father's principles that had never failed so far. Until he died (when I was ten: suddenly, at a roulette table at Monte Carlo) he had taught me confidence every day of my life.

Arthur Zeus, who could read minds, muttered the threats I knew he wouldn't hesitate to carry out. He might have fired me right away except that I was doing well and had by then brought a million dollars' worth of business to the firm. I was moving fast and hard against the day I'd have to let up. I didn't question his judgment. He didn't need waddly lawyers with swollen ankles or lawyers on the phone with baby-sitters. I told him I understood that, but I hoped he'd give me a leave of absence.

I read about something called "in vitro fertilization," very new, very strange, and so far unsuccessful. The best clinic was in London, so we went there. An egg was removed from my ovary and put on a dish, where it awaited ravishment by Charlie's sperm. If life glimmered—which seemed unlikely—the whole fragile entity would be put into my womb to gestate. But nothing happened, and after some discussion we decided it was too expensive to try again.

As the rusty spots appeared with maddening regularity, I began to blame myself for what I saw as failure. Secretly I suspected that I was a fraud. Perhaps in my heart I didn't want a baby at all. Smart baby to refuse the sanctity of my voom! It was not safe in that dark, fell cave. The sour acid of doubt poisoned each falling egg. It was in an effort to purify myself, to castigate myself, that we left the beloved apartment, which I decided was sapping my fertility because I loved it too much. When we turned in our lease and signed the contract for the Rivertown house, I felt a crazed kamikaze excitement. There— now all my chips were down!

I told Arthur I would have a forty-five-minute commute, a very optimistic estimate. He replied that if I were one minute late, if I showed the slightest unwillingness to stay as long "as necessary" at night, if my work suffered or changed its nature, I could start cleaning out my drawers, and this only because I still didn't have any baby. I told him his doubt hurt me. Hadn't I been devoted—and devoted to him—for eight years? He only smiled.

Later I thought of that all-knowing smile. We'd moved impulsively, almost absurdly. The gods were not yet satisfied. Sacrificial acts were required. (Was this where we went wrong, did it start with the house?) We blundered into the place one bright Sunday and bought it without even haggling over the asking price. Shortly afterward, we moved into our charming, bewildering colonial, with perfect nursery and sunny country kitchen, in the sought-after Beaver Pond School District.

But what were we doing there, when did we even see it? We were up at six, sometimes not home till eight or nine.

Arthur was loading me up with complicated cases, as a test, and Charlie was hard at work on Ashtoreth, a hot whopping-new government project that took most of his time. The crates and boxes remained unpacked for weeks, then months, vast bulky shapes in the gloomy rooms like reprimands. When we were there—and often not at the same time—we wandered like ghosts, looking for the toaster or a pair of shoes. I had no experience with houses; I'd been raised in apartments and hotel rooms. None of it fell under my hand the way the city apartment had. Workmen and deliverymen would only come when I was at work, and then Arthur dumped the toughest case of my career into my lap.

Was it that? Was it the night I came home and found Charlie fuming with rage because he couldn't find his gray tweed suit? Or was it the raccoon in the kitchen, eating the trash, or the seventeenth pizza from the place near the station? Or the whole wretched combination? Whatever it was, that was when I hired Ellie.

· 3 ·

A LUCENT SATURDAY MORNING IN SPRING. CHARLIE AND I were having our coffee on the back terrace. Ellie was cleaning up the kitchen. Her pinkish face was visible through the window, and most of her hair was stuffed under a scarf.

Twenty-two Holly Lane had been transformed. Rugs were laid, chairs re-covered, a bathroom enlarged and modernized, bookshelves installed, and pictures hung. The church door was in a central spot in the living room, massive carving and renaissance brass lock standing out brilliantly in the afternoon sun. I used country colors—spring green, cream, dashes of burgundy, and deep black-brown.

I'd hired a gardener, and now ruby tulips pushed up in their bed next to the well cared-for lawn, and iris and geraniums were starting in pots on the terrace. The apples and magnolias were in glorious blossom, and the azalea hedge bloomed rich purple and red. Our lawn bordered those of our neighbors, Kerner and the Showalters, with no visible division, an oddity of our cul-de-sac. Tall beech and ash trees swayed overhead, under which I had once imagined doll picnics with tiny teacups, sprightly games of catch, snowball fights, and fall play among the leaves. Beyond, the ground sloped down to a patch of woods that bordered the river, where we'd envisioned instructive forays for berries and mushrooms.

It seemed less and less likely that I would ever be pregnant. Most of the time I was relieved, though sometimes I wistfully thought I would like a child—though of course not just any child, certainly not one like the Showalters' two sons or Ellie's pouty little brats. A daughter might be nice: one that looked exactly like me and loved me to death.

The back door banged and Ellie came out with a small tied-up plastic bag of trash, humble compared to our neighbors' great bags of popsicle boxes, giant milk cartons, and boxes of Tide. She held it firmly and matter-of-factly. Trash was trash. She was not given to wanderings such as mine. She was wearing a denim skirt and a red-and-white blouse. She looked healthy, young, attractive; when she paused to look out at the trees, probably forgetting we were there, the line of her shoulder, back, and rather broad hips curved appealingly.

We'd become friends of sorts—on my terms, of course. I'd been raised in Europe, where servants were servants. But imperious commands only caused Ellie's mouth to pucker in stubborn hurt, and I knew my mother's authority over her maid was based on something more subtle, something unavailable, possibly, to an American daughter. So I swung back and forth between bossiness and obsequiousness, coldness and chumminess. Ellie was not, after all, really a servant; she was a young woman who did domestic work. All we really had in common were bedrock female matters. She'd mentioned her easy fertility almost apologetically.

"Wish I could give you some, Miz Morse! I'm Fertile Myrtle!" At twenty-four she already had two children and had once had—voice dropping—an abortion about which she would always be guilty. Now she took her temperature every morning, or had until Bill left again, gone she didn't know where. She'd been glad when he left. It wasn't worth it. This time she was really finished.

"But what about money, Ellie?"

What was the difference? Bill managed to lose whatever he made at the tracks anyway. She'd get along. She'd been thinking about getting a small business, maybe a laundromat. But she needed a little capital. She had a brother who could maybe lend her some. She really wanted financial independence for herself and her two girls. Her hold on the economic structure, if it could be called that, was tenuous. One slip and she would fall through the bottom into the dark abyss of poverty and welfare.

My first response was to be rather cross. Why hadn't she planned? I asked clients the same question. But plan what? With what? How could she, with no money and a husband who drank, gambled, and swatted her around occasionally? Sweet-natured, a little spacey, she worked hard. I had no complaint about her. She smiled, hummed little songs, giggled at bad jokes, when she should have been frightened to death or stealing the silver. Divorce seemed to be out of the question, though I wasn't sure that would help things any.

"But Ellie, you don't have to put up with that sort of treatment just because you're a woman. There are lots of resources open to you: Gamblers Anon, Alcoholics Anonymous. The courts are finally starting to recognize the problem of battered women. You and Bill should go for couple therapy."

"Well, he's gone now, Miz Morse."

"Please call me Fran. We're both women. We have the same problems, in a way."

Her eyes widened. "Oh, now, Miz . . . Fran, I can't believe Mr. Morse ever—"

"Oh, no, Ellie. I didn't mean it literally. Charlie is an angel, the best husband in the world. I just meant *as women* . . . the whole sexist culture with its emphasis on power and violence . . . epitomized by the defense buildup of weapons that are only symbolic because, if they're ever used, that's the end of life on earth. It shows in the whole idea of dominance, which . . ."

Ellie's eyes glazed over. She turned her attention to changing the vacuum cleaner bag.

Kimberly, Ellie's five-year-old, appeared from the other side of the house. She'd asked if I minded if she brought her children sometimes, and of course I said I didn't at all. They might change our luck. She was followed by seven-year-old Jodi, a doughty child who was forever giving her sister orders. Ellie bent to retie Kimmy's hair ribbon, a sweet, unself-conscious gesture. I looked at Charlie, and he was watching her too. I couldn't get his eye. His hands holding the paper dropped a little.

She gave Kimmy's hair a final tweak and shooed her into the kitchen with the promise of a cookie. I didn't approve of her mothering methods of empty threats and shameless bribes. As she closed the door, she saw Charlie and me watching her and gave a little self-conscious giggle and shrug. She had the kind of looks that bloom early, then run off rapidly into pasty plumpness. I'd say she was just a shade past her peak then. At twenty-one, she must have cracked glass with her looks—the dark blond hair, the blue eyes and fruity coloring. She went inside. Charlie went back to his paper.

He had been doubtful at first—his mother had never had a maid. Was there so much to do, with only the two of us? But Phase Two of Ashtoreth (a satellite designed to explore the ozone layer, the greenhouse effect, and other threats to life on earth) claimed most of his attention around that time, and the improvements—dinner on time, a well-stocked refrigerator, freshly ironed shirts—were worth the doubts.

Along with order and a pleasant disposition, Ellie brought certain ineffable disturbances. I'd hoped she would free Charlie and me for whatever pleasures there were in Rivertown: tennis, long walks by the river, acquaintance with our neighbors, who by now must think us wild-eyed ghosts . . . though I hardly dared think of pregnancy. I'd imagined us doing more things together, but the truth was we were hardly ever there at the same time. I'd come home late to find him in the study working or asleep over a book, dinner plate on the floor nearby; or else he was out late and I dined alone on salad or leftovers. I sat in the kitchen looking out at the other houses, where dark shapes flitted behind curtains or a rare human figure moved quickly from car to front door, locks clicking, alarm light going on.

I didn't know, at the time, why Charlie had a new evasiveness, an uncharacteristic malaise that had nothing to do with being overworked, for he loved being overworked. Or why he sometimes avoided my eye, or why he was suddenly so passionately involved in the garden, spending all weekend driving around to nurseries for seeds and fertilizers, refusing to take me along because I might be bored. I'd never questioned him before, so I retired to bed with briefs . . . but it wasn't the way I'd pictured things at all.

Sometimes he lay awake in the darkness, hands clasped behind his head. The stillness was so deep I welcomed the occasional yowl of a cat or the swish of a car on the main road. His face was outlined in ghostly moonlight.

"Charlie, what is it? The house?"

"No, Fran."

"It's the same old thing." My heart gave a dull contraction. "The same old insoluble thing."

There was a long silence.

"Partly, Fran. But not only. It's more like a feeling of disappointment. Maybe our life in the city was too good. So now I expect you to wave your magic wand again and turn out a country version: a fire in the hearth, kids and dogs barking, the smell of an apple pie in the oven." His chest rose and fell. "A warm, welcoming house."

I sat up. *"Leave It to Beaver."*

"Maybe."

"Well, what do you expect, Charlie? What do you want me to do? Okay—we'll get a dog, okay? A big one that barks a lot. We'll adopt kids," I added desperately.

"We will not. It's my problem, Fran. It doesn't have anything to do with you."

On that note he went to sleep, but I lay awake. He'd been describing his own home—in Ohio—or the way he thought it was.

But I determined to be warm and welcoming. A few days later I picked up wine, cheese, and pâté on the way home, set them all out, and lit a fire. I found two of the wine goblets, put on the Beatles. But he didn't come home, and I spent the evening there alone, drinking up most of the wine and trying to read. I could feel the tension rise in my chest. I'd breathe deeply, push it down, forget it . . . up it came again like an angry fist.

"Where were you?" I yelled when he came in at ten-thirty.

"Take it easy! I had a meeting; then I had a bite with Dick Belden at the Oyster Bar. I told you all this, didn't I? Or did I?"

"You didn't. Or I don't remember." I followed him into the living room, where he looked at the plate of hardening cheese and darkening pâté.

"Frannie, I'm sorry." Together we took it into the kitchen, wrapped it in plastic, and put it into the refrigerator. As he closed the door he said, "You've never been like this before."

Later, the VISA slip for the Oyster Bar lay on the bureau.

I blamed the house. I hadn't been like this, I thought, not till we moved into this white colonial in this quiet, shady cul-de-sac where cars purred into driveways and newspapers landed with a slap on front walks. We had been unprepared for owning a house. It hung on us like a vast weight, demanding, insisting, forcing us to spend money on things we didn't understand: a new hot-water heater, insulation in the attic, storm windows. Besides the things that didn't show there were a hundred that did. The driveway had to be resurfaced, the trees pruned, the stair rails repaired, the wallpaper in the front hall replaced after a leak in the upstairs bathroom dripped down and ruined it.

"Well, everything's piled up," I explained. "I'm exhausted. And that damn girl is slacking off." It just popped into my head. Why had I said it? What was the matter with us anyway? Charlie and I had never sat around and waited for each other, or made each other explain. Now his grave look was frightening, a dark gap in the fabric of our lives.

"Slacking off?" he repeated, with what seemed like exaggerated anger. "She works her ass off doing all the things you don't do because *you're never here.*"

Without stopping to think about this I burst into tears. We'd both adopted the curious ethic common to new homeowners—that the country is good and the city wicked, that time was only spent in town out of brute necessity. Charlie could do some of his work on the computer at home, which I could not, giving him a certain moral superiority.

. . .

But how unreal was our country myth, as we sat alone amid our beautiful new decor or looked out at our lovely garden. Our house was a stage set with no actors and a muddy script. We had invited our city friends several times, but soon it became painfully clear that they would do anything to avoid traveling an hour for dinner and our company. Never had they come down with so much flu or had so many visitors from Europe. The exception was the Hellers, who would have come every Sunday if we'd let them, because they were always looking for some place to take the baby. But the Perskys refused to come at all, and the Lehmanns and the Moraleses had come only once, arriving at the door with the aggrieved air of people completing a forced march across Siberia. They'd gotten lost twice and been ill-treated by a gas station attendant, proving again, if it needed proving, that leaving the city was a generally poor idea. "For God's sake," they kept saying, "come back." We smiled with what we thought, we hoped, was affectionate tolerance, but what was really despair. How could we? We'd look like fools and feel even more like failures. Fran and Charlie, who'd lucked out!

It was true enough that I was exhausted. The house, the rusty patches, the commuting, all of it was getting to me. In a not-so-secret sense I would have welcomed a baby because then I would be pampered, my baby and I—coddled and admired and cared for, excused from responsibility. Without one I would plod back and forth to the station forever, to the office, to court, and back again; and Charlie also, slaving to pay for a new furnace and copper pipes.

I'd been working harder than I ever had, too, on *Gilmore v. Apple Valley Chemical*, a landmark case and my swan song at Zeus & Wenberg. It was my first departure from what is euphemistically called matrimonial law. It wasn't the kind of case we usually took, but it represented one of Arthur's periodic attempts to change the firm's image. Not too much, of course; our underpinnings were staid and conservative. But Arthur, a brilliant man, had an eccentric awareness of the injustices of the world, and if the chance came to correct one he was quick to take it—as long as it didn't interfere with his life. Mrs. Gilmore and her skin cancer was one of these, and with the customary flight into the sun required for such a cause he'd assigned her to me: a hard grueling job he knew well would put me to the test.

Mr. and Mrs. Gilmore had been forest rangers in the Adirondacks. Eight or ten years earlier, they'd begun to notice the pernicious effects of what they believed to be acid rain. Lakes had died, trees had died, great swaths of meadow had turned brown. Birds, once a plentiful chattering population, disappeared; small animals were found dead for no apparent reason. (Arthur had found some of the same things on his farm in the Berkshires.) The Gilmores had fashioned an original, ingenious technique for tracing wind and weather patterns with simple, easily available materials. Their evidence pointed to Apple Valley Chemical, a company that used nuclear waste as fuel for various chemical processes.

For years Apple Valley ignored the Gilmores' pleas and threats, claiming, with some justification, that their evidence was too thin and hokey to stand up in court. The Gilmores stepped up their efforts when Mrs. Gilmore began to suffer from the dermatitis that eventually turned into a disfiguring and fatal skin cancer. About two years before, Apple Valley had merged with Remus Inc. and changed its techniques, no longer using the toxic substances which, the Gilmores claimed, had caused the harmful fumes; since that time, the trees and lakes had come back somewhat, the birds were returning, the meadows were starting to bloom. But Mrs. Gilmore's melanomas spread. She claimed that her husband had left her because of the stress, her son had run away and was living on the streets, she was broke, and she had an incapacitating neuritis that made her unfit for work. She wanted five million dollars.

"She has no case," I told Arthur.

"So make one."

"For God's sake, Arthur, it all hangs on kites and balloons and that air dye, which sounds illegal itself"—an invention of Mr. Gilmore's, which colored the air to show wind patterns. "And nobody's ever suggested anything about acid rain and cancer."

"We'll suggest it. I hate this shit. I have a dead pond

behind my house. Have you ever seen a dead pond? It's a nause-ating sight. You'd better drive up and look at it."

"She's going to die anyway."

"The money will go to ecological causes in the state." Arthur stared at me, cold marble eyes in an enormous fat face. "It just doesn't fit, Rivertown and babies and din-din for Charlie. You're here on probation, Fran. Make something out of this case and I'll consider keeping you. *Consider.*"

He could still strike terror into me. I went cold from head to foot. I hadn't known my hold on my profession was so fragile. There were other firms, but being let go from Zeus & Wenberg would be a gigantic black mark on my name . . . Fran Let-terman, who was receding into the distance to make room for the new, confused Frantic Fran.

"But why me?"

"Women's issues," said Arthur. "And you used to be good."

I went shaking into my office. But who had I been kidding? I screeched in at the stroke of nine, distracted, and shaved a few minutes off the end of the day to make my train. I sneaked phone calls to the gardener, the stonemason who was fixing the walk, the washing machine repairman. Charlie meant to help, but somehow these things fell to me (as Arthur's farm chores fell to his wife). I was walking a thin line, and I knew it.

Now I wept in the kitchen.

"It's that damn case. Arthur is making me a sacrificial lamb to one of his causes, and the case is bizarre anyway, hopeless; he knows it as well as I do. He's just getting back at me for daring to have some life of my own—"

"Don't ever call Ellie Ferguson a 'damn girl' again," Charlie said.

I watched his back leave the kitchen and go toward the stairs. What? I turned out the light and followed him.

"Charlie, what are you talking about?" I was running up the pearly stair carpeting. "What does Ellie—"

"Nothing," Charlie said. "*Nothing.* Drop it!"

"Drop what? What are we talking about?"

He wouldn't answer. He slammed into the bathroom, then

came out and announced that he was sleeping on the daybed in the "nursery." To my bewilderment he would not explain.

"Haven't you ever wanted to be by yourself? That's allowed, isn't it?"

"Well, of course. But I don't understand—"

"Fran." He looked half impatient, half bemused. "You don't have to understand everything. Turn your head off, for Christ's sake."

At breakfast I said, "Let's move back to the city."

"No!" Charlie shouted, slamming down his coffee cup.

I'd sworn to myself I'd say it out. "Please listen to me. You're obviously unhappy with our life here. So am I, and it's silly for us both to be miserable. I'll put the house on the market and start looking for a co-op."

On Charlie's face was a struggle. "I'm not unhappy. I love this house. You can't solve your problems by moving somewhere else."

"But what are our problems, besides—?" I stopped. That one was enough, it seemed.

He closed his eyes as though in pain. "Stop blaming yourself, Fran. You're just being . . . yourself."

"The usual empty womb."

I supposed I sounded bitter, a tone Charlie couldn't tolerate under any circumstances. He wiped his mouth, got up and grabbed his briefcase, and left without a word. Once outside he apparently remembered the same thing I did, that we drove to the station together. Without looking back he slowly got into the car and sat there waiting for me to lock the door of the house. His head was bowed. He had that common mien of suburban husbands: trapped. Beaten down, like an old mule tied to a plow.

I ran down the walk and got into the car next to him just as Ellie drove up in her ten-year-old Ford with a dented fender. Waving cheerfully, she got out of the car with Kimmy, clutching the usual shopping bags of who-knows-what that she trundled back and forth. She wore jeans and a white T-shirt; her hair was tied back in a ponytail. The little girl was in a pink pinafore. Spring morn! And here sat Charlie and I in our city darks, our expensive car, our grim faces and sour devious minds, our heads

23

full of ozone and old women with cancer. We couldn't help smiling at her. Who wouldn't?

On the way to the station I said in a low voice, "Charlie, do you want me to quit my job?"

The most remarkable thing happened. Charlie clutched the steering wheel so tightly it came off in his hands. Thank God we were only going five miles an hour and he was able to stick it on well enough to get to the gas station. The man at the Arco station was stunned; he'd never seen such a thing before. Mr. Morse was pretty strong—boy, and this a late-model Subaru! And broken right off, too.

"Charlie, we have three minutes to get to the train."

Charlie was looking at the wheel. "Go ahead, Fran. I'll get the next one. I just want to make sure . . ." Whatever it was hung invisible in the air. "Maybe Bruno can even fix it now. Or else I'll line up a rental car." He kissed me briefly, and I ran down the hill to the station. What had happened?

Later, when I called Charlie's office, his secretary told me he wasn't coming in till after lunch.

Could I really have asked Charlie that question? The idea was unimaginable. My job was my life. If it wasn't I wouldn't be able to do it. And it was more demanding now than ever.

I'd known that *Gilmore v. Apple Valley* was going to be tough because Arthur was so invested in it. He wanted poor old Mrs. Gilmore, crippled, shaking, covered with dreadful skin lesions, in court. He wanted to play it for all it was worth, refuse their inevitable attempts to settle, and make sure it was in all the papers.

"But what for?" I asked him.

"Because after a lifetime of being a whore I want to do a thing or two I believe in."

"But this is just—" His look stopped me. Those little gray eyes, like nails. "All right, Arthur. Though I'm not sure how the jury will react to a half-dead woman being wheeled into court."

"They will accept anything in the name of justice."

What a strange man I worked for. But I had my orders. I had never been very concerned about environmental problems.

24

I secretly believed they were greatly exaggerated by pinko ideal- ists and crazed sixties-type activists. I read *The Wall Street Jour- nal*; I was a child of my times. I was sorry for Mrs. Gilmore and her string of disasters, but—well, those were the breaks. In my secret heart I believed in the right of Apple Valley–Remus to spew any vile gases it wanted into the air. It wasn't my air, after all. You didn't have to live downwind. But I worked on it, read about Spaceship Earth and its fragile ecology, even drove up to look at Arthur's disgusting pond (though how it got that way was yet to be confirmed). And she had a point, and a thin, rickety case. Five million I wasn't so sure, but I'd try.

There is always a flush of pleasure with a new case: like that of a painter who suddenly "sees it" on the blank canvas, or at least sees how to go about seeing it. I had some lucky breaks: a recent study on toxic fumes and cancer; a couple of other cases of skin cancer in the area, 50 percent higher than the norm; and five cases of leukemia and lupus. I worked fast and hard, staying late in the city to work at the library.

But I began to smell something fishy as soon as I drove up to the house where Mrs. Gilmore now lived—if barely—in Queens. I was greeted by an offensive young man, her son Ross; sitting in a chair by the window, half alive, was poor Mrs. Gilmore, trembling with Parkinsonism and covered with skin lesions. Even to my unskilled eye she was not long for this world. Nor was she, as the saying goes, playing with a full deck. I had trouble getting straight answers from her, even when I threw the son out of the room—the son whose nose for money had brought him home to his mother after all these years.

"I doubt if she can testify," I told Ross afterward outside the house.

"Sure she can. She has to be drilled."

"I don't think she even understands what's going on."

"Well, Mr. Zeus told me that's all right. Let the jury look at her! Put *me* on the stand."

"What's your excuse for running out on your parents for five years?" I asked.

"So who's going to know that?"

"The defense attorney, Mr. Gilmore. He's a friend of mine. He's learned everything by doing his job. Frankly, you look very

25

poor. And in this particular case I think it matters, since you stand to inherit."

The case disturbed me. I walked around with it and slept with it and ate with it. I've sometimes wondered if Arthur was trying to lure me back into my profession, in a sense, by throwing me a case he knew would capture me, which would prove to be so much more fascinating than "babies and Charlie's dindin." (And that's why Arthur is a genius—a lesser man might have thrown me a hardball, almost as punishment.) And what a juicy one! Full of conflicts and paradoxes, like life: full of twists and turns, good guys turning into bad and vice versa . . . for the Apple Valley attorney was as nice a guy as you could hope to meet.

"We don't spew shit into the air, Fran. We have emission controls, which we put on without anybody making us, even before the merger with Remus. We have day care . . . profit sharing . . . we're a model company. We happen to manufacture household chemicals. We'll settle with the Gilmores, even though I think they're a little nutty" (my secret opinion too).

"We want Mrs. Gilmore to go in front of a jury."

"Well, I see where you're coming from, but why *us*? I could point to half a dozen factories that violate every rule in the book . . . not to mention the nuclear reactors. Now that's where the real dirt is coming from!"

"I'm sorry," I said. I really was. I had to harden myself all around for this one. But I was good. I knew how to fish among all this right and wrong, nice guys and rotten guys, greening and greed, for those thin shining threads of the law. And I knew better than to give in to anything else. What mattered were my charts of kites and balloons and puffs of purple and orange, pictures of dead fields and dead animals and ponds with fish turned belly up. I believed in our system of justice. The truth *did* come out in court, not in speculations or theories; these things were too ambiguous, too evanescent. Bit by bit, thread by thread, I would tease it out, deftly present it, and lay it before the People.

Charlie was working in the garden, whistling as he pruned shrubs and pulled up weeds.

"Charlie, are you . . . cutting back?"

"Watch what I'm doing, Fran. Right here, where the five leaves are."

"Not the roses, Charlie. Your job."

He examined the leaves carefully. "I told you Ash Two was cooling for a while."

So he had. "I'm not yet used to your new obsession with growing things."

"Well, I guess it was always there. Couldn't do much about it in town." I couldn't catch his eye. "I'll be working mostly here on the computer, then starting some new research in a month or so."

"Well, it's a good thing, because you'll be around for Lulu while I'm on the rack for the next couple of weeks."

"Lulu?" He put down the pruning shears.

"She's coming tomorrow. I told you."

"Is she staying here?" Charlie asked.

"She always stays here."

"Not always. Once she stayed in the city."

"She stayed once at the Drake and hated the noise; she's too used to quiet. Come on, Charlie, you have to remember; we had this whole same conversation three weeks ago. What's the matter with you? Actually I think she'll be good for us, shake us up a little, remind us that there's life away from Rivertown."

Charlie looked stunned. I was surprised, because he liked Lulu. "How long is she staying?"

"Who knows? Till she gets bored, I imagine."

Lulu was a good if somewhat unpredictable houseguest. She was enthusiastic and self-sufficient, well able to amuse herself, sometimes coming back from the city with some odd gift she thought we'd like, strange dark breads from the Lower East Side, yarn to knit Charlie or me a sweater (which never got finished), records of Glenn Miller or Edith Piaf, sometimes a special crystal with benevolent powers . . . about which Charlie and I were polite. She was more sociable than I am, besides having more time, and got to know the neighbors and the local shopkeepers. In her one previous visit she'd made more friends in Rivertown than I had in the whole year and a half we'd been here.

But there is no perfect parent. She was so European, with her odd rules about this but utter laxness about that; so impulsive, suddenly deciding to go to California ("Do you realize I've never seen the Pacific Ocean?"), bringing back memories of other whims and desires that had led to another move, perhaps another lover. When I told her this she'd been surprised. ("But Fran, I never left you; there was always Brigitte or Anny or Lucia"—the nannies and au pairs who had raised me.)

I was, besides, uncommonly tried by her metaphysical bent. Even her appearance was otherworldly. Lulu's streaked hair was long and straight, pinned back in a knot from which wisps forever separated. She wore watery silks of strange colors, flowing purple poets' smocks, black chin-to-ankle coveralls like a Turk. She disembarked from the plane in a sort of harlequin costume with diamonds of mauve and black, which brought back costuming from the past. Somehow her garments suggested, unsettlingly, other, deeper meanings. She'd humiliated me by wearing a green velvet cape with matching jodhpurs to my graduation from Miss Comfitt's Seminary in 1956, causing stares from other parents. We'd had an argument about it. Now I know that my anger had at least partly to do with the profound conventionality of all children. Why didn't she just *know*, like the other mothers? Why didn't some instinct point her toward beige suits, spectator pumps, blouses with soft bows at the neck? Why wasn't her light-brown hair in docile curls around her face, suggesting convention and maternal devotion, instead of streaming down her back or barely knotted, like a Valkyrie?

And that was just the beginning! Why didn't she have a cozy house with a kitchen where she baked cookies? Why didn't she talk to the other mothers over her breakfast coffee about suitable prom dresses, dates, allowances, and other matters urgent to young daughters? Why did we have to live in *Europe*? Why was she so hysterical, her conversation so strange, her interests so peculiar? Why wasn't she normal? Why, oh why, did my father have to die?

Lulu was sixty-two that visit. I'd been born when she was only nineteen. (Why wasn't she *older*?) The somewhat baffled expression that crossed her face when I talked about my work irritated me, but it also taught me patience. I spoke more slowly, as though to a small child—patronizingly, I know now, for Lulu's frown had nothing to do with intellectual limits but with mystification that I had chosen to devote my life to the law. How could I have turned out like this—a child of hers? An artist or poet she would have understood completely. A dancer, flutist, mountain climber, archaeologist, priestess, shaman, tennis champ—all these would have met with her approval. She admired doctors, nurses, and social workers who fought epidemics and treated the poor without charge, teachers and librarians, certain small shopkeepers, devoted mothers of ten . . . many things would Lulu have been thrilled about, including nothing at all. In spite of this she was proud of my accomplishments and knew Waldo would have been too. I had followed in his path rather than hers.

Charlie seemed oddly oppressed by her presence, which he had never been before. Usually he got along with her well, often better than I did. His shoulders again had that poor-old-mule sag, and his tight hands on the wheel as we drove home from the airport reminded me of what had happened before. I almost said something about it, but something stopped me—perhaps his jerky, nervous driving. How odd it was: always easier and looser than me about everything, he'd always been able to float into Lulu's astral world without losing his wits.

Lulu hadn't seen the house in its finished condition.

"It's very lovely, Francesca." We were in the upstairs hall.

"It still isn't completely done."

"Well, it looks it. Except of course for *this* little place," she added as we went into the baby's room, optimistically papered in palest green and white stripes—a sort of compromise in case the room ended up as a permanent guest room. "I suppose there's no news on *that* front."

"You would have heard if there was, Lulu."

"I can't believe it won't happen yet. It's curious how . . ." She looked at me and sighed.

"How what?"

"Well, how only *some* genetic things are passed on." She wandered over to the window, which looked out over the back yard. The kitchen wing of the house jutted out; the small maid's room used by Ellie in the daytime was just below, and we could hear her voice, probably talking to Jodi. ("No, stop, I said. No, not *now!*") Then it dropped to a murmur. "I mean," Lulu went on, "it was so easy for me. *Too* easy, in fact! It's strange. Maybe

I shouldn't even say it, but I started, didn't I? I mean fertility. But then I was younger, and I didn't . . . oh, dear. Never mind me. Frannie, I love your woods, I can't wait to wander there. Last time I noticed the strangest energies there, very spiritual yet sensual too; I could hardly believe it. Do you walk there much?"

"No time, Lulu. And I'm not dying to get full of burrs."

Lulu looked at me quizzically. "You are so like your father. It's remarkable."

"Hardly." I laughed.

She turned back to the window. "That girl is looking a little peaked," she said, as Ellie came outside. She went over and sat under a tree, uncharacteristically idle.

"How can you tell from here?"

"I just can."

She was right: Ellie looked red-eyed and rabbity as she left, clutching her shopping bags. "Good night, Miz Mo . . . Fran."

"You look tired, Ellie. Are you coming down with something?"

"Well, I think I might be getting a cold. I don't feel right."

"Thank God it's Friday, right? Feel better, now?"

We were in the kitchen, where I was arranging some cheese and crackers on a plate. Lulu sat at the table, watching her musingly as she went out the door. Her car rolled out of the driveway.

"Well, I doubt she'll be feeling better *immediately*," Lulu said, as she bit into a radish.

"What do you mean?"

Lulu smiled. "She's pregnant."

"Don't be ridiculous. She can't be."

She was pulling the cork out of the Cinzano. "But she is. I know she is."

I looked at her. "Have you any proof of this, Mother?"

"Her hips are bigger than before, and her breasts. But it isn't just that, she has the look."

"Ellie has been separated from her husband ever since she came here." The whole conversation annoyed me.

Lulu laughed. "For heaven's sake, so what? She must have a lover. She's a very pretty girl."

Was she? Young—yes. Strong and healthy—definitely. Pretty? I'd always considered her features a little coarse, though her coloring was good. I'd longed more than once to get her some decent clothes, ones that would disguise the little figure faults: heavy thighs and arms and a short neck. She was given to sleeveless T-shirts—a mistake—and tight jeans, and her behind was hefty. She wore her hair in teenage ponytails.

"Ellie's not the type to have a lover," I said, as Lulu poured us each a vermouth. "She's Irish. She's never mentioned divorce, even with that disaster of a husband. She's a good girl." What was I saying? What was a good girl? "I mean she's not— um, liberated, though I've tried to explain a few things about where women are now . . . to drag her out of the dark ages."

"Oh, Fran. Really."

"Well, what's wrong with that? Why shouldn't she be free too? She's already on the way. She's self-supporting, and now she has a financial goal. It would all collapse if Bill Ferguson came back through the door."

"It appears he has already," Lulu said.

I crunched the ice out of the tray. "She would have told me."

"But why should she? It's none of your business. I certainly don't ask Giulia about her sex life, nor would she tell me."

"It's different here, Lulu. Ellie is my friend"—the kind of friend you order around. "It's just chance that I'm not working for her. That's why I insist she call me Fran."

Oh, I know I was deluded. Such a friendship was impossible. Lulu looked down into her glass, moving it slowly back and forth as I talked of sisterly solidarity, her right, her body! It was possible of course that Ellie did have a lover, unlikely as it seemed: somebody she'd met in a bar and gone home with in a moment of loneliness and desperation, though she'd told me she never went to bars alone. Or a friend might have gotten her a date. But how strange she'd never mentioned it!

Lulu said, "The aura in this house has changed." She held her hand up as though to test it. "There's something going on here, Fran. I'm not sure what. But you'd better be wary."

A long, gray weekend. Lulu was visiting friends, and Charlie

31

brooded at the TV. Her arrival had visibly depressed him, which he tried to hide when she was around. We spent an interminable bleak Sunday, Charlie slack-jawed in the study watching a base-ball game. I didn't tell him about Ellie, he'd been so oddly defensive of her at times. I retired to bed with a pile of paperwork. As darkness fell he wandered muzzily into the bed-room, groping on the bureau and in drawers for nameless disap-peared items, silent and withdrawn.

"How was the game?" I asked, to break the silence.

"What game?"

"The game. The game. What was the score?" I felt my voice rising and scraping.

"I don't know what the fucking score was," Charlie said, grabbing his wallet and charging downstairs. I heard the front door slam, then the car motor coughed into life and buzzed down the driveway and away into the distance.

I turned over and lay facedown amid the papers, feeling intensely sorry for myself. To hell with him! Then for a moment I thought, or dreamed, that there was no rusty patch in my pants. I closed my eyes and prayed, though I was not in the least "regular." My reproductive machinery hopped and skipped around in a merry and unpredictable way, as though to make up for its orderly and disciplined owner. Could it be, after five years . . . ?

I played a game with myself and pretended that it was. Imagining It made me feel peaceful and protected and strangely powerful. I'd phone my office. "Arthur, you'll have to try Gil-more yourself because I'm pregnant." When he started to scream and swear, when he ripped out the phone, I'd gently hang up. I took a hot bath and daydreamed among the bubbles. Meg. Jessica. Stephanie . . . but "Steph" was too much like "staph." The old-fashioned ones, Laura or Mary or Faith . . . Faith Morse-Letterman. Mary Letterman-Morse. A boy would be Charlie Two—no, Three.

I'd order white nursery furniture and a layette from Saks. I'd forget about the law, Charlie would support me. I'd sit by the window and rock little Mary or Charlie and sing lullabies . . . and Charlie would love me again. As I put the baby down to sleep he'd come into the room on tiptoe, his eyes brimming as he looked at the two of us. His arm would steal around me as we stood together, looking down at the miracle in the crib. Our future.

· 4 ·

I DAWDLED AROUND THE KITCHEN THE NEXT MORNING, HAVING a second cup of coffee and pretending to read the paper. As I sat there listening for Ellie's car, a taxi drove up and discharged Lulu and our neighbor to the north, Adam Kerner, a professor of anthropology at nearby Grier College and a big, amber bear of a man I'd exchanged greetings with a couple of times.

"I met Dr. Kerner on the train," Lulu said, "and we shared a taxi. I've asked him to come in for a cup of coffee."

"Please do, Adam." He was an extremely interesting man, though this was not the moment I would have chosen to entertain him. Heavily bearded and shaggy-headed, he had sharp blue eyes under his thick eyebrows that I imagined missed nothing.

Lulu dropped her bag and valise. "Dr. Kerner is full of the most fascinating and shocking anthropological lore, all about primitive goddess worship and prehistoric fertility rites and—" She stopped and looked at me, her hand in front of her mouth. "Oh, dear."

"Mother means we could use a fertility rite around *here*. Maybe you could advise us about dancing around poles, or whatever you think might do the trick."

Kerner smiled. "You can chant in the moonlight too, but it probably won't work. There's only one thing that does usually."

I heard the wheels of Ellie's car come crunching into the driveway and tried to look unconcerned as her steps came up the walk and her key turned in the lock. When she saw the three of us, she jumped. She still looked white-nosed and red-eyed.

"Oh, g'mornin', Miz . . . Fran. Miz Letterman." Her gaze scooted between us in what seemed like terror. "Dr. . . . er . . . Kerner."

33

"Hello, Ellie," he replied in a friendly voice, as I glanced at him in surprise.

Ellie dashed toward the maid's room, her little domain, paper shopping bags crinkling. She was wearing a pair of very loose baggy overalls. She closed the door most of the way, and from behind we could hear her blow her nose.

"Are you feeling better, Ellie?" I asked.

"A little." The door closed.

"Well," Lulu said, cocking her head and glancing at me, "somebody here has *already* been dancing around poles."

Something made me look at Kerner, who, remarkably, did not look surprised. He only stirred his coffee thoughtfully. I went over to the closed door.

"Ellie, is there anything I can do for you?"

The door opened a crack, and I saw half her face. "Um . . . no." A choke and gulp.

"If there's anything wrong, maybe I could help." All I could see was a section of pink cheek.

"No, thank you, Fran." Her voice was strained. Her eye appeared briefly.

"Remember what I told you, now," I said, sounding weirdly merry. "Things that you don't share just get worse."

"Excuse me." The door closed in my face. Kerner cleared his throat and Lulu shook her head at me, making violent gestures telling me to back off. I went and sat down, swinging my foot nervously. Lulu remarked that it was getting late; was I going to the office? Then Kerner stood up, saying he had to go, and at the same moment the door of the maid's room opened and Ellie came out. She moved slowly, looking trapped; the room opened directly onto the kitchen.

Lulu smiled at her. "How about some coffee?" She gave Ellie's shoulder a friendly little shake. "You look like you could use some. I make it really strong."

Ellie smiled weakly and moved over toward the sink, where she began putting dishes into the dishwasher. There was a silence, while I tried to see her body through the overalls, and failed, and Kerner hesitated.

"Mother makes superb coffee," I said pointlessly. "But I'm afraid I'm better in court than I am in the kitchen."

34

"No matter," said Lulu, from whom I had learned small talk a long time ago. "Everybody's good at something. Ellie" —as she filled the mug—"is good at *many* things."

Afterward, Lulu swore she said it only to cheer the girl up, meaning, for instance, her skilled ironing and excellent pot roast. But she might have stabbed her in the back. Ellie whirled around, tears now vividly on her cheeks, wisps of hair coming out of her ponytail. Her eyes were anguished and accusing, and she gave a sort of gasp. She started to say something; what, I'm not sure— and at that moment Charlie came down the stairs and into the kitchen.

Something went between all of us like a bolt of electricity. Ellie's eyes fastened on Lulu, then me, then Kerner, then tore to Charlie in a rage. Charlie looked stricken. The color drained from his face, and he looked at me with a pleading expression I'd never seen before. Then Ellie cried, "Oh, leave me *alone*, I can't *stand* this any more!" running back into the maid's room and slamming the door. Charlie lunged after her.

It took me ages to get it . . . incredibly long, Lulu told me later, being less tuned in to this sort of thing: being American. Lulu, having become totally European, sighed and shook her head, making a moue of despair in Charlie's direction. It was true: things like this just didn't happen any more, did they? Everybody was too smart, or something. In Lulu's world . . . well, it wasn't the first time. What do you expect, if you hire such a pretty young girl? I stood staring as Charlie banged on Ellie's door, demanding to be let in. From within we could hear her sobs.

"Ellie, open the door," he kept saying. "We all have to deal with this together."

"With what?" I asked. Lulu looked at me incredulously.

Maybe I did know sooner, for a cold pool had formed some-where in my abdomen. It enlarged and spread upward, downward, all through my body and through the room. I knew without know-ing. Certainly I knew that something dreadful was happening. With a rather theatrical gesture to Lulu that said, "Take care of her," gesturing toward the closed door, Charlie grabbed my arm and steered me out through the hall to the living room.

I'd had trouble with that room. It was long, like a shoe box, and no matter what I did to it, it kept looking like a country-club lounge. "Charlie, what would you think of wall-to-wall in here? Just bring the hall carpeting right through, and then—"

"Fran." Charlie's face loomed in front of me, very close. I could feel the heat from it, as though it were a sort of lantern: burning eyes, open mouth breathing fire. "I never wanted you to find out like this. But I can't believe you haven't had your suspicions. I've never had a secret from you in my life, and I swear to God I never will again. I've been half crazy."

"I don't understand." But the part of me that refused to take it in was wearying of the fight.

"Fran, don't pretend with me. This is bad enough. I know you've thought of this. It's why you've been unhappy. I'm not stupid. I love you for it. Worse if you didn't care enough to be. I understand why Lulu is here. . . . God, this is a relief." He put me down on the sofa and then sat opposite me, holding my hands tightly. I heard murmurs from the kitchen. "You deserve to hear everything. I deserve anything you want to do . . . up to a point. It's over, Fran, all but the responsibility for her and the child. It was a terrible mistake."

No, I thought. It's a joke. Now I was icy from head to foot, from my stormy head to my stockinged feet, my toes nervously digging into the rug: icy with a terrible cold that turned to unbearable physical pain, as Charlie told me how sorry he was, how he wished he could undo it, how he couldn't believe I was as surprised as I appeared, how he'd be relieved at my anger, yes, relieved, how he had no decent excuse, only fire in the loins, how there was a rotten part of him that wanted to accuse me of responsibility by being so busy, so unavailable, always out late, but he knew damn well that was prevaricating . . . nobody had forced him, certainly not Ellie, I should get that straight right away; her only sin had been giving in and that probably had to do with loneliness, she was human, her husband had left her; it had only been a few times, and when she told him she was pregnant he—

I screamed then—screamed my head off, got hysterical, tried to kill him. Charlie looked stricken. I think it was the word "pregnant." *She* had no rusty patch; the crotch of her pants remained pure while mine turned up that foul symbol again and again, symbol of my incompetence, my failure! Or was it just the sudden rush of images of Charlie and Ellie in bed—and what bed, where, how, when, how often; did he love her; how *could* he?—and I gave the wounded howl of a woman who sees that men can lust without love and see no contradiction. Who knows what order it all came in, or which was worse? I grabbed a little statue from the coffee table—a little curling whale caught in mid-leap we'd bought in Nantucket—and tried to hit him with it; he wrenched it out of my hands, and I began flailing at him insanely. I don't know what I said, or even what I did: flung myself on the couch, had to be carried up to bed, where Lulu came with a cup of tea.

Sounds nutty, doesn't it? Rivertown, New York, the early 1980s. The master of the house, the pretty maid, the . . . wife. The what wife? Not frigid, not hateful, not ugly. The preoccupied wife, rushing to the office. Coming home late, but loving and sexy! All made more difficult by a mistaken move to the "country" which wasn't really country at all, but a place where people streamed forth to the city from their houses at 6 A.M. to toil for the privilege of starting out again at 6 A.M. the next day, forever to the grave. And poor Charlie—living with two crotch-watching women, waiting for rusty patches. No wonder he'd pulled the steering wheel off!

"He thought you already knew," Lulu said. "That Ellie told us in the kitchen. And *that's* why she was so upset . . . when it was really just the tension, poor girl, and of course the whole thing."

"I don't want her in the house!"

"She's gone home."

"Did Charlie go with her?"

"Francesca." She was acting like a mother for once, smoothing my hair back. "Charlie wants *you*. He's been very foolish. He's *very* sorry."

"You don't understand," I sobbed. "Charlie and I . . . we had an *unusually* good marriage . . . a perfect marriage! Better than most people's. We are—were—partners." More tears. More talk. More soothing: Lulu telling me that all men did it, for heaven's sake, it didn't mean a thing; me protesting that she knew nothing about America in the eighties, she came from another world . . . though I was beginning to wonder what this great difference was, the one I was always talking about. My head throbbed, my eyes burned.

37

"He prays that you'll forgive him."

"Never. Forgive him? I'll kill him! He's destroyed us—he's trashed everything we had." I felt dreadful, sick to my stomach and half faint. *"He has destroyed trust!"*

I half passed out, or went to sleep; I felt crushed by pain, devastated, wound in wires of betrayal that cut when I moved or even breathed. I would never have believed I could feel like this: tough competent Fran, who handled everything. I'd sleep for a while, then wake up, wondering for a blessed fragment of a second why I was in bed . . . then remember. I'd let my mind wander, the monstrous truth would sink below the surface . . . then it grabbed my mind again in its cruel grip. Lulu came in and out, and Charlie once. Oh, God. I would kill him, and Ellie, then myself. I'd find a gun; it wasn't so hard. People did it all the time.

When Charlie's face bent down toward mine I kept my eyes closed, then finally opened them and said, "I will never forgive you. It will always, always be there."

"No, Fran. There's a way out. If you'll just listen. . . ."

"Get out!" I screamed, covering my head with the pillow.

I slept for a while, or closed my eyes and endured terrible, jumbled dreams. Later I woke up, sitting woozily on the edge of the bed. The empty room swung slowly back and forth, then settled precariously at some point in the middle. It seemed hot, still, breathless; the air was unaccountably orange and hostile, lit by Charlie's lantern lust. This room that had always been so cool and restful, with its pale blues and cream, had turned against me. I wondered if I could live through this endless day, this intolerable life.

After a while I got up and dragged myself over to the window. Ellie's car was gone. Down on the terrace, Charlie and Lulu were deep in conversation. He seemed to be explaining; she was listening, when he didn't deserve a moment of anybody's time. Certainly there was nothing he could say to me. I looked at myself in the mirror: a small, pale face with deep purple eye sockets, a wrinkled blouse I took off and threw on the floor. Let him pick it up. You were, in the end, on your own. You suffered alone, you died alone. The two people I cared about in the world were talking together on the terrace.

I broke our sacred rule about the bedroom and lit a cigarette.

I left it smoldering in an ashtray. Then I got up, washed my face, and dressed for the city. I took out a suitcase and packed it. As I left I wrote Charlie a note, which I taped on the door: CHARLIE I WILL NEVER GET OVER THIS.

Then I went downstairs and out the front door, got into my car, and went toward the parkway.

Driving is one of the illusory joys of suburban living. Its false sense of freedom helps to counteract the more real miseries of mortgage payments and infidelity. Fuck him! I yelled as I sped down the Sawmill River Parkway. In the city, I put the car in a garage and checked into the Drake Hotel. I ordered a double vodka martini from room service. I hate you, Charlie Morse, I said as I drank it.

It was a bright, breezy spring afternoon. I decided to phone the office and tell them I was sick, then go to a museum. I'd have dinner at some lovely restaurant and find an old movie. I could phone Pam Morales or Jill or, better yet, Terry, who had caught her husband fucking his secretary. I'd drop into Saks and Ann Taylor. I'd sit in the sun and eat a chocolate bar.

Terry said she'd love to see me but she hardly ever got out of bed . . . a luxury financed by her ex-husband, who was paying dearly for his little slip. She'd quit her job, and restaurants gave her panic attacks.

"But Fran, if you wouldn't mind picking up a barbecued chicken or some Chinese and coming over . . ."

"Come on, Terry. My treat."

"Oh, no. Even the thought makes me sick. I'm not safe any-where but here."

The last thing I wanted to do was hang around Terry's sloppy, smoky bedroom eating Chink out of containers. But I was too curious; the anguish burned too hotly. I had to talk to someone. I took orange beef and Tung Ting shrimp and a bottle of Chablis. She greeted me wanly but affectionately, her long pale hair strag-gling down over her old bathrobe.

"Oh, you're an angel. I live on Diet Coke and chicken pies. Gristede's sends it over."

"How long have you been like this?" The place was a disaster. She'd never been much of a housekeeper, and now chaos had taken over completely in the form of piles of dirty clothes, newspapers, old coffee mugs, and a rank cat box.

"Like what? I've just been a little tired. Here, sit down"— shoving the cat and a couple of dirty towels to the floor.

"Terry, Charlie's gotten the maid pregnant."

Together we indulged in one of those we-two-are-miserable confession fests so dear to women. In payment for Terry's cries of horror at Charlie's crime and her hindsight opinion that there had always been something about Charlie, she couldn't say exactly what, that made her not so surprised he'd done something like this, I listened to the most graphic description of the moment when Terry found *them* on the floor of his office, to which she had a key . . . the timing had been, oh, too perfect! David had looked up, seen his wife—but couldn't stop! He'd tried, ending up with everything out in full view; *that* was what she couldn't forget.

Suddenly my head began to spin, and I went into the smelly bathroom and threw up, while Terry, holding her Diet Coke, murmured sympathy from the doorway.

"Oh, Fran. Charlie's such a bastard. My lawyer was fabulous, very radical lib, the first consult is for free. I'll write down her number."

"It's too soon. I don't know yet."

"I'm glad you came, Fran. It helps to talk. Come any time."

Pam Morales laughed when I told her about it later.

"Oh, we've been hearing about David Persky's outside orgasm for months." I was in my bed at the Drake, head throbbing, feet cold, shivering.

"She's out of her mind."

"Oh, I don't know. But she has an obsession—she's lucky. I know it's a shock hearing about it for the first time. It has a certain . . . immediacy, the way she tells it. Pungency! Listen"—her voice dropped—"at least he *does* it. Julio doesn't do it at all any more. Not with me, not with anybody. We just go to bed and read, sometimes a little huggy-snuggly."

I woke around midnight, my heart slamming against my ribs. The Hellers had moved, but Jill Lehmann was home.

"Oh, Fran . . . oh, I wish you'd called before. I'm frantic . . . moving to LA on Friday. I have a job with CBS. I've had it with

New York." Her comment on my crisis: "I've heard worse. Why don't you adopt the baby?"

"You aren't serious."

"Sure am. Why not? Listen—good luck. Come and visit me on the Coast."

I tossed and turned, lay stony in frozen terror, and finally went to sleep for one blessed hour at dawn before I had to get up and go to the office.

Arthur looked at me sharply. "You look lousy."

"A little tired, Arthur. I'm fine, just need some coffee."

"Charlie called yesterday looking for you," he said, "and again a few minutes ago."

Never had we interfered with each other's professional lives, and he knew what Arthur was like. I'd sworn I wouldn't call him, but now I reached for the phone in my office.

"How dare you! I'd never hint of our problems to your office, and you know it."

"I didn't know what happened to you. As far as I'm concerned we're still married," he said.

"I'm staying in the city for a few days. I have to think."

"Think all you want. I'm ready to talk when you are."

I wobbled through the day, then went straight to the hotel and ordered a kind of childhood dinner of creamed chicken, mashed potatoes, peas and carrots, a glass of milk . . . and chocolate cake. I who never ate sweets. It all tasted very strange but good, and I ate it in bed with the TV on. I fell asleep early and woke around one in the morning, my heart banging, and didn't get back to sleep till six—ruining myself for the next day. Midafternoon, as I ordered my fourth coffee, Pam called.

"Want to go out later, hit a few bars?"

"Bars. You and Julio still do that?"

"Oh, not Julio, just you and me. Feel like getting laid?"

I sat down slowly. "Are you serious?"

"Good God, Fran. What do you think I do to stay alive? He doesn't care; he understands."

How far I'd gone from this world! I'd forgotten that there were still people who went to bars, sidled up to each other, paired off for the night, enjoying timeless, unrecorded, off-screen delight. That was the joy, the knowledge that it was off the record; you

41

could get away with it. Charlie had been the only man in my life for a long time. But—look what he had done to me!

Not that an evening's dalliance would even approach reciprocity. Charlie had had a full-fledged affair; there had been feelings; he had started a baby. In no single night could I compete with that. All I'd wanted to do, when I drove off to the city, was to cry with an old friend or two, wander around Manhattan, and try to recapture—I don't know, lost youth, hope, or whatever, and it was still what I wanted to do, except . . .

So Pam and I went to the bars and picked up a couple of guys (which was laughably easy), and I took mine back to my room at the Drake. I was lucky; he didn't beat me up or kill me. He wanted to sniff coke and play dressy dressy—me in his clothes, him in mine. At this moment I knew I'd aged. Rivertown had entered my blood. I was exasperated rather than shocked. Did we have to go through all that? I told him to gather himself together and leave . . . nicely, politely, because I suspected he had a nasty side. Sorry, I said, we just missed each other's signals. I was pretty straight, separated from my husband, lonely, etc. I sweet-talked him out the door and double-locked it.

It was pleasant to walk to work, to arrive with a container of regular and a Danish as I had for so many years. I was all right for the first part of the day, but starting at around three or four the evening began to loom before me like a blot: another movie, one of the girlfriends, or the hotel room. I had stomach pains and headaches: light bothered me, noise bothered me.

I'd leave the office around six, start up Sixth Avenue, and something would trigger my anxieties: some sad rope of a human being hanging against a wall, the little Styrofoam cup on the ground; a delivery man peeing in the street; a knot of ethnic teenagers I was sure were plotting my demise. All the misery, the rage, the fear, the greed . . . I'd lost my bearings in the city. It alarmed me, as though I'd forgotten how to speak English or lapsed into dreadful physical shape. I was getting soft and suburban. Rivertown was the problem, the bad virus, the reason I couldn't walk up Fifty-sixth Street without being filled with unaccountable anxiety. I knew suburban women who were afraid to drive to the city, even some who were afraid to go there on a train; they were afraid of everything else too—their husbands, their children, the dark, their own evil thoughts. They were like sick children locked up in their houses, allowed to go and amuse themselves at shopping centers, fearing to go farther . . . and I had started to be like them.

On Thursday Lulu called.

"Fran, this is getting ridiculous. I don't know which of you is being sillier."

"Silly? The bastard has betrayed me. He's completely wrecked my life."

"Charlie wants to talk to you, which he can't do when you keep hanging up on him."

"Whose side are you on, Mother? How can you even talk to him?"

"I'm on the side of your marriage, you foolish girl."

She persuaded me to go back—just to talk. I hadn't much liked New York this time, and the house was half mine anyway. If anybody left, it should be him.

It was hard to bite the bullet, swallow the poison. One by one the promises are broken. The things we thought we'd never do, we end up doing willingly; sometimes we never lay eyes on the things we thought we couldn't live without. It was the first hard choice. Nor was it pure . . . part of my struggle was done with a calculator. In the end I decided just what I could live with, what I could stand, and then prepared to stand even more. I'd said it to clients: "Assume the worst and you'll begin to be prepared, because what happens will probably be twice as bad." And ignore the seductive musical voice that says, "But it will never happen to me!"

Charlie met me at the door. He was pale and his eyes were puffy and purple; his shirt looked vaguely grimy and unpressed, his tie spotted. There was a stricken, desperate look about him that gave me courage.

I'd decided to lay it on the line.

"These are my terms, Charlie. I want to go back to the city. We'll buy an apartment and live as we did before. Rivertown has been a disaster. I barely have a job; Arthur may fire me yet. We've been trying to fight nature. Somehow we're not supposed to have children. I don't even want children any more. I want you. It kills me to admit it, Charlie. It's the hardest thing I've ever said. It's disgusting and pathological . . . but I'm in no mood to play games. I love you, I want you more than a baby or anything else, and the only way it's going to work is in Manhattan where we belong. I don't want a divorce."

Charlie's expression didn't change, and I wondered where my reward was for this painful admission, and why my little speech had sounded so artificial. Why did this solution appear sad, damp with failure, rather than clear and triumphant? I wasn't even sure I meant it. I hadn't found anything new about the city during my week there. What stood out like a welt was the doomed condition of single women.

"The affair with Ellie is over. That's the first thing," he said. As he spoke the agonizing piece of ice that had filled my insides slowly began to thaw. I turned my head away and smiled. I'd prayed and it had worked. But I remained stern.

"That's good news, Charlie. You've got your wits back."

"The other thing is, I've decided to keep the baby."

There was a silence.

"I'm not sure I heard you correctly." We'd stopped for a light.

"I think you did. I want my child." His frontal gaze was firm.

"Without consulting me."

"That's right."

Chills went through me. "Stop the car."

He pulled over and I reached for the key. "It's a long walk home," he said.

"You're in excellent shape," I said. "Get out."

"For Christ's sake, let's talk about it."

"There's nothing to say." I couldn't speak with a knife in me. Another knife. I would be like one of those Arab fakirs who walk around with swords and daggers stuck under the skin, clattering and clanking, all inserted by Charlie.

"I was hoping—I *am* hoping—that you'll realize what a wonderful solution this is."

"You're crazy," I whispered.

"She's waiting to hear, but I swear I won't talk to her without your being there if you want. The decision is *ours.*" He explained that an abortion was out of the question because the TV evangelists had convinced Ellie that it was murder. "Fran, just think about it. It can be *our* baby."

I shouted, "Yours, not mine! Get out of this car!"

Let him walk home, and let Ellie wait miserably by the phone! I slammed down the accelerator and left Charlie plodding along River Road.

Why, oh, why had we ever moved? We'd been so perfect, so in touch. How could I have ever wanted a baby at all? Parents had such grief, such woe . . . perfectly nice decent people watched their children die of drugs or AIDS or disappoint them in a thousand subtler ways. It wasn't worth it. Mankind was on some unstoppable downward slide, plunging toward stupidity and violence and self-destruction. I didn't want any part of it: probably I never had; it was only Charlie's attention I'd wanted, Charlie adoring me for doing what he wanted—or some picture of the perfect family I'd never had.

In the house, I went up to our bedroom. After a while the downstairs door slammed and I heard him coming upstairs: Charlie, the potent old mule. He appeared in the doorway.

"It's a disgusting idea," I said, softly and coldly. "I think you're worse than she is for thinking of it." How quiet it was in Rivertown: only the wind in the trees and a few crickets.

"No," Charlie said. "It saves everybody."

"God, I hate you!" I shouted. "How can you even ask this of me?"

I slammed the bedroom door and threw myself against it. It would look like her, for God's sake: all blond and dimply. If I did agree—I'd been trained to consider every possibility—every day I'd look at that little curly Ellie face. I would never be able to forget. I'd rot away, corrode with the rage I shouldn't feel. I'd be fired. It was a miracle I hadn't been fired already.

When I took it to kindergarten, the other mothers would be half my age, with knowing eyes. I would react badly to the whole thing. A child would bind me, make me privy to small-mindedness and nastiness, petty snobbism and country-club power struggles, as, frustrated by my own lost life, I'd push the child to ever higher accomplishments. For I knew myself. I wasn't tolerant or patient or even very fair-minded. Never would I let a child of mine do its own thing. I was churning, driven, ambitious. I scarcely knew how to rest, and I expected the same of everybody else. I would take it out on the child. For it would fall to me to take care of it, that I knew—au pair or no au pair—not to Charlie in this false family scenario. I'd hate him for tying me to Ellie forever.

And I'd been the one who thought of it! I remembered that morning in Venice, when I'd gone with him to Florian's. I'd looked at him as he sat at the bar with his espresso and the paper. How much I had loved him then!

Chilled Smirnoff, straight, helped me gain strength to face the hallucination that was my life. My breath remained dewy, my back straight . . . if my eyes were somewhat shinier.

"She's not getting any less pregnant," Charlie said a few days later.

"Good. I hope she's puking her guts out."

"Ellie has agreed to the plan, and now all we need is—"

"There is no plan," I said. "You talk to her. You still see her. You lied to me—again. You told me this was between us."

"Around the sixth tearful what'll-I-do? phone call, I decided it was wrong to add your cruelty to the whole difficult situation. The waiting is torturing her."

Then he told me how important fatherhood was to him. The Morses went back to the Revolution at least. They had fought at Gettysburg and Ticonderoga, and one had been with John Brown . . . all confirmed by old portraits and daguerreotypes on the walls of their Ohio house, that faded brown past they were so proud of. The only grandchild was his sister's brain-damaged, institutionalized daughter. I might sneer; I always did at things like this. But family was important to the Morses.

It was hard for me to sympathize with the dour old couple who hadn't wanted Charlie to marry me.

"There was a time when you loved my family and felt that you were part of it too. Or so you said," said Charlie rather inaccurately.

"Well, not after your father made it clear that I'm an outsider. That my blood isn't blue enough."

With my strange antecedents and slick otter looks, I'd never fitted in. Lulu was Italian and French and Russian Jewish and—shhh—a drop of Hindoo, as she called it, a bequest of some sprightly long-gone great-something who'd lived in India and been intimate with some fellow in white jodhpurs and a turban, right out of the Raj, and those telltale dark liquid eyes kept turning up. Blood, blood—didn't we all let it divide us up and sow hate? But probably it was seeping out too; in a few generations everybody (if there was anybody left) would look vaguely alike, with orangeish-brown skins and flat noses and almond eyes and aimless black hair, and morons every one.

Once, many years ago in Venice—I couldn't have been more than eleven—Lulu had taken me to a séance. It took place in the dark, fragrant lair of her closest friend, Signora Maude Brill, an English psychic who lived near San Giovanni Evangelista, where a hundred bells rang every day at noon. Maude had lain on her tapestried daybed, closed her eyes, and crossed her arms on her thin chest. Candles flickered; Omar, her small bald assistant, strummed his balalaika. The air was perfumed with sandalwood. Maude chanted some strange words, trembled all over; her whole body seemed to arch. More thrilling chords on the balalaika.

"Lu-i-i-i-sa," she sang, "I am Melanie Sanders."

Lulu's hand gripped mine. "She is experiencing levitation."

"I don't see."

"Look, Frannie. Her body has lifted off the pallet." But Maude's flowing dress merged with the daybed.

"Lu-i-i-i-sa," Maude chanted, "respond if you are there. This is your Aunt Melanie."

"Oh, Aunt Melanie!" Lulu breathed. "I remember you well!"

"Little Luisa! Do you remember the day I gave you my best cameo, threaded on a black velvet ribbon?"

"Yes, yes!" exulted Lulu. "And do you remember I used to call you Woofy?"

This was the relative who'd had the romance on the shores of the Ganges, surrounded by a thousand flickering candles floating in the river. Woofy had been swept away by passion. She'd come home with a little brownish memento—my Aunt Olive, named for her shiny black eyes. Dark Olive was always yanking my hair and telling me it was rude to disagree with her.

"Of course I remember," Woofy replied. "You were a sweet little girl, Lulu, but shy and fearful."

"You told me to be proud and free," Lulu whispered, "like you."

"Moth-er." I tugged Lulu's hand. "Is she still risen?"

"Woofy, this is your grandniece Francesca."

"She is different from you, Luisa—her eyes flash; she is proud and strong. There is a strange color in her aura, some foreign thing . . . something secret and dangerous!"

"Like you, Woofy." Lulu's hand, cold as ice, clutched mine.

"I fear her path will be rough and wild. I suspect"—more balalaika, more puffs of incense—"she holds the ancient Gnostic secrets of our line." And Woofy went on to say that Lulu and I were direct descendants of the dark Lilith, destined to grow tall and strong, rich and powerful, fight wars, use men as lovers and slaves . . . at which point Lulu protested and Woofy retired, rather crossly, saying Lulu wasn't ready for family secrets or worthy of them either. Maude returned; the arched body became horizontal.

"Moth-er, what are ancient Gnostic secrets?"

"I must say, Maude, I'm not sure these messages are suitable for Francesca."

Maude only shrugged. "You should know by now that the spirit world is a wild and unpredictable jungle."

I needed Woofy: I needed ancient Gnostic secrets. I needed something to get through this long black tunnel with no light at the end. Secretly, I suspected I was wrong. A better woman would agree to this perfectly sensible solution, a better woman would even love the child. Didn't this prove I was unsuited to this herculean task? Why did he ask it of me, then?

The next evening Lulu rapped sharply on the door and walked in. "I want you to listen to me, Fran."

"You're on his side," I wailed. "I've heard all the arguments. I'm bad, I know I am."

"For heaven's sake be quiet." She closed the bedroom door, then came and sat down on the bed, where I had flung myself after work. "I know your feelings are hurt. But there are other things to consider."

I shoved the pillows behind me and sat up. "It's my decision, Mother."

48

"There are others' feelings as well as yours. Another life has started . . . and I'm afraid I agree with Charlie. That poor girl can't keep it."

"Poor girl!"

"I'm surprised you still know so little about men. As a lawyer you should have learned a few things. They aren't terribly different. Your Charlie is showing a sense of responsibility about his mischief, that's all."

Lulu then told me that I had been . . . not exactly planned. Not what every child imagines: eagerly awaited, joyfully welcomed. Waldo had been married to Peggy when Lulu met him. Ordinarily, of course, Lulu would never have gone near a married man. But, well, there were circumstances . . . and they were at sea, on the *Normandie*. She was so young, so vulnerable, being shunted off to yet another relative—lost, almost like Ellie! And Waldo as I well know was so charming, so brilliant . . . handsome as a sun god! She knew there had been a strong ray of love destiny . . . and that, coupled with a recent disappointment, opened her up to him. And so it had happened. Luckily for her, and for me, it had ended happily.

Lulu told me all this with the air of someone relieved to be unburdened of a great secret. She held my hand as she released the information, holding it tightly in case I collapsed in tears. But I was thrilled. It proved my parents' love and my father's sense of responsibility to the woman he loved. I had brought all this about!

"He didn't hesitate for a moment," she said, "when I told him I was expecting a child. He was a good man, Francesca. And so is Charlie! Oh, the stories I could tell. . . . Poor Maude Brill lived in sin with a painter when she was only a child; her family didn't want her. When she got pregnant he left her and she had to have an abortion; she was only sixteen. . . . And my God, the Italian men! I know for a fact that Cipi de Rimini has four children out of wedlock, and Beppi Lusardi has at least two. They might send a check from time to time, but only on the condition that the women keep their mouths shut. It's awful, but nobody really thinks it's so strange, because that's just the way men *are*, and don't tell me it's any different here. The point is to see that the children are cared for, the poor innocents."

And so forth. "You've been married for ten years, Fran, and I know you love him. Forgive him." She squeezed my hand. "No situation is perfect, *mia cara*; most are very . . . imperfect. It's hard when the first big thing goes wrong."

When she left the room I lay on the bed, my mind spinning, gyrating around in those early days when I'd met Charlie and fallen in love with him, entering the bondage I couldn't leave . . . and that was love we'd had, all right. I was soaked in it, I breathed it and ate it. Oh, precious house of crystal cards, my apartment with Charlie tucked into it, my glassine friends and their clever mots, their trilling laughter, their baffled souls . . . my bank accounts and CDs and carved church door and monthly rust spots. I was only forty-three; was it too late to find somebody else? Go back to town and steal a glassine husband? But I knew too well what was in town.

Charlie had always been more cautious than I, more careful—until this recent disaster. Though a couple of years younger, his spirit seemed older, his words fewer and more valuable. I'd believed him to be wise, occupied with serious matters fit for someone whose work led him to the very boundaries of human knowledge. So I thought, that day, mistakenly, that he was wise about this too, that he saw something beyond me. I thought his vision exceeded mine—though I know now he wasn't aware of the things that fired him.

Charlie said through the door, "We'll get an au pair. A nanny. I know I'm asking everything of you. People shouldn't ask such things of other people, I know that."

Oh, God. "I can't, Charlie. I'm not good enough."

"You're the only woman who is."

"I'm not. I'm selfish and resentful and I'd hate its little blond curls."

"Fran, open the door."

"It would be stupid like its mother, and I'd hate it."

"Frannie, open the door. I love you. I want you and the baby too."

"You want the baby more, don't you?"

A silence. "Yes, because as long as I love you there's very little chance for another one, and I'll always love you."

I crept toward the door. "It would kill me."

"Oh, no, it would make you wonderful. It would make you so . . . so wonderful that I'd never be able to do enough for you. Give you enough. Love you enough. How many women have that?"

"This is torture, Charlie. It would be easier if you beat me up. I can't do it. I can't, I can't, I can't!"

"Open the door, darling," Charlie said.

I looked at the knob for a very long time, then slowly, infinitely slowly, put my hand on it and turned it.

· 5 ·

SHORTLY AFTERWARD ARTHUR FIRED ME.

With a curious burst of principled thinking, I told him I wouldn't put Mrs. Gilmore on the stand; the whole thing was a farce. Ross, her son, had been working on her and telling her what to say, though she could hardly talk. She had no comprehension of what was going on. I told him I hated the whole thing and we should settle with Apple Valley–Remus.

"If you don't put her on the stand you're fired, and I'll put her on anyway," Arthur told me.

Tears sprang to my eyes, which I knew he hated. How shaky I was getting.

"Arthur, please. It's a sleazy business. You're better than this," I said, sealing my doom.

"You can't take the flak. That's what I was afraid of. You've gone soft. The job has to be done, and the media have to be there; that's what it's all about."

"You're using that woman."

He looked at his watch. "I'm sorry, Fran. You're a good lawyer. But I need the best."

The best—the ones who ground their heels in old ladies' faces. That was the nature of the business, wasn't it? What did it matter? Mrs. Gilmore was so miserable anyway, what difference would a day in court make? If only Ross wasn't so . . . if only the Apple Valley lawyer hadn't been so . . . but it was really me, and I knew it.

And it happened. I watched dully, incredulously, as it all slipped away: Mrs. Gilmore, balloons and air dye, venal sons, and strangely liberal counsel. Arthur wheeled her into court himself, argued a vast, unreasonable settlement out of the jury, and kept the whole thing in the papers. Apple Valley was forced into bankruptcy, Mrs. Gilmore died, and Ross Gilmore is now a wealthy man. Arthur calls it an environmental triumph. I call it a puzzle, a negative of a positive, a positive of a negative. I sat home and read about it and saw Arthur's big, broad face filling the TV screen as he was interviewed in front of the courthouse.

Unfortunately I made a fool of myself. I refused to leave and kept telling myself Arthur wouldn't carry out his threat. I had just wanted off the case, that was all; people had done it before. I kept working, and then one morning Arthur marched into my office.

"Oh—Arthur."

"I expect you to leave by tonight."

"I can't believe you mean it." I felt as though all my blood were draining out. "I wanted out, that was all. When Jim Harrison wanted out of the Voorhis suit, you had no problem with that."

"By tonight, Fran."

"I'll be here every morning at eight. I'll take an apartment in the city—" I began raving. "Or we'll move back. You can't do this. After all these years, and for the first time I can't handle one. I know, my personal life has been a little—um, demanding. But it's all okay now. I promise. I promise. Listen, give me rotten old *New York v. Bonner.* I don't care if it's thankless, I don't even care if you don't pay me. I'll just—"

"By tonight," Arthur said. "I can't stand listening to you degrade yourself. If you are willing to work for nothing, you're worth nothing."

Scrape—he turned on his heel and left. I sat at my desk shaking and tearing a matchbook to pieces. Several sympathizers tried to console me with lunch at a nearby bistro, where I got seriously drunk. I truly felt that without Zeus & Wenberg I was nothing. How could he do this to me, how could he be so unfair?

I ended up alone at the big round table at Bistro Boulogne with a cup of hot coffee in front of me and instructions to drink it. When I had done so I staggered out—the bill for the Last Meal having been paid for by others—walked around for an hour or so, and finally got on a train and went home. When I arrived at the office the next morning, all my things—and there were a good many of them—were neatly piled out by the receptionist's desk, and Jim Harrison was on the phone in my office, not looking as embarrassed as he should have. "Well, Fran, I'm sorry, but you know you kind of had a deadline." And did I then leave gracefully? No! I had a tantrum and was practically dragged out by Arthur and deposited in the hall, where I stood making a fool of myself, shouting accusations at everybody and ordering them to send my stuff home by parcel post—which they did, God knows why. I suppose that was my gold watch.

So that was the way Zeus & Wenberg remembered me: screaming my head off as I was being bounced. The unmentionable dark side of the fast track.

"I have my rights too," Ellie said in a small voice. The three of us were in the study, Charlie at the helm, I in the new subservient role that seemed, on the surface, to be appropriate. Ellie, pink-eyed and teary, seemed glued to the wing chair. She looked graceless and desperate, caught in the betrayal of her own body.

I'd had clients like Ellie, girls who didn't think past Friday afternoon. I'd spent a lot of time trying to change their ways, but for the most part they seemed as hopeless as she was. My job had been to pick up the pieces and try not to lose my temper. Here was one occupying the center of my life.

I had given in to Charlie and been rewarded by being fired. I still smarted over this brutal unfairness. It was too much at once. I kept expecting to wake up from the nightmare, but on and on it lurched—this plan, this decision. Every morning it was there; first in the form of Charlie making love to me when I was still half asleep, with a new passion born of gratitude. I'd sense something malign but try to keep it out of sight till we'd finished; if it surfaced immediately, like the Loch Ness monster,

53

all sexual desire would drain out of me. Either I'd lie there cold and stony, sighing with exasperation as Charlie exerted his marital rights, or get up, whatever condition he was in, and get dressed, ignoring pleading cries and moans of misery.

After I'd had some coffee I was better able to discuss this enormous impending change in our lives, but only if, on some level, I didn't really believe it was happening; these were other people we were talking about. Then Charlie would go to work and I'd be alone, Lulu having gone to visit friends in Vermont. As the day wore on, I'd know it wasn't other people we were talking about, it was us. I'd changed my mind a dozen times.

"Of course you have rights, Ellie," Charlie said, in the new serious, impersonally sympathetic tone, which, I couldn't help noticing, brought tears to Ellie's eyes and stiffened her back at the same time.

"Of coursh," I echoed. Sometimes a word didn't come out right. It had been so since my leave of absence, as I liked to call it. My sabbatical. No, before that, when the Smirnoff became my companion. Just a tiny shot after breakfast made all the difference. But I was perfectly comprehensible, I knew what I was saying. It was just the s's.

"After all, it's my baby," Ellie said.

"Well, Ellie, nobody's arguing about *that*," Charlie said carefully. "Yours and mine." They both looked at me surreptitiously.

"The main responsibility is mine in the end. You understand what I'm saying," Ellie said.

"Well, I'm not sure I follow you, Ellie," Charlie said, in his high school principal voice.

She sat up, twisted her fingers, stared into her lap. Charlie glanced at me, possibly a signal to behave like an attorney. But this was Charlie's dance. I was worthless. For all these years Zeus & Wenberg had made me real, jolted me into action, put money in the bank. Now I wasn't worth the space I took up.

"I have this friend," she said in a rush, "and she worked for this man in a store, and he—well, it was the same thing, she needed the job"—Charlie winced—"and she caught something from him. And she was really sick and the man wouldn't pay, or even return her phone calls. He was real rich; he could have taken care of her so easy. And she hasn't been quite right since."

"Ellie, do you think I'm like that?" There was a dead silence.

"I don't know." Her voice was very low.

"Well, I don't know how to reassure you." He took out his handkerchief and slowly wiped his face. His hand was trembling. "Maybe the man's wife didn't like it. But Fran is sitting right here. From this moment on, we'll take care of you till after the baby's born."

He looked at me inquiringly, and I nodded gravely, then caught Ellie's eye.

"The best medical care. Maternity clothes . . . vitamins . . . all the tests, whatever's needed. We'll be available to you day and night, like a second family."

I closed my eyes; perhaps it would make me invisible. I'd thought so when I was a child.

"Maybe even a little compensation to make up for . . . your trouble. You can even keep working here if you want."

He faltered, and Ellie reached for her handbag, the contents of which always ended up in her lap or on nearby surfaces: glasses, gum, wallet, tissues, nose drops, keys.

"This is what I thought. Rita was right, I guess."

"What's the matter?" Charlie asked in surprise.

"I don't know. It just feels like—I don't know, you're trying to run over me. I mean, you took advantage of me before; I was just a girl working for you. I won't go into *that*. Now you're trying to do it again. Fine! You tell me what to do. I get pregnant and have the baby, then hand it over to you. You wave good-bye! Maybe I could come over and see it on its birthday."

"But you don't want—"

"No, I don't want it, two kids and no husband is enough trouble. It's just"—her face was red and there were tears in her eyes—"I thought you were *decent*, Charlie."

I dropped my glass, and the crash sent Ellie to her feet and toward the door, Charlie after her.

"Ellie. Fran. Look, this is ridiculous. If you're not satisfied about something, why don't you just . . ." I heard them arguing in the kitchen, heard the door slam. Charlie came back in.

"Jesus. I don't know what her problem is. On the phone she was all right."

I only smiled. "You still love her."

He looked haggard. "I never loved her, for God's sake. She was around; we were having trouble. We've been through all this."

"What trouble? That I couldn't get pregnant?"

He was breathing audibly. "You were making me into a stud. You were prying and suspicious and bitchy and—"

"Where did you do it, Charlie? In our bed?"

Color drained from his face. "No."

"Where? In the maid's room?"

"No. Yes. So what? Who cares?"

"So I can imagine it, that's why. Pink Ellie. Is she pink all over? But I don't need to ask. She wears shorts up to her crotch and those little halter tops."

Charlie's voice was subhuman. "She perspires easily."

"In February?"

I laughed loudly, then began to cry. It was twenty past the hour, when some believe a fairy flying through the room leaves a silence in its wake. I got the tear fairy. The truth was I was tired of my own conversation, but I couldn't stop.

"How often?"

He was moving toward the door. "Only a couple of times."

"Ten, Charlie? Fifteen? Thirty? Two? How many? Was she willing or did she fight you off at first? Did she come on to you?" But I couldn't imagine her doing so. She wore a tiny gold crucifix around her neck. So it had all been Charlie. But maybe I had her wrong. Maybe she untied her halter. What did I know? Perhaps that was the worst, not knowing—those speculative pictures I'd have in my head for the rest of my life.

Charlie stared at me furiously, turned, and stalked out of the room. I heard the kitchen door slam. I ran into the bathroom, to the toilet, and threw up.

We were a strange trio. Ellie kept coming to work, unaccountably, I thought, till I reminded myself she needed the money. She was quiet, distracted, unresponsive to my gestures of—well, to be honest, I didn't make any gestures of friendship. I was as sulky as she was. I missed my job terribly. I didn't know what to do with myself for all the hours of the day and wondered how other women filled them.

I could not bring myself to think about our domestic situation. It was Charlie's problem; he could solve it. I ignored his frequent pleading glances for help when Ellie refused to speak to him.

"Fran, for God's sake—" he'd start.

"How's Ashtoreth?"

"I told you, going into Phase Three. Listen, Fran, about Ellie—"

"Pass the salad, Charlie. Just give it a toss." Our eyes met. "I gave in. What else do you want?"

"I need your help," he said.

I closed my eyes. "I'm sorry, I can't give it."

I saw Ellie talking to Kerner once or twice. His academic hours were odd, and often he was raking leaves or mowing his lawn first thing in the morning, when she arrived. I couldn't imagine what they talked about, or whether their conversations were in any way responsible for Ellie's unusual quiet thoughtfulness.

One afternoon Charlie arrived home early.

"We're going to talk," he said to me, but he meant Ellie. "This is ridiculous. This isn't going to work unless we cooperate."

"It certainly isn't." Ellie's voice was muffled as she folded sheets, one corner tucked under her chin. I was sitting at the little desk in the hall, doing some paperwork; I was half in this scene, half out of it.

"Ellie. The thing can't be undone. I'm trying to make the best of—"

"Excuse me." Politely but coolly, she turned the sheet, blocking him from sight. I silently cheered. The gesture annoyed Charlie, and he grabbed her arm.

"Stop pretending I don't exist. Talk to me, damn it."

"Don't touch me," Ellie said warningly, as I half rose. "You don't understand *anything*."

Charlie's hand dropped, and he looked at it as though surprised at its behavior. "I'm sorry. I'm trying, but I'm not very good at seeing through walls."

I put down my pen and walked past them into the kitchen, where I took down a glass and got out the vodka bottle.

"Oh, great," Charlie said. "Terrific. Get sloshed." He looked from Ellie to me and back again. "I'd like to have a simple, practical discussion. Is that too much to ask? With the future of another human being at stake, we should at least be able to—"

"Here's to human beings." I raised my glass.

"That's right, Fran," Ellie said, unusually emphatic. "Charlie needs to be reminded about human beings; he forgets they exist."

Charlie took his jacket off very slowly and deliberately, hanging it on the back of a chair. "I'm not sure what that means. I'd appreciate it if you'd explain. I've told Fran there are to be no more secrets."

"Fine. All right." Ellie put down the last sheet, neatly folded, and faced Charlie. "The Libbers are right. I never knew. If you're a woman, if you're poor, you're trapped."

"She's trapped," I said to Charlie.

"It always happens. Rita has a friend who lost her children in a terrible custody battle, and—"

"I don't see what that has to do with anything," Charlie said.

"No, you sure don't," replied Ellie, blowing her nose. She didn't look very well: her hair was dull and dry, her skin waxy. Her waist had thickened and her breasts were larger. "I told you about my friend who caught something from her boss, and he wouldn't even—"

"Ten thousand," I said to Ellie. "Plus the other expenses, of course."

She looked at me, then started on the towels. "That would certainly help."

Deep shock was creeping over Charlie's face. I told myself he was an impractical scientist, locked away in labs while others ran the world: I told myself men didn't shop, so they didn't realize what things cost, as I'd found again and again in my divorce settlements.

I told myself a few more things, but they rang hollow, and I felt as though I'd never known Charlie before when he said

58

sanctimoniously, "You can't measure a human life in dollars and cents." He looked at me. "There are laws against the buying and selling of children."

"The law is what you make it, Arthur always said."

Ellie threw me a quick grateful glance. But I'd done enough for one day, and I went out to the living room so the lovers could fight. Ellie would accuse Charlie of blindness and cruelty, Charlie would counter that she was selfish and manipulative, even that she'd possibly engineered the whole thing to get his money. Let them see each other as they were! I'd revealed myself enough, hadn't I, with my hysterics, my unemployment, my failed voom? Let us all be naked before the Lord; let none be worse than the others in this ignoble transaction!

After a few minutes of raised voices, I went back to the kitchen. Ellie, her face flushed up to the damp tendrils of blond hair on her forehead, was silently, angrily, gathering up her crumpled shopping bags, while Charlie fumed at the sink. As she went out the door, our eyes caught. I have often thought of that look. It was a warning, a pact, a truce. Her summer-sky eyes were knowing, almost prophetic. There was no hate; too much was at stake.

Charlie stood watching her leave, breathing audibly through his nose, his hands jammed into the pockets of his chinos. He wore a slate-blue sweater, and he was still the best-looking man I'd ever seen. Ellie's car scudded out the driveway and screeched down the street.

"Want some vodka?" I asked him.

He turned slowly to me. "I can't believe this. I didn't think she was that kind of woman. This is extortion."

"Actually it's the first intelligent thing I've seen her do."

Charlie bristled, grabbed the vodka bottle, and stormed out of the room. I heard him locking it up in the dining room cupboard, with a tiny brass key he kept on his key chain. I didn't care. I had another one stashed away.

"I'm going to work."

"Good idea, Charlie."

He came over and stood in front of me. "There was nothing unreasonable about asking her if the child was mine."

"Did you really ask her that?" I was instantly sober.

59

"Well, of course I did. For all I know she's been . . ."

I turned and ran out of the room and up the stairs. I'd had enough. In the bedroom, I fell into my wing chair by the window. Lord, how many things we had to solve! Where to start? Probably simply. I could knit the baby a little blanket, if I could only remember how to knit.

It was twenty minutes before the hour. I put my head down on the table and cried.

I'd gone slightly to pot. I was smoking again, and now the house had that faint acrid smell that both Charlie and I—now only Charlie—hated so.

My hair is best short, almost like a boy's; the black helmet suits my features, which are fine-cut and regular. Now it hung over my ears, making my face look small and lost. I had zits for the first time since I was seventeen. My nails were broken, I hadn't shaved my legs . . . I was a mess. I'd found a mangy old cat in the woods one day. Now it slept on the bed, which Charlie, when he was there, would not permit. I'd named it Baby.

This was a revolutionary condition for me. I'd been taught by French and Swiss au pairs that it was a sin to go to sleep without hanging up your clothes, running a rag over your shoes, brushing your hair forty strokes and your teeth fifty. I was the sort of woman whose bras and pants lay in neat piles in the drawer, whose sweaters were folded with tissue paper . . . and I'd always hated animals.

I was never really drunk, just slightly furred, enough to dull the bizarre world around me. Charlie claimed concern, but I didn't believe he'd care if I fell down the stairs and killed myself or went down to the river and swam to oblivion.

"So what, Charlie? You'd marry Ellie and have your baby."

"I don't *want* to marry Ellie," Charlie said. "God knows why, but I love you."

"God knows why!" we marveled together. And Charlie imagined the new baby would fix everything.

A dark and furious night, rain beating on the roof. Charlie was away at a meeting. I lay in bed watching *Star Trek*.

The kitchen door clicked and I froze: Baby stood, his yellow eyes flashing, his tail up. I pulled on my bathrobe and crept slowly out into the hall. Slowly I stole down the carpeted stairs into the living room and picked up the little whale statue from the coffee table.

"It's me, Miz . . . Fran," came a low voice from the kitchen. Ellie stood there. Bruises, a black eye, puffy face; only a monster would not have been moved at the sight of her. "I'm sorry to come, but I had to get out of there. I used my key."

She told me that Bill had arrived home unexpectedly, sized up the situation, and dealt with it in his customary manner. But why had she come here instead of going to the large, sloppy, loving family to which she undoubtedly belonged?

"Where is he now?" I asked.

"At home," Ellie replied. "With the girls."

"He's probably breaking their necks."

"Oh, no! He'd never touch them!" She looked stunned. "He's a *wonderful* father!"

"He's a prick, Ellie. He should be in jail." When she stiffened, I said, "Well, look at you. How do you get yourself in these messes? You'd better stay here for the night," I added, indicating the infamous maid's room.

Ellie glanced around. "Is Charlie . . . ?"

"He's away." The deep relief I felt when she asked made me realize how little I trusted him still.

"I just thought, because of the baby, I should . . . and Bill doesn't know your address. But you can understand how he'd feel; he comes home and there I am, four months gone." She shook her head. "He took one look and knew. In a way, I deserve—"

"Don't be ridiculous, Ellie."

She collapsed into a kitchen chair. A tear crept out of her eye, and she blew her nose miserably. "I just had to tell you, Fran. I'm not sure I can take it. I thought it would be all right, because you and Charlie . . . it's not like my friend; *that* man acted like he'd never seen her before. You and Charlie may have your problems, but I believe you are both decent people."

Something tightened in my chest as I listened to her. I

thought of poor old Mrs. Gilmore, like Ellie's friend—a piece of garbage who'd proved useful to somebody.

"And I'm not perfect, I'm willing to take my share of the blame, though it was mostly—"

"Please, Ellie. No details." (But I longed for details!) I found myself staring at her straight little nose, her plump arms, her large breasts as never before, trying to get inside Charlie's head—or his loins. She was three or four inches taller than I was, and around thirty pounds heavier.

"When I told Bill about it—"

"You *told* him?"

"Well, of course, what else could I do? He said—um, that I shouldn't have the baby, and if I did we were through. That he'd get a d-divorce."

"Ellie, listen to me. Let's go to the police and find a doctor right now. I'll get dressed. We'll take Polaroids of those bruises, just in case—"

"I don't want a divorce!" cried Ellie.

"But if he beats you up—"

"He doesn't beat me up like *that*. He lost his temper and hit me a few times, and I'm pregnant by somebody else, don't you see? He's got a *right!*" She looked at me impatiently. "He's the father of my children! Anyway, who's to say divorce would be any better? I know this girl, Sandy, and she got a divorce because her husband fooled around"—she glanced at me, bit her lip—"I mean all the time, not just once. So she lived alone with her kids and worked and finally met this guy she's seeing now, but *he* won't marry her because he's married himself, and he won't get a divorce. I just say this, Fran"—she unzipped her jeans halfway, breathing a sigh of relief—"just to say there's always something. Sandy said 'divorce doesn't solve anything, you just get another set of problems.' "

I went over and grabbed her by the shoulders. "Swear to me the baby is Charlie's. On a Bible"—which we didn't own. "If it's Bill's, if you saw him sometime and we don't know, I'll kill you, Ellie. I swear I'll sue you, and I know how. I'll ruin your life."

But she went white. "You don't trust anybody either, do you? I feel sorry for you and Charlie, I really do. You're cold and suspicious. . . . I haven't seen Bill since before I came here, though it's none of your business!"

"Well, why should I trust you? I thought you were cleaning my house and instead you were taking off your little halter and your—" Her expression stopped me. "All right, tell Bill we're trying to pick our way out of this as best we can, and most people wouldn't be as"—I was going to say nice, but that didn't seem accurate—"as *responsible* as we are. There's another life here."

"Well, I know that, Fran. And so does Bill—though you might not believe it. Like, last night I told him, 'Bill,' I said, 'you'd better not dare do anything that might harm this sacred human life!' Well, that stopped him! He was brought up religious, much more than me—he'd die rather than hurt this child in my womb. You don't know the Catholics; to them every baby is holy, almost like Jesus . . . they don't care how it was conceived, though you might not believe it."

How Ellie unfurled before me, each layer revealing depths I'd never suspected. "I do. I don't. I don't know."

"I mean, the Christ child's parents weren't even married, only bespoken. And mostly men only like their own babies, but Catholic men are like women sometimes in that way—motherly, almost, or maybe I mean spiritual. Bill is a *very* spiritual man . . . more than me; my family was never religious. What I'm saying, Fran, is that maybe there are times when the Lord would rather take back a little soul sooner instead of later, to spare it misery and grief, there's already so much—and so I thought I could mention it to you because we're both women. I just can't do it, with Bill back and all, or I'm afraid I can't. I have the other two kids . . . so if something happened to this baby, like if I had a miss or something, it might not be so bad, do you think?"

I was stunned at where this twisted path had led: through the woods, among the spirits, past the madonna and the holy infant, straight to the point. I cleared my throat.

"I'm not really sure how the Lord would feel, Ellie. Nor do I care."

"Do you think it's murder?" Ellie whispered.

"I think it's sanity."

Slowly she got up and went into the maid's room. I heard her digging in her shopping bag, heard the water in the bathroom running. In a few moments she stuck her head out.

"But if Charlie ever found out—"

"I assure you he never will."

Ellie smiled at me, for the first time in weeks.

· 6 ·

THE OFFICE OF DR. SEYMOUR DORÉ (PRONOUNCED DOUGH-ray) was on Route 3, a wide avenue many miles long lined with discount outlets, mini-malls, used-car lots, muffler shops, rug shops, video shops, seedy motels, car washes, pet clinics, fast-food restaurants, gas stations, fake colonial furniture outlets, and pretentious chain restaurants with such ethnic cues as thatched roofs (Polynesian), purposeless ropes (seafood), or huge wooden doors (steak). Though Route 3 was of course real—more real, probably, than Rivertown's zoned-for-colonial center, designed to give the well-heeled inhabitants the illusion that we lived in an eighteenth-century paradise—Route 3 had, to me, terrible, disturbing qualities that grated on my nerves. I dreaded visits to this ugly, utilitarian stretch of road.

Why did I care that nothing on Route 3 matched, that a round pink nail salon curled like a snail next to a huge used-car lot fluttering with silly pennants, facing a supermarket near a medieval frozen custard stand like a Tuscan fort . . . but between which was a pathetic little copse of spindly trees on a bit of unpaved earth?

And why was I so sensitive to the stink of cars, so threatened by the bright directional lines and arrows in the street forcing me to decide where to go before I knew where I was going—and where was that?—but without which I'd end up in the next town, though where the next town was, or if there were such things as towns any more, remained problematic. Route 3 was the chugging, clanking, cancerous artery you had to ride to survive, for the needs of most local residents refused to stay confined to the choice and showy wares of Center Rivertown and demanded snow tires, Big Macs, and porno videos.

But Charlie and I were not on Route 3 shopping for snow tires or discount jeans. We were on an unforeseen errand . . . though isn't life itself a string of such errands? Dr. Doré was the price of our now inevitable baby!

He had ambushed Ellie in front of the abortion clinic as she made her way toward it, frightened, guilty, accompanied by the unfortunate but intrepid Rita. Rita had fought hard to get her charge past the feverish demonstrators, who waved pictures of fetuses and said things like, "Think what you're doing!" and they might have made it if the leader of the mob, Doré, hadn't had, like, charisma. Before Ellie knew what was happening he had gotten her to agree to at least think about it, and Rita was left sputtering among the pro-lifers.

A couple of weeks later Ellie phoned to say that she had decided to have the baby after all, but only if Dr. Doré, having promised to keep the circumstances of their meeting and Ellie's momentary lapse into godlessness a secret, was "in charge" of the whole thing. And that Bill of the curly hair, mischievous Irish eyes, and ruddy cheeks, not to mention flying fists, had agreed. And that I was supposed to bring Charlie around to this so-called plan, without, of course, mentioning the abortion clinic . . . and so ended the happiest two weeks of my life.

Clinique Doré was in a mini-mall, stuffed between Van's Video and Shoe Wonder. A baby-blue building with a mansard roof, it looked like—might have been, must have once been— a Pizza Hut! Now there were window boxes of geraniums and ivy and a tiny brass replica of a baby on the front door.

Charlie and I went in and sat down. The building had been redone with cottage cheese ceilings and cheap motel decor. A crucifix hung over the receptionist's desk, and framed prints of liquid-looking nonobjective art hung on the walls. A white-noise machine covered specific sounds from within. On the foam-rubber sofa, Charlie squeezed my hand.

"Fran, I—"

The door opened and Ellie came in, consigning his thought to obscurity. She wore a bright printed dress and sandals, and her hair was very "done," curls rigidly sprayed into orderly disorder. She was carefully made up, with too much blusher and mascara. I liked her better the other way, with her T-shirts and ponytails. I wore a rather stern dress of navy blue linen, with a white collar suited to a barren wife, and I'd gotten a haircut. Our eyes met, mine accusingly; hers wavered, then moved quickly away as she gave our names to the receptionist.

Bill followed her in. Certainly tall, certainly dark, eyes definitely blue. But the rose of his cheeks suggested the tiny broken blood vessels of the boozer, and the naughty, heartbreaking Irish smile was, to me, the provoking sneer of a wimp. I concentrated on not judging the synthetic tweed sportcoat, shiny pants, and patent leather shoes. I didn't find him handsome. He was too coarse and crude, lips too red and tongue (also red) too constantly visible. His bonny blue eyes locked with mine and I had trouble pulling away. It wasn't a seductive gaze; it was more like Hello, fellow cuckold. It was insolent, irritating, and right on the mark. Bill Red-Lips, Fran Hindoo-Eyes. Charlie and Ellie Never-Mind. Lost in the stars, those two couldn't be trusted. Bill and I would take care of it all. . . . I sighed miserably.

We'd barely mumbled unnecessary introductions when the door opened and Dr. Seymour Doré appeared. Of medium height, shorter than Charlie or Bill, he wore a black three-piece suit, white shirt and black tie, and pointed tan shoes. He had a large, soft, earnest face and burning dark eyes, milky white skin, wavy black hair in a neat part, and hands that I was immediately aware of; also large and soft, they often moved slowly around, seeking a place to land: Ellie's back, Charlie's shoulder, the chairs that he moved into a circle for us to sit on. The office with its indirect lighting, curved Naugahyde sofa, and free-form sculpture didn't seem to go with him.

He and Ellie smiled at each other. His look was godly, hers a little preening.

"We're here at Ellie's request," Charlie said rather crossly, "and I'm not sure what the point of this is."

"People never do at first," Doré said, smiling. "And I'll bet Ellie dragged you here by the hair." He was not so dumb. I looked at him, then at Bill, who appeared slightly stunned.

66

"What are your credentials, Dr. Doré?" Charlie asked.

Doré immediately reached into a desk drawer and took out several printed pages which he handed around: his résumé. I glanced at it. Parsippany Law School, a psychology degree from some obscure place, a couple of years at a medical school I'd never heard of. His training was "ecumenical," his interest in "the legal, medical, and spiritual interfaces of our society, especially fertility and adoption."

We all read them. There was a moment of silence as Charlie stared furiously at Bill's crotch, which bulged between widespread legs in tight pants, a stance that did not seem accidental. And Ellie, in her innocence, ignored the surrounding stench of male animal and only stroked, slowly, the arm of the Naugahyde sofa, sending occasional admiring glances around the mocha-carpeted, track-lit office, where the statues, I now saw, had a certain suitability: one suggested a mother and child, another could be a pregnant woman.

Doré's face wore an earnest, honest, how-can-I-help expression, lips parted slightly as if to suggest open options—though he'd already managed to close down the only one that made sense. Under his milky exterior, something burned and challenged, something almost hypnotic.

"Ellie says you arrange adoptions," Charlie said, "though we're not sure that's exactly what we want."

"I was away on business," said Bill suddenly, "and when I got home I found this . . . situation. This mess." He looked at Ellie, whose finger was moving slowly down the curved spine of the Birth figure. "This goddam mess."

Charlie looked at him. "Sorry. I'm sorry."

"Well," said Bill, "you'd better be more than sorry."

"I've done a lot of soul-searching. I behaved badly. Inexcusably. I feel very bad about the whole thing." He looked unhappy, and I knew he meant it.

"Well, just for starters," Bill yelled, "how about *very very* bad? How about like *shit?*" Doré's dark, burning eyes flicked back and forth between them.

"Yeah. I wish I could undo it. I can't. Fran and I had been having some difficulties. You'd left Ellie—"

"I was on a *business* trip! Guys like me make business trips too, you know. Just because I wasn't sent to some fancy hotel with limos and women and—"

"Let's try to stick to the point, Bill." Doré had a rich, theatrical voice.

"I was away trying to find work to better our lives. To improve things for our children. . . ."

"Well, you never told *me* that," Ellie said.

Bill seemed to increase in size. "Don't give me that crap. You knew perfectly well."

She looked around nervously at the three men.

"Did you know where he was, Ellie?" Doré asked. A silence so heavy you could almost feel it. Then she shook her head minutely, almost invisibly. "Is that a bruise on your face?"

"Oh, no. It's nothing. I just . . . fell against the door."

We all looked at Bill, and he sat back in his chair. Charlie gave him a disgusted look and said, "Fran and I want to keep the child."

"Do you agree to this, Ellie?" She nodded, and Doré smiled a slow, vast smile. "And you, Fran. I suppose you've tried the usual reproductive . . ."

"Obviously."

"I see." He gave me a lightning-fast head-to-foot glance, as though to check out this supposed infertility. "And of course you agree to this."

"Why else would I be here?" My foot was twitching.

"These questions may sound redundant, but I've found it's better if everybody says what they want up front. Bill?"

Bill was staring at his ankles. "She's not going to do it for nothing."

"Nobody ever said she was," Charlie snapped, as I tried not to smile.

"Twenty thousand or she won't do it," Bill said.

I picked up my bag. "If you'll excuse me."

Doré moved in neatly with a glowing description of his friendly little clinic, while I sat on the edge of my chair, picking at my handbag; then he moved on to the well-known North County Hospital, failing to mention that it was about to go bankrupt, where the baby would be delivered by the distinguished Dr. Ramahutti of Pakistan . . . the total fee being only ten thousand, not counting counseling, which he recommended, and other extras.

I got up and walked out of the room.

In the Burger King where we went for coffee afterward, I tired to talk Ellie out of the Clinique Doré and interest her in Dr. Lamborghini, the fine ob-gyn man I would have chosen for myself. But it was too late. She *wanted* to go to the friendly little clinic where they would understand, and nobody would give her funny looks the way they would in some cold fancy doctor's office. She trusted Dr. Doré; she didn't trust any of us. Then Bill told her she was being an asshole because here I was offering her the best, and she kept insisting on this stupid Indian jerk. . . . Charlie told Bill not to talk to her like that, Bill said he'd talk to her any way he wanted and Charlie'd better back off, and I lost my temper and told Ellie she could have the damn baby in a field for all I cared. Charlie and I would adopt; the deal was off! And as we were all yelling about that, Ellie cried, "Don't you see, this is why we *need* Dr. Doré!"

In the end, the delicate balance of forces between us, some unmentioned, ended with a contract paying Ellie ten thousand dollars and Doré five. Bill's noisy threats stopped when he was told we could all go to jail for baby-selling, and Charlie had always been glad to leave money matters to me. Because I had less to lose than Doré or Ellie, I was able to set the price; if the aborted abortion plot ever came to light, I'd shrug it off. In the end, power comes down to raw nerve.

The contract gave Ellie the illusion that there was something legitimate about our strange transaction. The baby was bone of her bone, flesh of her flesh—the way she saw it. She was *giving it over* to Charlie. Though Charlie believed the child to be his already, I advised him to keep such controversial, difficult thoughts to himself and keep his eye on the ultimate goal.

Charlie and I were in love again. We phoned each other in the daytime, held each other close by night in the four-poster bed.

"I never thought I could love you so much," he whispered. "Nobody ever did as much for anybody as you've done for me."

"I'm probably out of my mind."

"Every man wants to be forgiven, and you've not only for-given me, you're allowing me to have the child."

"Don't go out and start another one, Charlie."

"Oh, no . . . it was like a test, you see. . . . It never has to be made again. You were better than me. You forgave, and you accepted."

"And I want a windmill too," Kerner said.

He was leaning on my desk—my new desk in my new office over the coffee shop, where I was attempting to start a law practice. I shared the space with Phil Bollinger, an accountant, and Beulah Markowitz, a real estate agent. I never entered it without hearing Arthur's metal voice deep in my brain: "Having fun in the office over the coffee shop, Fran? Which is more challenging, the house closings or the zoning laws?" It was not, of course, what I was used to. After years in a hermetically sealed thirty-seventh-floor office in the city, I now looked out onto the town square with its gazebo, the Episcopal church, and a piece of the wide, greenish-gray river that flowed from the northern mountains into the broad plain. On the other side of the river were the malls, the developments, and Route 3.

My progress was slow. Downstairs on the shiny black door with the knocker was a little plaque: F. LETTERMAN, ATTOR-NEY-AT-LAW. While my office mates chattered on their phones, I sat there idly, pretending I was busy and trying to make a phone call to Charlie or a friend sound like official business. At lunchtime I went downstairs and had a tuna-fish sandwich, rather than going home to eat, and I ordered up coffee as though I were too busy to go down and get it. People in Rivertown moved cautiously, and I hadn't been around long enough. There seemed to be little need for legal services. Beulah had sent me two cases, a man on Holly Lane who wanted permission to put solar plates on his roof and a house closing: dull stuff compared to the city. But Beulah said, "Oh, it's all here, I guarantee you. There's plenty of action behind those white picket fences. Last year the wife of a big corporation head, they live in that mansion just south of the bridge, she was caught shoplifting in Saks. She had seventeen pairs of panty-hose and eight bras under her fur coat! And the mayor"—her voice dropped confidentially—"was found in a compromising situation in the back of the antiques shop on Juniper . . . with the handsome young owner! How about that? Now, don't repeat it, Fran."

Kerner, the man who wanted the solar plates, had been turned down by the zoning board for the third year in a row, largely because of the strenuous objections of an anonymous neighbor who believed that unsightly metal objects on Kerner's roof would depress the entire real estate market, if not collapse it completely. "He should spend the money having his roof repaired," the person opined in a typed, unsigned letter. I found it galling that this nameless villain could bring progress to a halt in such a way.

"I haven't heard anyone use the word 'progress' in years," Kerner said. "I never expected to hear it from some hard-boiled Manhattan lawyer."

"Well, I was supposed to try this case that raised my consciousness." I told him about Gilmore. "I guess I thought Rivertown would be kinder."

Kerner smiled. He wore a white shirt, a bright red tie, and an academically frayed tweed jacket. His beard was multihued: brown, gold, gray, white; his mustache was a shade darker and more of a piece. Beulah, from whose examination no one escaped, had told me a little about him. His wife had left him a couple of years before because, she said, he was completely mad. Darcy Kerner had once confided to Beulah that it was one thing to invent a brilliant seminal theory about human behavior and another to expect people—his own family—to live by it, which Kerner had done. Like an old Shakespearean actor who has come to think he was King Lear, he could no longer draw the line between his creation and reality. You didn't notice it, because he seemed so nice, low-key and rather self-effacing, but underneath he was a roiling, mad revolutionary. Darcy had taken the children and gone back to Chicago, where she came from, and married a CPA.

"Would you and Charlie have any objection to a windmill?" he asked.

"I'd love it and Charlie wouldn't care, or he'd like it because he could show it to his son and explain how it works. But the nameless wretch will shout even louder."

"How about a BLT?" he asked.

I'd finished feeling sorry for myself. It was time I stopped hiding away and got to know Rivertown. I'd feared clacking yentas and churchly wives seeking volunteers, kaffeeklatsches and ladies' garden groups, without admitting to myself that neighborhood and amorphous kindness were among the things we had moved for. Even Charlie had struck up an acquaintance with our neighbor on the other side, Sheldon Showalter, who was teaching him to shoot woodchucks.

We'd settled into Ellie's pregnancy. She still came three days a week, for light work only. It made sense. It was a hot August, her apartment had no air-conditioning, and the girls could play on the swing set and in the kiddie pool. She'd be away from Bill, where I could check on her. I was good to Ellie. When she looked woefully at the stuffed garbage bag, I took it out. I carried the laundry basket and watched her daughters while she lay on the living room floor with her feet higher than her head.

I liked having her there—coming home around five to find her putting a roast in the oven or making chicken salad, with Charlie safely at the office. Ellie's appeal diminished as her pregnancy advanced. Her hair was stringy, her face puffy, and her ankles swollen. She complained of hemorrhoids, and an allergic rhinitis kept her nose runny and a fistful of tissues in the pocket of her smock, dropping behind her like Gretel's crumbs, so she could be easily located. Her face had broken out, and her back hurt.

I secretly rejoiced at all these things that might have been mine. But because of Charlie's vision—to put it euphemistically—*Ellie's* legs ached, *her* nose ran, *her* sleep was interrupted; in four months it would be Ellie who would grunt and pant and sweat, cry out for something to dull the pain, expel our baby in all the foul smells and exudates nature deems necessary for childbirth. In the meantime I could wear tight-waisted dresses and high-heeled sandals and bikinis, my hair remained dark and silky, my ankles slender and bony as a bird's and brown from the suntan that was so easily mine, while Ellie burned or blotched. In shorts and a T-shirt, which I changed into after work for my daily run, I knew Charlie could hardly fail to notice the difference.

"When's the baby due?" Kerner asked, as we sat down in our booth.

"Around Christmas." I cleared my throat. "You know, Adam, that morning you were there—well, we were all a little hysterical." I glanced at him. "I suppose everybody in town knows it's Charlie's baby."

"It's Ellie's baby," Kerner said.

"Well, Charlie did have a little something to do with it. But what I meant was, you probably think we're all crazy."

"I wouldn't say that. But I would say"—he leaned back and crossed his arms—"that you might not have thought it through, which could be dangerous."

"But we have, Adam."

"Is Charlie a nice guy?" he asked. "I mean, a really decent guy? I don't know him that well."

"Of course." I was surprised. "He's—uh, very happy right now. Very thrilled, very grateful to Ellie."

"And Ellie's spirits?" He waved at the waitress and ordered two BLTs and two iced teas.

"You probably know better than I." There was an uncontrolled note of bitchiness in my voice that surprised both of us.

After a thoughtful moment—Kerner never hurried—he said, shrugging, "Well, she came to me at first because she wasn't clear on titles; she thought I was a medical doctor. Ellie didn't really understand that she owns her own body; she had some idea it belonged to other people, or God, or I don't know what."

"So *you* suggested the abortion." I stared at him as the waitress put down the sandwiches.

"I know I sound interfering, but it's hard for me to keep out of it, Fran. I teach and write and lecture about this sort of thing. I have certain beliefs, which some consider radical. . . . Tell you what, I'll drop a copy of my new book off at your house."

"In a plain wrapper?"

He laughed. "Just to encourage you to go after my windmill."

"What's it called, Adam?"

"The Penile Delusion: An Examination of the Wilting Patriarchy."

Ellie's spirits were not, in truth, as good as one might expect. I couldn't put my finger on the problem. When I handed her the first check for five thousand dollars, she winced and made a gesture of covering her eyes.

"What's the matter?"

"I don't know, it's just easier with—um, smaller checks, like the ones I work for. Then I can say: okay, so much for food, so much for gas, this is for the girls' lunches. I used to make little piles of it till Ch— Mr. Morse told me I shouldn't leave it around." Oh, God, he'd been to her apartment. She glanced at me. "Well, I just mentioned it to him once, that I divided it up in piles on the bureau—and you don't have to look at me that way, Fran, we *talked* sometimes, for heaven's sake, it wasn't just—"

"All right, all right! Here, take the fucking check"—which I was still holding as she eyed it doubtfully.

"Why do you have to use that language?"

"Because it makes me feel better."

Slowly she took the check by one corner. "I don't know, it scares me."

"You've got to learn to trust yourself. I advise you to put that money where Bill can't touch it. You know he's going to walk out on you again."

"Well, I don't think so, Fran. He promises he won't. He says he's learned his lesson"—whatever that was. "Anyway, you know how he is. He said it would be disloyal of me not to share the money with him, him not working and all." Bill's income from driving a truck was unsteady and had a way of disappearing. He often had ideas for "deals" that would bring riches if he only had some "venture capital." But according to Ellie, he lacked follow-through. "Seymour—um, Dr. Doré—said he could give me suggestions for good investments."

"Did he really. Such as what?"

"Well, he thinks it's very important to put your money into something you believe in, something that does good." The

74

bastard. I fought to keep a straight face, without which I would learn nothing. "And he isn't, like, pushing me or anything, but he told me about this place in the country where poor people, people without much, can lead a simple, spiritual life. It's called Life Farm, and he says it's a beautiful place and very spiritual. And sometimes the people there travel around to work for other causes, they aren't selfish, they don't take anything without giving something back. And they work so hard, you can get a good return on your money—" I tried to remain expressionless, but she caught my eye. "Well, I knew you wouldn't like it. You don't trust anyone."

"Ellie, please put it in a bank. Any bank."

Inevitably Bill had an idea too. His was rather ingenious. A salad van! Ellie would buy a used van, which they would paint white. His friend Buddy could decorate it with a big green pepper on one side, a tomato or a head of lettuce on the other. A salad bar on wheels! It might even play a little tune. He could be the Good Greens Man. When they weren't selling vegetables, they could take the kids on vacation and stuff.

I studied Bill as he outlined his idea between bites of a salami and cheese on rye from my refrigerator, where he felt increasingly at home. It wasn't bad. It had a weird symmetry, a surface cleverness. I didn't know Rivertown well enough yet to predict whether it would work.

Ellie said she'd think about it, an assumption of power that didn't please her husband. "If he had a project like this it might stabilize him, see. Settle him down."

"She'll decide." Bill, standing behind Ellie's chair, reached one hand down toward—not quite on—her left tit, grinning at me. I hadn't really thought about it before, but Ellie had undoubtedly fucked Bill; his big Irish cock had been jamming at the cervix within an inch of our baby, spreading only God knows what germs. Could Bill contaminate our gene pool? A tiny Bill Ferguson would lie in our white wicker crib—shiny shoes, pseudo-tweed jacket, and all. Our daughter would scorn Saks baby clothes and demand turquoise tulle and plastic shoes; our son would reject Harvard for the mall, where he would hang out with the guys, a pack of Camels stuck in his T-shirt sleeve, jiggling to rock from his earphones.

Ellie's irritability grew with her size. She became more provoking all the time, eating things she knew she shouldn't, drinking a beer when I was around because she knew I'd say something about it. When I did, she'd counterattack. "I hope you're getting rid of that filthy old cat."

"Baby? Never." Baby stalked balefully to his favorite spot, a recess in the wall where the garbage can was kept, where he could be sure to pick up the smell of onions and coffee grounds. He settled down to chewing his mange spots.

"Charlie thinks you should give it away," Ellie said.

"Charlie and I are very clear on everything, including the cat. Please, Ellie, I don't want to fight, it's too hot."

"Well, he told you already, I heard! It has mange and fleas and it's starting to rip up the furniture. It's dis-gusting. I wouldn't have a baby in the house with that thing."

"You aren't going to." I thought of telling her that if I kept gorillas in the house it was none of her business, but I didn't. "And cut the little hints about Charlie." Not that I really cared; I knew it was over. Who'd look at her now? And Charlie had never been happier. He talked of the first tooth, the first step, the first car. He spent a day at the Beaver Pond School and pronounced it pretty good but weak in science; he started running again to get back into shape. He started a small trust fund for little Jenny/Charlie Three.

What was the matter with Ellie? At six months she was supposed to be blooming. I watched her ironing very, very slowly. A slow tear crept down her cheek and she wiped it away with the back of her hand.

"What's the matter?"

She gulped. "I feel like a machine or something, for you and Charlie. Eat-this. Don't-eat-that. Put-your-feet-up."

"I know, it must be hard." I went over and put my arm around her. I felt as though I were comforting a large baby. "I know I'm a crabby bitch, but I can't help it. You're so good to do this, Ellie. . . . Charlie and I are so lucky. And we'll share the baby; you'll be its other mother, or its auntie. It'll be partly yours. You can visit it all the time and keep it for weekends." I hadn't discussed any of this with Charlie and didn't intend to.

She slowly spread out Charlie's shirt collar. "I wanted to

work partly to get out of the house; he leaves his shoes and his dirty clothes all over the place and expects me to pick up after him. Sometimes he drinks a lot of beer, or he and Buddy go out to a couple of bars, and then when he gets back he wants, he wants . . . and ever since, since . . . I can't stand to have him touch me. He says it's his husbandly right, but Sy—I mean Dr. Doré—says the only one I should listen to is Dr. Ramahutti, because my health and well-being and that of the baby comes first . . ."

"Of course, Ellie!"

". . . and so I thought it would be all right to come here, and the kids like it. But you pick all the time, Fran, and you give me headaches. And Charlie—now I'm pregnant it's like I'm not even a person, as far as he's concerned." The iron threatened to burn the shirt, and I grabbed it and turned it off. "I mean, of course I don't expect anything in *that* way . . . but now he looks at me like I'm a stranger, polite and cold; it's *crool*. After all, I'm the mother of his child!"

"I told Charlie I'd break his neck if anything ever, ever went on between you."

"Well, I know that, not in *that* way! But he could be friendly. The other day he bumped against me in the door and he jumped like he was bit, like he couldn't even stand to touch me." She was sniffling, half woe, half allergy. "And I caught him looking at me the other day, disgusted and amazed, as if to say, What did I ever see in her? I know I look lousy, I always do, my looks come back at the end . . . and Sy"—Sy!—"says it's not good for me to be upset. He's showing me how to meditate but I can't do it, everything runs around in my head . . . and so, Fran, it might be better if I got another job."

I couldn't believe what I'd heard. "Are you joking?"

"Oh, no! In fact I've already called the—"

I stalked out of the kitchen in a babyish rage. Up the stairs to our bedroom, a sea of pearl broadloom with an antique four-poster in the middle, where I flung myself facedown. The whole thing was a disaster; our child would be an idiot. She was part of our family. Didn't she know it? Sharing our food, washing our underwear, ironing Charlie's shirts, having our baby. The idea of her leaving and immersing herself so intimately in another family's life was unacceptable. I heard her slow step on the stair. As she arrived at the top with ironed clothes, I growled, "You'd better think how your new employer might feel as you blow up with the child of your last one."

"Well"—she drew herself up—"I *am* a married woman. They wouldn't know."

"*If* I didn't tell them. *If* you could even get another job without my reference. And most people wouldn't treat you as well as I do; they'd work you like a dog. 'Clean behind the couch, Ellie! Bring in the wood! Leave your kids home! No, you *can't* leave in time to pick up your daughter at school!' " Ellie looked stricken. "But go ahead, find out for yourself. It's time you learned something about the real world; you're going to be out in it soon enough. In fact, you don't know how good you've got it!"

Ellie and I stared furiously at each other, and she caved in first.

"Well," she said, in her hoity-toity, I'm-a-lady voice, "Maybe I'll reconsider. On one condition, Fran."

"What?"

"That you never forget that *you don't own me.*"

· 7 ·

LULU, BACK FROM HER TRIP, DECIDED TO STAY ON. SHE PHONED a friend in Venice to make arrangements.

"Yes, Cipi darling. . . . *Molte grazie.* . . . How lucky Beppi can do it. He'd better keep Giulia a couple of days a week; she needs the money. Now, Cipi, how's my darling Bernadetta and the grandchildren? *Si . . . si.* . . ." Then some rapid whispered Italian which I knew was about me.

Lulu's friends were mostly named things like Cipi and Beppi and Lippi and Gino; they had beautiful Annas or Lucias at home and usually, by now, several grandchildren. Sometimes she shed a few tears because they would never, never divorce. They were usually handsome, sometimes rich, and always "fun." They chattered, gossiped, told jokes, danced, knew wines, and would do anything for Lulu. They had been around, sometimes with other names, since my father died. They had taught me to joke, to joust, to manage at parties, to swallow shyness and fear, to be charming, to land on my feet. The Beppis and Cipis, the Jean-Lucs and Harrys, had once been her age; she had grown unaccountably older while they remained young; she'd just never found one to grow old with her. And she had told me she would never marry except for love, proving how very American she really was.

"I'll talk to Beppi myself tonight. I assume this is not to be mentioned to Lucia. . . . Of course not, I won't even ask, but I hope he doesn't get stinko. I hope he doesn't drink at all. Oh, he should know about my terrible fridge, it hardly cools; I just use it for milk and butter and fruit." Pause, gasps, giggles. "Did she really say that? . . . How could she make such a fool of herself, she knows better than that! It's like that time at Torcello, remember? . . . Cipi, my nickel is running out, give my love to everybody."

She hung up and made her naughty-girl moue that always irritated me. "If it's all right with you and Charlie . . . and Beppi's paying a pretty good rent. I couldn't bear not to be here for Act Three, so to speak."

Lulu had bought the palazzo around twenty years before, for not much money as palazzos go. ("You're on your own, Francesca, there's no point in my keeping the apartment"—the one on East Thirty-fifth Street, the closest thing to a real home we ever had.) And no one, mind, called it a palazzo but Lulu, and romantic as it sounds, nobody would *want* it except Lulu. It's cold, drafty, and damp as the canals rise inexorably; green slime covers the marble step which is the boat stop, and in summer it smells of . . . rot, I guess, since the whole city is rotting away. With my new practical know-how, I'd advised against it: it would lose its value, it would simply fall apart. It took me many years to understand—if I do yet—that Lulu's needs and desires are far, far from mine, that things that matter to me don't concern her. Her finances were mysterious then and still are. My father had left her something, certainly enough for my education and the travel she couldn't stop doing. I suspected there were other sources, an old lover or two who helped out—which was more inclined to happen in a culture where women are still protected and frequently have no vocation—and for that reason she managed in a way that lone women somehow could in Europe. Her furniture was threadbare, the description of the fridge to Cipi optimistic. But something always came up, and she knew she wouldn't be allowed to starve.

Though Charlie's and my upbringings were so different, we felt one great lack in common. We both had "light parenting"— Charlie lost between his two sisters, me in some mini-Grand or Chez Somebody with Yvette or Marie while Lulu danced the night away in her endless search for love. Neither of us had ever experienced those close passionate ties, or only in our dreams— movie dreams of a mother who'd fight Indians, rob a bank, throw herself across the tracks to save her child, which all mothers are presumed willing to do. Though I've never known one, I've known people who believe their mothers would do such things, which is probably what matters. But we didn't know that, Charlie or I, when we whispered these secrets on our pillows.

Lulu took charge of Ellie. She listened to her woes, took her to Macy's and bought her a corset for her back, made her rest every afternoon. I watched all this with mingled relief and galling jealousy.

The three of us went for dinner one night to the little French place, Bistro Beaumont.

"That poor girl has nobody." Lulu sighed.

I'd assumed, without really thinking about it, that Ellie had some large loving tribe of parents and siblings, aunts and uncles, who gathered together for family rites. I'd thought she had a family a little like Charlie's but more cheerful, perhaps, or at least more shanty Irish, devil-may-care, who drank a little too much and sometimes fell off the straight and narrow but, absolved by confession, tolerated things like having the boss's baby.

"They're mostly in Delaware," Charlie said, sliding danger-ously close to the amount of Ellie-ism I tolerated—a line almost certainly doomed to be erased. "There's only an aunt and uncle around here. They're not a very close family."

"Well, that's funny. You'd think they would be." I stabbed at my *médaillons de veau* in irritation.

"Of course it would be more convenient if they were," Lulu said. "But *this* way, there's nobody around to help her." She shook her head. "She doesn't even talk to her mother in Wilmington very much. They talk sometimes, of course, but her mother just isn't very interested. Ellie's told her it's Bill's baby. And the mother just says, 'Oh, not another one, how are you going to manage?' and 'Don't ask *me* for help!' "

"You seem to have all the details," I said, in a sour voice. She'd learned more about Ellie than I had in months.

"Well, I feel sorry for her. Everybody working over her all the time. As I say, she has nobody."

"What about Rita?" I'd had too much to drink. I felt the black cloud building up inside my head, the one I managed to keep down most of the time. Sometimes I didn't have the strength.

"Oh, Rita. She has her own problems."

I was into my third martini. "Nothing I do is good enough, is it, Lulu? Nothing. A lot of people . . . a lot of mothers might think I've led an exem . . . plary life. Exemmmm-plary. I'm independent, I'm a professional woman. I'm married to a man other women would die for." If they didn't know too much about him. "The only thing I've ever failed at was getting p-p-pregnant." I was crying and trying to order another drink at the same time, which Charlie prevented by shaking his head and making gestures at the waiter. "And that's all that counts with you. Don't think I'm not sorry. Don't think I don't wish *I* was the one due in December. . . . You'll never have a real grandchild; Charlie will never have a child by his wife. . . ."

"Francesca, calm down." Lulu never got used to my occasional outbursts. I had them every once in a while, but more often recently. Charlie hated them. He sat there tying his napkin into a knot.

"Look at me, Lulu. Just look! I'm forty-three and I look ten years younger. I'm thin. I'm pretty. I'm wearing a two-hundred-dollar little-nothing dress and I have plenty more in the closet. I have Charlie . . . what do you want?"

"Fran, knock it off," Charlie said.

"Knock it off . . . it hurts too much. Am I made of stone?"

"Fran, I am very proud of you. I brag about you to my friends." She gave Charlie a bewildered look.

"You've never understood, Lulu. I don't think you can. I'll spend my life falling on swords to get your attention . . . to get a word of praise, just a word! I'll probably die just to try to get your attention."

Charlie was throwing bills on the table. "Let's get out of here."

In the car Lulu said, "You did this once in the lobby of the Grand Hotel in Lucerne, but you were ten years old. I think it's time you outgrew this sort of behavior."

"No, it was Cannes, that horrible mother at the pension in Cannes, the one with the blue-black hair and clothes the same color and the hatchet face and the homely daughter in plaid who sniffled all the time—is that what you want? Well, sorry I can't accommodate you. I'm sorry I'm not pathetic enough or in some horrible mess of my own making like Ellie. . . ."

I don't know what else I said. Lulu became very quiet, then told me if I kept this up she was leaving for who knows—Venice, Route 3, Mars—baby or no baby. At home we had coffee and chocolate ice cream in the kitchen, and I ended up weeping and apologizing and crawling off to bed. The next day we all pretended nothing had happened, except Lulu suggested that meditation might help me if I would only open my mind to it. And she meant it about leaving; she hated "scenes."

One day I came home to find a note: MEET ELLIE AND ME AT CLINIQUE LOVE LULU.

Pondering my mother's elliptical message, I bolted for the car and Route 3. Was Clinique Doré in the mall with Shoe Wonder, or was it the one with Laundry King? Eventually I found it and ran into the waiting room.

"Frannie, I'm glad you came. It was the husband"—raising her eyebrows skyward, a gesture she often used to express hopelessness about the male sex.

Bill had suddenly arrived, she told me, while she and Ellie were having a cup of tea, demanding to speak to his wife in privacy. Lulu had gone into the dining room and listened while they argued. After waffling for weeks, Ellie had turned thumbs down on the salad van—for which Bill let her have it, disappearing shortly afterward. After having a look at her, Lulu thought it would be prudent to bring her over for a checkup.

"She's still in there, but I've seen much worse; Giulia used to come in every Monday morning beaten absolutely bloody, and she refused to leave him; they consider it the husband's right . . . though I don't agree with that at all."

"Mother, for God's sake!"

"It's nothing, Fran, a couple of bruises and a cut or two, a few stitches and she'll be fine. It was partly"—her voice dropped—"a situation I've heard of before during pregnancy: men are so used to having *what* they want *whenever* they want it, and she's been told to say no if she doesn't feel like it . . . and she told me she *never* feels like it."

Clinique Doré had thin walls, and I had the sense of invisible, teeming life behind them. There was a strange familiarity about the place, a tantalizing déjà vu.

"Did you call the police?"

"No, Ellie didn't want to. She has some friend whose husband was physically abusive, and when she called the police—"

"Was it Rita?"

"I think so, why?"

"It's always Rita."

"Well, the police wouldn't do a thing for Rita. The husband just said she'd fallen downstairs and the police believed him, and Ellie said that was what always happened, and I'm sure it's true. And Rita had said to get to a doctor and have a picture taken—"

"How did Rita enter today's events?"

"Ellie called her for advice. So we came here, and she's being seen by the *dottore*, but you know, Ellie has some funny ideas."

"What did she do with the money?"

"I don't know, Fran. Though she mentioned investing it in a home or—"

"A farm."

"That could be it."

I dropped onto the sofa, trying to fend off a tension head-ache. From all around there were little cries and murmurs, little squeaks and soft bumps, little bubbling, trickling, squishing sounds. Were they siphoning out fat? Babies? Dropping mothers and babies on the floor? I imagined phantom pizza cooks slam-ming paddles and squishing dough, flinging it merrily up in the air, blobs of dough big as infants . . . ghostly Indian doctors with babies on paddles.

I'd learned to listen in Rivertown, listening to our house, always trying to separate benign sounds from threatening ones. Now our sump pump beat like my own heart, the tiny rattle of the radiators in winter signaled warmth and order. I listened to my car, searching for precise words for Bruno at the Arco sta-tion. I'd heard an old man clearing out catarrh and an excited mouse giving a speech to many people hammering . . . but here in Clinique Doré nothing made sense, though I thought there was a faint odor of pepperoni.

I looked more closely at the art on the wall . . . which turned out to be not art but pictures of fetuses at various stages, one for each month, fitting in with Sy's beliefs. I found the seven-month picture. Charlie Three's eyes were closed just like those, his tiny fists doubled up against the imminent onslaught of civilization, his bald moonlike head encasing a brain already preparing for wisdom, confusion, and insanity, his tiny legs flexed as though in mid-leap. There was something mystical about him . . . haunting, suggesting other kinds of life in other worlds, magic powers.

"The problem is, Fran, she won't—"

The door opened and Ellie appeared with Ramahutti, a smiling, servile Indian who could be my cousin, fragrant with rosewater. Ellie had a black eye and a couple of bruises, and there was a Band-Aid on her cheek.

"The baby is well, Mrs. Morse, by hand examination," Ramahutti said. "The heartbeat is strong. Mrs. Ferguson's little cuts are not serious."

"Well, Ellie. How are we going to get you through the next two months? Maybe I should keep you on a leash." It didn't sound as jovial as I'd intended, and her eyes darkened.

"I reported the matter of the amniocentesis to Dr. Doré," Ramahutti said.

"What matter?" I asked.

"Mrs. Ferguson has refused this simple test."

Ellie's mouth was pursed into an I-won't-budge expression.

"Dr. Doré said it was perfectly all right," she said. "He's *so* wise and *so* understanding."

"He is *such* a fruitcake."

Lulu gave me a warning look. "It seems that Ellie has some strong convictions about the invasion of her body."

"If only she'd had them a few months ago. Come on, Ellie, everybody has amnios and at the same time we could find out the sex. It's in the contract, you have to."

"My body is my empowerment," Ellie said, drawing herself up.

Ellie won the round. As she, Lulu, and I walked out to the parking lot, I suddenly asked, "Ellie, did you by any chance get this from Dr. Kerner?"

She had. "He's so brilliant, he knows about these tribes all over the world and their strange customs and all, and things they do with their babies, and they're never separated from the mother for a minute till they're five years old . . . they sleep in the same bed and the husbands can just *lump* it."

"That's very interesting, but I don't understand what it has to do with anything."

"Well . . . it's hard to explain. But Dr. Kerner thinks it's nobody's business what sex the child is, and it doesn't matter anyway."

"Well, it doesn't really, but it would be fun to—"

"And he doesn't even think it matters *who* the father is, in a theoretical way. It all has to do with men trying to own women . . . and it goes back to how, thousands of years ago, they worshiped the Great Goddess and everything."

We were in the parking lot. It was a bright, crisp fall afternoon, the kind of day we'd moved here for. Even Route 3 had a bright, fluttering clarity, a parade air: a hundred colorful pennants snapped over the used-car lot across the street, little swirls of paper leaves twisted across the ground, the trees on the hills

85

beyond were a tawny gold. How clear and simple everything appeared to be. How muddy and mysterious it all in fact was.

"You must have misunderstood Dr. Kerner. He'd never say . . ." But he would.

"He's such an interesting man, Fran," Lulu said. "Some of the things he says remind me of things I've heard Maude Brill say."

I ignored this traitorous remark. "Ellie. I will say this only once. I don't care what Dr. Kerner says. For two more months you belong to us. If I want to hang you by your heels in the village square, so be it. As for your money I don't care either, though today's financial move has gotten you a black eye and a bloody nose, and you seem anxious to end up in the street with a tin can in your hand . . . and I have a few things to say to Dr. Kerner." I was sputtering.

They both looked at me coldly. Lulu, ignoring me, settled Ellie in her car, making sure she did up her seat belt. She closed the door and we stood watching her as she drove off.

"Shame on you," Lulu said.

When I tracked Kerner down, I told him sternly to keep his wacky ideas to himself.

"You agreed with me before, Fran. I have no intention of censoring myself. Have you read my book yet?"

"Adam, that book is six hundred and thirty-five pages long."

"If you read the first two pages of Chapter Three, you'll have a pretty good idea of the bones of the theory. And the summary at the end of Chapter Six. I'd be very interested in your opinion." His intense blue eyes stared at me. "I know you're smart, Fran. Just let your mind go."

Lulu and I drove over to Ellie's apartment one evening, an attempt at reparation. Despite the faux-Miami exterior of 2941 River Tide Boulevard (Route 3's more pretentious name), a meanness lay within. Low ceilings, orange walls, plastic philodendron, a feeling of claustrophobia. It all stank of cigarette butts, which were plentiful, and rancid cooking oil. Through the thin walls came the sounds of televisions, crying babies, angry voices, coughing, scrapes, thumps, the familiar Route 3

86

rag. The elevator seemed to be made out of thin plastic. When it cracked open at the fourth floor, I saw Jodi and Kimberly and a couple of other kids hanging around down the hall. When she saw us, Jodi hastily hid her cigarette. They returned my greeting with a sneaky, surreptitious "hello."

"Don't you have any homework?" I asked brightly.

"I did it already," Jodi said, looking at me with hate.

"She's only in the second grade," Lulu said, ringing the doorbell.

"I had tons to do at your age," I said. "Three hours each night. In Europe kids get a decent education."

Ellie had never looked worse. She was enormous—a huge blob of an abdomen with an exhausted, wretched woman attached to it. Everything had lost its luster: skin, hair, eyes. Her eyes were permanent founts, unceasing little oozes, the way water seeps to the surface in the woods to gather into tiny streams. That luscious, fruity skin was lifeless and broken out, and the once-blond curly hair was a handful of dry straw tied back with a rubber band. I'd expected a cold greeting after my recent behavior at Clinique Doré and had come in part to apologize. But so low was she that she stared at me dolefully and sighed as though I were just another inevitable woe in the long string that spelled out her life. She smiled wanly at Lulu and invited us in, then waddled down the hall to the living room on swollen ankles.

I'd never wanted to be anywhere less. A small box of a room with the sounds of traffic coming through the window. Cheap rugs, cheap everything. Lots of everything. Piles of magazines, a huge TV set, heaps of family clutter—kids' clothes, games, sneakers, books, plus TV Guide, stray socks, loaded ashtrays, a pile of pennies, assorted junk mail, hand lotion, an Ace bandage, Bill's fake-alligator shoes, bulging over the fourth toes, some snapshots, wads of tissues—the things I was always hiding in my house were the substance of Ellie's apartment. The remains of an unappetizing-looking dinner sat on the coffee table: take-out ribs and beans, cans of Coke, and chocolate chip cookies in a bag.

On the green foam-rubber sofa sat a thin woman in glasses. Her frizzy black hair burst around her head in a large Afro, her

87

thin coral-pink mouth matched her pants suit. She looked at me as though I were Satan.

"This is Rita," Lulu said to me. I'd known an instant before she said it. "Rita, this is Fran."

"Hello," I said. Rita made a sound as she assessed how best to deal with me.

Ellie lowered herself carefully into a chair. As I looked around the room she said, as though in reply, "I haven't heard a word from Bill."

"He was simply driven out," Rita said.

"I can see how Bill might react strongly to Ellie's pregnancy," I said carefully. "He's not a very secure person."

"He's been pretty patient on the whole," Lulu said, sitting down next to Rita.

"Well, that's a very strange statement, that Bill isn't secure," Rita said to me. "I don't know why he shouldn't be. He's very handsome and attractive to women. He's extremely smart and enterprising. Most people would admire his idea of greens on wheels, even though it never came to fruition. He loves his wife and is a wonderful father. But after a certain point, *anybody* would say to themselves, I can't deal with this."

"Are you feeling all right, Ellie?" I asked rather pointlessly.

"I feel horrible. My back hurts and Dr. Ramahutti says the baby is big, and my legs ache. I can hardly keep anything down, and I have to do Number One all the time, about four times a night, so I hardly get any sleep."

"Do the support stockings help?" Lulu asked.

"Oh, I guess a little. But I'm just all wrung out by this one. It's like it's sucking out all my energy and strength. With Kimberly I was working right up to the end, you know, at the gourmet shop where I was part-time, and I'd pick up Jodi at my neighbor's and take her food shopping, and then sometimes we'd go out for dinner or we'd see some friends. I couldn't do that now for anything; I'm tired all the time."

"*That* was a little different, last time," Rita continued, staring fixedly at me. "*Then* she had a normal home and a supportive husband. This shocking and stressful illegal situation she's in now would be too much for anybody. Ellie is completely unprotected. I only pray that since she's made this decision, the whole

88

thing goes off without any more difficulty and she can return to her life. And that Bill returns to the marital home."

I'd pretend she wasn't there. "You're welcome at our house any time you want to come, Ellie. Not to work or anything, just to come where it's quiet, look at TV, or take a walk in the woods or around the neighborhood. You could bring the kids the way you did before."

"Now *that's* a very strange offer," Rita said. "I can't imagine why Ellie would be more comfortable there than by her own place, or by me. And I don't know why you make such an offer, Mrs. Morse, when your home on Holly Lane, in the Beaver Pond School District that's supposed to be so terrific, must be full of painful memories for Ellie. . . . It's where it all started, among all you nice people." Zap. "Myself, I wouldn't take Beaver Pond if you *gave* it to me."

"Are you taking your vitamins, Ellie? I'll get you more if you need them. And did he tell you, you should lie on your back with your feet—"

"Hey, who's the doctor anyway, Mrs. Morse?" Rita's voice was rasping. "It seems to me you better keep out of the medical business. Dr. Ramahutti is a very distinguished obstetrician and an extremely sympathetic person as well, and Dr. Doré is truly one of the finest human beings I ever met. I've talked to them both and I was very glad to hear that they are entirely on Ellie's side and prepared for legal defense if necessary."

"What?"

"I didn't say it would be necessary, Mrs. Morse. I never made such a statement. It's strange that you should suggest it." The woman was crazy. "And you a lawyer. You should know what the law is intended for, to protect the poor and innocent. To keep people like Ellie from the shark's jaws."

I was getting depressed too. It wasn't just Rita. It was the amount of Rita-ness, somehow all part of the salmon walls and salmon polyester and flickering soundless TV that Ellie kept furtively glancing at, the painting of an Irish setter on the wall, and the smell of barbecued ribs and beer and Vicks and cigarette butts. It was more than the Route 3 rag. It wasn't fair to condemn people for their poverty or their bad taste . . . but why

89

was there *so much*? It all seemed to be part of a vast encroaching debris slug of wrong-heartedness, weird assumptions, distorted values, loss of connections, boredom twisted into aggression.

I would have even welcomed having my fancy life shown up by something simpler and better. What had happened to bare houses and bare-bones goodness, to Mother Hubbard and the Cratchits, the tortoise who won the race, the values taught by Miss Comfitt, my old headmistress, who spoke daily of good and evil? When had simplicity been corrupted? What had happened to that fine old belief that want brings wisdom, that the accumulation of possessions carries a certain risk, and the devil makes us greedy? I'd been taught these things as a child, but now they sounded as strange as Oriental music.

Jodi came in the door and tried to creep unnoticed into her room.

"She smokes," I told Ellie. "I think you should know." Jodi stared at me in loathing.

"I have advised Ellie to sue." Rita droned on. "Nothing personal, Mrs. Morse. But it seems to me there should be some recompense for the grief and misery you and your husband have caused this family. The law recognizes that money is equal to grief and suffering, and the courts now make large awards to those who abuse others, as punishment for irresponsibility. I have this friend who was unable to conceive, and she went to a doctor who put her on a drug which gave her quintuplets, and one died and it wasn't right, and she sued because she couldn't afford to raise them, and she got two million, even though the lawyer took most of it. And she deserved to win! What kind of doctor—"

"Let's go, Lulu." I looked at Ellie. With one eye on the TV, she scrambled in her chair. "Don't get up. And . . . Rita." I stared back at her. "You know something? You talk too much. And that is only the barest, barest beginning of what's wrong with you."

Lulu got us out of the apartment.

"Lulu, if I get through this I'll never do anything bad again."

■   ■   ■

Thanksgiving Day: pale luminous sky, pewter clouds in low streaks, brown leaves eddying around the lawn and the waiting swing set. Wild geese on the edge of the gray, choppy river, chipmunks in the woods, chestnut and bittersweet and a couple of other berries I hadn't yet identified. Shouts of kids playing, the faint distant hum of the parkway. I'd grown fond of our nature preserve now that I had time (a byproduct of working locally) to appreciate it. I was discovering solitude. Just Baby and me: I carried him back to the house, his claws digging mistrustingly into my jacket.

As I came in Charlie said, "I hope you've thought about what to do with that cat, Fran."

I laughed. "Not funny, Charlie." Then the doorbell rang.

"I'm not laughing," he said, as he went out to answer it.

The start of Thanksgiving Day: the mahogany turkey, the dish of ruby cranberry, the bright green broccoli, the fragrant pies.

Charlie raised his champagne glass. "Soon there'll be a spe- cial little person in this house," he said, smiling at me, then at Ellie, who didn't smile back. "Somebody who belongs to all of us."

Ellie looked better. She was one of those women whose looks change from day to day, from month to month. I'd seen her go from a fresh, pretty girl to a bedraggled frump. Now something else was happening. The thick waxy skin of a few weeks ago was pale and translucent, the dry hair combed loosely back and almost pretty. Her summer-sky eyes were clear, and the cinnamon-brown top she wore suited her. Jodi and Kimberly wore matching skirts and sweaters in pastel colors.

"My *brother*," said Jodi, who hadn't forgiven me for telling about the smoking. "My *sister*."

"We've talked about that enough, so be quiet," Ellie said sharply. She sounded sensible and businesslike, saying it quickly to avoid an uncomfortable pause. She looked better, she *was* better; in the kitchen before dinner she'd told me she was getting used to being without Bill. It was easier with the girls without him. She was dealing with the fact that he was a "chauvinist" and irresponsible. Could some of my remarks about the liberation of women have sunk in?

Something less tangible was happening to Charlie. He'd put on a little weight, but it wasn't fat; instead he seemed . . . denser, fuller perhaps, a glass slowly filling up with something rich and strange. His color was stronger, his movements more deliberate. His features had thickened slightly. What was this liquid? I'd been attracted by the mysterious quality I'd thought was *mind*, the spare intellectual devotion of a man who helped plan satellites to look down on an imperfect world. But I could hardly find that any more. Was he filling up with fatherhood? After a second glass of champagne I found whatever-it-was irritating, and I kicked him under the table to stop the stupid toasts. He ignored me.

"Jodi, would you like stuffing and broccoli?" Lulu asked.

"I hate broccoli," Kimberly whined, "and the stuffing has icky things in it."

"Dates," I said.

"Kimberly." Ellie's voice had a warning edge.

"Aunt May makes better stuffing." The little girl pushed a piece of turkey around on her plate. "I wish I was there."

"But you are not, Kimberly," I said. "And if you sit here you'll have to have the manners to taste everything once." If Ellie had her way they'd live on Twinkies. "I was brought up to eat what was put in front of me without complaining."

In a moment of supreme misjudgment, we'd invited our neighbors: Sheldon Showalter, who shot small animals with his Luger and was trying to sue the town because he'd sprained his ankle in the station parking lot one night when he was drunk; his wife, Johanna, a thin blond woman with desperate eyes who ran the village knit shop; their two sons; and Kerner, who looked frayed and uncomfortable. His jacket had seen better days; his sweater had a hole in it. Johanna had told me he let rooms out to make ends meet. Though a distinguished author and lecturer, he had failed to get tenure at Grier because he insisted on teaching penile delusions and such audacious matters instead of straight anthropology.

I'd looked at the designated sections of *The Penile Delusion* and found that, like cognac, a little went a long way. The nuclear family, he said, had been established thousands of years ago so men could claim ownership of the children and the property. Fatherly love was not natural but, rather, an artifact of civilization: mothers were the true owners of their children both before and after birth, to abort or not, to keep or give away. This power had been veiled over and obscured by men, but women should understand it and insist on it . . . acceptance of paternal influence should come only in proportion to increased equality in other areas . . . and hundreds of pages more, but then I closed the book. This dangerous man was sitting at our dinner table.

"Fran feels strongly about nutrition," said Charlie, as Kerner stared at me. You couldn't tell what he was thinking. "She always says, 'You are what you eat.' "

"You are not," Kerner said.

"But don't you think, Adam, that people who eat unhealthy food generally look . . . I mean, healthy people: you just know. . . ." Damn him. I wrenched my eyes away. "Taste the broccoli, Kim."

"I don't want to."

"Taste it."

Kimberly cautiously put a microscopic green sprig into her mouth and chewed, tears welling in her eyes. We all sat watching her breathlessly till she swallowed it, gagging and red-faced, and grabbed for a glass of apple juice. "Pheeeuuwee, it's *yuk.*" There was a terminal silence as they all looked at me.

Sheldon Showalter looked particularly stunned. "We have never—*ever*—forced our children to eat anything." It was hard to say what the result of this was. Their sons, around ten and twelve, did not seem to have needed such discipline. They cleaned their plates and waited breathlessly for more. They almost ate the china. They watched Charlie's carving knife skillfully slicing the snowy breast as though their lives hung on it . . . and it was more than food they were hungry for.

"We keep only natural things in the house," said Johanna. "Isn't that right, Shel. The boys snack on fresh vegetables and yogurt." She seemed very jittery, dropping spoons and spilling gravy.

"Takes me ten minutes." Sheldon poured himself more champagne. " 'Glop' we call it: yogurt and cottage cheese and chopped crudités. We always keep it around."

"It takes *you* ten minutes," said Johanna, after *I've* shopped for the vegetables and the low-fat yogurt and the farmer cheese at the dairy, and then I hear about how the knives aren't sharp and the cukes are no good. . . . I'd say each bowl of Glop takes more like two hours."

"Two hours," said Sheldon. "Well, now, isn't that terrible. Two hours." His gray eyes were tortured and shifty, his salt-and-pepper hair short and stiff. He kept setting his jaw determinedly, as though it tended to come undone, and sending me puzzling slinky looks. He was on his fourth glass of champagne, I was on my third. *"Po-o-or* Johanna."

"Tell you what," Charlie said. "After dinner we'll go for a walk in the woods." He smiled at the four kids, getting a definite nonreaction.

Kerner cleared his throat, giving Ellie, next to him, a brief smile. He must be bored to death with this idiotic conversation.

"Uncle Charlie has been boning up," he went on mercilessly. "The thrushes. The warblers. The mushrooms and toadstools and fall berries." He raised his glass. "To the season of the harvest!"

"Come on, Charlie," I said. "You don't know what a shrush is. Neither do I. What's a shrush?"

"A brown songbird." His smile froze as he looked at me. "There's a woodpecker down there too. Chipmunks. That little patch of woods is crawling with life, you just have to know what to look for." He raised his champagne glass for another ghastly toast. "Next year there'll be a little high chair, right there. And little Jenny or Charlie Three will be in it."

Anxiety: the cold wet hand that reached out of the darkness and grasped my soul, the automatic discharge of a thousand incoherent fears attacking like killer bees, turning the air brown and malevolent. Anxiety was panic that often struck when life was sweetest. Here we were on the brink of having everything we wanted. What was the matter with me? My eyes met Ellie's. Hers were glistening. She turned away, thinking no one had noticed. But I'd seen her eyes, her mouth flattened with fear.

I got up and went into the kitchen, where I stood rinsing dishes, swallowing hard and trying to pull myself together. In a moment Kerner appeared.

"Why did you do that to the kid?" he asked, wrapping up the turkey carcass.

I got out the dessert plates. "It's not going to work, Adam."

"You might be right."

I'd wanted reassurance. "I'm a powerless barren woman, so I act like a bitch to other people's children."

He covered the bowl of stuffing and put it in the refrigerator. "You read the end of Chapter Three, but you did *not* read Chapter Six," he scolded. "You don't understand it yet. I did *not* mean women only have power from motherhood. I meant, women as a sex have power from the *ethos* of motherhood. It's different. And I'm not really talking about men and women, but male and female principles."

I looked at him and whispered, "I'm scared." He put the dish down and put his arms around me for a moment; it was like being embraced by a huge tree, the trunk rooted in the earth, the branches enfolding me. I thought he smelled like the woods, but I was pretty drunk. He dropped a brief, beardy kiss on the top of my head.

"It's not bad, being a parent. You'll be bigger than the kid for a long time, don't forget."

I managed to smile as I took in the pumpkin pie and ice cream, but the texture of the evening, fragile to start with, was falling apart. Sheldon was too drunk to eat dessert, and he kept making nasty remarks to Johanna and the boys. Their marital myths began to come clear. Johanna was sinful, wasteful, slothful, gluttonous. Sheldon was pure and righteous and disciplined and strong. Ellie was, I think, trying to hide from what she already knew. She looked pleadingly at Charlie, and he smiled his deal-with-Ellie smile—avuncular, responsible, but very this-is-it. Those-are-the-breaks. He'd developed it at first to shut me up, but now I think it was real. She was only a vessel for his child. She knew it but couldn't accept it, it was so strange.

Stumbling around in the woods, I held Ellie firmly by the arm to keep her (and myself) from falling, delivering ever more urgently my usual advice on the prudent use of her money, such as starting a laundromat or candy store.

"I'll do the legal work for nothing. You and Rita could be partners."

"Thank you, Fran. But I have other plans."

"You'd better be careful. You're going to end up on the street, you jerk. And when you do, don't come crying to me." I went crunching and snapping down to the water, alone. A gaggle of Canada geese screeched and flapped a little way out as I pitched pebbles at them. Every pebble sent them squawking. What a fun walk, what a Norman Rockwell day we were having. This was what we'd moved here for. The drink was wearing off, and I was sinking fast.

A tear oozed into each eye. Charlie and Sheldon were deep in conversation, Sheldon making rifle gestures toward the Canada geese. Lulu and Johanna were in the house cleaning up, and Kerner was now walking with Ellie. She was talking animatedly as he chewed his unlit pipe, nodded, and listened, studying her with those piercing eyes. I watched them from my rock. It had nothing to do with fucking research. Was every man on earth an idiot? Did they all turn to pulp over cute little blondes, even pregnant ones?

I left them all there and went back to the house for another drink. In the study, the four kids were watching TV, but when I stood in the doorway and waved, none of them would look at me.

· 8 ·

At last, a call from Ellie: "It's starting."

A cold, crystal-clear night, a counterpane of early snow. The sky was black and deep, strewn with stars. I grabbed Charlie's hands. They were warm, throbbing, almost electric.

"How do you feel?"

"As though my life was about to start. As though I was about to be born."

"Have you been dead up to now?"

Charlie pulled on his coat. "She just mentioned Lulu and me, Fran. You don't have to go."

96

"You don't have to go to the manger, Balthazar. Just stay home and sniff your myrrh."

"All right, but for Christ's sake stay in the waiting room."

"Don't tell me what to do, Charlie. Our child is about to be born and I'm the one you should be considering, not Ellie. I don't think you trust me," I said as we got into the car.

Lulu, wrapped in her cape in the back, leaned forward on the seat.

"I did a chart on the baby, Frannie," she said quietly. "I hate to be a doomsayer, but we must be *very* careful tonight."

"Oh, Mother, please."

"It's the Sagittarius Vale," she said in a low voice, "and I pray she'll deliver after midnight."

We sped through the night as I'd always imagined, and the advantages of Ellie's going through this, rather than me, were clearer than ever. I secretly found the idea of childbirth disgusting. Had this personal delicacy affected my ability to conceive? Nothing sounded less appealing than being strapped to a rack in agonizing pain while a live creature fought its way out of my crotch as a wreath of grinning people watched; or to see my slender, well-cared-for body turn into a collection of spare tires, pendulous breasts, and clots of knotted veins . . . nor did the idea of nursing appeal in the slightest. Then I wondered if Lulu had felt the same way. Her hand gripped the back of the seat nervously, the silver snake ring she always wore glinting when we passed a light. We crossed the bridge over the deep, dark ribbon of water that divided Us from Them, as Beulah put it.

At night, Route 3 was a panoply of mismatched dark hulks fronted by dozens of tacky signs, glaringly lit. North County Hospital was a sprawling pink building in faux Spanish, set back from the road. It looked like a cheap hotel in the Southwest, now sitting, oddly, in snow. We skidded into the parking lot. In front was a Christmas tree with pink balls and blue lights.

Charlie and Lulu scooted off to Ellie's room while I waited, as ordered, in the lobby. I was the only person sitting on the vinyl couch, adding to the overflowing ashtrays. A huge stuffed Santa hung over the brightly lit nurses' station.

Charlie reappeared shortly.

"She's eight centimeters dilated."

"Did you measure?"

He ignored this. "I have to be in there. She doesn't have anybody."

"She has Lulu. And I'll bet Rita shows up, and the aunt and uncle . . . they'll all be here, wait and see. Are you going into the delivery room too?"

Charlie was glaring at me. "It's in the contract. It's all been settled."

"Which end are you going to stand at?"

"You've been drinking," he said in a low voice. "It's unbelievable. Do you ever think about anybody but yourself?"

"I'm talking about Ellie Ferguson's cunt. If you're going to stand there watching while the baby comes out of it." I'd only drunk a little. I glanced over at the redheaded male nurse, who quickly dropped his eyes. "Don't look at me like that, Charlie. It's a very important question."

A pause. "I'll stand at her head."

Charlie left and I sat down. In half an hour or so I couldn't stand it any longer. I crept down the hall to the labor room and stood by the door, then quietly moved inside. Ellie lay on the bed sweating, face pale, teeth clenched. Her hair was in strings. In her blue hospital gown she hardly seemed like a person, but a massive mound with a shred of helpless, weak little person attached to it. The mound dominated everything. Charlie saw me.

"Fran, I told you—out."

"I'm sorry, Fran," came Ellie's voice, very thin and high. "I don't think I can do it if you're here, I don't know why."

"But Ellie, maybe I can—"

"Fran." Charlie grabbed me and bundled me out the door. "Go get something to eat."

"But Charlie, all I want—"

"God, Fran. Keep out!"

"Well, Charlie, she's going pretty fast. Can't I come in to see it born?"

"Jesus, this isn't a peep show!"

He left me shoving coins into a coffee machine and trying to make conversation with the nurse, whose name was Vincent.

In a few minutes he came back. He looked more and more like a prospective father from the movies: pale, hair ruffled, a little wild-eyed. He took a puff of my cigarette. He barked at Vincent.

"Where the hell's Dr. Ramahutti?"

"Oh, he'll be here any minute."

"God, she's going like sixty," Charlie said. "Fran, listen. I need you to calm Lulu down, she's raving about Sagittarius."

I put my arms around him and kissed his cheek. "Of course. Why don't you get some coffee and doughnuts, there's a machine over there."

I jogged down the hall to find Lulu outside the room.

"Francesca, she's going so fast I'm afraid she's going to have it before midnight."

"Well, Lulu, we can't hold back the clock."

Lulu glanced around. "She said you stopped it. If you could just come in and talk to her. . . . It's a quarter of. If she could just wait twenty minutes."

"Lulu, are you serious?"

"Completely—and you'd be too if you'd read what I did. Oh, I wish I could speak to Maude. I tried to get her before but she was out."

Ellie lay on her back, her face wet, her eyes dark holes of pain and patience. She looked frail, as though her little limbs— limbs that had always seemed healthy and husky—might break under the strain. Her body was hot and slippery, her gown in wet knots. The blond crotch that had tortured me was now a portal to the truth. I went over to the bed and took her hand. She looked up at me, panting.

"Ellie, try to hold on for a few minutes, okay? Lulu thinks it would be best. Just till—um, the doctor gets here."

"Where's Sy?" Ellie gasped. "He promised to come."

"He's coming, dear," I lied. "Wait for him." Lulu pointed frantically at her watch.

"Nobody's coming," she said, her last words before another contraction swept over her. Her face changed and she cried out. The baby was so far down her legs were forced open. Lulu took a look and said, "Oh, my God, she's having it."

I went out into the hall and yelled. Vincent's bright pumpkin head shone in the dark hall as he sprinted along. He ducked

99

into the room, took a look. "Jeee-sus!" He pushed an alarm bell, and a drastic-sounding bell rang somewhere.

"Excuse me." The doctor, a young female resident, shoved Lulu out of the way as Vince turned the light on. "Wow, she's ready. No time for an episiotomy. . . . Come on, now, Mrs— who is she? Mrs. Ferguson. Push, now, a great big push. Atta girl. Bear down . . . okay, rest a minute . . . the top of a little head's right here." Unexpected tears came into my eyes.

"Ooooh . . . ow-ow-ow-ow-oooooow!" Ellie howled, her eyes wide and frightened at the enormity of what was happening. "Ohhh, God!" A cry from eternity. We all gripped her. I've never forgotten that hotness, that body stench rising like earth gases during an earthquake. Her body was the earth, her straining muscles, her wild grimace, her departed eyes. I'd forgotten Charlie completely till he darted into the room, wild-eyed, frantic, awestruck, at the very moment the baby slid out, accompanied by a scream that almost knocked down the walls . . . at just one minute before midnight.

The next morning Charlie whispered, "I've never been so happy in my life."

I smiled. Something had happened to me in that room too: a profound, unexpected feeling of connectedness, as though I'd been sending out frantic roots and tendrils all my life and had finally struck some dark, rich, fertile loam, some underground river of mythic connection with the rest of my sex. I felt a new tenderness toward Ellie.

I didn't get to the hospital till almost five. It was Route 3's best hour. The Christmas tree cast purple shadows on the white snow, and the pink cast of a winter dusk lay over everything. The lobby and the halls were quiet. An aide passed with a cart of dinner trays. I smelled beef stew, roast chicken . . . boarding school food. I smiled at little dishes of ruby Jell-O and rice pudding.

Ellie's room was a semiprivate whose second bed was empty. A translucent curtain sequestered her. Standing by the window was Rita. She stiffened and tightened her thin lips as I came in.

Ellie looked so beautiful I caught my breath. Her skin was

rich and a little flushed, her dark-blond hair combed back in waves, her summer-sky eyes clear and bright, set off by the pastel blue hospital gown. What a contrast of her chameleon looks with her rather placid, even personality! She held the baby in her arms. Most hospitals don't allow visitors around babies, but little lapses like this were what kept North County from being fully accredited. The little shapeless, fuzzy-headed creature looked blindly up at her. Her full breast, a pale moon, was available. The baby was too young to nurse; its tiny head only rested against it. As I came near the bed, Ellie's arms tightened around the baby. Her eyes were guarded.

"I've named him Monty," she said. "Montgomery Charles."

"Ellie, I think you're terrific." I wanted to tell her how much I admired her but couldn't find the right words. At the same time I was struck by her terrible dependence. There seemed to be nobody but Rita, who was tapping her fingernail, annoyed and annoyingly, on the metal table: poor infuriating Rita with her cash-register job and retarded son and whatever it was that she—for I was sure it was she—had caught from her boss. They lived in a world of strain and struggle I would never know.

Recently I had been asked to defend Center Rivertown against the county's proposal to fill the old Van Willem Hotel with welfare families, a case I could have won blindfolded since nobody wanted all those junkies and lowlifes within easy view of the colonial train station. I hadn't agreed to it yet. Was I, like Arthur Zeus, developing principles? Beware principles, he himself had said. But then where would they go, the Ellies and Ritas and worse; what would become of them? The poor in other parts of the world lived in shantytowns. But no shantytowns were welcome here, even on Route 3, where they'd pull down property values and scare the customers away from Milo's Muf-flers and Hai Thai.

Ellie and Rita looked at me in some curiosity as I smoothed the pillow behind Ellie's back and gave a cursory tidying to the bedside table, chattering about North County Hospital and its dubious amenities. The food didn't look bad, but if she liked I'd bring her over some soup or a sandwich. She should tell me if she needed anything. I told her that in spite of past difficulties

I wanted to be her friend. I had been selfish, thoughtless, even cruel; I wasn't the best person in the world. I hadn't truly understood her problems. And I hadn't seen the bond between all women. She mustn't worry about anything. The baby would have two mothers . . . but tears were streaming down Ellie's face.

"I can't give him up," she whispered.

There was a brief, fragile silence.

"You don't have to yet, Ellie." I smoothed back her hair as Rita watched me with a sort of baffled disgust. "Of course you don't yet. We'll wait. You mustn't worry about anything. Just take care of the baby."

"No, Fran. I can't give him up at *all*." She spoke in a sort of gasp, as though her heart were thudding. "You don't know what it's like, a boy and all. . . . I can't."

"Ellie, dear, I know. Keep him a few weeks."

"I don't mean a few weeks, I mean *forever*. You always change what people say."

"I don't. It's just that you've had a huge hormonal change." I was playing for time—and a lot of things were going through my head. "What you're saying is irrational. You can't possibly—"

Ellie's eyes hardened. "I'm not irrational."

"Perhaps this isn't the best time for this discussion," came Rita's unwelcome voice. "I must say, Mrs. Morse, I'm really astonished, and slightly puzzled, by your response. It is certainly very reasonable. I expected something quite different. I even advised Ellie to wait a couple of days before mentioning this, but she is a very honest, very emotional person, perhaps too emotional, and she couldn't rest till she'd stated her feelings. I know personally how badly she feels, how hard she fought against the tidal wave of maternal feeling. Nor did she ever dream—"

The baby made a couple of little squeaks and Ellie tried to interest it in her nipple, with only fair success.

"Monty," she whispered. "Here, Monty. Like this." Rita and I watched. I hadn't really looked at the baby before. Like all newborns it looked like a plucked chicken. The irony was that it was, at least in theory, mine. Ellie wiped her eyes with the back of her free hand and gently, reverently, touched its red, scaly little cheeks. "Darling, dear Monty, I love you," she whispered. It didn't sound corny. "I'll give you and Charlie back every cent of the money."

"Ellie, stop that kind of talk. You can't even take care of yourself now."

"Well, Rita's going to help." She looked frightened. "I mean with Monty. She can babysit and I'll work . . . maybe I can get a loan and go back to school. Or I could go to Wilmington by my parents." Rita's and my eyes met with terrible understanding. "I know what you're thinking, Fran. I know you. You only think things are important, never feelings, and you have to get your way. You think I'm a fool the way you always have, you think I gave in to Charlie and got caught and everything out of stupidity. But it's more that I give in to my feelings, and you pretend you're so tough. You say you love Charlie, but why did he come to me?"

"Now, now." I was being sorely tried. "I don't know, and I don't want to discuss it. If you really want Monty, keep him."

The triangle of light from the hall widened as Charlie opened the door slowly. When he saw Ellie holding his son, his smile was transformed, like some worshiper in a Renaissance painting. He walked over to the bed, holding out his arms to Mary and the Christ child.

"May I?"

Ellie handed him the baby. Gently he took Monty and held him to his heart, his eyes closed in paternal bliss . . . an artifact of civilization, according to Kerner.

"Dear, darling little Charlie. You're here at last."

Ellie glanced frantically at me. "His name is Monty."

Charlie was deaf to everything. "I can't believe how perfect he is. I was talking to Dr. Ramahutti"—who'd been stuck in a snowdrift the night before, he said, while Sy was stuck in another. "He said they sometimes have red marks on their faces or elongated heads, but this baby came too quickly for that."

"Charlie, we shouldn't tire Ellie," I said. Monty/Charlie yawned, and the sight of that rosy silken orifice and tiny cat's tongue blinded Charlie to all else. Then Ellie cleared her throat nervously.

"Charlie—um, there's something I have to say to you." She looked terrified. But Rita was not so dumb. She pinched Ellie's arm.

"You've had enough," she said. "You're exhausted and emotionally overtired. It can wait till tomorrow." She looked at Charlie. "I hope you have no objection to my giving her orders, but nobody in this hospital pays much attention to her."

I stood up. "Come on, Charlie, Ellie has to rest." It took another ten minutes to get him out. In the hall I said I'd forgotten my gloves and went swiftly back into the room, put my mouth to Ellie's ear, and said, "Take him and get out. And don't *ever* tell on me." I turned and left. I could feel their astonished eyes on me as I left the room.

On the way home, Charlie picked up a bottle of Beaujolais to have with our steaks. We all toasted our new life, and after dinner Charlie found the ornaments and wanted to go out and get a tree. Lulu tried to be cheerful, but her eyes were worried. She jumped every time the phone rang and glanced up every time a car passed on Holly Lane. Charlie alone was happy; I of course was Judas.

How elusive happiness is! It teases and tempts, but one more thing is always needed, one more day. It grows only in incomplete soil. Charlie didn't know the half of it as he picked over strings of Christmas tree lights. Lulu was mumbling over her beads, like an old Arab woman.

I grabbed Baby and took him outside, away from this false cheer. The snow was pure and perfect, the air sharp and transparent. Together we stormed across the lawn, kicking up snow behind us. I went over to Kerner's, but his house was dark; he'd probably left for Chicago to see his kids.

"Baby, I'm so bad," I said. "Bad as you are. Worse because I know better." I hugged the resistant creature, then let him go. He galloped back, leaving a wild trail in the snow.

Slowly I followed. I could see Charlie through the kitchen window. He was on the phone, has back toward me and his hand sawing up and down stiffly. Baby tore in, leaving trickles of melted snow on the kitchen floor, as the radio played "Jingle Bell Rock." Lulu, at the door, looked straight to my bones.

"Ellie's taken the baby and gone without a trace. Charlie is on the phone with the police." Her voice was low. "It's started, Francesca."

T·W·O

I WOULD DO ANYTHING FOR FRANCESCA. NOT, AS SHE WOULD claim, out of a sense of guilt for denying her stability as a child, but because she is all I have. But she and I are as unlike as two people can be. She is hard-working and determined, I am fatalistic and lazy. She is practical and down-to-earth and I am spiritually inclined. While I have a rather serene disposition, Fran's nature is passionate. She is very like her fiery, driven, exciting father . . . or, in truth, the man she *thinks* is her father, Waldo Letterman. Her real father was the room steward on the *Normandie*.

But who's to know, and what matter anyway? Though Peggy Letterman never did give Waldo a divorce, he was a beloved husband to me and a better father to Fran than many children have in normal households. She was his only child and he loved her dearly. After the war was over, Waldo, Fran, and I had four glorious years traveling in Europe till he was struck down in the casino at Monte Carlo under mysterious circumstances. The cause of death was never established and everything went to Peggy, but he left a generous trust fund for Fran's education. He'd always appreciated her quickness and taken her intelligence seriously. We got tutors for her wherever we were—Paris, Gstaad, Venice, even during that strange year in Cairo. What a pity it is he didn't live to know about her academic success and brilliant career. How thrilled he would have been that she took after him, for I never went to college—unless you count the art-finishing school where I spent two years. The room steward, Laurentian, must have been very smart and certainly overqualified for his job.

I stayed in Europe with Fran for two years after Waldo died, searching for spiritual sources to replace him and give me strength to live the rest of my life. I decided that after Fran was educated and on her way in life, I would return to Venice.

During this time, Fran went from a friendly, tractable child to a disagreeable brat who had to be virtually hauled on and off trains and in and out of hotel dining rooms. "Give me this time, Fran," I begged. "I need to heal." But children are unreasonable. She'd dig in her heels or have one of her tantrum fits. "I hate you!" or "You don't understand me, you never have!" or "You always treat me like a baby!" and "Papa would let me do it . . . wouldn't make me go . . . never was so mean . . . said I didn't have to." She doesn't look much like me. She's smaller, thinner, sleeker, darker. Her mind works differently. She's a cat that always lands on its feet.

Eventually I settled in New York. When Fran was fourteen, I put her in Miss Comfitt's Seminary in Massachusetts. It was time she had some training in manners and principles. Miss Comfitt said she needed a "structured environment." At first I worried that Fran, with her passionate nature, couldn't endure the prison atmosphere. But it agreed with her. She worked hard, was president of her class and head of the debating team, the hockey team, the French Club, and the Young Republicans. She developed the high perfectionist standards she still has—or did until this recent peculiar business.

It's almost incomprehensible to my friends here. Cipi says, "All this fuss over a *baby*?" He has five children and seven grandchildren. I didn't ask what *he* would have done—probably turned Bernadetta in for a new one! His attitude was the same when I arrived back here to find all the liquor gone, along with two Tuscany chairs and a painting. And the place filthy, I don't know what he did with Giulia. Though Cipi was apologetic— "Darling, I was in Milan; I never dreamed he was such a *maiale*"—he shrugged it off after five minutes. As for Monty— "Forget it, Lulu. It does no good to worry about one's children. You'll only break your heart."

I can't get that poor girl out of my mind. Something struck me about her the first time I laid eyes on her—a vulnerability, a femininity perhaps, entirely lacking in Fran. She reminds me, as Fran never did, of myself once: adrift, trusting, a sitting duck. The scattered family, the lack of real ties: in my case, sent off to school here and there, never knowing what to do because there was no one to give advice. How lucky I was it was Waldo; how much worse it could have been! (But Ellie Ferguson isn't so lucky.) And what did Waldo want with me? I was nothing. Pretty, but so innocent, so ignorant! But then, that's what a certain type of man wants, that quality of needing protection. Once women cultivated it. But I doubt if Fran could understand that.

Charlie can think of nothing but his baby. When I left he was barely going to work. He's afraid he'll never see his son again. Ellie has dropped out of sight like a stone in a pond, with all three of her children.

As soon as I was settled and got my boat (untouched by Beppi, thank God) back in the water, I rowed over to see my darling Signora Maude Brill over near San Giovanni Evangelista. Many of us here couldn't do without this remarkable woman. She is deeply, passionately spiritual, a true psychic in a profession where there are so many fakes and charlatans. I found her in her little lair, dark and scented with sandalwood. Her long, thin body was bent like a crane over her charts. I sketched the recent circumstances for her. It was a hollow satisfaction to have it confirmed that the baby's chart, which I did the afternoon of its birth, was entirely correct. As she discovered the malevolent black energy lurking there, a look of the gravest fear passed over her face.

"I've heard of this Sagittarius Vale, Lulu, but never seen it myself," she said slowly. "And to tell the truth I never wanted to."

She led me back into the nether regions of her house, where a couple of dim lights lit up shelves of musty volumes: Maude's fine, well-known library of the occult, so excellent, in fact, that people come from all over the world begging to use it.

"Some of the medieval philosophers and alchemists warned

against this exact combination, if what I'm thinking of is true."
She pulled out a crumbling brown volume and carried it carefully
to the prie-dieu by the cobwebby window, where she began
going through it, muttering to herself. "Capricorn . . . Pisces
. . . ah, here it is." Her round British face became grave. "Are
you strong today?"

"I'm not sure." A chill went through me.

"I'm sorry to distress you, dear Lulu, but you know it's safer
to be warned. It's better to know why terrible things happen,
isn't it? There are people who never realize. . . ." She turned
pages as I watched fearfully. "Here. 'The Sagittarius Vale is
associated with a configuration of violence and disaster. When
December twentieth falls in the above pattern' "—she showed
me an old astrological chart of the winter sky—" 'mysterious
maleficencies almost invariably take place. There are recorded
floods, fires, earthquakes, massacres, plagues, shocking crimes,
sinking ships, babies born dead, and'—something"—she was
translating—" 'large numbers of admissions to insane asylums,
collapsing buildings, virulent diseases,' and so on. The first case
of plague was discovered in Rome on December twentieth . . .
the famous Hanging Gardens of Babylon fell down on December
twentieth."

"I don't think I want to hear any more, Maude."

"All right. But you have to understand, Lulu, that it is all
connected to the mystery of Francesca's conception and her
Gemini birth, which lies zodiacally opposite the new child's.
And you can't forget that Waldo died"—she grasped my hand—
"on that very date."

I was trembling. "I have to go, Maude." All I wanted to
do was get out of that place.

"Go ahead, dear, just let yourself out. I'm going to keep
reading. This is interesting indeed."

Deeply shocked, I left her to delve more deeply, which she
loves to do: all of it being financed by the prudent investments
of her late husband, who had laughed at matters of the occult.

Back in my rowboat, I calmed down and told myself that
it was all nonsense anyway. It was dusk, the hour when the
Venetian light turns pink and mauve, the stone of the buildings
turns purple and soft-looking, everything becomes muted. Boats

jammed the smaller canals, and the air was full of the shouts of the deliverymen and gondolieri, the sputter of motors. The air was damp and cool. Though my sign is Fixed Air, my true medium is water; this is why I live here, where I can travel on it every day, sleep next to it at night, and breathe its strange sensuous odors always. It revives me and opens my mind to new insights—even when I don't particularly want them.

And my mind insisted on going back to that foolish night in 1938: a pair of sparkling dark eyes, a voice with a mysterious accent, a slight, straight, graceful figure in a navy-blue uniform going down a narrow flight of stairs from the top deck as I watched from above . . . our eyes caught as he turned at the end. I was alone, on my way to visit more relatives who would pretend to welcome me. I'm afraid it didn't take much: some champagne, a couple of dances, a few lies and compliments. I'd never been with a man before and didn't really like it, but I suppose I thought that in time, with love and patience, it would get better.

On the grand old ocean liners, every night was a ball in formal dress: the orchestra playing, a dance floor crowded with elegant people giving little screams of glee at every pitch and roll, vast wasteful buffets and endless champagne. Though the ship was half empty, there was a heightened, almost desperate air of celebration as Europe braced herself for the doom that was to come. But I hardly thought of that. The next evening I couldn't even catch his eye, and we sat at different tables. I picked tearfully at my food and watched him dancing with a laughing woman in white.

But my table mates wouldn't allow me to brood, and one big blond man pressed, in a friendly way. Did I know Paris well? He and his wife hoped to explore some of the less familiar neighborhoods and smaller museums of the city. His manner was, at least on the surface, one of kind disinterest, though it didn't hurt that I was pretty and lost-looking, with a touch of mysterious sadness. Soon I did dance with him and was constantly with him and Peggy for the rest of the crossing. The last evening he fixed it so we were alone together and managed to get me to bed with him.

I suppose I behaved like a slut (especially since this experience was no better than the last one!). But the cold betrayal of Laurentian had only heightened my need for love. I hadn't learned about consequences. So I didn't fight too hard. Was it so surprising for a girl who had no one to tell her what to do? Like the perpetual houseguest I was, I tended to do what others wanted, to be agreeable in order to be liked. There might have been more lovers and silly affairs if Waldo hadn't turned out to be the kind of man he was.

Then he was guilty: he hadn't meant for it to happen, though of course he had. I wept and felt like a fool, for now I would lose my friendship with the two of them. I swore off sex forever and decided to enter a Parisian convent immediately, as soon as I found a suitable one, like a Henry James heroine.

In Paris that summer the talk was all of war. My aunt and uncle were forever discussing the German situation and wondering which rumors to believe. One night at a restaurant Waldo and Peggy walked in and sat down with us. Uncle James knew Waldo through his business. Peggy was a thin, nervous woman, unsure of herself, in great contrast to Waldo's vital, glowing warmth and confidence. They'd known each other since childhood, he told me later, and been pushed together by their families. They had no children. I kept stealing glances at Waldo, and he at me.

My Aunt Grace and Uncle James had to watch, with a disapproval they didn't hesitate to voice, the twists and turns of Waldo's and my falling in love. I think the lowering shadow from the east increased their tolerance, the atmosphere of increasing danger that made convention seem unimportant; as well as their fondness for Waldo and sympathy for his anguish. Peggy fought us every inch of the way and took her revenge by keeping him legally bound to her forever. I felt sorry for her, for she had no resources in herself, nothing to fall back on. She was all sour, twisted hate.

It was not smooth at the beginning. The affair was propelled by Waldo's passionate love as I held back; my foolish young heart still yearned after that dark seducer in a navy-blue uniform who'd talked his way into my cabin and kissed me senseless. Though I knew Waldo was a man of great sense and intelligence, highly respected not only by my uncle James but many others in the distinguished circles in which he traveled, these qualities meant less to me, at the time, than white teeth and a sense of rhythm. But a month later, after a visit to the doctor, I was on the phone to Waldo, then in London, my trembling fingers nervously dialing, then twisting the wire. "Mr. Letterman"— that's how ridiculous I was; I was afraid to call him Waldo!— "this is Luisa Christien. I was wondering if you'd be back in Paris soon. I want very much to talk to you if I may." Waldo pressed, and by the end of the conversation he'd extracted the whispered admission: "I'm expecting a child."

"I'll be there tonight," he said.

I was terrified. I thought of an abortion and hoped he could help me get a safe one, or some arrangement (from novels) about having the child in secret and putting it out to nurse with a countrywoman—where I would visit it every so often in a black veil.

Many men would have disappeared at this juncture like a puff of smoke. But for Waldo this was a joyous event. This was the child he thought he'd never have. He was prepared to take all responsibility. I remember the evening he stated his case to me. He virtually put himself on trial, defending both sides and skewing the opposition. He loved me, I must know that. There hadn't been an hour since he'd first seen me that I hadn't been in his head. He was now prepared to leave Peggy and marry me. But on the other hand, I should consider how unfair he was being. He was twenty years older. Did I truly want this child, conceived out of his overpowering, thoughtless lust? I must be very, very sure. If I wished he would arrange for an abortion . . . though he looked sad and frightened as he said it. I should further consider the war, the effect of the inevitable scandal on my aunt and uncle, the disruption of my life plans (there were none), as well as the sheer chanciness of throwing in my fate with someone I hardly knew. On the other hand—Waldo was a lawyer through and through—I should know that he was not accustomed to having affairs with other women. He had been a blameless husband to Peggy, who was barren through no fault of her own, and never thought of leaving her till he saw me;

he was prepared to provide for me very handsomely, though our lives would be peripatetic.

I said yes. Not because I had any judgment at all, or because I was in love with him, or even because I cannily weighed the odds and decided to take the risk, but because I didn't know what else to do. People are so often punished for making decisions in such a stupid way—but the stars were right, and how lucky I was! In a few months I was very much in love with him.

By then Waldo insisted we all leave Paris; he was privy to information most people were not. Fran was born in New York, and Waldo settled us in the apartment in Murray Hill while he traveled around in his capacity as legal adviser to the military. He stayed home when he could. His instinct was right. I was untaught, but strong enough for him. He taught me everything and, when Fran was old enough, began teaching her. We talked continually of the end of the war when we could go back to Europe, where we both wanted to be.

They were having blackouts then, and when the siren went off, we all went down to the basement shelter and waited for the all-clear. I remember all too well one night when Waldo was away. Fran was about four. The tenants were all filing down the long, narrow stairs, lit in a shadowy way by high ceiling lights. Fran was in her little blue bathrobe, holding her doll as she turned the corner below me. I looked at her thin, pretty little pixie face, those dark piercing eyes, her catlike graceful walk. I saw another face like that, going down another flight of stairs, turning to look up at me from below. I knew beyond a doubt. I must have frozen in my tracks, for the woman behind me asked, "Mrs. Letterman, are you all right?" And Fran was looking up at me with what seemed like terrible, unchildlike wisdom. I was very young; it was before I knew or thought about the seen and the unseen, the known and the unknown, the interconnection between us all. I felt a chill to my very marrow.

At that moment I swore to myself I'd never tell what I knew. As the years passed, and I was punished by seeing the unmistakable resemblance she had to her father, there were times I wavered, thinking Waldo must see it; her build, coloring, personality, everything was different. But he only said, "She's all you, Lulu," and even seemed to take pleasure in her very uniqueness, which most men wouldn't have done; they want to see themselves in their children, as though they were mirrors. Sometimes I wondered if he'd even care, he was so deeply attached to her. But I didn't know.

Then in Venice I met Maude Brill. She was very young, of course, just starting out, and worked for the city doing *restauro* on old frescoes, at which she was very skillful. She told me that she was overwhelmed by the curious and undecipherable energies that were released when she removed even the tiniest bits of dirt and paint; whole clouds, vast auras of other ages, full of long-hidden knowledge of such dark disciplines as alchemy and Gnosticism, flooded her mind. When she could barely think about anything else, she took up spirituality as a profession. She has only told me the smallest bit of what she knows, believing that each soul must make its own journey. But she has told me, as she did today, that spiritual knowledge can only be received when one's soul is "swept out," as she calls it, of personal clutter—and this remarkable woman knew, without my telling her, about Laurentian. I begged her for the advice she never gives, for Signora Brill only tells what she sees in the stars or what comes into her mind when it is "receiving."

Now the war was over. Months passed; years passed. Waldo, Fran, and I traveled to many places. A strange old man deep in the Musky in Cairo told me that he saw an "obstacle" in my path, a "darkening *nube* that threatened my happiness"— and once a Romany Gypsy turned my hand down, put her cards away, and said, "There are secrets that must never be told." Waldo said I shouldn't listen to such nonsense, but I couldn't help it.

Oh, how often we want just one more thing! The lie between Waldo and me was the one blot on an otherwise perfect life: our love, our beloved little daughter, our travels and fascinating friends everywhere. Wasn't that enough? I was too foolish to know that it was. And so when Waldo mentioned, one night in Monte Carlo, quite casually, as he had before, that Fran "was becoming a beautiful, catlike Lulu," I blurted out the truth about my sorry little escapade on the *Normandie* only a day before we had met, ten years before—ten years we'd been lucky to have. I'll never forget the expression that passed across his face: a stillness, a shadow, as though he'd seen his own grave! He said nothing, gave no word of reproof. Would that he had!

I cried, "I would do anything to undo it, Waldo. I have never seen the man since. You are Fran's father by the best and only meaning of the word."

"I know. It's all right, Lulu," he said.

The only merciful thing, the only shred of silver lining in this wretched tale, is that I only had to watch the new quiet, shadowed look on his face—a look that cut me like a knife— for a few hours. At the roulette table at the casino that night he crumpled over and died. They never really established the cause, and there was even a passing suspicion of foul play. And it was on that black Sagittarius night of December twentieth!

I was devastated by what I thought I'd done. Except for Fran I might well have committed suicide. I was horribly attracted to bridges, high windows, high rocky cliffs over the sea . . . then I'd look at her, and the dark excitement would disappear. Finally I took Fran back to Venice.

"You did not kill him, Lulu," Maude said. "He might have even known. But there is some connection . . . I'm not sure what. You must be very careful every year at this time." How right the Gypsy was; there are secrets that should never be told! "I have never believed in this modern idea of honesty between lovers," Maude went on. "Some matters are simply too frail. Your Aquarian curiosity got you into trouble—as well as your guilty longing for confession. You had everything else. Did you have to have that too?"

T·H·R·E·E

ELLIE'S DISAPPEARANCE WAS AMAZINGLY COMPLETE FOR A GIRL who trailed crumbs and Kleenex, and—well, illegitimate babies. Uncharacteristically, she had told no one: not Rita, not Doré, not her mother in Wilmington. She and the three children just dropped out of sight. The police gave up in a few days, and the FBI showed no interest.

As hope ebbed, Charlie sank into despair. Unable to sleep, he wandered around the house, worked at his computer, or sat in the kitchen drinking coffee and staring at the door, as though waiting for the bell to ring. He asked how I felt about taking out a second mortgage and hiring private investigators to find her. I told him I'd never agree, and the sooner he could forget the whole thing and move on, the better. His face closed down when I said it.

Our marriage hung on Ellie like clothes on a line, or perhaps two lines. Charlie believed that Monty's return would make the flowers bloom again; I knew better. He believed all our linen had been washed and dried in the sun, but I knew what was still in the hamper. Like most men, he believed his confession about his affair, and my seeming forgiveness, was redemption. He forgot the continuing inconvenience of memory.

What surprised me most was his surprise.

"Didn't you ever think of this?" I asked him.

"Of what?"

"That Ellie might find it hard to part with the baby."

"Well, she made a deal. Life is tough. You don't get compensation. Did anybody write you a big check when your father died?"

"No." I found some cigarettes in the desk drawer.

"You were expected to cry a little, then move on, right? That's what Ellie Ferguson is expected to do—and she gets ten thousand bucks besides. It's not bad when you consider everything."

"It's not the same."

"Sure it is."

"Deals fall through all the time, Charlie. Then people make new ones."

"Fran, this is my son. My son!"

"But he's hers too."

He threw up his hands. "She signed the contract, didn't she?"

"The contract was illegal."

"So what?" Charlie shouted.

How had Charlie gotten so deeply paternal? As a divorce lawyer, I'd sadly concluded that most men were pretty poor fathers. They lost interest in their children after a divorce, stopped supporting them, and sometimes dropped out of sight completely, often going to a great deal of trouble to do so. The ones who remained involved and responsible were rare birds, and keeping up their relationship with the children seemed to cost them tremendous effort—though I'd never understood why it should. The custody suits waged by fathers were usually, underneath, about money or revenge.

But there were a few like Charlie. There had been one in the paper who sued to stop his estranged wife from having an abortion, so he could keep the fetus and have it implanted in the womb of his new girlfriend. There was the gay man in Australia who had a fetus somehow implanted in his pelvis to grow there before being delivered in some approximation of a cesarean section. There were fathers who kidnapped their kids and took them to other states or even countries, beyond the reach of the mother's legal pursuit. There were—somehow connected—Doré, and his ilk.

Even stranger, these opposite forces could exist in a single male breast. Right-to-Life fathers turned their backs on children after a divorce as much as others, and unwilling fathers, whose sperm had crept out and attacked while they were asleep, had been known to become admirable parents. The young man trying to replant his fetus in a new mother, talking all the time about his "freedom of reproductive choice," might balk at poopy diapers, long nights with earache, or evenings with algebra, and he was just as likely to walk out without a backward glance, leaving the pieces for the mother to pick up. What made men the way they were? It distressed me that, at forty-four, I still didn't understand them.

It hurt and angered Charlie that I was only half loyal to his cause and semisympathetic with his unhappiness. To him, *we* had made an important decision, *we* had evolved a plan for our future, and I wasn't holding up my end. But I couldn't feel true partnership if some of our assumptions had been as wrong as I now believed. I was puzzled at the whole strange conundrum the thing had become. Something was happening to us, Charlie and me. The earth was splitting, slowly, silently, and Charlie and I were on opposite sides of the crack. The plates would shift, tectonic motion would drive us miles apart. I kept staring at the widening crack, wondering if there was time for one of us to jump to the other side . . . but it wasn't going to be me.

One evening Kerner came by with his latest blasphemy, *The Myth of Paternity*. Charlie and I were sitting in the study in the dark, or mostly dark. I'd seen Adam coming and tried to wave him away, but he rang the bell anyway.

In the light of the desk lamp, Charlie looked sadly at the new, shiny maroon book cover, with Kerner's picture on the back and a couple of respectful blurbs. He sighed and shook his head as he leafed through it.

"Kerner, I don't see how you can write this crap." We'd been working on a bottle of Scotch. "The way I feel about my son is no myth. It's real."

"It's real enough, but academic. It's the *concept* you love."

"I wasn't holding a concept in my arms, Kerner."

"Sure you were. The whole thing is conceptual. That might have been the baby of the woman in the next room."

"Adam," I said.

"I saw Monty born," Charlie said in a low animal voice.

"All right, the *man* in the next room."

"Monty is *my* son. My *son.*"

"Oh, I know, Charlie. But he's still just an idea, is all I'm saying. A fetus is an idea, in effect. Nobody sees it, we only imagine it. If we saw it, it would be dead." He looked mildly at our staring faces. "You're a scientist, Charlie. You're at home with concepts."

I said, "Adam, you're seditious."

Charlie poured himself another drink. "All right, Kerner. Run your so-called theory past me, okay? Tell me about goddess worship. Why should they worship goddesses instead of gods?"

"You tell me, Charlie. Why would they consider women superior?" Charlie looked baffled. "Is there anything they can do that we can't?"

"Oh," he said in a moment. "They can have babies. Is that what you mean?"

"Exactly."

Charlie laughed. "Well, they can't do it alone, can they?"

"No, but in those days they didn't know that. They thought it was a supernatural power. They fell down and worshiped women's genitals."

"Can you prove that?" Charlie asked.

"I wasn't there, if that's what you mean."

There was a brief silence. "Well," Charlie said, "so now we're smarter; we've learned it takes two."

"But it doesn't really. Women don't need us, Charlie, especially these days. They can just drop in at the Harvard sperm bank."

Charlie's semipolite smile slowly faded. "That sperm didn't just spontaneously generate in there. The girls didn't cook it up in their test tubes."

"No, but you have to admit it's pretty easy to come by. 'Spreading the sperm' is a common male fantasy. I've never known a man who rationed it, have you?" He lit his pipe, after glancing at me for permission. "Women have a frightening unrealized power."

Charlie was staring at him in thinly disguised horror. "So

they can have babies. So what? The poor ones end up on the dole. That's about as powerless as you can get."

"Exactly," Kerner cried triumphantly. "That's how we punish them. We hold the economic reins, which is why we formed the nuclear family in the first place. Either we own them, and try to control their bodies, or we dump them in the streets . . . and do you know why, Charlie?" Charlie's face was skull-like as he slowly shook his head. "Because we *envy* them. Have you ever heard of couvade?"

"Jesus Christ," Charlie said.

"No, couvade. In some tribes, the father gets symptoms of pregnancy. He feels sick and he might even blow up, and sometimes he even goes into labor with his wife and delivers . . . nothing." Charlie was pale. "Isn't it remarkable the way people have coveted things from each other since the beginning of time. It's our great motivating force and our great weakness."

"But you don't," I said to him.

"Yes, I do," Kerner relied. "I covet knowledge."

If we had been rich, and if Charlie had been a different kind of person, he might have launched a vast campaign to find Monty: pictures on milk cartons, TV spots, and billboards. Or, more likely, he would have gritted his teeth, made himself forget, and talked of adoption. But Charlie was a loner. He worked alone, he made decisions alone. He'd probably manage to die when I wasn't around. I had always admired him for following his star, and when he decided to go off by himself and look for Monty it was entirely in character, and I didn't argue. (Once I would have been hurt that our marriage was not enough for him, but I'd pretty well gotten over that.) The hopelessness of it hardly mattered. We both knew that he had to do it or he'd never rest again.

Phillips Olimpia valued him enough to give him a leave of absence. He gathered up his index cards of carefully worked-out probabilities, packed a suitcase, and drove off—promising to phone every two or three days.

After ten years of marriage, I'd forgotten the pleasures of being alone: the swingy freedom, the delightful self-centeredness. The days seemed longer, as though Charlie absorbed hours when he was around, and the house bigger and more open without him and that massive companion, his obsession. The air was clearer and cleaner.

When Odysseus was off fighting the Trojan War, many aggressive suitors made moves on Penelope. I was not such a choice prize, but scarcely had the sound of Charlie's motor faded than Sheldon Showalter started turning up at the back door, on the terrace, over near the trash cans. The ruder I was the friendlier he became.

"I think you're lonely, Fran. I just get the feeling. And I've discovered that Johanna is . . . mmm . . . having an affair."

I knew about this and was sworn to silence. Johanna was getting it on with Phil, my office mate.

"Oh, I don't believe it, Sheldon. There are other explanations for all those things"—meaning the string of clues that Johanna was inexplicably leaving. "The handkerchief, somebody probably left at the Knitty Gritty"—the knit shop, where Sheldon correctly believed Johanna held her trysts.

"I know you've been looking at me, Fran. Don't hide it."

"What?"

"Come on, let's stop fooling ourselves."

"Are you serious?"

"Of course. Beautiful Fran. You're like a cat, a sinuous Siamese cat . . . and what claws!"

I wrenched myself from his unwelcome presence. What about the other side? One week he was away on a promotion tour of his book, and the week of spring vacation, a boy and a girl in their early teens appeared around his house. Not little Kerners, as one might normally expect, but little Woolseys, his wife's maiden name. On Kerner's insistence! The four of us went out to a Chinese restaurant one night, and the kids seemed pretty good and only a touch crazy . . . and very smart. They kept glancing at me, and then his daughter asked him how Lucinda was. He said she was just fine and she sent her love. Without Charlie's looming gray presence all sorts of things were being revealed!

A cold, clear February day: *Markowitz v. Rivertown Lodge*. Beulah Markowitz, Realtor, versus all-male Rivertown Lodge, which wouldn't admit her to membership because of her sex. Beulah believed that behind the gray stone walls of this local citadel of dullness many secrets were whispered that, with access, would keep her "in the loop" and double her business. Separations, divorces, illnessess, business reverses, pregnancies, deaths—the first hints of life's major passages could lead to new listings, help her catch the ear of owners who just needed a little persuasion to sell. I represented Beulah, and we were making it into a local feminist cause célèbre.

There was a crowd around the courthouse, and the parking lot was jammed as we arrived. Beulah was thrilled that so many women had turned out. Didn't we have every right to be bored and fed vile food in the musty rooms of the Lodge under the mounted elk heads, to listen to the grunts and belches of overfed male WASPS? I was grateful to her for retaining me—my first big local case—and glad of the distraction . . . for in my briefcase was a letter from Ellie Ferguson.

There was a fine mix of little old ladies in tennis shoes, middle-aged ladies in tennis shorts, and Johanna and other local tradeswomen from the dress shop, the notions shop, and the bookshop of Center Rivertown. The librarian was there, the town clerk, the waitresses from the coffee shop, and the young couple who ran Bistro Beaumont. They held discreet posters: LODGE FOR LADIES TOO; TIME TO BE FAIR; WE WANT TO BE WITH YOU! There was even a brief, ragged rendition of Olivia Newton-John's "Let Me Be There."

The letter had been sent to Lulu, who sent it on to me. I'd only had time to glance at a line or two before I had to leave the house. I was secretly, guiltily thrilled.

Beulah grabbed my elbow. "Fran, what on earth is that?"

She pointed to a group of women approaching from cars parked out on the road. Not Mercedeses, not Subarus or Toyotas, but old Fords and dusty Chevies. And the women were—well, strictly not our class Dear, as they say. Poly pants and stretched velour tops, wrong-colored hair, pink down jackets. Plastic handbags. Some, Beulah pointed out, were not even Caucasian.

"What are they doing here?"

"It was in the paper, Beulah."

"This is an issue of Rivertown *proper*."

"Well, maybe they don't agree. Listen, as your attorney I advise you to look friendly and welcoming." I smiled and waved as I walked over toward them, hand extended. Beulah followed with a sort of curled-lip sneer. "I'm so glad you ladies could come," I said. "We must show solidarity *as women* even if we don't necessarily want to join Rivertown Lodge *ourselves*." I said this rather loudly for the sake of the tennis women. Cameras clicked, lips buzzed.

"Well, maybe we do," said one of them.

"That's why we came," said another. "We're women too."

"We think there's something else to be addressed here. We live in Rivertown too."

"But you aren't homeowners, are you?" one of the tennis ladies asked.

"We rent. So what?"

I grabbed Beulah. "Come on, we haven't time for a revolution."

"Why, the nerve of those people!" Beulah panted, trying to keep up with me. "Fran, go more slowly. To think that *renters* . . ."

At the top of the court steps, just before I shoved Beulah inside, I glanced back to see a mild melee with a few waving posters: RENTERS ARE WOMEN TOO. A black bushy head, a thin angry face . . . Rita.

I couldn't keep my mind on the case. The Force wasn't with me . . . and the Force was necessary to win. Between that angry, knowing face and Ellie's unread letter, the simple threads of this case became hopelessly snarled. Why would Rita want to join the Lodge? Or Ellie? How could these women afford it? Was it even a feminist issue at all?

After lunch, I hid in one of the cubicles in the ladies' room, and took out the letter Lulu had sent me.

Dear Mrs. Letterman: I hope you don't mind my writing to you. You gave me your address in Italy—

"Fran." Beulah's feet, in shiny brown pumps, appeared in front of the door. "That *is* you, isn't it? Now I'm not telling you how to try this case, but there were a few times I thought you should have objected, as when he said blatantly sexist things like 'Women wouldn't be interested in the topics of conversation at the Lodge'—whatever *that* means—and 'We like steaks and chops and we don't want dinky little tuna salads.' And then all that stupid crap about the cost of putting in a john for us."

I came out of the cubicle. "Beulah, who is trying this case?"

She was poking at her grayish-blond frizz with a comb. "Well, I just thought—"

"Let me take care of it. One wrong move, and Judge Wildhammer will throw the whole thing out of court."

"All right, all right. But those women. Do they have to be in there?"

"Yes, Beulah. They are your sisters."

"Oh, *God!*" She laughed. "Spare me! If they join, I'm leaving town!"

Dear Mrs. Letterman:

I hope you don't mind my writing to you. You gave me your address in Italy so I guess it's all right. I feel you are the only one who would understand. You were always kind when others were not. I don't mean to say anything against Fran, I know it hasn't been so easy for her.

I hope you believe me when I say only desperation would drive me to do what I did. Every hour was worse. I just wanted to die. And I know it sounds worse that I planned it out, but with three kids you have to think ahead. I arranged with one of the hospital nurses to take me to a certain bus terminal. [We had phoned or checked out every means of transportation but this . . . and I had managed to forget Nurse Vincent.]

I had to be with Monty. He is so sweet, he hardly cries at all, and he has his father's eyes. Every day he does something new. He is in good health, and so are the rest of us.

You probably wonder where we are, but I must keep my location a secret. (The postmark doesn't mean anything because I got somebody to mail this for me.) I have gone by my brother and his wife, where we are staying. [Brother! Nobody had mentioned a brother . . . but wait, hadn't Ellie once mentioned him, a long time ago? He was the one who was going to supply her with "venture capital."]

Sometimes I think, Mrs. Letterman, that life comes down to finding people you can trust. As I said, I felt like I could trust you. And the other person I trust is Sy Doré. I know none of you liked him much. But to me he was always kind, fair, and wise, and he treated me with respect. So now, Mrs. Letterman, I am leaving here and going to Life Farm. Sy said once there would always be a home for me there. Kenny thinks it's a wonderful idea, and he's taking a day off from work to drive us there tomorrow, three hours away.

Maybe I sound crazy to keep running. But I can't leave my little son. Somehow I am afraid Charlie will catch me in the end, but I want as much time with him as I can.

Thank you for reading this, Mrs. Letterman. I hope you'll forgive me for what I did.

Sincerely,
Ellie Marvin Ferguson.

Lulu had added, P.S. Isn't this something? Suppose she decides to come and stay with me?

We lost Markowitz as I'd known we would. I told Beulah that we were ahead of our time, that the case would be easily won in five years, that we "made a statement." But Beulah didn't really care. She didn't really want to join the Lodge any more. She thought the judge had made up his mind beforehand, and that was that. Her heart really hadn't been in it since the day of the trial.

And I think I know why we lost. There was a huge batch of "amicae curiae" letters from women, all saying in essence that the status quo should be preserved, that the old boys had a right to their own lair, and their wives liked getting rid of them for one night a week. And a few hints about "what Rivertown *was*" and how we should be slow to make changes.

Those Route 3 women had scared them to death. Suppose Markowitz won . . . and somehow those women managed to join . . . and then they'd come driving up in those dusty old Dodges and Fords and barge in, and before you knew it there'd be Coke machines in the front hall and TV and—well, the wrong kind of people. Everybody was a little edgy because the country club had just started accepting Jews. And those crude husbands would throw beer cans around and start fights and make unpleasant suggestive remarks to nice women, and then, God help us, we might as well set fire to the place.

"Fran," said Charlie, "I'm in a motel in Roxbury, Mass. I miss you."

"I won't even ask."

"Well, you don't need to. But I have a good lead for tomorrow, a woman who just got moved to a trailer camp."

"When are you coming home?"

"Don't know, Fran."

Dear Mrs. Letterman:

We are now safe at Life Farm. My brother drove us all the way here in his Mercedes. He asked me if I needed any money, and I told him I had plenty but I didn't feel right about the money I had from Charlie. He said, "Who's Charlie?" and I'd forgot. Then I had to tell him the whole thing. He almost fell out of the car.

Then he said the whole thing sounded like a felony to him, and I should either give Monty back or else the money. I told him I'd die rather than give up my little son. We argued for half the trip. Then he said since I refused to give him up, I should send back the money and he'd give me the same amount, but it was to be a big secret all around. So we decided to do that, and he said he'd put ten thousand dollars in Escrow so he could "launder" it before finding a way to secretly send it back to Charlie. I could keep what I had. So I said okay. I swore never to tell where he lives, because Mom and Pop would drive him crazy.

"Good luck, Sis," he said. "You'll need it."

You should have seen Sy Doré's face when we all walked into the office at Life Farm! He looked so happy and kind I was sorry we hadn't come here at first, but then I was afraid he'd tell Charlie. I still wasn't sure. But after we talked he said I needed time to myself so he wouldn't tell for a while anyway, and I knew I could really trust him.

He and I had many meetings without Fran and Charlie before. We talked of many things and his deep religious beliefs and his wish to bring people to the Light. He told me I had unusual spiritual capacity. And he said there was something special between him and me. He calls it Spiritual something. It's as though we met someplace once, even though we really didn't.

Life Farm is a simple place in the mountains. There are other people here who are lost and have troubles like me. Old Mr. and Mrs. Friggs run it. There is a big main house and some small log cabins. There's a cow and some pigs and chickens and a couple of sheep. We all share the chores.

The atmosphere here is very religious. I never prayed so much in my life! I didn't have much religious education but boy am I making up for it!!!!! And that is putting it mildly. Truly Sy is a spiritual leader. His faith shines from that kind, wise face as he stands on the Rock where he gives his sermons. The subjects are simple but very applicant to daily life. He assigns us each a sin for our Personal Struggle. Mine is Bodily Temptation. I almost blush as I write it. But I have a special prayer I say every night, and bit by bit I am conquering the devil in my flesh.

I guess I'm really bending your ear, Mrs. Letterman. My mom used to say, "Ellie, I don't want to hear any more." If you feel that way please just throw these out. I'll probably never see you again, and so I wouldn't ever know.

Sincerely,
Ellie M. Ferguson

"She is Eve," I said to Lulu on the phone, "and this time the snake is spouting passages from the Bible."

"What did Charlie say?"

"Well, he hasn't called," I lied. "I didn't get around to reading them till today."

"I can't wait to hear what he makes of all this. You know, I think Ellie is a very talented writer. It's like *The Perils of Pauline!* And wait . . . *wait* till you read the ones I sent off yesterday!"

"Fran? I'm in Worcester for a couple of days."

"I wish you were here."

I wasn't sure I meant it. I couldn't even wait to get off the phone to read the latest letters. I had my Smirnoff's on the rocks, a turkey on rye with Russian, and a pint of chocolate chip ice cream, and, it being a cold night in March, I'd lit a fire.

"Any news?"

There was little that I chose to tell him. There had been another tiresome encounter with Sheldon during which he called me his "kitten" and admired my breasts—of which there isn't much to admire. And I'd finally gotten Kerner his solar plates and windmill by some simple, brilliant blackmail: the recalcitrant member of the zoning board had turned out to be Phil Bollinger, my office mate and lover of Johanna. When I hinted delicately that I knew what he'd been up to in the back of the Knitty Gritty, he turned white and tried to buy my silence with a fancy lunch at the Rivertown Inn. So it was easy to strike a deal, and Kerner was delighted. . . .

"Not really," I said. "I miss you. Come back soon."

Come back soon. Don't come back. I didn't even know what I meant. A cold, sleety March rain was beating on the windows, and I curled up on the sofa in front of the fire.

> *Dear Mrs. Letterman,*
>   *Last time I wrote you on impulse, without even stopping to think. And I had feelings I'd never had before about God, and goodness and Sin and many other things. But I*

was not completely honest with you. I made Life Farm sound like this happy place with many people praying together, and farming and growing things and all that.

Well that's the way it's supposed to be but I don't know. There's only nine people here now, the Friggs, who run it for Sy, and me and my three, and Janey and Oscar and Evelyn, these people from around here somewhere. It's so cold we have to run to the barn to do the milking and feed the pigs, and most of the time we are in the big house painting and cleaning and plastering. The Good Dirt is frozen solid. We're supposed to find spiritual meaning in our work but sometimes you hardly can. There's three meals a day to cook and washing up and sorting the garbage for the compost heap. There's the laundry, but the washer is broken half the time.

Sy brought this other woman yesterday, Marietta. She's about seven months along and she told me she hates her husband. Sy thinks she needs the pure atmosphere of the farm. She didn't do any work, just sat and mooned at Sy.

So it's a whole lot different than it sounded when Sy told me about it. I pictured it like Little House on the Prairie with a nice little one-room school for Jodi and Kimmy. Well, there's a school all right but it's eight miles away and the girls go by bus or in the Friggs truck. I began to wonder because they didn't seem to be learning anything. And Jodi was acting insolent with this stupid farmer imitation, and Kimmy cries every night because she hates it.

One day I went over to see what was going on and Mrs. Letterman, that place is a dump. I don't know how they can call it a school. It's dirty and the teacher is some kind of farm woman. She doesn't know anything, all she teaches is about rain and crops and cow disease and stuff like that. And I saw Jodi hanging around with these farm kids, I don't like the look of them and there's something sneaky about them, and when I ask her about them she won't answer me. She's almost ten now and it's time she started behaving like a young lady, but what am I to do?

It's hard to talk to Sy about it. He just says to Trust

him. He says what I really have to think about is giving Monty back. [Well, what had I expected? But my stomach curled into an unpleasant knot at this inevitable end to my little game, in which I'd pretended she'd get away with it.] The first time he said it I went and cried for an hour. Then I went to the Prayer Rock and cried for a while. Sy came along and said, "Sometimes it's hard to do the right thing, Ellie. But remember Jesus Christ returned to his father, not his mother." He put his hand on my head. When he does, those feelings go through me like electricity. I told him I couldn't give Monty up. I'd stay at Life Farm and scrub floors or till the soil or clean the chicken house. I didn't care. He told me it wasn't fair to Charlie or to him because it made him an accomplice. And anyway Monty is a boy and needed his father. I should pick a time to give him back, maybe a month, and pray and get ready. "You can make yourself do what's right, Ellie."

All the time I was sitting on the Rock and Sy's hand was on my head. It moved just a little, like he was stroking my head just a little. It was like he was pouring warmth into me with his hand. I knew what he said was true, God's truth was coming right through his hand. So I told him yes, I guessed he was right. When I said it, his hand pressed harder, then went down to my neck for just a minute. My whole body was flooded with holy warmth and light.

I don't know what to do, Mrs. Letterman. But it sure helps to write to you.

With sincerest regards,
Ellie

Dear Mrs. Letterman:

I must write down the events that have happened to me, though I might never mail this letter. You will probably think I'm bad and weak. But once you told me you understand about Temptation too.

Life Farm is no more, and I am transformed.

This morning Evelyn and I were out feeding the chick-

135

ens. I had Monty in his sling as usual. It was a little warmer, the kind of day when you know spring is coming. Then Oscar, this tall guy, comes down and said, "They're gone. The Friggs stole all the money."

I was very surprised. He said the safe was open and empty. He said, "The place is finished. I'm leaving." Evelyn shakes her head and says what bastards they are. I asked where they went. I thought it was terrible but Oscar only shrugged.

So we went back up and Oscar, Evelyn, and Janey said they were going to walk into town and get the Trailways bus. The Friggs and all their stuff and the truck was gone. I thought it was mean to walk out on Sy after all he did for us. I said, "Remember the way you were when you came here? We were all Spiritual Orphans. Are you going to run out on him now?"

But they didn't care. They told me good-bye and good luck and left. I don't know what happened to Marietta, I never saw her again.

So Monty and I stayed there, and later in the afternoon Sy turned up the way he does without any warning. He drove up while I was sitting on the porch feeding Monty. He got out and looked around. They'd taken everything. When Janey, Oscar, and me were down in the fields they just grabbed everything and ran.

Poor Sy looked like he was going to cry. His face trembled like a child's. "Everything," he said. "They took everything, Ellie." He looked around the place. "They must have been planning this for months. They even took my papers. I'm destitute. I'm as I was when I arrived on the face of this earth."

Then he told me all about his life. He was always a shy quiet child, his head was full of strange things. Then when he was fourteen the thing happened. He was walking in a field at dusk alone as usual. All of a sudden the Virgin Mary appeared in front of him in a vision. She told him he would be one of her Holy Apostles. Then she disappeared in a flash of light. When the Lord explained it to him, Sy swore to dedicate his life to spreading the Word, especially the lessons of the Virgin.

"It's hard, Ellie. I've been tested again and again. But I always come through, stronger and more faithful than ever. But"—his voice got lower—"it's hard, Ellie. It's painful. Give me your hand."

He came over and sat next to me on the porch steps. There was a late sun shining over the empty farmyard, and I wondered who was going to milk those poor cows in the morning and feed the chickens. Sy reached out his big, beautiful hand and I put mine in it and so we sat, him on the lower step, the baby nursing. I felt as though my hand was on fire.

"Sy," I said shyly, "once you said, when we were back in your office, that you felt a special something between us. Well, I feel it right now."

He looked up at me. And then . . . I only tell this because I know I'll never see you again in my life, Mrs. Letterman. Because it is very embarrassing—but then so is everything else too. I looked into his dark, shining eyes in that square sincere face. There was a look there, as though something spiritual was happening to us right then. And all of a sudden I knew what he wanted—something very strange but beautiful in a way. At that moment I would have done anything for him.

"I need your succor, Ellie," he whispered.

So I slowly reached over and undid the other side of my nursing bra. It was like my hands did it by themselves, as though I was hypnotized. Out came my breast bursting with milk. Sy's face got closer, his burning eyes looked so deeply at me I almost fainted. I felt ripped in half. I wanted him to do it but was afraid, I guess. When his mouth closed over my nipple I felt a transport that shook me from head to foot. Can any woman have more than I did then—with her child at one breast, her loving man at the other?

In a few minutes Monty was asleep, so we put him in his little crib and walked inside together, where Sy made passionate love to me on the couch in the office. As you know Mrs. Letterman I am not innocent. I have been with two men in my life and two others before I was married in high school. But not a single one has ever made me feel the way Sy Doré did. This gentle, kind religious man turned into a mighty bull, thrusting and thrusting into me till my cries echoed throughout the mountains! I will try not to go into details, but Sy is very well endowed when in a state of arousal, and I felt as though he was filling me right up to my brain which was hardly working any more! I was an animal like him, grasping and grabbing and begging for more as I looked up at that face swollen with passion! We were locked together like two beasts! And to excite me more he sometimes sucked at my breasts again, those breasts which belonged to Monty, swallowing that thin milk as though it was nectar with a blissful smile on his face.

"This is life, Ellie! This is elixir! This is manna!"

Then the school bus stopped letting out the children and I heard Kimberly's footsteps running up the hill from the road. Sy and I rushed around putting our clothes on and trying to appear respectable. I could hardly think straight. I told the children there was going to be a change of plans but I didn't know what. Jodi came slouching in with the new country-idiot manner she had. I told them everybody left and it was just the five of us.

Then Sy said he and I were going to pray together alone. So we cried, and were repentant about what happened, but Sy said he thought we were helpless against it. He also thought that this was no ordinary lust but a spiritual transport that would be a sin to deny. I was surprised that he didn't think it was just a mistake and we should try to separate—though I didn't know where I'd go next. I guess I never expect men to stay around after they've had their pleasure. But Sy was different. He'd had another vision, he told me, at the peak of his pleasure; and now he knew that the milk was Holy Milk from the Virgin Mary, and his transports were really the Lord speaking through his body.

"We have a duty to stay together for a while, Ellie. We have been chosen." I wasn't so sure about that, but I was hot for him, that's for sure.

He suggested we go off alone together for a while to a special place he knew. I thought I should be with my children, and that my breasts belonged to Monty. But Sy thought they belonged to "us." I was a wonderful mother, that had been proven! But now I had a higher duty. It was time to take Monty to his father. The girls could stay with Rita.

We discussed it with Jodi and Kimmy, who couldn't wait to go home even if they had to stay with Rita. They hated Life Farm. But what about my baby?

I knew I had to make this decision myself and I went for a walk in the woods while Seymour went to town with the girls to get Kentucky Fried Chicken. I took Monty out of his sling and held him in my arms. For him I had risked everything. The truth was I was a little skeptical of this holy duty idea. I didn't know how you could tell. But at the same time my head was so fuddled, all I could think of was Sy and the way everything felt and how soon we could be together again, and I felt like I was a little crazy, and thought maybe that had something to do with it—I'd been taken over by a higher Power. So maybe I shouldn't be with my children till I was more myself again. I didn't see how Sy and Monty could share my milk. And I was ashamed of myself because it was just Bodily Temptation all over again, and Sy wasn't helping very much with that— though maybe he had an explanation which he usually did for everything. Well, I knew what I was going to decide anyway. I was weak and I knew it.

I opened my blouse and fed Monty for what might be the last time.

"You'll be happy, Monty. Your daddy loves you very much." I kept saying it to him but really to myself. It didn't seem fair that a woman should have to choose between her man and her baby, but you know, you almost always have to. It makes me wonder about everything.

Very best regards and hopes for your continued good health,

Ellie M. Ferguson

I folded the letters and sat there staring into the embers for a long time. The rain was drumming on the window, and I could feel my heart beating, very slowly.

I got up, put on my raincoat, and went out the back door.

As I rang the doorbell, I peered into Kerner's kitchen. I'd often marveled at it. A wooden table in the middle under an unflattering ceiling light, fixtures from thirty years before . . . so long ago they'd come back into fashion. Somebody had lots of vision or no vision, depending on how you looked at it. There were four matching tin canisters with wooden knobs, a quaint gas oven, a sink with grooves on the side so the water would run over toward the drain. The pots and pans were aluminum tag-sale, and there was even a percolator on the stove, the kind you timed with your watch. Under the sink was a big plastic dish saying DOG. From within, DOG barked wildly.

Adam, very rumpled-looking, appeared at the door.

"Fran. What a nice surprise."

"Hello, Adam."

"Let me just finish something, and we'll have a beer."

I followed him through the hall and the two parlors back into his lair, a place of seeming confusion but, I knew, actual order. Stacks of books and papers, a word processor, a clutter of pictures on surfaces and on the wall—Darcy and the kids in various stages of what looked like a good American marriage: sitting on the beach, singing carols around the Christmas tree, standing in front of a station wagon in bathing suits. There were a couple of a long-haired, sad-eyed woman, who, I realized with some irritation, must be Lucinda.

I watched Kerner as he sat down in front of the computer and tapped silently at it. His work, and his face, were in a pool of lamplight in an otherwise dark room. I hadn't thought this through too carefully. I hadn't thought it through at all. What to think, what to say? Some things were better ad-libbed.

"Shut up, Parry," Kerner said to the dog. He looked up over his glasses and smiled. "Paracelsus. A medieval alchemist."

"I know."

"You do?" He looked down, peered at the screen, tapped some more, then looked up at me again. He leaned back in his chair. Damn the beard. I couldn't read his expression—probably one reason he had it! I got more and more nervous . . . almost dizzy. It was possible that this wasn't a good idea, but I didn't really care. Booze has a wonderful way of giving even mediocre ideas a shine. Even bad ones have been known to look good. But whatever this was, there was no turning back. I was tingling from head to foot. The more I looked at him the more excited I got, till I wondered if I'd ever been happy, if I'd ever really been alive before. I'd thought I had, but now it all looked pretty faint and faded. Snapshots with torn corners, creased across the middle.

He got up slowly, glasses down on his nose. He switched off the computer . . . if he lost a chapter it was my fault. He was wearing a baggy green sweater over a white shirt. I was in my raincoat. Freeze frame! Part of it was the nowness, the new-ness, the clear urgent present. Time was hard on marriages, they got dull and creased. Did people ever live them for a lifetime? There was Darcy, framed and slightly faded. He'd told me it had been an amicable divorce. He'd asked more of her than she could deliver. After all, why should she share his obsession or even understand it? (But *I* did.) Most people didn't. (But *I* did.) Why hang on to the tail of a comet, unless you were crazy—as I must be? I'd never thought I was, but I hadn't, very often, felt the way I did then. You could reach out or hang back, hide or go for broke.

When he came over to me I threw my arms around him. A few dizzy moments later, he said, "Just because we want to isn't enough yet." When I protested crazily, he said, "You like answers as much as I do, Fran."

"I don't care." I couldn't bear to let go of him—my tree of life.

"If it's any good it'll keep."

How to explain this encounter? In twenty minutes I was back in my own kitchen, tears streaming down my face, Baby in my lap. I was laughing too. I was humilated; I had been rejected; I had made a fool of myself with a kind neighbor who'd had more sense than I did. But I could never again say nothing had ever happened to me. My body ached . . . but how much worse if it never did! My head was whirling, I hardly knew what to make of what had happened . . . but what a spin it would put on my life, and his too! The casual waves as we passed on the way to work, the knowing smiles, the secret bond! And the new silver lining to my life that I would need badly. The phone rang, and I grabbed it eagerly.

"Hel-*lo.*"

"Fran, I'm in Hartford."

I gulped, closed my eyes, shook my head.

"Fran?"

"Hi, Charlie."

"I wish you were here. It's raining, it's rotten . . . but there are some new kids at one of the local schools here, just about the right ages, and—"

"Charlie, you can come home now. Monty's on his way back."

F·O·U·R

MONTY: A SMALL RED FACE, KNOTTED INTO A FURIOUS SCOWL. Red nose; pink maw open wide in hunger, fear, or something more ineffable. A bottomless pit always needing food, a pitiful bottom always needing a change.

I had managed to avoid the reunion. When Doré called, I handed the phone to Charlie. I tried to cover up an increasing dread by calling nanny agencies and running out for formula and disposable diapers, which we already had, hoping Charlie would interpret my actions as eager anticipation. The night Doré delivered Monty I claimed life-or-death work at the office . . . but was really at Rudy's, a bar in Blue Falls, getting mildly drunk with Beulah Markowitz. We kept toasting my last night as a free person, while Beulah told me about her druggie daughter and her hostile son as testimony to the rewards of parenthood.

"I'm not trying to depress you or anything, Fran. Everybody else goes through it."

By the time I got home I was grateful there was only one Monty and managed to feign great enthusiasm.

Until it happens, nobody realizes how a tiny baby can shake up a previously well-run household. Habits and systems collapse, prerogatives are reshuffled, schedules sent spinning. Monty was magnetic and distracting. It was impossible to forget about him, even when he was asleep, He was like a TV set that wouldn't turn off.

I was as bad as Charlie. It wasn't that I loved Monty. I

didn't even like him very much. It was some visceral response, beyond my control. I would do anything to stop those cries, which cut into me like tiny silver whips. I understood why people went mad and smothered their infants with pillows or beat them to death. Like most well-intentioned people, I disliked seeing these vicious tendencies in myself and resented Monty for bringing them out. I suspect Charlie felt some of the same, though tempered with love. His tolerance for crying was lower than mine. One peep and he was up from the dinner table or in from the yard to scan Monty like a detective and diagnose the pain. I could bear the cries for about five minutes; Charlie, about one.

Monty was restless, driven by an inner engine that never turned off. Johanna pronounced him "hyper." He crawled all over his crib and, as he got older, his playpen. He tried to get out of any space he was put into and, once out, applied himself to demanding the attention he unfailingly got. If the TV was on, he yelled or babbled. If our dinner was ready he gurgled or crowed and looked cute, tearing Charlie from the table. He woke early and called and chattered till one of us went into his room. If I sat down to do paperwork in the evening, he howled his way into my consciousness.

I watched Charlie for signs of disinterest now that his conceptual fetus had become a red, squalling, needy human child. Not only did he smoothly bridge the gap but something remarkable happened to him. His glass was filled at last. He was even a different color, deeper, more intense, flushed with love. He stood straighter, his shoulders broadened, the muscles in his arms firmed before my eyes. Gone was the laboratory slump, the bemused, faraway expression I knew so well, to make way for a new tender emotionalism. Tears came into his eyes as he looked at Monty, and when the baby grabbed his graying forelock in its tiny fist, Charlie laughed crazily, blissfully. He'd never been like this, even in the palmy early days of our marriage.

I hadn't really believed this would happen. I'd thought Ellie would starve in the street before she gave Monty up; when it became clear that wasn't so, I told myself that Charlie, like so many fathers, would rapidly lose interest and either give Monty back to Ellie or somehow put him up for adoption—the legality of which, or even the likelihood, I didn't examine too closely. I had been wishing Monty away, but each day confirmed that not only was he with us for good, he was the most important thing that had ever happened to Charlie. Charlie was in love.

When, in the rare moments that I could capture his attention, I tried to discuss this with Charlie, he only listened to me in mild puzzlement. What was my problem? He loved me, he loved Monty. If he paid more attention to Monty, it was because Monty was helpless and dependent on us for his very survival, and I was totally self-sufficient. I didn't—in fact—even need him, financially. We were and had always been equals, right?

Right. Then why were my feelings always hurt? And why did I feel so lovelorn? Fatherhood suited Charlie; it made him twice as attractive, three times as sexy. Don't ask me why; usually it has the opposite effect. But when he came into the bedroom at 3 A.M., with the baby on his shoulder, wearing only his briefs, I got turned on . . . then was rejected because there wasn't time or Monty wouldn't shut up or was just too distracting to forget about for long enough to have sex. I found myself watching him as he leaned over the crib or spooned up farina, wishing all this was for me. I'd reach over during the night. "Fran, I'm exhausted. In the morning. . . ." *Snore-snore.*

There was, during those early days, a certain camaraderie as we balanced our jobs and searched for a satisfactory nanny, took turns with night feedings and followed the directions of the pediatrician. Once we had talked philosophy, but now I settled for the pros and cons of disposable diapers and the dangers of earache, the question of strained peas and the general delight, wonder, and perfection of Montgomery Charles, where all Charlie's conversation eventually led.

Finally, after a string of disasters, we found Angelina. She was from Peru, rather dark and mysterious, in one of those tie-under-the-chin hats. She talked a lot about UFOs, which were plentiful around her village. In fact some of the residents had come there from other planets. I instructed her to lay off the UFOs around Charlie. She nodded; she understood about the unenlightened.

She hugged Monty to her broad breast, and Charlie and I, at last, attended to our neglected careers.

By this time I had a small, rather unexciting practice: a few estates, a couple of divorces, and some house closings. I was practicing law like an old country doctor: a little of everything, and not really sure what direction I wanted to go in. I sensed that there were more exciting pulses somewhere, if I could only hear them: some subterranean tom-tom beat, the distant sounds of revolution, beyond the parkway hum and Saturday fire whistle.

Rivertown, with its sweet village green, yellow school buses, and planters of petunias and trailing ivy, was a fantasy town, a movie vision of the American dream. Only forty miles south were dark pockets of wretchedness, of poverty, crime, drugs, hopelessness. Once, I'd brushed up against this misery every day of my life. I'd passed the shadowy shuffling figures, dropped coins and bills in the plastic cups, read the lettered signs describing some downward spiral of misfortune. I'd stiffened my mind, sighed at this continuing evidence of human weakness, blamed the welfare state, the decline of the family, community mental health policies, the drug trade. If my heart caught as I looked out the taxi window at some ragged creature pawing through a trash basket, I tended to become annoyed and blame the creature for being there and upsetting me.

In Rivertown it was possible to forget all this. Here the darkest sins were the panty-hose thief, the mayor's peccadilloes, or the occasional suicide or domestic abuse case—not trivial things, certainly, but eternal and somehow inevitable experiences of human life. A man three blocks away had swallowed a bottle of sleeping pills and was found dead in his backyard. There were explanations: he'd lost money in the stock market; his wife had a lover. But how do you explain a wretched creature dead in a subway station, his only shroud a sign saying he couldn't get a job? I don't know. What can you say about a mother of three living in a welfare hotel or even in the streets . . . just where I was always telling Ellie she'd end up if she didn't do something about it.

I was constantly inspecting Rivertown's seamless surface for cracks. Route 3, for all its ugliness, was not a crack. It was rampant commercialism, zoned out of our little dream town but crucial to its support. It was a depository for idiocy and vulgarity where Doré fitted in perfectly. But even offensive Route 3 better accommodated human oddity and perversion and failure and hope. With all its inanities, its frontal assault on the senses, its mindless motions going nowhere, it had vitality while Center Rivertown looked embalmed.

I'd expected that when I did detect a crack in Center Rivertown, the exudate that seeped out would be the familiar stuff on Route 3: McDonald's would fight its way into the town square or some developer would build ugly condos next to the church, and we would all weep and wail. But when the cracks did appear, the view within was breathtaking: the issues were serious, primitive, resonant with history. Three mothers managed to remove a few books, all regarded as classics, from the library shelves on the grounds that they were too dirty for the eyes of their children. This being a comparatively enlightened area of the country, the books were soon put back. I brooded less on the stupidity of the mothers than the fearfulness of those who had given in to them in the first place—the people who hadn't wanted to "offend." I didn't know how you could live without offending. Around the holidays, feelings ran high when the Jews put a menorah in the square next to the old wooden crèche. I heard people I knew and thought I'd liked saying things that appalled me with their bigotry. Then, like magic, both crèche and menorah disappeared, the crack sealed over, and there was silence again.

When Monty had been back a few months, the matter of the Van Willem Hotel surfaced again. To my surprise, this time it was the homeless who wanted my services. They'd come to me because of my reputation as a civil rights lawyer, which was gratifying if unfounded. Their leader was a handsome but quite peculiar young man who was trying to organize a County Underprivileged Movement, to prove, if nothing else, that such people existed. Of lineage even more mixed than mine, his name was Banya and he reminded me a little of Michael Jackson. And he knew how to talk.

"There are seven who sleep under the train station, Fran; six in the park; and about a dozen in the Van Willem"—a major point of contention among the commuters, who objected to scuzzy heads and staring eyes, of decidedly ethnic cast, in the hotel windows directly opposite the station. It was hard to believe he was even standing here in my office with the view of the square and the Episcopal church. He wore shredded pants, a moldy old jacket, and sandals, and his hair was done in dozens of little braids.

"Tell me, Banya. How do you find time to fix your hair like that?"

"Man, I have a *lot* of time. If you don't have a home or job, it gives you *many* more hours every day."

"It's a hopeless case. They'll shoo all of you over to Blue Falls," whose character was better—somewhat better—suited to Banya and his ilk.

"I don't know about that. That developer, he want to turn the Van Willem into a cheap dump. I got proof he intends to gut that fi-i-i-ine old Victorian building, strip off the moldings, put in Sheetrock walls and a cheap bar, and them false ceilin's. He's not sayin' so, but he intends to make it into a real tacky operation . . . then the county gotta put us there anyway 'cause it's on the list."

"So what's your proposal?"

"We stay there and restore the place, real historical and natural-like. We'll sand down the wood, strip off that ugly wall-paper, take the layers of varnish off that fi-i-ine old banister down to the originate oak." He leaned back and grinned. "I bet you're surprised I know about all this jazz. I used to work for this antique dude."

"But what then? They'll want to run it as a classy hotel and they'll still throw you out."

"Then we call in the media." He reached into his pocket and pulled out some filthy, mushed-up papers. "Here's Mr. McIntosh's plans." He glanced over at Phil, who was pretending to work. "I borrowed them," he whispered.

"You borrowed the developer's plans?"

"Well, I thought it'd give you the idea faster. That bird intends to cheap everywhere. You see here: instead of copper pipes he's gonna use lead . . . lower the ceilings . . . and with those joists the stairs will creak and maybe even fall down. Tinfoil for bathroom fixtures. No air-conditioning . . . the little things, Fran, nuts and bolts, screws, the cheapest you can get. And guess who pockets the difference?"

With difficulty I tore my eyes from this fascinating document. "Give it back or I won't have anything to do with your case."

"Oh, I will, Fran. I don't know what came over me. I just happened to be in his office, and there next to me was the copy machine."

"You are incorrigible. I have to think about it."

I wouldn't think for a minute. I knew I'd do it, even though I'd probably never receive a nickel. The poignancy of the situation was irresistible, the complexity exciting. Sometimes my profession seemed to have a life of its own, pushing me along unexplored paths, challenging me to look past the obvious into the dark tangled heart of complicated issues.

The Ashtoreth project had been dropped by the government but had then been picked up by Phillips Olimpia, a conglomerate that owned everything from manufacturers of rockets and rocket fuel, components of nuclear weapons, and top-secret chemistry and bacteriology labs to newspapers, breakfast cereal, and cream cheese. Charlie's recent spotty attendance was either ignored or forgotten, and Phillips Olimpia offered him a job doing more or less what he had done before. Would Charlie enter the fast track, leaving less time for Monty? Yes; he had to set a good example for his son and make money besides.

"But what is this conglomerate going to do with a rocket satellite?" I asked.

"I think they're going to use it for advertising," Charlie said, as he soaped Monty's hair. "Close your eyes, dear."

"Advertising?"

"That's what I heard."

"On TV?"

"Well, of course. . . . Daddy's going to rinse now."

"Do you mean pictures of a distant earth, girt with clouds, a few galaxies in the distance, and a spectral voice saying, 'Ashtoreth: ancient god of . . . what?"

"Hold still, darling."

" 'Ancient god of . . . Babylon, Ninevah, and Tyre, now

brought to you by Phillips Olimpia, purveyors of toxic waste, porn magazines, and your favorite breakfast food, Sawdust Crisp. Quality—then and now!' "

Charlie ignored me. "Here, Monty, wipe your face."

"Charlie, did you hear me?"

"He has soap in his eye, for God's sake." Monty, screaming, buried his face in the towel. I felt like braining both of them. When Monty was in bed I tried again.

"Charlie, what do you think of all this?"

"Of what?"

I explained it all over again.

"I don't know what you mean," he said.

"Don't you think it's the height of Reagan-era disgusting?"

He looked at me. "Well, what else would they do with it? It's going up, that's all I care about."

"Is it? That's all? The purpose has changed from benign to malign. Don't you care?"

"Not particularly. I'm in love with the technology; that's all that matters to me. And what do you care, anyway?"

"I do, and you should too."

I picked on Charlie more and more. I could hardly help myself. It exasperated me that he was so contented. We'd both stopped drinking and smoking when Monty arrived—a parental pact—but now I started having a drink or two before dinner. This made my tongue sharper and caused Charlie's face to stiffen and retreat as it did when he was angry, but it forced him to pay more attention to me.

"Talk to me, Charlie. I don't know you any more. You're making a rocket that's going to advertise toxic waste and kiddie porn, and you don't care."

"It's better than this stupid plan of putting bums in the Van Willem."

"You've never been like this before," I said.

"Sure, I have. So have you. You're the one who's turning into a bleeding-heart liberal. Go live in the ghetto if you're so crazy about down-and-outers. Live in the Van Willem."

"I'm not going anywhere, Charlie. If anybody does, it's you."

"This is *my house. My land. My son*—"

"It's half mine." I poured myself a second drink and felt Angelina's eyes on me. "Suppose I did move out, Charlie. Or refused to move out. Suppose I divorced you and took you to the cleaners?"

"Go ahead, I wouldn't give a fuck. I'd bring Monty up in some simpler place—Maine or the Adirondacks. I don't need all this." He waved his hand. "You can't stand it that I have something you don't."

"No, Charlie, I can't stand it that Monty is the center of your life and I'm not. What would you do if I told you I was pregnant?"

That got him. His whole face changed. "Fran."

"It's not true," I said. "Dumb joke." Then I started crying. "It's the only thing that makes you see me."

"Don't you see," he said despairingly, "that Monty is yours too, that he's *ours*?"

I hated myself for behaving the way I did. Every day I'd resolve to stop, but every day there would be all that paternal love filling the air like poison gas. When he was home he hung over Angelina, correcting her, telling her what Monty should be wearing or eating or doing. Angelina's face grew darker. Then one unfortunate day Monty pulled Baby's tail and Baby let fly with claws that left two tiny scratches on Monty's silken cheek.

Charlie grabbed Baby. "That's it. I'm taking him to the Bide-a-Wee or wherever you take them. Or the river."

"No, Charlie. You are not."

"That thing is a menace. It's filthy and unhealthy. A quarter of an inch farther over and it would have been his eye."

To my horror he slung the wildly protesting Baby over his shoulder and started for the door, me after him.

"Charlie, I mean it. You're crossing the line."

"You fight for the goddam cat and you won't pay any attention to your son!"

Well, it wasn't pretty. We said things we shouldn't have. Then I slapped him, and he grabbed me by the shoulders, shaking me till my head snapped back and forth like a puppet's, saying "Shut up, shut up, shut up." Baby tore out of sight, and then Angelina appeared with her suitcase and the Peruvian hat on.

Nothing, not even a raise, would induce her to stay. She liked peace, we were too much warriors. Shaking her head, she called a taxi and, possibly, a UFO to take her to a better planet. I watched miserably as the taxi bore her off.

It was a chastening experience for both of us. Charlie took days off, which was not recommended for a new employee or, in fact, any employee of Phillips Olimpia. I had to spell him or else he'd be fired. Johanna helped out, and we struggled along with unsatisfactory high school sitters.

We made up, as couples do, with a passion born of fear of deeper revelations. We talked; we admitted we needed each other. Violence is not a recommended solution for problems, but it does have the advantage of blowing off anger and leaving a residue of useful guilt. Charlie admitted that he'd been insensitive to my feelings, I allowed that I'd been a bitch, and we resolved to do better.

To make his word good, he threw himself into cooking and laundry, even taking responsibility for the house in a new way that lightened some of my responsibility for details. I did what I could, but I had a lot of work around that time.

One evening after this balancing act had been going on for a month or so, I came home to a radical lib fantasy, a sitcom in reverse. Charlie was in his apron cooking dinner, Monty playing in his playpen. Tired wife comes in, kicks off shoes, slings handbag into one chair, jacket into another. Makes for the bar, sloshes a little vod on some ice. "Wow! I needed that!"

Charlie smiled as he stirred a pot and checked the broiler. In a couple of minutes he'd served me a lovely piece of grilled swordfish, fresh asparagus, some crackers and Brie afterward. He put chilled wine on the table.

"Charlie, this is delicious. I wish you could do it every night."

"That's just what I want to talk to you about," he said.

"What?"

"Well, I was fired a few days ago, Fran. And I didn't mention it because—"

"Fired." I went cold from head to foot. "Fired. For never being there?"

"Well, more or less. But listen—"

I'd lost my appetite. "We'll move back to the city; there are nannies in the city. This is ridiculous. The kid is ruining our lives."

"Fran." Charlie gently took my hand. "Just listen for a minute. I've been thinking about this. And you know, it might not be so bad."

"It can't not be bad. We need the money. We'll starve. The bank will take the house. There we'll be on the corner of Main and River Road, shaking our tin cups—unless you can think of a better spot."

"Fran."

My stomach was churning. "Charlie, it's getting so I'm frightened every time you open your mouth."

"Oh, come on. Just listen, I want to ask you a serious question. What correlation is there between your earnings and your job satisfaction?"

"Job . . . mine?"

"Are the cases that pay as interesting as the ones that don't? Now, be honest."

I said warily, "Well, that depends. The homeless bums would be a lot of fun, but they wouldn't pay a nickel. Probably the answer to your question is no."

"What about *Markowitz*. Was that fun?"

"It was, Charlie. So the answer is not necessarily; there are exceptions. She paid plenty." I still didn't get it.

"Was Zeus and Wenberg an exception?"

"Well, that was a big firm in the city. . . ." I was beginning to understand.

"The last thing I'd do is push you into something you didn't want to do. That's why I'm asking you. That's why I'm pushing your tolerance just a little farther. . . . You're something, Fran. Most women wouldn't put up with what I dish out. I love you for the way you love me and stand by me." Charlie studied me, his shirt-sleeved arms folded over his butcher's apron. His forelock had gray sprinkles, his skin was not as satiny as it had once been. His hazel eyes looked out from under bushy eyebrows. I still loved the bastard. "I've thought of quitting for weeks, but it wouldn't have been fair without talking to you. Then they started trimming the dead wood." He refilled our wineglasses. "I *can* get another job. We *could* get a nanny. It's all up to you."

My head was spinning. "You want to stay home. And you want me to get a job with a hot law firm in the city and make a lot of money."

"And I love you for being so direct."

I pushed back my chair and went groping for ice and cigs, breaking our rules. *Clink-clunk, burble-burble. Crinkle, ssstrike, puff, ah!* The sounds of sin, of escape, the tiny lifeboats of escape in life's stormy waters.

"Are you sure about this, Charlie?"

"There's no question in my mind."

"It's not so easy. They like kids right out of law school." My voice was thin and watery.

His face slowly lit up. "They'd snap you up."

Slowly he walked over to me. As on the day I'd agreed to have Monty, I didn't know if it was good or bad, grand or disastrous. All I knew was that when Charlie wanted me to do something enough, I couldn't say no. Perhaps this was what marriage was all about, and the problems came when you tried to evaluate any of it. The odd thing was that I had always thought I was in charge. But Charlie had something, whatever it was, that I had to have.

As might be expected, the legal community was not holding out its arms to me. I was forty-four. And Arthur Zeus had dropped me from my place under his golden wing. I hadn't measured up. I had turned my back on the fast track, I continued to live out of town. Nor was Arthur interested in having me back.

"You blew it," he said.

I decided not to go back to divorce law; I was burned out on the battles of the hearth. Eventually I took a job with the legal department of Blazer, Blackjar & Monument, a real estate firm. Zoning. Air rights. Struggles with the Landmarks Association. Smashing down, building up. How far back from the street. And always the wink, the bucks under the table, the deals-within-deals which usually turned out to be the contents of the package. It was like a daily swim in Arthur's polluted pond.

And I gave up my office in Rivertown.

F·I·V·E

I'M ASHAMED TO WRITE ANY MORE TO MRS. LETTERMAN. I'M ashamed of everything, like there's never been a worse person than me. If I sit by this road the rest of my life I'll deserve it. If the bus never comes—if I just die here with the flies and the hyenas and those gaucho guys—everything that happened since I opened my legs to Seymour Pierre Doré that afternoon at Life Farm, it all was a terrible mistake.

Nothing like that ever happened to me. Sy says I never "came" before. I guess I didn't. I never was that crazy about sex before. It's nice to lie close to a man, and hug and kiss, and feel warm and cozy. But they all want to stick it in; sometimes I think it's the only thing they care about, just stick it in and stick it in. It's different when you're on the receiving end. Or it was till Sy made love to me that first time. It was like he was a child looking at me with those adoring dark eyes, and that made me so hot! I blush even to think about it.

With Bill—well, he is my husband. And Charlie Morse is all right. I knew he wouldn't harm me, and I was stuck with that if I wanted the job. But Sy—well, it was like I went crazy. Anything he said to do, I did. He wanted "all of me," he said. My Virgin Mother's milk should only be for him, because that was how the Lord wanted it. So it was for six months when I might as well have been in a crazy ward.

Jodi and Kimberly didn't mind staying by Rita. I endorsed Charlie's last check over to her for my girls' expenses. Sy lied about losing everything he had at Life Farm, because now it turned out he had enough to support me.

I cried when he left to take Monty over to Fran and Charlie. I thought I couldn't do it. I had to nurse him one more time, and Sy was watching, and he made me weak with excitement. So I kissed my baby one last time and handed him over. My head was full of all those things again, and I knew I didn't deserve to keep him. Sy took him in the car while I waited at Rita's. Then he came back and picked me up.

As soon as I was in the car he put his arms around me and thrust his tongue deep into my mouth.

"I've wanted you ever since I saw you at the abortion clinic that first day," he said, in his deep, melodious voice. "I knew it was just a matter of time till we would be alone together."

That whole trip was like a crazy dream, or maybe a nightmare. We stopped at a different motel every night. Sy and me were like two animals. it was like a sickness. I was much hungrier than him all the time, of course, and he joked about how I was giving him breakfast, lunch, and dinner. It seemed like there was something bad about what we were doing, but he always told me how holy it was, how it was different for us because the Lord told us to. I was like a person hypnotized.

First it didn't matter where we went, so we just drove around and picked up burgers or pizza as we went along. Sometimes we stayed in the motel room all day, but even if Sy wasn't hungry he made sure I ate. One place in North Carolina we didn't go out for twelve hours, just kept getting Cokes from the machine in the hall and those little bags of peanuts and crackers and stuff. Sometimes I just stayed in bed—God, I was so tired all the time—and he went out and brought stuff back. Then he could pick it out because he didn't like it when I ate garlic or hot peppers.

Then Sy said he wanted to take me to this little town in Mexico he read about when he was young, where the sun always shined and everybody was always happy and loving to everybody else. He had decided when he found the right person he'd take her there. So we headed straight south.

Ciudad Flora wasn't much like Sy thought it was going to be. It's hot and dusty and there are chickens and burros all over the place. There's a church, and this café where they all go at night to see the cockfights: they put spurs on them and set them at each other; it makes you sick to your stomach to see it. We stayed at the Bella Rosa Hotel. It wasn't so bad, but you couldn't drink the water and I didn't like the food. But still whatever he wanted was fine with me. Nobody there looked very loving or happy like in the book he remembered, they just looked poor and sad and mean. Sy and I prayed for them every night.

After a few weeks there everything began to go wrong. I wanted to go and see more places, Acapulco or Cuernavaca, but Sy said what difference did it make where we were if we had each other. Anyway, Ciudad Flora was cheap and we had to think about money. Well, that was the first time I heard about that, he always acted like he had a million.

It was boring to just walk around the plaza or ride around the country all the time. There were no newspapers or magazines, and the TV only got two channels in Spanish. And after a while I got sick of all the sex and really sick of feeding Sy. I told him I wanted to stop that part and he got very hurt and sad and talked about the Holy Milk and all that again. I said if he'd ever had to feed somebody he'd know it wasn't so easy; you got tired and you had to eat so much, and I was sick half the time from the food, and then I got the runs. Anyway, I'd always felt there was something unnatural about it. He got mad and upset and said I was being cruel to him. But finally he agreed to stop. But it wasn't easy, we were both so used to doing it, and when you don't nurse your breasts get sore and dribbly, so he'd end up doing it again just for the relief.

Then I told him we just had to stop everything for a few days so the milk would stop. He cried and got down on his knees and begged me to let him; his estranged wife (the first time I heard about her) never would let him and he'd always dreamed of finding somebody like me to have this experience with. In fact he didn't even care if he dropped dead right then, because now he knew what true happiness was. The rest of his life was going to be a big letdown after this great physical spiritual experience, etc. If I let him do it just a while longer he'd take me to Cuernavaca. It would be cruel to stop then, especially since Ciudad Flora had turned out to be such a dump, though our love had made it special, etc.

But I couldn't keep doing it because I was starting to hate myself for it. I'd taken my breasts from Monty, and I felt like some sort of criminal. I was beginning to be less hypnotized too. I wondered what I was doing in this place with this man.

I felt trapped because Sy had the money, and whatever I needed, toothpaste or anything like that, I had to ask him for. Well, I'd worked for my living before and I'd do it again. So I started working for the woman who ran the laundromat, while Sy hung around and watched the cockfights with these gaucho guys. I guess it was the work, hauling the wet clothes out and putting them in the wringer, but my milk dried up by itself. I was so glad.

When Sy found out he had a fit. He needed his "succor." He told me I'd done it on purpose, I was a bitch, a cunt, and a few other epithets of that nature. I said obviously I didn't do it on purpose, Nature had done it, but he said whoever had done it, it was like he had been stabbed in the heart.

Then he started going out for hours. The laundromat woman told me he'd better be careful, he didn't understand the customs, and women here are like owned by somebody, a husband or father or brother. I told him, but he said I should leave him alone. I shouldn't tell him how to deal with this "betrayal." He talked as though I'd done something against the Lord, I'd turned out to be like all the rest; he'd thought I was different. I'd fooled him. He'd seen the Holy Light in my eyes the first minute he saw me, but now I was a whore like all women. He might as well sink deeper into the Slough of Despond.

Well, I was fed up to here with him. When he was out the gaucho guys started hanging around me and asking if I wanted to go dancing. I had to get another lock for the door of the hotel room. The woman at the café told me Ciudad Flora is a rough place and not safe for a woman alone, especially not a blond American.

Then one night when I was locked in the room, looking at the TV and wondering what to do next, Sy pounded on the door, white as a sheet.

"There's been a misunderstanding," he said. "Somebody's

coming after me with a gun"—some brother of a lady he'd been having a perfectly respectable conversation with at the café. He grabbed his clothes and stuffed them into his suitcase. "Anyway, it's time I got back to my neglected work." And he talked as though I'd steered him off the path of righteousness.

"But what about me?"

Halfway out the door he said, "You're tough, Ellie. You'll be all right."

I guess I was a little slow at understanding. I ran down the stairs after him as he ran out the door—leaving me with the hotel bill—and got into the car. Well, he wasn't joking! Out of nowhere came these guys and they started shooting. He gunned the car, and I watched it turn onto the highway and take off at around ninety miles an hour.

I didn't know whether to be glad or sorry. God knows I was sick of him, but he sure left me in a mess. I couldn't pay that hotel bill if I worked at that laundromat for twenty years. I was afraid I'd end up in jail. The laundromat woman didn't understand what I was doing there anyway; she thought I broke some law. She didn't know why anybody would want to leave *el norte*.

At first I thought I'd just die in that place. I thought I was being punished for what I did. Then one day I started crying and told the Laundromat woman everything, or almost everything, in broken Spanish and English. She listened with no expression on her Indian face, like they do. For all I know she thought I was crazy. I kept sniffling and crying, and she didn't say anything for the longest time. Finally she said, "Come."

She took me to her hut, and I waited there till dark. Then her brother came with his cart and horse. She told me he'd take me up to the next town where I could get a bus to the border. She gave me a little bag of tacos. I thanked her again and again, and told her she could have anything I'd left in the hotel room, clothes and some jewelry. So she ran off to get it before the hotel man discovered everything and took it himself.

So I got in the brother's cart and he brought me to the bus station. I gave him $10 and said I had to keep the rest for the ticket, and thank God he didn't kill me or anything. He just put it in his pocket and turned around and left. I thanked him and blessed him in Spanish. He didn't say a word the whole time.

The guy behind the counter says the next bus goes to California, so I guess I'll take that.

S·I·X

FOR THE NEXT COUPLE OF YEARS I WAS TO WORK HARDER THAN
I ever had before. I left at seven to drive to the city and often
didn't get home till eight or nine. I'd stuff down some dinner,
spend a couple of hours doing paperwork, and fall into bed
exhausted. I'd be up again at six to sit in another traffic jam.
On weekends all I wanted to do was nothing—and there was
no such thing with the kinetic Monty in the house.

I'd be flopped on the bed or the terrace and he'd barrel in
from somewhere. "Fan"—he called me Fan—"read." Or "ball."
Or "sing." (He meant swing.) Sometimes I'd tell him to go find
Daddy, but I tried to do my part to give Charlie a little time
off. It wasn't easy to be a first-time mother at his age with only
a cleaning lady to help. So I'd amuse Monty for a while. I wasn't
easy about it. I wasn't used to kids at all.

I kept staring at him to see who he looked like, but it was
hard to tell. He was just an average rather nice-looking little
boy who never sat still and had an attention span of about a
quarter of a second. His hair seemed to be like Charlie's in front,
and I suspected he was going to have Ellie's heavy thighs and
arms. A lump would come into my silly throat. Their son. The
culmination of their love . . . or their sex. A few thoughtless
screws and this magic had happened, this complex, beautiful
combine of two human beings into a third. Was there anything
as real as a child, was there anything that could be explained
away less, rationalized less, avoided less? Would Charlie ever do

anything more important? Or me? On and on I'd muse, till Monty screamed, *"Fan! Play!"* with his boundless confidence.

At first Charlie, joyous and somewhat bewildered by what he had brought about, set out to demonstrate that he had done the right thing. I'd been prepared for male incompetence: he would stand in the kitchen making vats of spaghetti sauce while yelling at me for the ingredients; he'd ignore bathtub rings, ruin clothes with bleach, collapse under the strain of midnight teething. But he was a natural, jiggling Monty on one arm as he ordered fish over the phone and remembering to take out the frozen orange juice. He was as compulsively neat and clean as I was and knew what we liked to eat—simple grilled meat or fish and fresh vegetables—and his salad dressing was superb.

I wasn't possessive about my turf; I did not, like Johanna, talk of "letting" people into "my" kitchen. So Charlie quietly took possession. He replaced my brands of food with his and replaced the plumber, the dry cleaner, and the electrician, even though I had gone to some trouble to find good ones. I said nothing. Charlie seemed to be a happy man.

"I never can thank you enough," he murmured in bed. "I'd do anything for you, Fran. You know that."

He even seemed to have balance about the baby. His love was tempered by moments of human exasperation. Sometimes he handed Monty to me, saying, "Feed him, will you? I can't look at any more strained veal." Because he included me so casually I got to like the kid a little and spent some time every day playing with him. But the real magic was between the two of them.

Watching them together, I often found myself thinking of Waldo. How special and blessed fathers were. Mothers were unquestioned and inevitable as the earth. If they did something wrong, we never forgot. But fathers came from some star. Everything they did was more than had been asked. We forgave them their mistakes and thanked them for existing.

How smart of Waldo to die before he and Lulu started hating each other or developed problems like Charlie's and mine, how lucky to have had such a perfect marriage, how cruel of him to die when I loved him so. My mind swam with vague memories of *bateau mouche* excursions, roadside picnics in Tuscany or the Alps, and that big, blond square man who lit up dark hotel rooms, always smelled good, taught me to eat oysters and artichokes and *tête de veau*, who talked to me about the French Revolution and Saint Francis and Karl Marx when I was too young to understand most of it but just loved the sound of his voice. Sitting on my rock in the woods, I recalled little scenes: a lunch with a lot of people somewhere near Versailles where I'd been, for some reason, ashamed; a cross-eyed mam'selle who suddenly left me alone because her lover turned up, leaving me weeping in a Nice hotel; swimming in a cold Swiss lake while Waldo watched from the shore. I remembered him and Lulu, both so beautiful, grandly dressed for a ball. I begged to go but didn't really mind that I couldn't. I was so proud of this magnificent pair, these two perfect creatures that were mine. In my bathrobe, I stood in the hall and waved and waved as they got into the little golden cage of an elevator. "Good-bye, darling!" they called. "Good night, precious! *Chérie! Précieuse!*" My father had never stopped teaching, pointing out, asking questions. He'd left sometimes, but he never failed to come back when he promised, till that last time; he'd taught me how to stay. I had learned constancy from him. But he left a wound that never healed. I was still trying to read his mind for hidden messages. Was there some vital principle I had overlooked? I remembered, like the rush of my own blood, his tone of voice when I had transgressed. Once I ran away for a day in Paris, my adventure consisting of three movies and too many *pâtisseries*. The sadness of his voice upon my return was more effective than any scolding. I wondered what he'd think of my life now, especially since I'd chosen his profession; or if he'd be able to explain why I wasn't happy, though my life wasn't any worse than most people's. But Waldo's reply was muffled.

As the months passed, there were subtle, almost indefinable changes in the nature of our partnership. Charlie became . . . I suppose the word is *watchful*. He watched me as well as Monty, and he became a little teasing about . . . what? My untidiness—which didn't exist. Now it amused him to think that it might. If I walked in and dropped my jacket and bag on a chair, which I had always done, he'd pick them up, with a little wag of the head, and hang up the jacket. He kept an eye on me as I scraped dishes and tied up the bag of garbage. When I cleaned up a spill Charlie came along and cleaned it up again, with what I think is called a "twinkle." "Have to use the cleanser, Fran—like this." As though I'd just crawled in out of the woods! He even watched me with a tolerant smile as I went into the living room, as though I were an unruly puppy who might rumple the pillows or piddle on the rug.

At first I was amused. I would have become unamused very rapidly except for one thing: I had seen Charlie's face from the doorway, unguarded, as he watched a documentary about his Ashtoreth . . . vast, absurdly grand, glinting in the sun, on the launching pad. His brains and talent had helped make this marvel. His face was so sad, so nakedly yearning, that I turned away, almost shocked at what I'd seen. When I went over to sit and watch it with him, he turned it off.

"Can't we watch?" I asked.

"It's over."

"But it wasn't. They were just saying—"

"I'm not interested in it, Fran. That's all over. I was just . . . curious to see how they handled it."

"And?"

"They did a lousy job."

I followed him into the kitchen, where he grabbed the cutting board and began chopping an onion.

"But there's nothing wrong with your being interested in this. How could you not be? After all—"

"Monty got another tooth today," Charlie said, without looking at me. "I'll bet you didn't even notice." He glanced at me, daring me to say any more about it.

Charlie now lurked around whenever I was with Monty, making sure I behaved correctly.

"I don't think he likes that book, Fran."

"He loves it. Look at him, he's tearing the pages."

"That doesn't mean anything. He really likes *The Little Engine That Could*. Why don't you read that?"

"Because I'm reading this."

If I did something right, Charlie smiled or said an approving word. Attempts at discussion proved to be fruitless.

"Don't you want me to play with him?"

"God, yes! It's just that I know better what he likes and what he doesn't."

"I'm not going to check everything with you, Charlie."

"I don't expect you to. But I just don't want to confuse him."

Nothing you could put your finger on. Just enough to annoy me. But then, I was tired and everything annoyed me.

One day when Charlie was shopping, I took Monty over to admire Kerner's windmill. It had the neighbors buzzing. The Showalters hated it, and somebody around the corner said it made the neighborhood look like a theme park.

Kerner and I had stepped around my moment of frailty. We didn't ignore it or avoid each other's eyes, for by then our friendship had other roots. We behaved as though my late-night visit was a little *folie*, an aberration in an otherwise good behavioral record. We had a couple of little exchanges: I mentioned my unfortunate penchant for getting drunk under stress and doing things I shouldn't do, and Kerner waggled my head, laughed, and said it was a good thing I stuck close to home and chose my victims wisely. I got a little red, then laughed too. I won't say that was the end of it, but it papered it over for the time being.

Kerner was working on a new article about something called "genetic fingerprinting," by which paternity could be established beyond a doubt for the first time.

"It's a two-edged sword, Fran. On the one hand it would be invaluable for rape cases, and perhaps even to catch runaway fathers and make them pay. On the other hand it would be the end of that fine old medical truth, *pater semper incognitus*. The father is always unknown! It's woman's single, sole weapon against men. Women have got to understand this, but they get so many things wrong. They don't seize the moment."

"But what are they supposed to do, Adam? If the guy finds out the kid isn't his, he'll take off."

"This is *exactly* where there must be *radical social change*," he said in his strong voice, stamping for emphasis. "The *only* hope for our deteriorating society is for men to understand that the small and helpless ones need to be taken care of, period. Without their cocks being involved." And I should *never* confuse men's behavior with patriarchal attitudes. It was a matter of continually "grasping the dichotomies," which was *very* important—stamping again. Then he told me about his last article, "The Sexual Sop," which was about how men con women into thinking they control sex, so they can blame them for getting pregnant and deny them abortions as punishment. But usually it was the underdog who did the manipulating—so what did I think?

I'd had half an eye on Monty, who was crawling around, eating grass, and pulling himself up on Kerner's leg. As he made off toward the windmill, Charlie's car rolled into the driveway. Monty was sitting there laughing at the ridiculous thing as Parry, Kerner's dog, came hurtling out of somewhere, knocking Monty over in an excess of affection. Monty banged his head on a rock and howled. By the time I was on my feet, Charlie had dropped the groceries, charged across the lawn, and snatched up the screaming child.

"There, there, darling. Daddy's here." To me: "Call an ambulance!"

"But Charlie, he just bumped—"

"Show Daddy where it hurts, darling. God, are those teeth marks? The dog bit him!"

"The dog did not bite him!" Kerner roared.

Charlie was aiming for the car. "I'm taking him to the emergency room." Yelling over his shoulder: "Well, are you just going to *sit* there?"

I followed him, throwing a God-help-us look back at the bemused Kerner.

At the emergency room, Charlie fulminated so at the Hispanic intern, who recommended cold compresses, that they sent down a resident, possibly to calm Charlie down. But the resident put a single stitch in Monty's head . . . leaving Charlie shaken and distraught at the idea of a flaw in his son's silken forehead. After we'd hung around there for three hours while Charlie demanded ever higher consults, I announced that I was calling a taxi and going home.

"Go ahead, walk out when I need you. Some partnership, Fran. He's supposed to be your son too." And "I don't want him over there ever again. That fucking windmill could have *chopped his head off*, if the dog didn't *kill him first!*"

I didn't care. I had to get up at five-thirty. In the morning he kissed me and said, "I'm sorry, Fran. I overreacted. I don't know what's the matter with me."

The changes that took place in Charlie, and in the house, were subtle, twisting, deceptive.

It had long been established that Monty came first. I knew there had to be fences and gates everywhere to keep him from falling downstairs. And rubber duck stickers in the bottom of the bathtub to keep him from drowning. And coffee tables cleared of all conveniences and eye-pleasing objects such as ashtrays and curios and art books, and all sharp corners, such as the four on the dining room table and many others around the house, permanently padded with pieces of old blanket and masking tape. I tried to understand the need for a permanent sea of little wooden and plastic toys on every floor, I was patient as I wrestled the potty seat off the toilet so I could use it.

I knew, too, that it was going to cost. Charlie wanted two thousand dollars' worth of alarm system on the house, citing mostly imaginary local crime—at that time, a first for Rivertown. But more significantly, it just wasn't Us—or the Old Us. The Old Us, that fun couple, would refuse to get one and then be robbed and then say now we would never get an alarm because statistically we were safe, and we'd be a little amused and triumphant about it all. We were not sheep—or had not been. Now we were, and two little red eyes were installed by the front door. Once I would have demanded why Monty got all this expensive protection when I hadn't, but I no longer rose to the bait; I was too tired.

Then the Ashtoreth satellite was successfully launched into orbit. If America was bored with the government's space shuttles, something about this object of private gain appealed to our country's capitalist heart. And Phillips Olimpia's publicity was good. They made it sound as though Ashtoreth were some great, benign giant that would orbit the earth, watching us with its friendly eye, protecting us from evil forces, and sending down interesting and instructive messages. As always, style won: packaging eclipsed content, and nobody noticed the inanity of the whole thing.

Charlie gave up the pretense and watched it all day, and that night we had TV dinners. Charlie had sworn this would never happen. Now it had: our domestic watershed.

Ever so slowly we began to sink. Bit by bit we got like the Hellers: spilled apricots and spinach, bag of dirty diapers stinking up the front hall, damp half-eaten cookies—Charlie's number-one tranquilizer—everywhere. I was always tripping over a stroller or a jumpy-seat. I could endure a certain amount of disorder, with difficulty I could stop looking to my house for aesthetic gratification, if I knew it was temporary. But spills, dirt, and messes I could not bear. Once Charlie had felt the same. I became irritable the minute I walked into the house, where lunch dishes sat in the sink and a spilled can of Coke decorated the front hall.

Charlie got a little scruffier and put on a few pounds around the middle. He had a new way of skimming the headlines of the *Times*, taking a fast look at the sports and not reading the rest. The TV seemed to be on more. Charlie stared at it after dinner and often went to sleep in the chair. I never saw him reading a book any more.

Somehow things we'd always believed in were disappearing; things we'd scorned proliferated. There was a plastic reindeer on the front lawn, a five-foot Miss Piggy in the dining room. The Bach and Chopin Monty had been treated to for the first two years of his life gave way to whining country and thumping rock. Cotton gave way to nylon, *Sesame Street* to the *Gong Show* and *Make-Believe Ballroom*. And what about the day I came home early to find Charlie and Monty staring slack-jawed at *As the World Turns*, eating Twinkies? I stood there watching them, for once beyond speech. We'd promised not to fight in front of Monty, so I burst out later.

"Is this what you do all day? God, I'm out there breaking my ass for Blazer and Co., commuting two hours each way in the fucking traffic, for Twinkies and the *Gong Show*. For the sight of you in a plastic apron."

"It's practical."

"No, Charlie, it's *easy*. It's *hard* to think straight. It's a daily struggle to see past the cultural garbage and commercial TV bilge. We're *all* threatened by it." I found myself thinking of Ellie's old apartment. "If you really want to do something for that kid, show him something better."

"Oh, lay off," Charlie said mildly. There was a new, alarming blandness about him. It was getting harder and harder to rouse him.

"Charlie, put him in nursery school. Go back to work."

"He needs me at home. He's only two and a half."

"Charlie, talk to me."

"We have a child. Things are bound to be different." His voice was monotonous.

"But why do you have to buy him mint-green socks?" I pleaded. "How can you give him Gatorade?"

"Because I don't have time to run around looking for pure this and pure that. Because the price is right." He laughed. "I never thought I'd see the day when you care how I bring up Monty."

"Well, I do. And it's more than Monty."

"It's not so easy," Charlie said in a low, slightly sulky voice. "It gets a little boring, to tell you the truth."

"Put him in day care!"

"I'm not going to put my son in one of those places, with every Tom, Dick, and Harry you can think of."

During this exchange we happened to be out at the Bistro Beaumont. Donny Showalter was baby-sitting. I looked at this man I always seemed to be excusing from something: knocking up the maid, quitting his career, and now, worst of all, losing sight of certain delicate, hard-to-define but crucial threads that had not only connected us but defined our joint identity and explained our marriage. He was changing before my eyes. His old strong, silent, Lone Ranger intelligence, his very integrity, was evolving into . . . what? A sodden, dank, distant passivity, half couch potato, half mindless consumer. Worst of all, he had no more passion.

"You used to be crazy," I said in a low voice, "but I didn't care. I loved you. I forgave you, I even admired you for going after what you wanted. You didn't care what anybody thought. I admire obsessions, Charlie. I wish I had one. I'm like an empty motorboat turned on high. You were my obsession, and now everything's leaking out of you . . . everything interesting, exciting, valuable. You're a husk."

"Jesus Christ," Charlie said mildly, looking at the menu. "Lighten up."

"I won't. You act half drugged. Are you taking something?"

He laughed a kind of bright, honest laugh. "Asked by the Vodka Queen!"

"Charlie, can you hear yourself? 'Tom, Dick, and Harry.' You've never been a snob."

He put down the menu. "I'll have the lasagna and the veal parmigiana."

"Are you deaf? Are you numb? You are going to answer me before we order." I could hardly believe this conversation. "Who are these Toms—"

"Waiter." He waved his arm. "I'm ordering. You can do what you want."

"Then pay the bill yourself."

That got him. I marveled at the effect of this simple statement. His baffled, helplessly angry expression taught me more than I ever wanted to know about the classic nuclear family. Then he glared at me and capitulated, and I learned more.

"Go ahead, Fran. Make my day."

"Your father used to talk about 'every Tom, Dick, and Harry,' which meant anyone not of his ethnic or religious group, which meant practically everyone."

"So what?" He began tearing into the bread. "He wanted to protect his kids. I want to protect mine. You'd feel the same way."

"It felt great when he wanted to protect you from me."

"Well, Fran. You have to understand. You were kind of rich for his blood. He was used to, you know, conventional people. I mean if you—" He stopped when the waiter came by and we ordered.

"If I wanted to protect my child from Toms, Dicks, and Frans."

"Well, try and see it from another point of view, okay? You have certain things you value. Maybe it's just a male thing. I know I care more about my son and my land than anything else in the world. I want Monty in the right kind of school, so he meets the right kind of people. Isn't that why we live where we do? We wanted the Beaver Pond schools. Come on, admit it. Shel Showalter agrees with me completely."

I watched Charlie plowing through pasta dripping with melted cheese and veal dripping with melted cheese. It was for him and his kid I was killing myself at a job I wasn't even very crazy about. Now I was hearing creeping racism. But I exacted my price, my own arsenal. Like many breadwinners I had become not-so-subtly sexist. I mildly considered Charlie's feelings, but only as something to be dealt with, handled, pacified. He could have this but he couldn't have that. If I gave in on this he'd lay off about that. His choice of a life in itself made him inferior . . . which I wouldn't have admitted then but knew now I believed. After all, he acted inferior; he was bland and content, he had no interests beyond the house and Monty, he was throwing away his intelligence on what he pretended was the complex, psychologically delicate matter of whether—if he went at all—Monty should go to Goosy Goosy Gander, Mother Bumpy's, or Happyland Preschool, and what Johanna and the other mothers thought, and whether to get a morning or an afternoon interview, and what Monty should wear. The very inanity of all this made me feel protective and tender.

But during this instructive passage, when I could glimpse the world through male eyes, I saw tears and gaps in what should have been a seamless and satisfying cloak of power. For one, I was locked into my job like a cog in a machine. I had to keep going, keep moving and make the money, for everything rested on my frail shoulders: the house, the food and clothes for three people, our very lives in Rivertown, of which I was becoming unaccountably fond.

In a sense responsibility is harder than dependency, for a dependent can always blame the boss. While Charlie took Monty to Daddy-and-Me and made Chinese chicken salad, I marched in the ranks, afraid to miss a single step, to trip, God forbid to fall, for I would fall a thousand feet, a mile, right out of the running, past all the bright young law students and ruthless killer males who would trample on me without a thought. I could be fired! Fired from a tiring, crushing, basically stupid job and never find another one. Once I would have been stimulated by the war games of Blazer, Blackjar & Monument, but something in me was changing. I was tired of the urban battles, the power struggles, and the money-grabbing greed fests and orgasmic deals of the business world. But I didn't dare think about it, and I'd have bet my bones that most of the men on the parkway and the train were in the same bind. And every year was worse, the chasm deeper, the disappointment greater . . . that mysterious disappointment that I seemed to see in the eyes of almost everyone older than I.

Toms, Dicks, and Frans.

Charlie had taken me home to Ohio, where I'd learned about middle America. A football game at the high school, a tailgate picnic, an evening in front of the TV looking at sitcoms. Ten o'clock service at the Episcopal church, lots of greetings and gossip afterward on the steps. A big Sunday dinner at three that knocked everybody out for the rest of the day. At Miss Comfitt's Seminary, I'd written Lulu making fun of such rites: later I'd married them.

Charlie was the only son. There were two sisters, one heavily into drugs, the other living in Alaska and mother of a Down's syndrome child. It took me ages to understand what all this had to do with his parents' fat scrapbooks of crackling pictures and simple politics, which at the time I'd thought I agreed with. Because they seemed kind, I thought they liked me; because they loved Charlie they were polite. Because I'd been taught to make small talk, there were no cool silences to puzzle me. I was young and very much in love. . . . I left Ohio gushing; I loved them. No less appealing was their unflinching solidity during a time when the rest of society seemed to be on a collision course, when madmen were shooting down our leaders and the Vietnam war was ripping the country in two. The Morses paid little attention to any of it. How I loved their house . . . the chintz-covered sofas with floppy pillows, the window seats and cubby-holes and attics and corners, the big easy dining room with a china cupboard in the corner. Charlie introduced me to such artifacts as driveways and forced-air registers and church suppers and lawns.

Charlie was different when we were there. If he were a glass, the clear elixir of mind flushed away to make room for the rich, hot fluid of family life. He was more present, more aware, more sexual. He noticed everything I did, heaped on praise and blame, made suggestions, flew into little rages. When accused, he told me, with justification, that I was different around Lulu—people got silly around their parents. But it wasn't that; it was the way, in Ohio, his impenetrable coolness some-how filled up and overflowed, sizzling and spilling . . . and since I didn't understand it, I thought it was heat from a family hearth I'd never had.

First they said I was a Jew, then they said my father had been a Communist. I was a Jewish Communist!

I was stunned when this was revealed, which it was, half inadvertently.

"You do have a little Jewish blood from Lulu," Charlie said, trying desperately to repair the irreparable.

"So what? Tell them I have lots of it, and tell them to go fuck themselves."

"Fran." Charlie's voice was hot and sour.

"Tell them Waldo was a Communist spy. I'll tell them."

"Don't you dare," Charlie said, in a dreadful warning voice.

"My God, how can you listen to this? How can you protect them?"

Charlie tried to excuse them on the basis of age and back-ground. He told me there were many people in the country like them, which I couldn't know because I'd been raised in European hotel rooms. But slowly he changed, saw it as it was, turned his back on them, and we were married. And, as often happens, soon there was a truce because they needed Charlie for their lives to have any meaning. They welcomed me with qualified but passable kindness . . . almost admirable on their part, because by then I hated them. Those were the rough stones, the underpin-nings of our marriage.

· · ·

Banya, my pigtailed, homeless friend, came by one night after dinner, horrifying Charlie and fascinating Monty, who screamed, *"Fan's fend!"* Fan had a friend! And what a funny cute one, with those rags and pigtails! He had come to nudge me. McIntosh, the bad developer, had lost the sale; the fate of the Van Willem hung in the balance again.

"So Fan, I come to ax you—"

"I'm going to do you the biggest favor of your life. Don't say 'ax.' The word is 'ask.' "

"I *said* ax."

"If you ax me they'll send you to jail." I didn't give up till he got it right.

"Ax," Monty shouted.

"Lord, do he always yell so loud?"

"He's a very aggressive kid." I sometimes wondered how he got that way. Charlie wasn't particularly aggressive. "Listen, Banya. I'm not practicing law here any more, I'm working in the city."

"But we already started to fix that place up. It's all clean now. And we working on that fi-i-ine old woodwork."

How sweet. How idiotic. How badly I wanted to go to bat for them—much more than I wanted to struggle over a certain office building in a downtown landfill.

After he left Charlie said, "I don't know where you found that character, but I don't want him around here again."

"Oh, come on, Charlie. he'll come if I want him to."

"Well, not when Monty's here. He's an unwholesome creep."

"Monty loves him, and it's good for him to see a black face occasionally. Which you'd like to think don't exist."

"Don't be silly, there are two black families in town."

"Both tokens," I retorted.

Toms, Frans, and Banyas!

We argued more and more, or at least I did. I'd goad him and goad him till he got furious. I couldn't stand the way he was. His beautiful brain was weakening, slithering, turning mushy, his head was filling with Morse.

One fall day, in an unguarded moment, he told me that

the experience of fatherhood had made him reconsider abortion. If Ellie had gotten one, he never would have known, etc.

"That's disgusting, Charlie. How do you feel about contraception? Are you against that too?"

"Of course not." It was a Sunday, and we were walking up Morgan's Hill Road, alone for a change. "What an asinine question."

"Did you use it with Ellie?"

I hadn't even known I was going to say it. Charlie stopped dead. It was a gray, raw October day, with a biting wind. From where we stood you could see the river beyond the half-bare trees, broad and gray. The ground was a matted carpet of gold and crimson leaves.

"What an incredible question." His voice was furious.

"No, it's not."

"It is, Fran. It's a no-win question." He yanked at the scarf around his neck. "If I say yes, then I planned it, because I never use it with us. If not, I'm a bastard and I didn't care about her."

"You're already a bastard, as far as that goes."

Charlie strode on up the hill in his tweed jacket and desert boots, me at his heels. We were in a rather empty area near the cemetery on top of the hill. If Charlie was really sick of me it would be a pretty good place to strangle me. At least he was responding; it might be worth it. Finally he stopped at the cemetery entrance.

"I didn't use any, because I believe it's up to the woman. Okay, Fran? Women have the babies, so it's up to them."

"Then why isn't it up to them to have abortions?"

He looked at me for a long time, beyond anger. "You're changing the subject."

"All right, Charlie. I aced you." We started walking again, Charlie slightly ahead, swinging along and staring at the ground. "Charlie, what was it about Ellie? I mean, I'm not so bad, and I was"—I couldn't say "am"—"crazy about you." I mean, was it some quality, or . . . ?" He was looking at me in disbelief. "I know I'm a pest, but I don't know what to do with all this."

"You could make tapes." His hands were jammed into his pockets.

"Just tell me this one thing. Then I'll shut up."

He stopped and looked at me for a long time. There were little puffs of fog in front of our faces. Finally he said, "It was her innocence. Didn't you know that?" He started back down the hill and I followed, my mind churning around. "Her sweetness. Her tendency to screw up."

"What?"

"Oh, you know what I mean. She cleaned all right, she did her job pretty well. But, oh, she'd always forget something—the noodles in the soup, or half my shirts. She ran out of gas in the driveway once. She forgot one of her kids, left her with a neighbor . . . you know how she was."

I did. A cold pool slowly formed inside me. "This is what appealed to you? The empty gas tank and the wads of Kleenex?"

"Well, she seemed so . . ." He reached out suddenly and grabbed the low branch of a tree, pulling at it. "I thought she needed me."

He strode down the hill ahead of me. I watched till he turned the corner out of sight. I didn't ask him any more questions that day, but that night, for some reason, we made love.

We had another contretemps over Baby, ending again with threats of expulsion by Charlie, who thought Monty might lose the next fight.

"Baby stays. I'll watch him."

"You can't watch him while you're at work."

"I'll quit and watch him." Monty stared as Charlie and I looked into each other's souls. How I would love to quit.

"Very funny, Fran."

"I'm serious. I hate Blazer. I want to practice here again."

"We can't afford it."

"Too bad, Charlie. You're able-bodied. That's been proven beyond a doubt!" I looked at Monty, who had hardly ever heard angry voices. High time he did! "Sometimes daddies go to work, Monty. Isn't that funny?"

"Monty, go to your room and play," Charlie snapped. At least I'd gotten a rise out of him. "Go to your room and in a few minutes I'll come and read to you." When Monty left he said, "Don't you *dare* drag him into it."

I began to cry. It was the sex, it made me feel all warm

and vulnerable and ruffly, like a baby chick. "Monty always comes first!"

"We got into it together."

"Well, hardly, Charlie!"

"I mean after she was pregnant. Anyway, we would have adopted, or used one of the new techniques. At least Monty is part somebody's."

"Suppose I'd gotten pregnant by somebody else? Then what?"

Charlie gave me a disgusted look. "That's completely hypothetical."

"So what?"

There was a long pause. "That's different," he said. "I would have been *very* unhappy. I mean, of course I know *you* were unhappy. But I couldn't have accepted the—" He stopped.

"Well, why not? Let's assume I got pregnant by some decent, intelligent man—Bruno at the Arco station. Or classier, if you like." He wouldn't look at me. "Come on, Charlie. I'm pregnant by . . . Robert Redford. Prince Charles. Misha Baryshnikov."

"I told you it's different. The whole point is the name. The line."

"And I don't have a line."

"No, you don't. You've said so yourself. You're a wild combination. That's why I . . . you don't care about all that kind of thing, and I do."

"I know you do. No wonder you were so happy when Ellie got pregnant. Your child wouldn't have to have my messy mixture." I was trembling. "Hindoo. Russian Jewish. A few European countries. Why did you marry me, Charlie?"

"Because it was *too late*. Because I was crazy about you!" Charlie yelled. "Even with the mystery half."

"Mystery half. There isn't any mystery. Lulu can track every one of them."

"I'm not talking about Lulu."

I laughed, but it was a strange-sounding laugh. "Really, Charlie. I don't even know why we're having this idiotic conversation. This disgusting conversation. But then we've had worse! Waldo was impeccable, for God's sake, disgustingly impeccable, a WASP through and through, like you, Charlie. Once we all went to East Anglia so he could trace his ancestors. I mean, in a way I think it's shit, but in another way I suppose I like it because I married it, I just like it because it was Waldo's, and as far as I'm concerned he could do no wrong, you know that."

"I'm not talking about Waldo either."

Did he say it? I'm not sure. I just kept chattering compulsively about Waldo while Charlie stood there and looked at me. And at some point I got it, as any idiot would have years before. Big, golden, furry Waldo: small, slender swarthy me. Tall handsome Lulu, with light brown hair and hazel eyes, definitely chesty and hefty in the rear: small, thin black-haired me, with Hindoo eyes and olive skin . . . but I had no Hindoo eyes because there was no Hindoo blood in my veins, nor was there in Lulu's; it was only Cousin Olive who . . and Lulu was fair with a fine Semitic nose, but hadn't she said . . . I didn't know what she said. Maybe it was just . . . but who *was* I like, then? My God, who was like me?

I was wound up, tense, couldn't sit still: nobody else was like me. In pictures I looked like a changeling, a Heathcliff they'd found somewhere. Though there *were* certain resemblances to Lulu: our voices were the same, though mine was sharper and faster, and once Charlie had said at the beach that Lulu and I had the same legs; he could have picked us out anywhere as mother and daughter. When he said it I'd been thrilled, looking at our four legs stretched out on the towels— the same proportions, though mine were smaller and a different color, but certainly the same. We were one, Lulu and I; we had each other. We had a line.

I had a shameful, furtive understanding of Charlie's obsession. It was about connection. They couldn't take it away from you; you were marked for good. It was disgusting and I wanted it; I didn't want to float free across the face of the earth. I wanted connections and community, denied now by Charlie and once by Lulu.

"Who are you talking about, then?" I whispered.

"I don't know, Fran."

I'll never know whether Charlie told me or whether I suddenly got it. Or whether my mind had finally grasped what had only been a gauzy suspicion, an undefinable yearning that I had attributed to either Waldo's death or general alienation, or to nothing I would ever understand. Now I hated Charlie for having known something for a long time—for I was sure he had—about me which I didn't. It was as though I'd been walking around for years half naked, or with some deformity visible to everybody but me. Or as though he'd said, You know, Fran, you have this huge birthmark all over your face. I thought you should know. You aren't as good-looking as you think. For somehow he'd communicated this unthinkable thing to me, though I can't remember the words.

I was devastated. I never thought Lulu told him, though I know now she did. She told him I wasn't what he thought, or what I thought—in fact she didn't know what the hell I was. A piece was missing, gone forever . . . and that was when Charlie decided to keep Monty. Ellie seemed pretty safe with her blue eyes and blond hair and her Catholic background. I don't mean he set out to get her pregnant on purpose; even Charlie wasn't that bad. But once she was—well, he grabbed the moment and probably considered himself lucky that my mongrel genes hadn't taken. Or couldn't, as though nature refused further cross-breeding!

It brought back humiliations from the past, things that had marked me as different from everybody else. Parents' Weekend at Miss Comfitt's, Lulu alone and wearing green velvet jodhpurs. "Isn't your father coming, Fran?" "No, he's . . . um . . . dead." What bothered me was our whole unconventional style. It was unimportant to my ignorant mind that my life had been far wider and more interesting than the other girls'. None of them had heard the thunder of hooves at the Palio or swum in an icy Swiss lake; nor had those pudgy banker fathers half of Waldo's brillance—Waldo, who was, really, only my best friend. But secretly I longed for their white brick houses, their hometown high school to remember, the big brothers and football games and neighbors and chocolate cakes and Christmas parties, the line. Sweet smiling Mom and jovial indulgent Dad, the fire on the hearth, and love all around. I'd thought I could marry it—and lost it instead.

S·E·V·E·N

THE BIG THINGS, WALDO ONCE SAID, COME AT LITTLE moments. "Watch for them, Lulu," he told me, "for your life can break while you're looking at it, and you won't even hear the sound." It was one of the last things he said to me . . . not accusing, not angry, instructive as always. By the end of that December night he was dead, crumpled over on the green baize of the gambling table.

Fran has been here. She had another fight with Charlie. I guessed that she was jealous of the baby. She took a few days off from her job. She looked exhausted as only she can: jet-lagged, sallow, rings around her eyes, thin set little mouth. I tried to fatten her up a little, but she only picked at the food. Something was obviously on her mind.

The first night she was here I swept her off on one of those fine, foolish evenings, a party that flowed through the city for hours, losing a few here and picking up some more there. It was the usual crowd, Cipi, Beppi, and the rest: dinner at a place near the Arsenale, after which we all got on boats and sang, feeling very drunk and ridiculous. Cipi was as outrageous as ever in a velvet jacket and that white mustache, very protective of Fran and me . . . but God how I wish I'd never slept with him! It was only a couple of times ten years ago, but he still starts sidling and grinning after a few drinks, winking at Fran as though he owns me and singing at the top of his lungs on the boat, hanging on to my hand. Thank God Bernadetta wasn't there;

she was at home with a sick relative, she always is. . . . She was once so beautiful, she could have had anybody, but then Cipi was once irresistibly handsome. I doubt if he was faithful to her for a month. She and I have become quite good friends. I know she knows; I'm pretty sure she no longer cares. Who hasn't he slept with? At least I had the sense to stop, and managed to do it without losing his friendship. She tells me they haven't shared a bed in years.

There was also a French editor and two American women and an Englishman who has a gallery and a miserable-looking Yugoslav journalist, and a fat Milanese businessman with his bimbo and three or four ageless, aimless, nationless people, the usual hangers-on, all stupid and wagging their tails and laughing too loudly. They were goggling at Fran and me, trying to figure out if we were important enough to bother with or if I was like them. I thought, I *am* like them. A little older, surer of myself, but just as aimless, as nationless.

We went to Florian's, where I hadn't been for months. Last time I was here, some American fashion woman, all done up in boots and sunglasses and a great silky sweater with a cowl up to her nose, got very friendly, put her arms around me, and began kissing me in the most shocking way until Cipi dragged her off, saying, "Leave her alone, Betty; my God, you've lost your senses." It took me ages to realize she must have been one of those women. I thought they wore men's suits. Lord, there are some strange people around these days.

Cipi was trying to persuade Fran to go and see Maude Brill, and Fran was shaking her head and saying it was all nonsense. He reminded her that Maude was once a talented *restauro* and all that, and how each little chip of dirt and paint hid extraordinary auras of Gnostic knowledge and ancient wisdom, and Fran just pooh-poohed it. Then he said, "You must have some secret you wish to solve, Francesca."

"Oh, I do." And she turned and looked straight at me with those big dark eyes. "But that's not how I'll find it out." And she kept looking at me till I turned to speak to the Englishman. I felt her watching me still.

Later we rowed home through the dark canals, the little *luce* swinging and making patterns on the damp stone walls as we passed. She was so quiet I thought she was asleep; there was only the swish of the oars. All the shutters were closed. Then: "Lulu, there's something I have to know. It's from looking in the mirror."

"You'll have to explain, Fran." I felt my hands grow cold.

"Do I really? I would give anything to believe you. If I could pray, which I can't, I'd pray you're telling the truth and that I'm imagining things. But I don't know."

"Don't know what?" I hated myself for stalling, but I was frightened to death—of my own daughter. There was a long silence.

"You're like Woofy, aren't you. I'm like Olive."

"I don't—"

"Lulu, for God's sake!" she cried. "Who was my father?"

My heart was pounding. I felt faint. I'd tried to tell myself this moment would never come; she'd never ask. This was the knowledge that had killed Waldo . . . or so I half believed. We arrived at the house and I tied up.

"You owe me the truth," she said as we got out.

"Fran, try to understand. It's the Sagittarius Vale. And Maude says it's the most dangerous—"

We were inside the house. "Don't give me that shit, Lulu. Just look." She grabbed me and pulled me over in front of that old pier glass in the hall, turning on the lamp. "Look at us, Lulu. Don't you see?" It was still very dim and she turned on the ceiling light, but that doesn't brighten it much. But you could see the difference—the coloring, and something about the whole aspect. I'd thought about it often enough! She's small, thin, wiry, tense, and I'm softer, lazier, tending to fat these days. "Just look," she persisted. "I look a little like you, but not much. Who else do I look like?"

"Fran . . ."

"Tell me! Or do you even *know* who it was?"

Without a second thought I slapped her. Then she screamed all sorts of horrible things, the way she does, and I told her she must not dare speak to me that way ever, no matter how aggrieved she was. We were still civilized adults and she was still my daughter. She said she wished she wasn't and I'd ruined her life, and told Charlie, and that was why he had to have a baby with Ellie, because he didn't want to look in his son's eyes at the *mistero*, the unknowable; and I said yes, I had told him, he had a right to know that day we found out Ellie was pregnant.

Then she cried, "But not me? You never told *me.*"

"So, would it have been better? Just look at you now, it's not doing you any good! The danger is in the knowing!"

She was breathing hard, sitting on the stairs, hugging her knees the way she did when she was a little girl. "I have a right to know, Lulu."

Did she? Oh, I don't know. But by then there was no going back. I sat down next to her and told her the whole story, even the part where I told Waldo on the day he died, and of course she looked at me as though I were Lucretia Borgia. Easy for her to be judgmental! One night aboard ship forty-six years ago. Was she so pure? Had she never given in to a stranger's passion? I'll never tell her about any others, that's for sure! Of course she had affairs with men before she met Charlie, she just didn't get caught.

"Now I know why I'm barren, Lulu. It's Laurentian's blood." She made a face as she said it.

"Ridiculous. Sometimes it's just the combination." Then I stopped, because Maude had said it was part of the spell, and what Fran said was true . . . but I wasn't going to tell her that, and I wasn't even sure I believed it myself.

Then she wanted to know everything I could remember about her "real father," which was almost nothing. I wasn't even sure if Laurentian was his first name or his last, or whether he was the room steward or the purser—only that he was a slender handsome man in a uniform who danced with the single ladies. Very dark, flashing eyes, black hair, some kind of accent, and "Mediterranean" sticks in my mind, there was mention of some port, Beirut or Barcelona or Piraeus, and dreaming of going to sea. . . . I don't know. His English was limited, but our common language had nothing to do with words.

Then I tried to embrace her but she pulled away. I told her how unimportant it was, and how Waldo had been a better father than most people ever have, and blood meant nothing. But she said it was very convenient my saying that *now*, after all the years of saying she'd inherited this or that from me or

Waldo, brains or temper or whatever, and then she went upstairs to her room.

I followed slowly, feeling a hundred years old. There's another full-length mirror at the top of the stairs. Fran said once that I had mirrors put into the palazzo before I even got chairs, but most of them came set into the walls. I loved them and their cloudy reflections; they always made me think of lovely people dressing for parties, giving a last twirl in the upstairs hall before making a sweeping entrance down the stairs. Now they gave me less pleasure. I saw a woman in a green dress climbing up slowly, wispy brown-gray hair, plump, old-womanish—though my legs are still not bad, and in the dim light the lines are not visible.

In the morning Fran appeared puffy-eyed and depressed. She refused to speak to me, only went off for most of the day by herself. She's always had to think things out by herself. She came back late in the afternoon and we had a silent dinner. The whole thing was beginning to irritate me. Giulia had made her best linguine with scampi and calimari, just for her, and she hardly touched it. She sat there staring out the window, ignoring any remarks I made. I told her she was acting like a spoiled brat. She had everything—a wonderful life and husband and career, and now she had a child. Many women would envy her.

She said Charlie was not wonderful but insane, they fought all the time, he made her work to support them, and a long list of other crimes. I told her whatever she thought, I admired Charlie's sense of responsibility about the baby—Italian men had children they completely ignored, unless the woman came and threatened them with exposure. I asked her what she wanted anyway, and she sniffled a little and said she didn't know, or she wanted everything to be perfect, or at least the way it had been ten years before.

At that she seemed to cheer up a little, and we went over to the piazza for coffee and pastry. Then she said she'd decided to find her father, no matter how difficult it was. I warned her I'd told her everything I knew, and the *Normandie* had burned forty years ago. She said she didn't care, she was a good detective. She didn't care what he thought. She just had to see him. He couldn't hate her or put her off. He was in his seventies now; he'd probably be thrilled to learn he had a daughter he didn't even know about. She'd never expose him . . . and so forth. Sometimes Fran can be very theatrical. It always surprises me, but maybe it's the reason she's good in court. That doesn't come from me, it must be from him.

I found myself getting anxious as her departure drew near. It wasn't about Laurentian. She has about as much chance of finding him as I do of becoming Queen of England, and so what if she does? But Fran likes projects, the harder the better—and that was taught her by Waldo, for where else could it have come from? I was on my own, for Maude was on her annual trip to Bhutan.

So it was with a certain nameless fear that I embraced her at the vaporetto station. In fact we'd done a turnaround. We'd changed places in a way: she'd come back to her usual strength and high spirits, and I was drooping.

"Please be careful, Fran. I sense the darkening *nube*—again."

"Don't give me your *fumisterie*. It's picturesque and all that, but it's nonsense."

I watched the motorboat go off in the direction of the airport. I was nervous about her flying and told myself I was being silly. I am only a half believer in omens. They amuse me. They are more fun than what one read in the papers. Sometimes I agree with Fran. But Maude had told me to expect visitations, because you can't hover indefinitely on the edge of the spirit world; they'll always find a way to pull you in.

I met friends for dinner over near the Rialto. That Betty woman was there, greeting me with outstretched arms and calling me "her soul mate." What a pest! But the Englishman with the gallery was along and utterly charming. I had a good time with him, but I was distracted and came home early.

Once in bed, I couldn't sleep. There was an odd, persistent picture in my mind: a woman stood on a bridge, watching me intently. I didn't know who it was. Finally I got up and looked out the window. It must have been almost three by then and dead quiet. The water of the canal hardly moved, and all the shutters were tightly closed. I leaned out farther to look up to the end, and my heart beat faster because there *was* a woman on the bridge, a blond woman, holding a little light up to her face as though to identify herself—but from underneath, and the shadows were so I couldn't recognize her. There was something strange about her standing there alone in the middle of the night just watching me. I closed the shutters and went back to bed, but lay there trembling.

I looked around my beloved room, mostly dark. I knew everything on the ceiling by heart: the molding, the faded paintings on the ceiling . . . shepherdesses, courtiers, clouds and trees and birds and *putte*, but as I lay there imagining them, trying to put myself to sleep as I do, I kept seeing the blond woman.

Finally I got up and went back to the window. It was the heart of the night, that deep, dark silence before dawn. The city was asleep. I leaned out and looked down the canal. Something was out there—a swish, a ruffle on the water. Then I saw a ghostly shape coming toward me, a boat gliding stealthily under the bridge, past the dark dinghies tied up by all the doors. As it came closer I saw that it was a barge, and there were two others behind it—all faintly, dimly lit, phosphorescent, a dreamlike procession coming toward me. All three were decked with flowers, the way they do for funerals. I wanted to look away, but I couldn't: and there on the lead one, on a bed of lilies and phlox, bright asters and daisies and a dozen others lay—thank God—not my adored daughter but Ellie Ferguson: white, still, her eyes closed, her dead child clasped in her arms, a wax figure in a white communion dress and high-heeled shoes, hair spread out in a halo on top of the flowers; the baby was all in white too, its little eyes closed like tucks in the flesh.

I watched unable to breathe as she floated soundlessly past, the purples, reds, and golds of the flowers glinting in the light of the beginning dawn. No one was driving or steering. The boats moved by themselves, slowly and steadily, trailed by the tiniest ripple, flecked with the early light.

I watched, my heart beating, as the next two came. I made myself look. There—and somehow I'd known it—was my beloved Waldo, pale, still, but just as he'd looked when I last saw him, wearing the dark suit I'd buried him in. He lay in a mound of poppies and chrysanthemums and blood-red asters. As the barge passed under my window his eyes opened, and his lips seemed to pronounce my name. Tears came to my eyes. "Waldo," I said, but the word seemed to disappear even as I said it.

Then the third barge of this sad, grisly procession I was being subjected to: and in a moment there below me lay Charlie amid roses and delphiniums and white tulips, as still as the others, dressed the same as Waldo . . . with tears on his cheeks, tears that rolled down out of his closed eyes. I waited for him to speak, but he said nothing.

I turned and slammed the shutters closed and threw myself against them, trembling. I didn't open them until that slight ripple had died away, and I knew the ghosts' barges were out of sight.

E·I·G·H·T

· 1 ·

MY FATHER THE PURSER. THE DANCER. THE OARSMAN, THE bos'un. The pride of the high seas. Why did he make me so sad? He didn't know I existed. I could have a dozen brothers and sisters.

My father liked a little nooky. The results of his nooky did not interest him. Just dip it in, then pull it out. He seemed strangely unsocialized as he went back and forth across the sea, dipping and pulling, flashing his beautiful white teeth, dancing his sinuous rumba. I could see him greeting people in one of his several languages. "*Bonjour. Como està? Wie geht's. Salaam alei-kum. Dobrieveche. ¿Cómo va?* Would the lady care to dance? To stroll on the deck? To screw? To drink champagne courtesy of Compagnie Générale Transatlantique? What is your favor, lady?"

Lulu didn't know what nationality he was. He looked Medi-terranean. Swarthy. He had a panther walk. Was he Italian? Egyptian? Lebanese? What kind of blood flowed in my veins? Where are you, Laurentian? I tried to imagine a white-haired Mediterranean type: Omar Sharif, Onassis, Zorba the Greek, Tevye. He might be alone, living out his life on a pension on a small Greek island. I'd find him in a shack drinking cheap red wine. I would approach quietly, simply. "Dad . . . you don't know me." Or: "This may come as a surprise, but . . ." Or: "Do you remember a night forty-six years ago, a pretty brown-haired girl on the *Normandie*—one of the last crossings that summer before the war?"

I was shocked but not surprised, furious but weirdly amused . . . and more understanding of Lulu than I had ever been. She was less guilty than relieved. A stone had rolled off her back, she told me. An impediment in her love for me had been removed. But I could barely meet her eye, so pained was I at her betrayal.

With a certain desperation, I picked through the pile for something positive. I was, I knew now, well over half European. My roots, those tangled roots that Charlie had luckily managed to avoid, were deeply sunk in some unspecified land east of the Atlantic. So were most people's, of course. But I had a particularly exotic mix. Strange and marvelous blood ran in my veins, fiery alien blood, the blood of Gypsies and cossacks, rabbis and artists, a blend that had served me well . . . one I might well be proud of, if I could only get those old shreds of Morse out of my head.

It was harder to get a fix on my father's character. He appeared to be less than admirable. But then I was seeing him only through the eyes of a rejected lover. Lulu described herself as an innocent, unworldly, lonely eighteen-year-old, shuttling back and forth between relatives. But I knew that girls of eighteen could be cunning as Circe. At that age I had already learned to spin webs to capture men. Where could I have learned such tricks, if not at my mother's knee? And I knew Lulu. She had been a flirt for as long as I could remember. She had probably been born one. Wasn't it possible she had lured Laurentian into her cabin—Laurentian, whose job it was to be polite and charming to lonely women? She might have seduced *him*! I could not have done such a thing at the same age only because I'd been brought up in America.

Lulu had said that after that one romantic encounter, he had danced with other women without throwing a glance in her direction. But maybe that wasn't even true. Perhaps he had been at her cabin door the next day, the moment he was off duty, and she'd rejected him for Waldo . . . then later made up the story she now believed herself! Perhaps he'd had some seizure while they were making love and remembered nothing afterward, wondering why the pretty girl in yellow was sending him reproachful looks! Suppose, even, her behavior had been so wanton that he was shocked, even embarrassed by having been held in sexual thrall for hours and driven to heights of pleasure he'd rather forget—being of some religious persuasion (probably Catholic) that frowned upon sexual excess! Suppose any number of things!

Or perhaps what Lulu had told me was true, and I had inherited a busy imagination from . . . somebody.

How different was my land from the one I'd just left, with its ancient stones and gentle brown hills. Rivertown in November was dun gray and silver, with a lowering sky streaked with dark clouds. Against the slow-moving, viscous river was a tracery of bare branches. There had been little rain and everything was dry and grimy. Dead flowers drooped in the planters on Main Street, and pieces of newspaper blew forlornly around the sidewalk in front of the building where my old office was. The Knitty Gritty looked closed. A handful of mail had fallen out of the box onto the ground.

Nobody was around as the taxi turned into Holly Lane. The house was still as I dragged my suitcase up on the porch and turned my key in the lock. On the plane, I'd tried not to think of piles of laundry and overflowing trash cans, breakfast dishes in the sink and an unspeakable bathroom. But everything was neat . . . incredibly neat. Jars were lined up on the shelves, cookbooks stood spine to spine on the kitchen shelves. The surfaces sparkled, the copper pans hanging on the rack had been polished. In the dining room the chairs were mathematically juxtaposed to the table, and two silver candlesticks stood neatly in the middle. The living room was equally tidy. The throw pillows were lined up like little soldiers, the Oriental rugs in rigid apposition. As I stood staring at all this, I heard somebody come into the kitchen.

"Fran?" Johanna appeared. She wore a spotty T-shirt and a pair of ripped jeans, and her hair hung in blond strings. Her eyes were sunk in blue bruises. "I saw the taxi; I had to talk to you right away. Oh, Fran—Sheldon's *left* me."

"I'm sorry," I lied.

"He came into the back of the shop and found me with Phil. Oh, God, what am I going to d-do?"

For some reason not yet explained, Sheldon had gone down to the Knitty Gritty, opened the door with Johanna's second key, and gone straight through to the back.

"At first we didn't hear him. I didn't even hear the door unlock. Then I knew it was him. I know those footsteps, *stamp-stamp*, like nothing could stop him. Then, Fran, it was so weird; it was like my head was in two parts. I couldn't stop *coming*. I looked over Phil's shoulder and there was Sheldon standing there, his face absolutely murderous.

"Then he shouted, 'You bitch!' and Phil jumped about a foot in the air. We both grabbed for our clothes. We were in the supply room in the back. Sheldon was standing there yelling and calling me a cunt and few other choice epithets, Phil was trying to find his pants. . . . I'm talking *major farce*, Fran. Sheldon began kind of pushing Phil, and Phil pushed him back, and they knocked down some of the balls of yarn . . . then I picked them up and began throwing them at the two of them, and they started it too. Sheldon's saying, 'I knew it, I knew it!' and Phil's telling Sheldon to cool it and 'All the guys do it,' which made me furious and I threw some more, and I was crying and balls of wool were sailing through the air.

"Then Sheldon said he'd expect me at home immediately, and he left. I must be some kind of nut case, because I touched myself just a little when I was putting my tights on, and I started up again! But Phil was white as a sheet, and he just gasped out something about 'disaster' and ran off to his car . . . and I haven't seen him since!" By then we'd opened a bottle of wine and sat down in the kitchen.

Johanna had come home just as Sheldon had ordered. And after that, it had been hell. Sheldon had even hit her a few times, or tried to. He must have learned his technique from an old silent movie. He sort of backed up, fists out, face livid, then pushed his jacket sleeves up over his wrists . . . then made a couple of lunges. She would remember that white, hairy arm flying out of nowhere to slug her till the day she died.

Then one night he appeared with two packed suitcases. He couldn't stand it. The scene in the Knitty Gritty haunted him. It might well drive him insane. She'd hear from his lawyer.

"And he doesn't want to see the boys. I talked to him on the phone and asked what they have to do with it, and he said he couldn't help it, but his feelings about them had changed, now that he knows *what I am.*"

"You're lucky to be rid of him, Johanna."

"But I *hate* it," she whimpered, dabbing at her eyes. "I get so lonely, and the kids are getting all fucked up. Donny is flunking everything and little Shelly is bed-wetting. And the worst of it is, now Phil won't even return my calls. 'Johanna, I don't want to be involved in your divorce.' He's afraid Sheldon will drag him into it, and his wife will find out. And I sit there every night watching television, and I get so *horny,* and I can't pay the bills because he doesn't send any money. I don't know which is worst."

"I really think you're better off without him."

"Fran, I wanted to tell you right away, while they're out. Sheldon is living here."

"What?"

"At your house. Listen, *I* can't help it, Charlie invited him."

"I'm throwing him out," I said.

"Fran, please be careful. He can be mean."

"I don't care what he is."

"I'll bet he's got his dead animals in your freezer."

We opened the freezer, and there were three small hairy animals in plastic bags—Sheldon's "small game."

I ran upstairs, Johanna after me. The guest room obviously had a new tenant. It was scrupulously neat. The bed was made up as tight as an army cot. You could bounce a quarter on it. Sheldon's pajamas were folded on the pillow. In the closet, shoes were lined up neatly, suits on the rod shoulder to shoulder. On the bedside table was a litter of medications, and *Business Week* and *Hustler* for nighttime reading. Lined up on the bureau with military precision were hairbrushes, comb, two pens, some breath mints, and a line of boxes: jewelry box, cigar box, a box containing chess pieces, a box containing toy soldiers. A box for keys and one for mail. . . . Johanna looked at them with tears in her eyes. "Shelly *loves* boxes."

I went on to Monty's room. It was as neat as could be expected considering the contents. There were enough toys for a couple of nursery schools, some still in their boxes. Fire engines, trucks, trains, a tricycle, a bouncy-seat, things to push and ride on and sit on. The bed was occupied by a couple of dozen stuffed animals. The closet was so full of clothes the door wouldn't close. A million little suits hung on a million little white plastic hangers. Little shoes on a pint-size shoe rack. Drawers of underwear and T-shirts and socks and sweaters.

We looked at this in silence, then crept down the hall to the master bedroom. I felt a curious relief: this was what I had expected. Unmade bed, clothes strewn around. Dust, dead flies, fuzzies. Rings from wet glasses on the tables. This was my room. I had chosen this four-poster, this highboy, and the sewing table by the window. I had bid for the slipper chair and the kneehole desk. Here I'd drunk tea in my little sewing corner, here Charlie and I had snuggled together and watched late movies. Now in the wastebasket were Coke cans and Sara Lee tins and Dorito bags, and there was Sara Lee lemon icing on the sheets and spots on the silver rug. It smelled strongly of unwashed male and dirty bathroom.

Johanna was on her way out as Charlie's car drove up.

"How's the odd couple?" she asked as she left.

Charlie ignored her. When he saw me in the kitchen he started, as though he'd forgotten I existed.

"Oh, hi," he said, giving me a rather aimless kiss. Then he wandered out into the hall and into the living room, where he flopped into a chair, rubbing his eyes. He picked up the remote—with me out of town, the TV set had been moved back into the living room—and began fiddling with it. Channels flicked silently on and off the screen.

"I had a lovely trip, and Lulu is very well, thank you for asking."

It went past him. "Oh. That's good." He settled down at a news program but kept the sound off. I turned on the lamp and looked at him. He was unkempt, pale, almost gray-looking. His hair looked flat and sticky, plastered down here and there with cowlicks in between. His eyes were dull and red-rimmed and there was some kind of rash on his cheeks, which were, I saw sadly, beginning to be jowly. He wore a shirt made of some cheap synthetic that forms tiny pills on the surface, and a pair of no-color, nonfitting pants. On his feet was an ancient pair of Keds.

Having faced, as I eventually did, the irresponsibility of my father, I felt a new sympathy and admiration for Charlie. I would stay on at Blazer's, I would "work on my marriage." I would be kinder, more understanding, more patient. I might even play some of Lulu's games and feign helplessness. I was too bossy and compulsive and bad-tempered anyway. I couldn't change my essential nature, but I could bend a little, shift, qualify. As for Charlie's bigotry, I'd try to correct it, lead him back to where he'd been before. It was obvious I'd just spent two weeks with my mother.

I sat down near him. "Now that I'm back, Sheldon can leave. I understand that you were lonely, and you wanted some help with Monty."

Charlie looked blank. "He wants to stay. He's been a big help, Fran, with certain . . . problems. I think it's better if he stays for a while."

"But I don't, Charlie." His gaze wandered to the TV. A game show, a couple of talking heads, an old *I Love Lucy.*

"He cleans," Charlie said, laughing at Lucy at the same time. "The guy is a maniac cleaner. Look at this place."

"Charlie, talk to me. Look at me."

"He cooks," Charlie said. "He's not a bad cook. And he's used to kids, so he's pretty good with Monty."

"What do you do when Sheldon is doing all these things? And where's Sheldon, by the way, and where's Monty?"

He stared in front of him for so long I thought he hadn't heard me. "That's part of it," he said finally. "I have trouble answering three questions at once."

I sat looking at him for a long time. I'd seen brilliance, anger, passion, I'd seen both kindness and cruelty. But I'd never seen him like this.

"Let's take them one at a time. What do you do while Sheldon is—"

The back door opened and feet came into the kitchen, shopping bags were dumped on the table—good hearth sounds, no matter who made them. Sheldon and Monty appeared.

"Oh, hello," Sheldon said, with faint surprise. To Charlie: "Everything all right, bro?"

Charlie gave a thin, grateful smile. "I'm all right."

Monty came into the room—didn't bound, the way he always had, just walked. He was bigger and bonnier than ever, with blue eyes, a blotchy red face, and darkening hair. When he saw me a big smile burst onto his face, which had seemed, a moment before, sad.

"Fan! Oh, *Fan!*" He came over and flung his arms around my legs, clutching me violently and hanging on to my skirt till he'd almost pulled it off.

"Easy, Monty. I see you. I hear you." He stuck his arms in the air and jumped up and down till I picked him up. "You weigh a ton, kid, and my arms have gotten weak. So how's life?"

"Monty go school."

"No kidding. Is Mother Bumpy's the lucky institution?"

There was a curious expression on Charlie's face as he turned and looked at Monty: a cautious gaze, an oddly unpleasant smile. When Monty flung his head toward him, Charlie quickly looked back at the TV set.

"Let's go, Monty," Sheldon said. He wore very clean, box-new L. L. Bean clothes.

"*I want Fan!*" Monty roared.

"You're going to have your bath, and then Uncle Shel will fix your dinner."

"No. Fan cook!"

"I'm a lousy cook, Monty. Don't you remember the horrible spaghetti I made you?"

"Yuk!" Monty said. "Puke!"

"I've told you not to use those words, Monty. Go up and start your bath." Monty went off with frightening obedience, and Sheldon went back to the kitchen. Charlie's head nodded forward as though he were asleep.

I followed Sheldon into the kitchen.

"Will you tell me what the hell's going on here?"

"I don't know what you mean." He was lining up boxes of breakfast cereal according to size.

"I want to know what's wrong with Charlie. Are you two getting it on with drugs, or what?"

He whirled around. "There are no drugs. What you are seeing is depression."

"He wasn't like this when I left two weeks ago. He was feisty and impossible. Could he be depressed because you moved in?"

"I have saved Charlie, since nobody else was about to." Sheldon's head was perfectly round, his crew cut salt-and-pepper. His features were WASP regular, with a thin, prim little mouth and a ski-jump nose. he wore a bright green T-shirt with an alligator on the pocket. "You'd run out on him—"

"I was visiting my mother, Sheldon."

"I'll bet."

I stared at him furiously, then decided not to get sucked into some ridiculous argument. I grabbed my suitcase, still sitting in the hall, and dragged it upstairs. I saw Charlie's still silhouette in the living room, his head falling forward. Upstairs, I considered the state of the bedroom and my marriage at the same time. Even if I spent the evening cleaning this place, what exactly did I want of that gray-faced ghost downstairs? Was he really mine, was this really Charlie? I opened the window, put some of the junk into the trash, and pulled off the dirty sheets, dragging them back down the stairs and stuffing them into the washer.

Sheldon served dinner in the kitchen. Some kind of frozen ribs with a lot of sweet barbecue sauce, frozen beans, and canned potatoes. I ate about three bites. In the heart of the health-food nut obviously lurked a junk-food addict—perhaps he'd had to move out to indulge it. I looked at Monty, chewing a bright orange rib and dripping toxic sauce down his front. It seemed so unfair. I'd been fed little quiches and *biftecks*. Often Marie or Anny had managed to find vegetables picked that very morning, believing children need good food to grow properly. Waldo introduced me to artichokes and Breton oysters. But how pointless it was to dream of vanished kingdoms. Monty was the future. This whole fucking scene was the future.

Monty wiggled and dropped sticky beans on the table. Charlie picked at his food and stared into space, and Sheldon lit a cigar.

"Sheldon, would you please put that out."

Charlie stirred to half-life. "He can smoke if he wants. It's my house."

"Only half, Charlie."

"I'll smoke half of it," Sheldon said, grinning.

I reached over and took the lighted cigar from between his fingers and dropped it into his glass of beer, where it fizzled to black death. There was a silence.

"I'll get you for that," Sheldon said.

"Me—your pussy cat?"

Sheldon festered.

Monty laughed "Fan pussy cat!"

"Not exactly, Monty. A big, mean cat, that won't be pushed around. A tiger or a panther."

There was something deeply disturbing about this meal, something I couldn't quite put my finger on. Well, of course Charlie was clinically depressed. Sheldon was running my house, and was a lousy cook besides. But it was something else—some vital lack, a song without the accompaniment. Then I knew what it was: Sheldon was taking care of Monty, and Charlie paid no attention to him except to sneak those looks at him from time to time—quick, calculating, appraising looks whenever Monty was looking in the other direction. When Monty turned toward him, his eyes were sternly on his plate. Once Monty, in an escalating determination to get some attention from the father who not so long ago had given him nothing but, hit Charlie's arm with his fist, and Charlie jumped as though he had been bitten.

"Don't do that. Don't touch me."

"Dad-dy," Monty said. "Daddy-o, daddy-o, diddly-o, dopey-o."

Charlie pushed back from the table and left the room.

"How about some ice cream?" said Sheldon briskly.

I got up and chased Charlie up the stairs. He stood in the

middle of the cold, tumbled bedroom as though wondering what to do next.

"Charlie."

"What did you do to this room?"

"Charlie, answer me. I want to know what's happened."

"Nothing. Where are the sheets?"

"In the wash, I'm putting on clean ones. Charlie, dammit, *talk to me.*"

Charlie bolted out of the room and made for the stairs. I sat down on the bed, holding my head and counting to ten. But as I tried to sort out the unsortable, I noticed something on the floor by the bed. Well, there were a lot of things on the floor, old magazines, a couple of soda cans, whatever I hadn't picked up before. This was a little packet of pictures, snapshots and a couple of newspaper clippings bound with a rubber band. Slowly I picked it up and undid it.

Most of them I'd seen before. The one of her in shorts and a big man's shirt, holding Kimmy by the hand: it had been in the Aspenhurst paper the day she brought Monty back. She looked young and fresh, the way she had the day I'd hired her, smiling, her blond hair loose and floppy. The big shirt sleeves were rolled up, and on one arm was a charm bracelet. There was the one of Ellie and Bill from the local paper, standing by their car squinting in the sun. Bill wore jeans and Ellie wore one of the infamous halter tops, and they were holding hands.

There were several taken around the house during better days: Ellie pregnant, out next to the woods; Ellie pregnant and me not, out on the terrace; Ellie and Charlie looking self-conscious—I'd taken that one. Every possible combination of the four of us, even one of Charlie and Bill on the front steps, each trying to look taller and manlier than the other. Ellie and me down by the river. Ellie and Monty in the hospital. Ellie and her kids . . . three or four of Kimmy and Jodi alone. one of Ellie alone. Three of Bill alone, two close-ups. One recent one of Monty in the bathtub and two on his swing.

I sat staring at this gallery for several minutes. It was the end of a long, very long day, which had started in Italy and brought me thousands of miles to something I could make no sense of. As I sat there Charlie walked in carrying the dirty sheets. When he saw me holding the pictures he dropped them.

"Give those to me." He grabbed them before I could blink. "How dare you go through my things?"

"Daddy Fan," Monty said from the hallway.

Charlie turned on him. "Go take your bath." Monty froze.

"Charlie, let's start at the beginning. I always go through your things, you used to love me for it."

"Well, things are different now. We've changed. I don't want you to ever touch anything of mine again."

"That seems excessive, Charlie. For God's sake come out and say it. It's Ellie again, isn't it? Love never really died. The thing I don't get is, why Bill and the kids?"

"I'm not telling you a fucking thing." He put the pictures in his pocket.

"You don't have to. You've never gotten over her."

I don't think I believed it even then. It seemed too recycled, somehow . . . but I couldn't come up with anything better. Charlie stared at me.

"You don't understand anything," he said.

He threw the dirty sheets back on the bed. My head was splitting and I was exhausted, but the idea of getting into those sheets was revolting. So we had a fight over whether or not to change the sheets. At least he was alive. Which did I prefer? Charlie more or less won.

"I'm not staying here," I said.

"Good. Go to a hotel."

So that was how I left Charlie—over some dirty sheets. He went back downstairs. I picked up my suitcase and was on my way out when a small voice said, "Fan, Monty play."

"I can't. And if you can pronounce the L in 'play' why can't you pronounce my name properly?"

"I dunno." He held a battered book. "Fan, read story."

"But I . . . oh, all right."

I read The Little Engine That Could for the fiftieth time, his head resting on my leg. When he was asleep I took him into his bed. I didn't understand why, when I changed him into his pajamas, there were blotches and welts all over his body.

· 2 ·

In the cul-de-sac we didn't move far.

The room at Kerner's was medium-sized, papered in floral rosettes on a pink background. The double bed creaked, and there was a sink in the corner. The bathroom was down the hall. There was only a hooked rug on the floor and my feet got cold, but there was an electric heater in the old, unusable fireplace. He said he'd endure Baby and he wouldn't let me pay him any rent, but would appreciate a bag of groceries from time to time. The place was mine to use. If I needed anything I should ask him or . . . Lucinda.

Dragging my suitcase up onto Kerner's porch, I knew I hadn't thought this through very carefully. I didn't want to sleep on the dirty sheets. I had to sleep somewhere. I felt a gesture of some sort was in order, though I would just as soon have waited till morning. Kerner was big and kind and warm. . . . I went to him as an animal goes toward a bonfire.

"Fran! Is anything wrong?"

"Well, Charlie and I need a little space."

"Do you want to—" At this exact moment a strange woman came up behind him. A type I hated, an aging Modigliani. Long face, long hair, long bathrobe.

"Oh, uh, Adam. I didn't mean to . . ."

"Come on in. This is Lucinda Wyatt. Lucinda, Fran Morse, my neighbor." Lucinda and I glared at each other, muttering minimal greetings. "Do you want to stay in one of the rooms?"

I hadn't even thought of it. "Oh—sure. Just for a day or two, you know. Till things cool down."

"Just get back?" he asked, leading me along the upstairs hall.

"Oh, Adam. You wouldn't believe what's going on. My father was the room steward on the *Normandie*, and Lulu doesn't know anything about him, and that goddam Sheldon Showalter is living in my house, and Charlie sits around looking dead, and I don't understand anything that's—"

"Adam, shall I get towels for her?" Lucinda called. Kerner and I were standing in what was to be my bedroom.

"I'll do it," he called.

"Keeps a sharp eye out, doesn't she?"

"Lucinda teaches history at Grier."

"And she has a Guggenheim fellowship to write her brilliant seminal thesis about the War of the Roses. You told me," I added, yawning. I also knew her car was often in the driveway.

"The Civil War," Kerner said, pulling a quilt down from a closet shelf.

I collapsed onto the chair with Baby. "This is just for a few days, till I get my act together."

"Stay as long as you want."

"Thank you, Adam." I tried to read his eyes, but they were hidden behind bushy eyebrows. "Could I have—uh, a glass of milk?"

"Help yourself, Fran. Take anything you see."

"Adam, could we—" I stopped as Lucinda materialized on the stairs. I was in the doorway of the room, Kerner hung in the hall. I thought of an art class I'd once taken called Relationship Between Figures. Ours was strong and searing.

"What?"

"Never mind. Good night."

I slammed the door, which was stupid. I imagined a triumphant little smile on Lucinda's ovate face. Her mouth would curl into a little U, her small eyes would become virtual slits. She and Kerner would go to bed and as they fucked she would tell him about Appomattox—unless that was a different war. I was much stronger on Europe.

During the next few days, I kept forgetting that I had left Charlie. I went to work, drove back into our driveway . . . and remembered. I woke up in the morning and wondered where I was, and I had trouble going to sleep in the room with the flowered wallpaper. At night, everything tumbled and whirled around in my head, a thousand questions with no answers.

On Saturday morning I walked across the grass as the postman was handing Charlie the mail, then followed him inside.

"Charlie, I've been thinking."

"Oh, hi." *Flip flip flip* went the envelopes on the hall table. More and more slowly, till he'd gone through the whole pile, which appeared to be mostly bills. As he finished, the pained eagerness in his face turned to resignation. Leaving them unopened, he wandered into the living room and dropped into a chair in front of the TV.

"I just wanted to let you know where I am. I've rented one of Kerner's rooms."

"Oh, yeah?" Game show. News. Rock Video. Cartoons.

"It doesn't have to be permanent." I raised my voice slightly. "It was kind of a blow, Charlie. Finding that stuff the minute I got back."

He settled on an old *I Love Lucy.* "What was?"

I was incredulous. "What we talked about in the bedroom. Just before I *left* you. Before our *separation.*"

Charlie dragged his eyes from the screen with difficulty.

"Separation?" He was searching through the mists of his mind. "Oh—Fran. Sorry, I have things on my mind. What time did your plane get in?"

"Three days ago." I was having trouble keeping calm. Charlie's face was puzzled, then an animal cunning crept across it.

"Oh, right. Now I remember." I knew he was lying. Whatever drug he was taking must be some kind of downer or amnesiac. The man was not functioning normally.

As he began pushing the buttons on the tuner again I turned and ran upstairs. Through the revolting bedroom, into the bathroom. In the medicine cabinet were only the usual aspirin, antacids, and allergy medication. I rooted around in nooks and crannies but could find nothing suspicious. The little packet of Ferguson pictures was gone.

As I came back down, Charlie was standing in the hall, going through the mail again. It reminded me of the daily mail grab at Miss Comfitt's, when we all raced from the dining room to claim what we hoped were love letters. There was a teen-age sweetness about Charlie's daily wave of eagerness and disappointment, the pulse of love in absentia, as he looked for his beloved's childish handwriting. Innocent Ellie!

Oh, how tired I was of Ellie! Ellie the klutz, the loser, the airhead, the mother of Charlie's child. It went beyond simple sexual jealousy. I felt betrayed in ways that neither of them would ever understand. Once I'd thought Ellie and I were bound by female commonality. But I'd found we had nothing in common at all. I'd never understood her passive, floppy, something-will-turn-up way of plodding through life. I didn't understand why she didn't want to better herself: improve her speech, get more education, stop chewing gum. I didn't grasp why the woman didn't use a diaphragm, why she ate Big Macs, what she saw in Doré or Bill Ferguson or even Charlie Morse, who augured nothing but trouble. Or if it wasn't even a matter of seeing anything but just lying down and opening her legs and hoping everything would somehow turn out all right.

But the worst of it was that if I were honest with myself, I had to admit that my record didn't shine either. I had opened my legs for the wrong people a few times. I deserved no points for sticking with the demented Charlie Morse—the truth was I lacked the backbone to get rid of him. I acted bossy and controlling, I made a lot of noise. But I always ended up giving in to him.

I was sick to death of Ellie because she reminded me of myself.

In the hall light he looked terrible, gray, with red puffy eyes and a three-day stubble. He slumped, he picked at his nails, he'd developed a smoker's hack. Whenever I looked at him his eyes either went out of focus or gazed at some point behind my head without seeing me. He finished the mail sorting with a sigh of futility.

"You look terrible, Charlie."

"I'm working something through, Fran. Makes me a little tense." Now he went toward the kitchen, leaving me, as usual, talking to his back.

"It's Ellie. Come out and say it, Charlie, I can take it. I've taken everything else. If you want a divorce I won't fight you. We'll make a fair arrangement and—"

"I don't want to talk about this." He poured himself a mug of coffee. "Maybe another time, okay?" He still wouldn't really look at me.

"And I'm quitting Blazer, I can't stand it any longer." Now

214

he was wandering back toward the living room. "You'll have to go back to work, Charlie. *Work. Do you hear me?*"

From the living room I heard the theme music from *I Love Lucy*.

Adam and I were raking leaves behind his house. I asked him about his marriage.

"Oh, I drove Darcy crazy," he said. "She couldn't deal with the evolution. Though involution might be more correct."

She kept pointing out his physical resemblance to the children. "Look at them," she'd say. "The coloring. The nose. Nobody has a nose like yours, it's like a lamb chop. The walk even. It's all there, what's the matter with you?" He knew, of course, but he wanted it *not to be important*: the main thing was that he loved them. She never really got it. Then she began to believe he thought they weren't his and was proving something-or-other by being so understanding. Then she became pretty paranoid, saying he was accusing her of being unfaithful, and then decided that he was unfaithful, which, he said, he had not been.

"Finally she left. It was like a turned-around version of Strindberg's *The Father*. Did you ever read it?" I shook my head. "A husband and wife disagree about the education of their daughter, and his will prevails. So the wife, in revenge, drops the smallest hint that the girl might not be his. The man goes mad from the doubt." He smiled. "Strindberg is considered a misogynist. But I was cheering the wife all the way. Now that, Fran, is female power."

"But what good is all this power, if it just drives men into a state of dementia?"

"A state of the sulks. You have to use it to change social values. You women are your own worst enemies. Darcy immediately married a macho guy; she loves being owned. I never ordered her around, I just tried to get her to think."

"Are you really so evolved, Adam?" I kept looking over toward my house for signs of life. I'd expected . . . something. Didn't Charlie at least want to argue? But there was nothing; it was as though I didn't exist.

215

Leaves were sticking to Kerner's beard. "I try my damnedest, Fran. I really fight possessiveness in myself."

"But people just *are* possessive. I'm a perfect example."

"No, you're bereft. Charlie has taken over everything in the guise of liberation. He's even got you financing his couvade. He's got you snookered. If he was really playing by the rules he'd have no interest in his illegitimate child, but he's got it all twisted. The child is yours, Fran."

As we watched, Charlie opened the front door to look pointlessly into the mailbox. I waved, but he only turned and closed the door again.

"You understand, you know," he said. "You helped Ellie. You get it, it just scares you."

"I helped . . . ?" I stood picking leaves off the rake. I felt awful. "I don't think so. Anyway, my brain isn't working very well these days, to tell you the truth. Too much is going on. I mean, people are so frightened and weak and silly and . . ."

"Don't cry."

"I'm not, it's just the cold." I swallowed. "I just can't think very well sometimes. Everything's so damn complicated."

"It takes time. Here, hold the leaf bag."

But people did think they owned each other. And maybe they did . . . what did I know? Lucinda's car came down the street and into the driveway.

"Is it serious?" I asked.

"Is what?" He was shoving leaves into the bag.

"You're living with a woman, Adam. I was just wondering if I'm going to have a new neighbor."

He stared at me, then grabbed the rake. "Do you care?"

I gulped. "I don't know. Yes. No."

"That's what I thought. The answer to your question is, I haven't the slightest idea."

He waved at Lucinda as she got out of the car.

"This is the worst mistake you've ever made," Blazer said.

"It's not working for me any more, Nat. I can't do it."

"Take some time off." Then he tried to tempt me to stay with a big steamy ridiculous case he thought would appeal to my pathological longing for "issues."

216

"Listen to this, Fran. This is major fraud, twenty-six million. You won't believe the people who are implicated, the heads of the three biggest brokerage houses on the Street . . . suggestion of mob connections . . . and some weird sex stuff too; one of them likes little boys, and there's some nasty hints about kiddie porn. Everything's been laundered through mega real estate deals, and there's a line of connection going right up to . . ."—stunning pause—"the White House."

"Sounds like a TV movie."

Blazer sat on the edge of his desk, his little white bangs almost touching his horn-rimmed glasses. "Fran, I love you like my own. Don't do this to me."

"Why should I do something I don't care about?"

"But why—*why* don't you care?" He shook his head in bewilderment. "People would kill for your job. For this case! There's going to be a major media coverage—TV in the courtroom! This is going to fly, Fran. And you'd look so good: in comes this little live-wire lawyer in great clothes—"

"To defend a bunch of crooks."

He gave me a thoughtful look. "Have you heard about innocent until proven guilty? Or did you cut that class?"

"Nat, you can see I have an attitude problem. The Force wouldn't be with me. I'm sorry. I have to get a few things in my head straightened out."

He watched me as I sat picking at the arm of the chair. "I'd be remiss if I didn't mention that if you change your mind again, reentry isn't easy. It would look like a history of instability."

The bell tolled for me as I left Manhattan for the last time.

"Charlie, talk to me." He was sitting out on the freezing terrace in his old leather jacket. The school bus had just picked up Monty. "Why have I been replaced by Sheldon Showalter?"

He sat there with his eyes closed for a full two minutes.

"Because he understands, without a lot of stupid discussion," he said finally. "He doesn't pick everything apart."

"That's not a very good answer."

"I don't care."

"It's unworthy of you." I pulled my coat collar up higher

and shivered. "I have a right to know, Charlie. Are you leaving me for Ellie Ferguson? Or for Sheldon?" He didn't look capable of going anywhere, for anything, or even of getting up. Nor was he loverlike or guilty. He appeared to be in agonizing pain.

"I need more time."

"But for what?"

"I just can't deal with you, Fran." His voice was almost pleading. "I wish you'd leave me alone."

He had a new way of closing down into complete expressionlessness. He sat absolutely silent, hoping, perhaps, that it would make me go away.

"Charlie, I've quit Blazer. I'm going back to my local practice that makes hardly any money."

"Okay," Charlie said.

"You'll have to go back to work."

"All right. Fine." His eyes were glassy.

"Can you hear me? Are you alive?"

Charlie didn't even have the strength to argue. He looked utterly weary, infinitely sad. I bored him to death; he just wished I'd go up in smoke. This was the worst yet.

I went into the house, swallowing the stubborn lump that came daily into my throat—especially when I was here. This was still my home, occupied as it was by foreign troops. I had loved it and nurtured it.

The upstairs hall was dark and stuffy. I looked into Monty's room, dark except for a little night-light in the shape of a mouse. At first I thought it was empty, then something moved in the corner. I turned on the light and saw him sitting in the corner on the floor, playing with something.

"Hi, kid." He hardly looked at me. "What's the matter? No hello for Fan? No. *Fran.* I'm not going to indulge your mispronunciation any more."

He looked terrible: dirty clothes, dirty hair, tear streaks on his cheeks, massively runny nose.

"Fan."

"What happened?"

"Monty bad." He looked miserably at me. "I ate . . . ate . . . double chocolate." He burst into tears.

"So what, Monty?"

"Daddy s-spanked me. It hurt."

I was surprised. "Well, you know, sometimes parents hit kids. It's not the best. It's not the worst. It happened to me, I lived through it. Come here, I can't stand to look at you."

I washed him up. What was wrong with his complexion? He was mottled, possibly from all the crying. But warning signals were going off in my head. Sheldon appeared in the doorway. For the most part he pretended I didn't exist, treating me like a piece of furniture.

"Come on, Monty. Be a big boy. *Hup-hup-hup.*" He clapped his hands as Monty looked at him doubtfully.

"Sheldon, what's wrong with him?"

"What do you mean? Charlie gave him a whack, that's all. He'll be fine. Come on, now—big men don't cry. Let's go down and play some ball."

He kept *hup*-ping at Monty till I left, ignoring a plaintive "Fa-a-a-an." I saw him leading Monty outside, a large baseball glove on one of his small hands. In Johanna's house, I saw a drawn curtain moved cautiously aside.

"Is Dr. Swinger there?"

"May I ask who's calling?"

"This is Francesca Morse, Monty's mother."

"One moment, please." *Mumble buzz mumble.* "Dr. Swinger is away. Dr. Fucci is covering. Is it an emergency?"

"Well, I'm really looking for information. Monty is a patient of Dr. Swinger's, and—"

"Do you want Dr. Fucci's number, or would you rather wait for Dr. Swinger's return?"

"Do you happen to know if Monty ever saw Dr. Fucci?"

"Well, I have no way of knowing that, Mrs. Morse. Why don't you call him and ask?"

"This is Dr. Fucci."

"This is Mrs. Morse, Dr. Fucci. I'm calling about Monty."

"Monty. Monty Morse?"

"That's right."

"Are you his mother?"

"I'm . . . yes, in a manner of speaking. He's my adopted son."

Buzz buzz mumble.

"Monty is no longer my patient, Mrs. Morse."

"Was he ever your patient?"

"I saw him once when Dr. Swinger was away."

"When was that, doctor?"

Pause. "Is this some kind of custody or divorce situation?"

"Well, yes, Mr. Morse and I are separated, and—"

"I see. Which of you has custody of Monty?"

I'd been afraid of this. "My husband does, but I just wanted to ask—"

"Mrs. Morse, I won't get involved in these things. You're asking for confidential information. And to be honest I haven't got time to go to court and testify, if that's what you want."

"Doctor, I'm his mother. I didn't say a word about testifying. I only—"

"Aren't you the Morses who had the surrogate situation?"

"That's right."

"Have you discussed this call with Mr. Morse?"

"No, and that's why I'm calling you. You see—"

"You wouldn't believe the grief I've been through over these things. Depositions, hanging around courtrooms while the lawyers argue, parents fighting in my office. You know, I feel sorry for these kids, but I can't put myself and my profession on the line any more. My advice to you is to get a good lawyer."

"I *am* a lawyer, Dr. Fucci."

"I'm sorry I can't comment. If I'm subpoenaed I'm stuck with it, but I don't say boo without consulting my attorney."

I was twisting the wire. "Can you tell me what physician—"

"—he goes to now. No, I can't. But try Dr. Swinger, we cover for each other."

"Johanna, does Sheldon ever hit your kids?"

"Well, of *course*, Fran. What else are you going to do with them?" Johanna kept the heat down to save money, and we were huddled by the kitchen stove. "But I don't think he'd ever hit Monty. He's so little, and he's not his."

"Well, something weird is going on over there."

"It's plenty weird; they're both over there falling all over that kid. They never even go out. . . . But you know, Fran, I think Shelly will be back soon. I know him, he's trying to fake me out. I'm talking *serious* contest of wills, like, who's going to give in first? This has happened before, you know—he moves out, I move out. But Fran, it's almost worth it. The last time, we gave the boys to my mother and we did nothing but fuck for five days. We were practically dead . . . all day, all night. We'd go into the kitchen in the buff, open some wine, fix a couple of sandwiches. . . . I mean, neither of us has touched another living soul since he left, and he knows it and I know it, so it's building up some head of steam."

"Johanna. The kid has red marks all over him."

"Well, he's always falling or knocking something down, and he has that white sensitive skin. I think he just bruises easily. I wouldn't worry, that kid is as healthy as an ox." She looked toward the window. "He's starting to look over here, Fran. We never move very far apart."

Adam and I had dinner in the kitchen on Lucinda's teaching night. I cooked it, and it wasn't very good, but it didn't matter. The man distracted me, he made me glow . . . and I'd missed him. We sat there and drank wine for a couple of hours . . . avoiding my ever-present, ever-more-boring marital problems, the troublesome gray ghosts in the next house. We had plenty of other things to talk about.

By then I had reconsidered spanking. Was it really so bad? The British nation—most of Europe, in fact—had thrived on beating up their children. I'd been spanked more than a few times. I hadn't liked it but assumed it had taught me whatever lesson it was designed for. Was it as bad as all the articles said, and when did old-fashioned spanking turn into child abuse?

Once, in an excess of Oedipal disturbance, I had called Lulu a crazy bitch, and Waldo had spanked me for it. Had he been wrong? My parents had believed that passions, ecstatic or disturbing or painful, should be kept under control. The feelings of others had to be considered. Was I so bad? If I still had tantrums in restaurants, if I still shot my mouth off, was it because I had been spanked too little or too much, or was it related at all?

And I was tired of sudden discoveries. Every day another study proved you shouldn't do this, eat that, behave in such a way. Child care was rampant with them. After you'd been around for long enough you got skeptical of all of them, probably proof that I was getting old. I was worn out by experts. Monty could use a few well-aimed whacks on the fanny. It was probably just what he needed.

We didn't hear Lucinda's car drive up, and she walked in as Kerner and I were holding hands and gazing into each other's eyes. Well, it wasn't really so romantic; he'd just reached over and given my hand a squeeze and was telling me he was my friend, I could count on him. But poor brilliant Lucinda was unable to grasp the difference between passion and friendship. She stood there staring at us with her little slitty eyes, clutching her briefcase to the front of her green turtleneck with little alpine designs on it, probably knitted by her mother. She tried not to look nonplussed. "Oh, hello," she said. "I didn't—I, er . . ." Adam invited her to sit down and gave her a beer, forgetting, in his confusion, that she didn't drink beer, then galloped around for wine like a large lumbering bear lost in the woods. It was here . . . no, it was there . . . oh, that was the red, she wanted white! Lucinda dropped her briefcase, dropped her glasses, and got her hair tangled in the string around her neck the glasses hung on.

Finally I murmured an excuse and went upstairs, where I crawled into bed with Baby. I couldn't see my house from the window. Kerner, possibly on purpose, had given me a room on the other side.

"Fran? Dr. Swinger."

"Oh, hello, doctor!"

"I just got back from vacation and found a note you'd called. You know Charlie hasn't brought Monty here for weeks. I see you two have separated."

"Well, sort of. Dr. Swinger, I just wanted to ask you something about Monty."

"Sure, anything. But my face is a little red here, Fran. I

don't know how it happened, usually I run a pretty efficient office—but I have this form here that should have gone out to Social Services a month ago . . . This is what happens when you don't do everything yourself. Let's see, now what was it? Oh, yes. There were marks all over Monty's back, Fran. Do you know anything about it?"

· 3 ·

DECEMBER TWENTIETH: MONTY'S THIRD BIRTHDAY. THE SKY was white and opaque, with snow predicted. A cold gray wind whistled around Kerner's house, stirring the windmill into action. I'd grown used to its gentle thumping and found it pleasing to know that nature's wind and nature's sun, captured by the solar plates, heated my bathwater.

Lucinda had gone home to New Bedford, Massachusetts, for the holidays. Through the bathroom wall I had heard raised voices for which I considered myself responsible. But it was difficult for them to fight, they were too polished, too academic, too evolved. The guttersnipe had been bred out of them, whereas I had a good dose from my daddy.

"Really, Adam, I don't want to be in the *way*," I heard. "I don't want you to feel as though I *have* to be here. I don't *have* to at all, I don't want to make things *inconvenient* for you."

Kerner's response was predictable male. "Lucinda, I *want* you to be here. If I didn't I'd say so. Fran's just a friend. She's in trouble, for God's sake."

"Well, Adam, the last thing I would want is to be a burden or an *obligation*. Our friendship is not based on that."

Then there was a silence, and I turned on the bathwater. There had been a certain cool at breakfast, Lucinda trying to look expressionless—not so difficult—and Kerner growling and mumbling. Then there was a further difficulty when Kerner, trying to pacify Lucinda before she left, managed to give her the wrong Christmas present. After foraging in the hall closet, he handed her an unmarked box.

"Don't open till Christmas," he told her.

"Oh, I can't wait." All thrilled, she ripped open the box and pulled out the tissue paper to reveal a pair of handsome calfskin boots, boots for walking across a field or down a country road. There was dismay in Kerner's face as she sat down and kicked off her penny loafers. But though she writhed and pushed, they were as tiny as Cinderella's slipper.

"Lucinda, I gave you the wrong box. These are . . . wait a minute." He found a similar box in the closet. I peered cautiously over to see if it contained silky undies, but it was a pasta machine, which understandably caused her eyes to darken. It was a handsome steel number you fed the dough into.

Lucinda thanked him briefly and left. He stood looking after her car until it turned out onto River Road, and longer. Finally he turned around, picking up the boots.

"I guess I blew that. These are for you."

I was very pleased. "I won't wear them when she's here; then you can say you got them for Alison"—his daughter. The boots were smooth and fragrant, the color of mushrooms or bark or stones. I took off my shoes and put them on, and they fit perfectly. "Thank you, Adam. They're beautiful."

"Just a thought."

"How did you know to get the right size?"

He said, "Once you left two perfect wet footprints on the bath mat."

Our eyes met, dangerously, and all the breath went out of me. We each moved in the general direction of the other, but halfway there the phone rang. For a minute we hung there pretending not to hear it, then finally he grabbed it and barked into it. His expression—which I was learning to read in spite of the beard—changed.

"It's Charlie." I took the receiver as Adam started clattering dishes in the sink and banging the lid of the trash can.

Charlie sounded low. "Fran, I wonder if you'd mind picking up the ice cream."

"Not at all. Are you all right?"

"Well, feeling a little overwhelmed. The whole class at Mother Bumpy's is coming, twenty kids."

"But you planned it months ago."

"Well, sure. But Shel—well, I depended on him to help, and he's on another planet. That bitch is flapping her tits at him. She picked Monty up this morning, and you could smell the musk three rooms away. I've warned him, but he won't listen."

"I'll come early and help."

Kerner dropped a frying pan.

"I'd appreciate it, Fran. Thanks."

I will say that then, charmed as I was by Adam, Charlie still had me by the gut—if not the groin. If he called I went. Never mind if his motives were impure. I was secretly thrilled to be included in the party. I could be useful, which I could not be here: Kerner's house was ancient, peculiar, inconvenient, and kept spotless by a laboring Martha who arrived by motorcycle and chased dirt as though she were excoriating evil itself, scolding us for untidiness and muttering her disapproval of the way I washed dishes.

Kerner banged the last dish into the rack and went thumping upstairs, me after him with a cheerfulness I couldn't hide.

"How much would you say, Adam, for twenty kids? You've done this more than I have."

I'd never been in his room before, only hovered in the doorway to ask where the linen closet was or how to work the heater. It was very plain, almost austere, with a plain brown rug, striped curtains, and heavy Victorian furniture. It smelled of wood and pipe tobacco and after-shave. I stood there pointlessly stroking the top of the bureau as he pulled things out of drawers and put them on the bed. Then he went into the bathroom, where I heard the clink of bottles and brushes going into his toilet kit. As he came back into the room he glanced at me, then opened his closet and took out a suitcase.

"Are you going away?" I asked stupidly.

"To Chicago. I told you."

"Oh, Adam." I'd forgotten. I watched him in gathering disappointment. A little scene had been hovering in the back of my mind: the two of us could hang out together, roast a little bird, raise a glass, sing a carol or two. It was the time of year when people commit suicide.

"Oh, Adam what?"

"I forgot you were going. I guess I thought—"

"What?" He went back to the closet, pulling out shoes in cloth shoe bags. Into the suitcase. Back to the closet, back to the bureau, moving faster and faster.

"I thought we might get a little tree."

"I always go, Fran."

"Where do you stay?"

"At the Lake House. It's near Darcy's."

"So you spend Christmas sitting in a hotel room."

He snapped open his briefcase. "I have papers to correct."

"Waiting for the kids to give you a crumb of their time." I was pulling a button on my sweater. I'd meant that to sound lighter than it had.

"That's one way to put it. I've explained, I don't have any pride or anything about my kids." The button came off in my hand. "What do you care? You have plenty to keep you busy."

With this he whirled around and began going through a mound of papers on the top of his desk, throwing some in the suitcase and some in his briefcase. Like Johanna my head was split in two. If I had been asked, at that very moment, to choose between Christmas with Charlie and Christmas with Adam, I would have converted to Islam. Since I was being offered neither, I would only go on to endure further capriciousness on both their parts. Kerner took off one jacket and put on another, took off his shoes and put on another pair.

"Are you going back to him?" he asked.

"No. I don't know."

He got up and slammed the suitcase shut. "Do you still love him?"

"It isn't love, it's just all the years. The *weight* of it. You know."

"Oh, I know." Back to the suitcase. "I sure do know."

Again the phone, for him this time. I went back to my room and changed into mommy clothes: a sedate skirt, dark stockings, a sweater with a Peter Pan collar—the kind of clothes I'd always wished Lulu would wear. I got out the present I'd bought and sat down to write the card. Kerner appeared in the doorway, tying his tie. He was wearing his better pants: Kerner's pants were fair, better, best, and awful. He pulled the tie in place, standing in front of the mirror over my bureau. I could smell clean clothes and after-shave.

I tried to concentrate on the card. Love, Auntie Fran. Love, Fan. Love, Mommy. Love, Stepmother? What did it matter? He couldn't read anyway. I felt Kerner's hand on my head.

"I'll try to change the plane reservation a day or two. We could at least have dinner."

He gave my head a little shake and disappeared.

I found medium confusion at my house. Without dutifully vetting my thoughts for sexism, I'd expected to find a chaos of crepe paper streamers, poppers, and noisemakers, with two bewildered males crying because they didn't know what to do with any of it. But Charlie had rallied and gotten it half done, and Johanna had volunteered her services.

I had expected . . . I don't know what I'd expected. The odd couple was full of surprises.

Charlie's description had been accurate. He kept trying to involve Sheldon, even get his attention, but Sheldon's heart was elsewhere.

"Shel, what do you think? Shall I put the poppers on the table or hand them out?" Sheldon didn't reply. "Shel? Shel! Shall I put the poppers—"

"On the table," Sheldon said.

"Do the streamers look all right? The kids might yank them down."

"They're fine."

"Do you think they'll pull them?"

"So cut them shorter, for Christ's sake."

"Charlie, it's fine," I said.

"Fran says it's fine," Charlie said. "Do you think it's time to pick up the cake? I don't want them to see it."

"So keep it in the box."

"I'll pick up the cake," I said, somewhat bewildered. As I went out the door I heard Sheldon say, "For God's sake keep hold of yourself."

When I got back with the cake and the high school kid who did magic tricks, Charlie was lying down. Sheldon was sitting in the dining room wrapping little presents for the grab bag.

"What's the matter with Charlie?" I asked.

"He's having another anxiety attack."

"Does he have them a lot?"

"Hardly ever, Fran, only two or three times a day." He kept craning his neck to look out the window. "And now he has to put on a nice face for all the mommies."

"I see." I didn't. "How long has he been having them?"

"Ever since he heard from the people in England."

"What people?"

"Oh, come on, Fran. The ones at the lab." He held up a set of jacks sealed in cellophane. "Would you say this is for a boy or a girl?"

"Sheldon, I don't have the slightest idea what you mean. Is this something about a job?"

Sheldon looked particularly spotless and perfect that day. His hair was freshly cut, too short for my taste; he looked almost bald. He wore a bright red L. L. Bean lumberjack shirt that still had the creases, and his chinos were immaculate. The area between his topsiders and his pants cuffs was bare. In the winter daylight, I saw how closely shaven he was.

"I thought he told you," he said.

"He told me nothing."

"Well, then, he has his reasons. And I don't want to be involved." His gaze wandered back to the window.

"You're already involved." I was furious.

"And I don't blab other people's secrets."

"Explain, Sheldon. Or I promise I'll kill you."

"That's the way you try to get everything, Fran. Threats, temper tantrums. If you ever tried being considerate or sweet or feminine for five minutes, your marriage might not be in such bad shape."

At this moment there was a thump on the back porch and Johanna came in with Monty, who was in a paroxysm of excitement—he'd been to two birthday parties in his life and knew what unadulterated bliss they were. He greeted me with great enthusiasm, dancing around the kitchen.

"*Fan!*" he yelled. "Monty *three* now!" He flung his little

arms around my leg. "Un-cle Shel-ly. Monty *three!*" He tore off
to squeal with joy over the Christmas tree. Sheldon returned to
his prize wrapping, folding every edge and curling the ends of
the ribbons with the edge of a scissors.

Johanna took off her coat, hanging it up rather slowly on
a hook by the back door. Sheldon stole a glance at her. She
wore tight jeans, and the white sweater I'd seen on her needles
for weeks would have better fitted Monty. She was carefully
made up and her blond hair hung in cascading curls. A deep
musk scent wafted from her.

"Can I help?" she asked brightly. "There must be tons to
do." She smiled at the admiring high school kid. "Let's get you
set up, okay?" She leaned over to help him with his boxes.
Sheldon half rose, then sat down again.

"Shel, what are we going to do about the musical chairs?"
Charlie asked from the hall. "We don't have anybody to play
the piano."

"You can sing, Charlie," Sheldon said, unkindly. He was
looking toward the living room. "Ask Johanna." His voice was
thick.

"You need skipping music," Johanna caroled from the living
room. "Got any skipping music?

Sheldon finished his wrapping and picked up the gifts to
put them in the grab bag. I happened to notice his silhouette:
sticking out. As he slowly walked out into the hall, I saw the
briefest look of panic on Charlie's face.

"I'll skip with them," Johanna said, hopping around the
living room.

The party, which had been long planned, was another attempt
by Charlie to relive his childhood. There was to be a sit-down
supper—he had even made chicken à la king. I hadn't seen any
in thirty-five years. There was that thick, pasty white sauce,
those rubbery cubes of white meat and spongy celery, those
bright flecks of pimiento. He'd made it himself from his mother's
old recipe. He served it on toast triangles, with peas on the
side.

Monty wore a red Eton suit just like one Charlie had had.
Ten minutes or so into the party, it was filthy—Monty being

Monty. He rolled on the floor, ran outside to wallow briefly in the dirt, and spilled everything he touched. Mrs. Morse had always had the magician before dinner and the games after, unless it was the other way around. Charlie herded the twenty kids through all this, occasionally asking Sheldon or Johanna—who were never far apart, though never together—for advice.

These party guests were more rambunctious than Mrs. Morse's had been. They tore around the house, dropping ice cream on the rugs and squishing jelly beans into the chairs, skinning their knees and weeping, shooting plastic guns at each other and getting chicken à la king in their hair. The happiest, most peaceful pair were upstairs playing in the toilet. Monty ripped into presents and flung them aside while Johanna and I tried to keep track of who had given what, in order to say thank-you's. The candles were blown out in only two puffs, and the magician pulled scarves out of shoes, found quarters in sleeves, and pulled a live rabbit out of his top hat while the party guests shouted with excitement. Later I found rabbit pellets behind chairs and under tables.

The other mothers, in ankle socks or miniskirts, seemed politely bemused by all this. Johanna explained that kids' parties now served pasta and featured computer games.

"This is like an old movie," she said. "Major nostalgia."

"Those girls are young enough to be my daughters," I whispered. "Monty could be my grandson."

But I suspected that they sensed something else: that Charlie's every word, every genial chuckle, every jolly hand-clapping direction and pat on the head was put on, that he was struggling to get through his grand production, and that the whole thing was really a balancing act intended to distract the world from the sickening truth, that he could barely look at Monty. The miracle was that Monty didn't seem to notice this at all but was having a glorious time.

I looked over at Charlie and Sheldon, standing together across the room. Sheldon, smoking as slowly as Bogart, was watching Johanna, who was now sitting cross-legged on the floor, reading a story to four kids. She looked pretty, earth-motherly, voluptuous. I had an odd flash of understanding: men did not only desire those obvious totems, the crotch, the tits, the behind. They lusted, too, for female warmth, softness, the smooth welcoming curves and fragrant hair, the soft skin that they could only possess vicariously. And not just men: anybody who'd been cradled to a mother's breast. And not just sexually: everybody desired those qualities to take refuge in when everything else didn't work, which it usually didn't—some soft, gentle place where everything wasn't such a fight.

Charlie mouthed my name soundlessly and jerked his head toward the study. I made my way through the melee and followed him in, closing the door behind me.

"I just wanted to ask you something," he said, trying to sound casual. "I got a call from a social worker this morning."

"Did you." So Swinger had done it. Social workers were real life, notes and files and reports, the hard arm of the law, the merciless diagnoses of family "dysfunction." I knew all about them, but I'd never been on this side of the fence before.

"She thinks Monty is being abused." He looked at me, then away.

"Where would she get an idea like that?"

"Well, how should I know? Some stupid mixup." He was pacing back and forth. "You've dealt with these social service people, Fran. You've told me the way they screw up."

"Sometimes," I said.

"She's coming on Monday. She wants you to be here."

"What time?"

Charlie grew paler. "Monty had a couple of marks on his back. There was this one episode, Shel lost his temper. He felt terrible afterward."

"Really!"

"He's been under a lot of stress. He's been carrying this whole household since you left. I just wanted to let you know that, you know, it was nothing. He's not a child beater, or anything like that."

"Charlie," I said.

"There was another time when he was wrestling with the kid and they knocked into a table." He was pressing his fingers together furiously. "It was stupid. Then I had to take Monty for his shots, Swinger said something about it, then behind my back he went and called these people. A big misunderstanding. So I

231

just wanted to ask you to back me up in front of this woman." He dug out his handkerchief and wiped his eyes.

"And say what?"

"Just say . . . hell, you know what to say. That neither of us are child abusers. He doesn't hit his own kids."

"Yes, he does."

"He only . . ." He glanced at me, then looked away. "Boys need a strong male model. He believes in firmness."

"Charlie," I said. "Please don't lie to me."

"I'm not lying. I'm just . . . trying to straighten something out. It's just one more thing, you see. I can't deal with it." His voice broke, and I wondered if he was going to cry. "It's already . . . I want to keep going, you know. Get back to work. I just don't need something like this. It's not the way it used to be, you know. It follows you all your life." His eyes were pleading.

"What does?"

His eyes searched my face. "You always know, don't you? You don't believe in the little white lie. Other women fake orgasms and flatter and play games . . . not you." He picked up the little curved whale statue from the desk and began fooling with it. "Other wives lie and manipulate, but *not my Fran*. I never could keep a secret from you."

"Not true, Charlie. You kept a whopper or two."

"Not for very long, then. You always find out."

"You want me to, Charlie. There are welts on the kid's back."

"Welts. *Other* women soften things. They use euphemisms. Look at Johanna! She plays the game. But not my Fran." He pushed his hair back. "Somebody else might say 'signs of physical trauma.' It doesn't sound so bad. But you, Francesca, are merciless. You zero right in." He glared at me, twisting the whale. "All right, I lost my temper a couple of times. A few times. He's an obstreperous kid, you know that. He's not any genius. He's stubborn. He yells; there might be a hearing problem. People get mad. . . . In fact I know somebody who has temper tantrums in restaurants; she gets drunk and insulting and has to be dragged out."

"How dreadful!"

"I get mad too," he went on. "My father did; he batted me

around. Maybe he was wrong, I don't know. But now they put you in jail."

"Charlie."

"Maybe that's where I should be. I can't even stand to look at him." His voice was thick and rasping. "I've gone for him a couple of times. Shel stopped me. Okay? I make myself sick. I wake up, go to the john, look in the mirror. There's the guy who hates his child. How can you hate somebody two feet tall who thinks you're God? Showalter said, 'I won't let you hurt him, but decide what you're going to do.' Oh, Jesus." His voice was shaking.

"You aren't telling me something," I whispered.

"I look at him, I've looked at pictures of his mother. Of Ferguson. Of their two kids. I can't make sense out of it any more. I hate them all. I'm afraid of myself. I shouldn't even have him. What do I do, put him up for sale? The people in that English lab didn't take up that consideration. That's your problem, buddy! Guv'nor!"

"*What* is?"

"*He's not mine.*"

That was the moment when the track started to tilt, when the angle got so sharp everything started sliding off. Things aren't firm, they tilt and wobble, shift, roll us toward the edge with frightening speed. Think of a huge, thin piece of plywood, rather poorly balanced on smaller supports: our world, which we have been told, and want to believe, is firmly fixed.

"Oh, don't be silly," I said, and left the study.

I stood looking into the living room. There was a post-party glow, a hostess fulfillment. Our house, after months or years of being a cave of disappointment, had been today what it was meant for. The fire in the hearth, the Christmas tree by the window. Outside was a snowscape, with drifts now covering the brown grass and dark branches outlined with white, a few stars in the clear night: the image of peace and security. The last parents and children picked their way down the walk to their cars . . . and good neighbor Kerner, in beaver hat and sheepskin coat, came up on the porch with a present. He gave me a large woolly hug.

"I can only stay a minute. Just want to deliver this."

Charlie watched from the doorway of the dark study as Kerner gave Monty his last present, a red wooden airplane. Monty, indefatigable, turned the room into a miniature universe, making plane sounds: *"Eeeairgh! Eeeairgh!"*

Charlie, glass in hand, walked over to him. "Kerner, those things you write. Do you ever think of the effect on your readers?"

"I always think of it, Charlie. That's why I do it."

Charlie moved closer. "You could ruin somebody's life."

"I think people ruin their own lives. It doesn't much matter what I write about."

"I wrote to that lab you mentioned. The one where they do they . . . do . . . they do . . . genetic fingerprinting." He had trouble getting it out.

"Let's not talk about this," I said.

"I didn't even have to," Charlie said, ignoring me. "It's been obvious for months. For years. But I'm a scientist, I like proof. So I sent them locks of hair."

"Aaaeeergh," Monty intoned, bringing the red airplane in for a landing. We all looked at him—dirty red suit, one shoe missing, big blue eyes wide, chocolate and red streaks on his face. Adam smoothed the hair back from his forehead, but the little boy looked at Charlie. "Hi, Daddy."

"And did you get it?" Kerner asked.

Charlie gave a hollow laugh. "And how."

"It doesn't mean anything," I said. "I don't even believe they can be so accurate."

"I have to go to the airport," Kerner said. He looked at Charlie. "You have everything," he said, turning to me. "Everything. Don't think about this, Charlie. It's just another concept. Live your life."

"I haven't decided yet what I'm going to do to you, Kerner. I'm talking to my lawyer on Monday." As Kerner sighed and started out, he said, "That's right, drop the bomb and let other people clean up."

"Charlie's right," I told Kerner in the kitchen, as he was putting his coat on.

"Do you think I'm ruining his life?"

"Not really."

"Do you think, if I canceled my holiday with the kids to sit here and listen to Charlie's nonsense, that it would make any difference? You know what I think, Fran. I don't think it matters a shit. In fact, now he's got a great opportunity for humanity. So do you."

"Oh, God," I said.

"It's not so bad. I think some people would like to be heroes, and could be heroes, but the chance never comes."

"I don't want to be a fucking hero." I wanted him to put his arms around me, but he didn't.

"You and Charlie might as well do something good." He put his hat on. "Merry Christmas."

"I still say you're partly responsible," I said.

"No. If I were, it would be the end of everything, all research, all knowledge. Everybody's feelings would have to be pandered to. For God's sake use your brain."

I stood there watching his broad, dark shape cross the white yard. Baby appeared from nowhere, slithering around my legs.

"Fran!" Johanna yelled from inside. "I'm giving Monty a bath; his mother's coming." I ran inside. "She wants to surprise everybody." She had the disreputable, exhausted Monty by the hand. "Come on, Piggy. Let's go."

"I must have misunderstood."

"She called before."

"But I thought she—" Even as I said it, an unfamiliar car drove up. Johanna hauled Monty upstairs. I could just leave. Let them all kill each other . . . for Charlie's eyes were dark and pained; he stood swaying back and forth in the hall, fingering the curved whale, emptying his glass. Sheldon, his keeper, slowly followed Johanna up the stairs.

"You're in love with Kerner," Charlie said.

"That's ridiculous." (But it wasn't.)

"You're having an affair with him." Charlie's voice was low and hollow, like an echo. "You left me for him."

"You're wrong. Charlie, listen. Ellie's coming."

"I know. It's going to be a bumpy ride." The unfamiliar car left; another one drove in.

"It's even simpler, Charlie. I left you because you hate me."

Charlie's pale face stiffened in anger. "I've never heard any-thing so stupid."

"No, it's true. It's in your face and every gesture you make." It all just popped out. "You hate me the way you hate Monty. Everything about me. My crazy background, my phantom father. My brains, my professional success, my savvy, my independence. Everything, Charlie. Even my looks. My liberal beliefs, my poor little homeless client. Even my cooking." It was all coming as a revelation. "The wonder is it took me so long to get it."

"You mean make it up."

"Well, isn't it true?" He wouldn't look at me. "Of course it is. Accept it, you'll feel better."

"Well, I see nothing's changed around *here!*" came a famil-iar voice from the doorway.

At that moment the tilt was complete. We all started slid-ing toward the edge.

"Hi," Ellie said. "Surprise!"

Bill was behind her. They both wore down jackets and carried large, half-wrapped presents, too big for any bag—a stuffed purple cat and a bright green dog. "We just thought we'd say happy birthday, and—"

Ellie stopped whatever he was going to say with a look. Bill hadn't changed much. A little jowlier, perhaps, a little thicker in the middle. His hairline had risen slightly. But he had the same cockiness, the same insinuating grin. Could it really have been three years? Look at Monty and count.

But Ellie had changed. Thinner, with the remains of a suntan, she had lost her looks. She might appear pretty from a distance, she might be called pretty—as blue-eyed blondes usu-ally are. But from up close she missed. Her features had thick-ened, their youthful tautness had loosened. Something about her mouth had changed, giving prominence to her front teeth in a way I didn't remember. It was not unattractive; it gave her face a new emphasis, a jutting determination. Her eyes, once as innocent as those of a Fra Angelico virgin, had retreated into the guarded expressionlessness of the fearful. She'd lost the look that got her in trouble. It had been her vulnerable quality that made us all want to protect her, take advantage of her, and steal some for ourselves at the same time.

"Ellie and Bill Ferguson," I breathed, as though their names would make them more real.

"Well, we're not the Fergusons, like *that*," Ellie said. "We're working things through." She took off her jacket and sat down. "I'm staying by Rita. Bill has his own place."

"Where's the birthday boy?" Bill asked, looking around, as he always had, for food and drink.

"Excuse me." Charlie plunged out of the kitchen, eyes on the floor, as though he had some urgent business in the next room.

"Well, excuse *me*," Ellie said, looking after him.

"He's got things on his mind," I said. "You know Charlie!"

"Well, I guess he's got a right. But you know, it's been three years." Her voice was low.

"Well." I clapped my hands together nervously. "How about a drink? While we wait for Monty."

Bill got out bottles and ice. "It's like old times. Remember how we used to sit around here, talking about the kid?" He cleared his throat.

"It was a ton of fun," I said.

Bill laughed. "You know, Fran, I thought about you a few times. There's something about you, the way you say things." He sat down at the kitchen table. "We had some laughs."

"*You* did," Ellie said. "None of that whole business was very funny to me. I was like a football all of you were kicking around. Every single one of you was cruel to me."

Bill looked at me and crooked his arms in the position of a violinist, mournfully drawing an imaginary bow across invisible strings. "It seems to me I've heard this song befo-o-ore," he chanted lugubriously. He wanted me to laugh, but I wouldn't, nor would Ellie.

"I'll never be in that position again. I'm taking this computer course. I'm going to be self-supporting, and so are my daughters. You can't depend on men, that much I've learned."

"Oh, don't start," Bill said. "This is supposed to be a friendly visit." Ellie gave him a clear, steely look. "And to straighten a couple of things out."

They knew.

"I forgot the way everybody drinks here," Ellie said, looking at my glass of vod. "On the Coast, people just drink white wine, or else fruit juice spritzers. We were in California, you know."

"I think I heard." Words were deserting me as the vast, ineluctable dreadfulness of the situation sank in. I felt as though I were dropping into ocean depths, weighted down, mask gone. I could only pray—if I prayed, which I didn't.

"Things are different out there. Everything isn't such a big deal. It's really weird to be back."

Then Monty appeared in the door. He had been scrubbed clean and was wearing blue Dr. Dentons. His wet hair was combed down neatly. He looked delicious. There are few things as appealing as a clean child. He was innocence, purity, something bright and fragrant growing in a field. He made me think, like Kahlil Gibran, how lucky we were to have him for a while.

Ellie and Bill both stood up. Monty looked at them briefly, with no spark of recognition. He came over and flopped on my lap, paying no attention to the scrutiny of his parents. Ellie frowned as though trying to read in a poor light, but the tiniest, subtlest smile stole across Bill's face. I knew that smile. I'd seen it in the city when we told our friends about "trying." It was the purest distillation of male proprietorship.

My heart turned to lead, sank in my body. Ellie grew pale and turned away, but Bill kept looking at Monty, no longer trying to hide his pride.

"Well, some husky little porker!" He picked Monty up and threw him up in the air, then slung him around. "What a big strong guy! Come he-e-ere—Montgomery, my lad!"

"Bill, please don't break his neck," I said. "We've gotten sort of fond of him."

"Somebody better be," Ellie said.

"Handsome kid, isn't he?" Bill said to me.

I could hardly speak. "Very."

"How's he doing in school?"

"Well, he does all right in blocks but he can't skip."

"He'll learn." He got down on the floor for more violent games, this time rolling around and wrestling and raising Monty up in the air on the soles of his feet. They looked alike. They both yelled. Their legs were even alike, from what I could tell. Ellie was staring at the floor, biting a fingernail.

Bill suddenly stood up and went toward the Jack Daniel's. "Is there any ice?" He yanked the freezer door open. "Where's the goddam ice?"

"Stop yelling," Ellie said. "I get so sick of your yelling. Charlie at least speaks like a gentleman."

"Sometimes." I watched Monty go over to the green dog, trying to pull off the paper. He struggled, then finally yanked it all off at once, falling against Ellie's leg. She pulled back as though she'd been bitten. Monty went down in a tangle of brown wrapping paper, screaming in frustration.

"Help him," Bill yelled. "Jesus, what's the matter with you?"

"Nothing." She looked at me while Bill rescued Monty. "I just don't want to be touched, that's all. I can't stand to be touched, is all. Ever since—"

Bill's face collapsed suddenly. He looked as though he was about to cry. "This is one colossal fuck-up. Damn it." He took Monty into his lap. "I mean, you don't know what to *do*. He"—jerking his shoulder toward the hall—"doesn't either. Poor bastard." Monty's head fell against his chest, exhausted, his eyes closed.

There were sounds in the hall. I sat up on the sink and held Baby, as though for protection.

"Well," Charlie said. "So you've all met." I didn't like the look on his face, or the way his jaw was working. He kept squeezing pairs of fingers, first on one hand, then the other. "How do you like him?"

"Good husky kid, Charlie." Bill was trying to cover his nervousness. "And strong."

"Dark hair," Charlie said. "Isn't that something?" Bill nodded, as though this were a perfectly sensible question. "Isn't it, Ellie?" Ellie kept staring at the floor, chewing her nail. "Ellie?"

"What?"

"I said, what do you think of Monty's hair?"

She was very pale. "It's fine, Charlie."

"Fran?"

"You're leading the witness," I said.

"Not funny. How about his eyes? Big, blue eyes. I think they're blue, anyway." He reached over to the sleeping child

239

and pushed his eyelids up roughly. "They're blue." Monty gave a little cry and turned his face to Bill's chest.

"Hey, don't do that," Bill said.

"Oh, sorry. Just wanted to compare. How about his nose?"

"Charlie," I said, "stop this stupid game."

"Like his nose, Ellie? Bill?"

"Stop it," I said again.

"No, I want to know. Look at him, Ellie. Does he look familiar?" Ellie wouldn't look at him. Charlie walked slowly toward her. "Do you think it's going to have a bump in the middle or not? And the ears. They stick out, don't they?" He was staring at her. "Yours or mine?"

I prayed she wouldn't answer, but he had her intimidated. "Mine. Mine stick out," she whispered.

"What about his hands? I can't make them out. What do you think?"

"I don't know." She glanced desperately at Bill.

"Come on, Ellie. I think you at least owe me this conversation. This is our son, isn't it?" Silence but for some odd noises from upstairs, a moaning or purring. "You must have some opinion about who he looks like. There are things about him I don't recognize—but maybe he takes after your mother or your uncle Louie. I never met them, so I don't know."

You could have cut the silence with a knife. Bill had gone rigid, as though the slightest move would reveal his resemblance to the child on his lap, though resemblances are easier seen when the face is awake and alive. I looked at Monty's face, trying to will it to look like Charlie. There was a forelock, and something about the hands . . . looked exactly like Bill Ferguson's.

Ellie was frozen. She'd turned white, then red: she had little subtlety, and no skill at this kind of verbal game.

"He looks like . . . me." She was breathing fast. "He looks like . . ."

"Who, Ellie? Not me, does he?"

She looked up at him as though hypnotized. "No."

"Then who?"

Ellie gasped, then stammered, "I didn't know."

"You didn't know?" Charlie was stunned.

"No, I thought it was all right. But Bill was there this one time, I swear I forgot. So I didn't know *then*. I wouldn't have lied. And Bill didn't say anything . . . and that's the truth, no matter what you think. So Bill raped me. What are you going to do about it?" She reached for her handbag on the floor. "You could send me to jail for being raped."

"Shut up!" Bill yelled. Monty was sprawled on one of his huge legs, nose running, breathing through his mouth. "Jesus. I can't believe all this. Jesus. Jesus." Monty woke up, his head flopping in exhaustion. Bill was banging on the table with his fist. "That's her favorite word. Rape. Everybody rapes everybody, according to her." His mouth was turned in a little upside-down U like Monty before he started yelling. "I never raped her. I swear to God, I never raped anybody."

"I was asleep. I'd call that rape." She was digging in her bag, and she came up with a fat envelope that she held out to Charlie. "Here's four thousand. You'll get the rest within a year."

"Ellie," I began.

"That won't do it," Charlie said. "Fifty thousand wouldn't do it. You've missed the entire point."

The color left Ellie's face. "We lived in a dump out there. He worked two jobs, I did too. We'll do it again till it's all paid off."

"I want you to understand, Ellie." He was twisting his fingers. "I thought, if I had nothing else, I'd have a son. My *son*." The vague sounds from upstairs became louder and more definitive: human sounds of sexual joy, a primitive song that rose and fell, rose again, higher this time. Charlie looked at me. "They're up there in our bed. *Our bed*. It's just for fun—she's on the pill. Ridiculous, isn't it? I swear to God it doesn't seem fair. I wanted a child. Millions of people get them, they don't even want them. They stick them in garbage cans . . . their own flesh and blood." His voice was breaking. "They beat them, starve them, burn them, chain them, lock them in rooms. A woman in Queens threw two of hers out the window. They found them lying on the pavement the next morning."

"You have a child, Charlie," I said.

"I have nothing. No job. No marriage. This kid to whom

I have no connection at all. At all. It's all gone out from under me." He looked around at us. "I have to get out of here," he muttered. Suddenly, he pulled open the outside door, letting in a blast of cold air.

"Don't, Charlie." I got down from the sink. Our eyes caught for just a moment.

"I don't know what else to do."

As he turned and stumbled out toward his car, Monty woke.

"Daddy. Take Monty."

"No, Monty. Charlie"—I ran out after him—"don't drive, please. Charlie, oh, please, you're drunk." He ignored me. "I'll follow him," I said, rather wildly, grabbing my coat from the hook by the door. "Watch the kid." I ran down the porch steps to the other side of the car and grabbed the handle, but he reached over and locked it. "You're wrong," I yelled. "You don't get it!"

The cold engine wouldn't start. As it finally kicked over, I stumbled across the snowy lawn to Kerner's where my own car was. I was dimly aware of a little blue figure coming out of the house, Ellie and Bill following . . . his parents following him; he belonged with them. Charlie's car sprang forward, scudded down the driveway amid billowing clouds of snow. As I pushed the accelerator, something stilled my heart. Did I hear a cry, or was it in my own mind, a requiem for the end of my marriage?

Charlie turned north on River Road. I couldn't keep up, and by the time I came up behind a car with taillights I couldn't tell if it was him. When I was able to pass I saw that it wasn't, and I didn't dare go much faster. I fumbled in my pockets for gloves; my hands hurt with the cold. I tried to read his mind: probably he was going to a bar, maybe across the bridge to a dump on Route 3.

I had to talk to him, to remind him what he did have. His wonderful though neglected brain. He was only forty-four. He was not a poor man. He could find somebody else and have a baby, men could do it till they died. Maybe somebody more like Ellie . . . but I couldn't accept it. If he wanted me back, I'd go. I'd never been able to say no to him. It was sick, it took me years to understand it, if I ever did. I'd have jumped out of a plane if he asked me to. It was not always easy to know what he wanted, and now I had to find out if he wanted me.

It was not even a matter of love with Charlie. It was the marital bond that tied us fiercely together. We knew each other's secrets. Maude Brill once told me that everything has a dark side: Christianity has Gnosticism, Judaism has kabala, and for Confucianism there was Taoism. There are things that appear to be true and we believe them, and for most purposes they are true. But there's always the heresy: that tiny hard thread that contradicts all the rest of it, and that's what's really true and operative, that's what really does the steering, like the tiny gear wheel the others run off. Underneath the surface reasons why Charlie and I had married was that miniature drama, that tiny Punch-and-Judy show that only we knew of. Underneath my bluster and confidence, I believed myself to be strange, swarthy, ill-fitting, always outside some gate that only he could open: while Charlie slowly filled with Morse, punishing me for the very qualities—adventure, mystery, danger—he'd loved in the first place.

River Road curved through a stretch of pines south of Blue Falls. I tried to follow Charlie's tracks, which were weaving and erratic, with too many skids. At the bottom of a little slope the woods ended and I saw the river and the bridge—an upstate bridge with few lights, narrow and delicate in appearance. From it there was an extraordinary view. There was periodic talk of widening it and building up the side rails for safety, thus sacrificing that moment in the middle when a driver could safely look up and catch a glimpse of the two banks—one with its tidy marina, its towns and patches of woods and winding roads, the other a blur of megalopolis bisected by Route 3, spreading borderless into the beyond.

At night it was spectacular. It could have been the marvel of this sight, they said later, that caused Charlie to look up a little too long as a car came speeding in the other direction on the way home from a party, pushing his car through the fragile barrier and sending it spinning over the edge, flying, almost floating, into the dark river below.

N·I·N·E

· 1 ·

VENICE WAS DAMP, COLD, HALF EMPTY, THE DARK FLOOD-
waters lapping up across the *molo* and into the piazza. The foun-
dations rotted further, stone split and crumbled almost as you
watched.

I wandered alone from square to square, along the churning
gray waters of the lagoon, deep into tiny streets and *fondamentas*,
over little stone bridges. Sometimes I sat in a *caffè* for hours,
bundled in my coat, or inside at some hidden table where I felt
alone, starting with surprise when the noon bells rang.

Often I thought about nothing. But sometimes my mind
ran in wild, ever-broadening circles, looking for something or
somebody to blame, or some exit along the road that would have
saved us. But there was none. In the dark waters of the lagoon
I thought I saw Charlie's face, desperate, drowning, calling to
me. When I tried to answer it disappeared.

Sometimes I sat for hours in the murky interior of San
Marco, looking at each detail slowly, intently, as though some
glinting mosaic held the answer I wanted. Sometimes I rode on
a vaporetto until it got back to its original stop, staring out at
the choppy gray waters through a curtain of streaming rain . . .
and sometimes I'd stop thinking of anything at all but the trail
of water down the glass window, the sound of the motor, the

squawk of the gulls, the sad, drowned-clown look of some frilly palazzo on the Grand Canal. Sometimes I wandered through galleries, but the brilliant blowsiness of the Venetian painters, the billowing clouds and robes and fat cupids and religious sunsets seemed grotesque. I sought out tiny precise crucifixions and flat nativities but gazed at them without thinking or extracting any meaning from them. I would have gazed with the same fixity at a comic book.

Sometimes I sat inside Florian's, wondering why elegant men hung around cafés, and why lovers had lunch together. Lovers made me sad, and slow tears ran down my face because for me, now, love was over, finished; never again would a beloved face smile, a loving hand take mine, or a familiar leg move over to mine deep in the night. Sometimes I wandered through the Giudecca, sometimes I sat in the Ghetto Campo among the tall buildings, in my mind climbing five or six flights to get to the top window where, if fate had willed it, I might have lived. I looked at the Holocaust drawings on the walls and mourned that I was nothing—not Jewish enough to burn with rage, not non-Jewish enough to please Charlie Morse, not anything enough to reproduce.

Sometimes, all I did was sleep until Lulu or Giulia brought me coffee or wine. I felt as though every limb was made of lead, heavy, immovable, fixed. I'd lie on my back and look at the ceiling with its faded chipped cupids and gauzy shepherdesses and streaks of dampness. I knew this ceiling well, and usually I'd slept under it with Charlie, and oh, with Charlie the night I saw the girl in the square nursing her baby, the girl who started everything . . . for I was always looking for scapegoats. We'd made such passionate love that night with nothing between us! Sometimes I just sat by the window and looked dully out at the activity in the canal below, the daily jam of boats delivering laundry or bread or flowers or merchandise to the stores, and flapping laundry, shouts, shutters banging, dogs barking, television sounds, voices from directly across where two women were cooking together, putting cakes on the windowsill to cool. Sometimes Lulu's cat sat in my lap, stone-still for minutes or hours.

In the night I'd wake up and see, for the hundredth time,

that small blue figure running through the snow after his daddy. The picture ran over and over, a defective film I couldn't turn off. I heard his cry and felt the coldness in my heart. Then I'd be in my car driving down the snowy road, watching Charlie turn onto the bridge. The scene was as clear in my mind as the night had been, but if asked, I would have said that Charlie made it safely across the bridge—for some merciful amnesia had blanked out what I must have seen, what I knew had happened.

It had all been so fast, Bill said. One minute the kid was in the kitchen; the next he'd jumped down and chased after Charlie outside. I was running toward my own car. Charlie couldn't have seen Monty as he gunned his motor, the wheels spinning a few times before they caught, sending up snow and dirt and gravel and . . . one big, mean rock. Monty screamed; his baby hands covered his face. Bill had pulled them away, to see underneath. The two cars were skidding up the street; Charlie and I were not looking back. Bill and Ellie took him to the emergency room of North County Hospital, where they did their best. They enucleated his eye. It was a freak accident; it happened one time in a million.

("And on December twentieth," Lulu said, "there are often pairs of tragedies, one worse than the other, so you don't know which to mourn—a further torture." On the night of Waldo's death, her uncle James, whom Lulu had loved very much, had been crushed by a piece of masonry falling off a building in London.)

I mourned Charlie. But as the days went by, I realized that I was mourning less the man himself, who, after all, had been a source of unhappiness, than the way I'd felt being married to him. I found myself drifting back ten, twenty, or thirty years, because whatever I had been before I knew him, I would return to.

The mortification I had carried around all my life came back and flowed around me. I was a child again, bold and sassy on the surface but frightened and envious underneath. Our frequent moves and new schools, along with Waldo's tutelage, had taught me social skills early but rattled the underpinnings of security. I was a good fake. I had been taught to express myself

249

clearly, an art better developed in Europe, as was the self-discipline I'd been brought up with.

But if Waldo had trained my mind, he'd failed to educate my heart. I was a pushy, selfish kid. I had few friends, usually ending up with little draggle-tailed unimportant ones who, for their own peculiar reasons, wanted to be ordered around. I'd been unkind and cruel. I'd insulted one about her looks in front of the whole class, I'd reported another's smoking and almost got her kicked out of Miss Comfitt's . . . and more came to mind. I had not been, I thought bleakly, a very nice person. All the time I tried—nobody ever knew how hard—to impress those lucky girls who seemed to have everything: the dates, the love of their classmates and respect of their teachers, and a life in some little town that included Fourth of July picnics and Sunday dinners after church. I thought if you were surrounded by symbols of security, if you lived in a Norman Rockwell world, you were automatically a good person.

Every few days Kerner called.

"When are you coming back?"

"I don't know, Adam. I haven't decided."

"Well, I miss you." I only smiled sadly. "Things are falling apart here, Fran. Somebody vandalized the windmill. Red and blue paint, those big bubble letters, like in the city."

"Oh, that's horrible."

"And it won't come off. Now I'm getting flak from Phil Bollinger again because it's an 'eyesore.' "

It all seemed so far away. "He won't dare do anything."

"Oh, and Ellie's back in her old apartment, and her parents came and moved in to take care of Monty while she works and goes to school."

"It sounds tough." I had told Ellie I would pay all Monty's medical expenses, the least I could do. "How's the kid?"

"Not so good. He's not pulling out of it."

"Just takes time. Now he's with his parents," I said, rather briskly. "He's tough."

"Well. I hope so. Come back soon."

I hung up. It was all like another world, unreal, out of focus and small of scale: the United States. Here I walked among monuments, past ancient churches and palaces that expanded the mind's dimensions. Here one perceived mankind rather than man. The spirit rose and stretched. There was consolation in knowing that I was not alone, that other women had lost loves and husbands and we were together in a great tidal wave of bereavement. Everyone lost, everyone suffered, only the lucky ones realized it—and I was lucky to have loved at all.

I paid little attention to Lulu's life. She gave up asking me to accompany her as she paid her calls, did her volunteer work at the hospital, or shopped. She seemed to be part of a warm community of friends, buzzing on the phone in the morning, paying calls and meeting people at church, for Lulu was a social Catholic. I envied her strength and the time she had put in since Waldo's death to be able to live alone, which I had now to learn to do. And I realized that she was no longer a sad widow or desperate flirt and hadn't been for years. She was a contented person with a busy life. Had she always been? Had I made up the other Lulu? When she was young, she had seemed never to be around. But now she was here when I needed her.

I could hardly believe how free I was. I no longer had to think about Charlie but could do as I pleased. I could travel. I could even search for my father . . . replace the fantasies with a real person. I could live anywhere I wanted: Manhattan, LA, DC, Paris, London. I could live in a tiny cabin on a mountain-top or a grass hut on some tropical beach, just Baby and me. . . . I could stay right where I was, for the time being anyway.

One morning at breakfast I heard myself saying, "Maybe I'll live here with you for a while, Lulu."

She looked up from her newspaper. "You're welcome to, if that's what you want to do, Francesca."

"I have to get everything straightened out, the estate and the house, and check out Monty. Then I'd pack up and come back."

She poured us each more coffee. "I'd be glad to have you. The room is yours if you want it."

She had not jumped for joy at my suggestion. "If I did, of course, I'd like to contribute," I went on, my voice rising a little. "I'm well off financially, and I don't want you to ever have to worry about money. I might put some money into the palazzo. You know, fix it up a little."

"I don't worry about money." She looked at me thoughtfully for a minute. "Would you like living here?"

"How could anybody not?"

"Some don't." She stood up, pulling her robe around her. "I have to get going. Are you sure you won't come along tonight?"

It was Carnevale, the night of parties, fireworks, and off-the-record trysts, the anything-goes night. I'd begged off as usual.

"I'm just not up to all that."

"What is 'all that,' Francesca?"

"Well, the wild celebrating. It would be hard tonight not to have a mate. But I'll be fine. I'm lots better, in fact. Venice is curative, it's the ancient dreamlike quality; nothing seems quite real." Lulu folded the paper, looking down. "Rivertown is so real, so full of reminders. I'd even thought of asking you to come and stay with me, if you wanted." Somehow I felt about five years old, which, these days, happened from time to time.

"A great many things to think about and discuss."

"Well, I thought . . . we've hung out together before, Lulu. We could do it again."

Don't leave me, Mommy.

She smiled. "It's an idea, certainly." She picked up the cat and started out. "Much to be continued, dear. There are many considerations." She crossed the hall, *clop clop clop*, and went up the stairs—glancing at herself in the hall mirror as she did so.

I watched through the window as she went off in a black domino and a mask of brilliant yellow, like a sun. The black material ruffled behind her as she rowed, fluttering in the early evening breeze. She could have tried a little harder to persuade me to go. Not that I would have changed my mind, I couldn't face Cipi and Beppi and Betty and the rest, babbling and singing and gossiping . . . and since Charlie's death I hadn't been able to drink.

At around nine I got hungry. Lulu had left an extra domino in case I changed my mind, and I put it on, with a purple silken mask, and went out into the crowded streets. The sky was full of bright red and green flowers, blooming, exploding, shedding their petals in gaudy showers: white rockets shooting up into the black sky, cold blue jewels, mushrooms that boiled, puffed like soufflés, and suffused. The weather was mild, the streets full of black dominos that billowed and fluttered, topped with bird faces, cat faces, masks with feathers and lace and glitter, masks on little wands like lorgnettes. I sat in a tiny pizzeria watching it all, the little dramas, the secret meetings, the games and temptations and betrayals and mysteries.

As I walked back toward home through a tiny street, a broad-chested man in a purple mask loomed up in front of me. He took me in his arms, murmuring endearments. *"Oh, Gina, mia Gina,"* he said. *"Mia cara."* For a moment I gave in and let the strange lips crush against mine and the unknown body press against me. His arms were strong and knowing. I demurely let myself be pulled farther back into his secret niche, an old doorway . . . but then he knew and gave a surprised laugh. *Scusi, scusi! Sbaglio!* I laughed, he laughed . . . then stood staring past me at the real Gina, who had just arrived. She was about my size, and her mask was exactly like mine. I left him saying, again, *"Gina, mia cara."* I fled, burning with envy.

I was still amused the next morning. How Lulu would laugh! But she wasn't up, and it was almost eleven. Then down the stairs came a rather short bald man with a mustache, wearing a bathrobe.

"Hugh Randall—British. You must be Francesca. I'm so awfully pleased. Delighted." He shook my hand firmly while I tried to figure out who he was. "Pity we have to meet under such unfortunate circumstances, the recent tragedy, simply awful, I'm so dreadfully sorry. Went through something of the sort myself."

He polished his glasses on a large clean handkerchief while I made polite sounds. The third bedroom was a wreck; how could Lulu put anybody in it? Getting it in order, in fact, would be one of my projects—after the new kitchen.

As we stood there, Lulu appeared on the stairs, smiling as though she were still wearing the yellow mask. Hugh smiled back . . . and I got it. He hadn't been anywhere near the third bedroom. Lulu walked slowly, magnificently down the stairs. Had we met? Yes, yes . . . actually Hugh was sorry to just sort of run into me like this the first time, so to speak; could have been a bit more ceremonious, wot? Ooooh, the party was lovely, Francesca, everybody asked about you. Everybody's concerned . . . and do I need coffee, badly! I see the sun coming out, anybody interested in a long walk after breakfast?

"Excuse me." I got up slowly, walked out of the room, and went upstairs, passing Lulu without looking at her. I felt her smile fade as I went up and into my room, slamming the door behind me.

Lulu came in. I had not been polite, she said. I told her I didn't like surprises or secrets. She replied that she had dropped hints, she had invited me along to places—such as the party the previous night—where I would have met him casually. But I was so busy being *pathetico* I was blind and deaf to everything. I told her I was not in condition to pick up all the little hints and winks and nudges that she and her friends used for communication. Their lives were all games and innuendos. Why hadn't she told me clearly and distinctly? Shout it in my face if necessary! How could she let me find out like this, when Charlie was hardly cold in the ground?

"Francesca, I understand that you are upset. But that doesn't require me to sacrifice my happiness. Now stop behaving like this."

It was ridiculous: I was after all a middle-aged woman. Hugh brought back memories of Harry Burns, who had moved into our Murray Hill apartment for a while and then disappeared with Lulu's jewelry and a few "bearer bonds" he was going to "reconvert" for her. Harry had taken me to the movies and given me a kitten. He, Lulu, and I had gone skating at Rockefeller Center; he had come over and cooked spaghetti and meatballs. He and Lulu had danced to records while I watched: first very fancy sambas and tangos, then a slow, graceful fox trot . . . when they sent me off to bed. I didn't care if he was a thief.

Hugh was just as determined to win me over, but now I put up more of a fight, He gave us a tour of his antique store and took us to Torcello and to dinner at his favorite *ristorante*, carrying most of the conversation with admirable cheerfulness and the same stubborn British determination that had put jewels in Victoria's crown. It was tough going, for I sat silent in choked-down jealousy and disappointment, and Lulu's mouth was tight with the fear that I would behave badly and humiliate her. But he was unusually patient. It was almost worse that he was a good man and very attached to my mother, unlikely to wander off next week and find somebody else. Nor did he seem to be gay. What was the matter with him? Could it be—nothing?

When I told him I was considering moving into the palazzo for a while, he beamed and said it was a ripping idea . . . while Lulu looked past my head at something going on in the square. When I mentioned my idea of modernizing the kitchen, he listened politely and looked inquiringly at Lulu, who said, almost despairingly, that it suited Giulia well enough, though probably the fridge should be replaced . . . and as for new covers on the furniture, well, Marcello would just claw them up anyway.

"Fran, this is Beulah Markowitz."

"Beulah! What's the matter?"

"*No*-thing! You're like my mother, who gets palpitations every time the phone rings."

"Well, I'm not in the next town."

"We miss you, Fran. Your desk is so empty . . . there are lost clients wandering around the hall."

"Really?"

"No, not really. Or just one or two. The little pickaninny with the pigtails."

"Jesus, Beulah. 'Pickaninny.' The language of hate."

"I had to tell him about the Van Willem; he almost cried."

The Van Willem, she told me, was to be an "upscale mall" with natural-food lunchroom, quilt-and-dried-flower shop, and branches of Ann Taylor and Merrill Lynch. And there was a whole new uproar going on about the admission of blacks to Rivertown General Hospital in the wake of the closing of North County. She could pretty well guess my feelings on the issue, since I was always for the underdog.

"It has nothing to do with underdogs, Beulah. Black people have as much right to medical care as we do."

"Oh, I know, I know, but you know how it is. I mean, I'm not like that, Fran, you know that. If a *nice* black family moved

255

in next to me, I'd never object. It's just that, you know, there's a certain type, and in a hospital . . ."

Life was returning to my desiccated veins. "Beulah, you are full of shit."

"Well, Fran, I didn't phone all the way to Venice to be insulted."

Then I got a letter from Johanna. Most of it was about her renewed happiness with Sheldon (with more detail than I wanted to know) but she also mentioned, in passing, that a group of mothers had banded together to take *Madame Bovary* out of the school library because Emma's death was unnecessarily violent, and the kids might get the idea of taking arsenic. And *Wuthering Heights* because Heathcliff was a "poor role model."

When I was fourteen, I had followed Emma Bovary to the chemist's, seen her frantic hands grasp the arsenic and stuff it awkwardly into her mouth. My knuckles had been white; tears hung in my eyes at her horrible death, the stupid grief of the husband, the sure doom of the child. And Heathcliff? He had moved me to my very depths, he had taught me passion. Like Cathy, I *was* Heathcliff . . . I *was*! A waif, a foundling, a mystery child. I would fight for him, I would make sure he was always on the shelf!

The truth was, Lulu's life was no longer for me . . . if it ever had been. Once Cipi, Beppi, and the rest had seemed charming, worldly, sophisticated beyond measure. They had taught me many things, and for this I was grateful. But I'd changed. Now they seemed superficial, their concerns narrow and provincial. While the world reeled under major upheavals, while populations starved, while man still failed to understand man, they thought only of their own amusement, or so it appeared. Now I barely smiled at Cipi's old jokes and wondered how Lulu, giggling happily with Hugh by her side, had stayed so young while I'd gotten so old. Perhaps I would always be the stranger in the corner: the dark Francesca, the dark Lilith, Laurentian's daughter.

Lulu took me to the vaporetto station. It was a Sunday morning and the shutters were just opening; a few voices were beginning to echo from inside houses. The clean clothes on the lines snapped in the breeze. I rowed while Lulu sat in the back of the boat.

"Fran, I wanted to talk to you without Hugh."

"No, you don't have to. I think he's super."

"Oh, not that, Fran. It's about the curse, Maude phoned me last night. It's played itself out; the baby's life is safe."

"Thank God," I said solemnly.

"Hugh thinks it's all nonsense, and that it was all just a coincidence." She scratched her nose. "I'm just not sure. I'm still hanging on the edge of the spirit world."

I turned and smiled at her. She wore a brilliant yellow shirt, and her hair was in a braid. "So, why not hang? You have the advantage of seeing farther."

She said thoughtfully, "You know, Fran, I think you're right. You just have to twist your mind a little."

· 2 ·

ONCE, WHEN CHARLIE HAD EXPRESSED PUZZLEMENT OVER MY fondness for Baby, Lulu had said, "She always picked the smallest, saddest one of the litter. All her pets had something wrong with them."

Now it was just Baby and me. I invited him to spread out—offered him his own bedroom. I put his box and bed in Monty's room, mostly cleared of toys and possessions. Bit by bit he managed to move them back to where they were before. I heard heart-stopping thumps during the night, and it was just Baby's bed going down the stairs. I grabbed the cat box just before that went too. Sometimes he slept on the foot of my bed, sometimes not. Sometimes he was there when I reached out during the night, looking for Charlie—and sometimes I found nothing but cool flat sheets.

I was dreadfully lonely. Lulu was in love. Sheldon was back with Johanna . . . even the Fergusons were considering reuniting. Sometimes Lucinda's car was parked next door. I began having crying jags. It wasn't fair. It wasn't right. I'd said before that there was no justice but never really believed it till now. I had done what Charlie wanted: accepted Ellie's pregnancy, was good to her, attended her *accouchement*. To protect Charlie's feelings I had kept secret her ridiculous letters describing her pathological affair with the unspeakable Sy, from which my mother had barely recovered. I had given up the work I loved and slaved for Blazer, Blackjar & Monument so Charlie could be a mother to his son. Still his car had gone flying off the bridge.

"With nobody to blame for your misery," said Dr. Bread, "now you must look to yourself."

Breadstein. McBread. Breadstick. Dread Bread. Beulah Markowitz had heard of him somewhere. I picked him out of a list because he was close to home, and I liked his office. He was good at torture. I paid him to torture me.

"You are not so good. You hid her letters hoping Charlie would never find the child. Yes?"

"No."

"You were attracted to your neighbor. You still are."

"No. Well, so what?"

"So nothing, Fran. But do not tell me you are a good girl because you are not. No better, no worse than most."

More tears. "I'm so sick of crying."

"Then stop feeling sorry for yourself."

This is not, I've since learned, very good psychiatric method. But Bread is no fancy shrink from a prestigious teaching hospital. He is a caricature, a maverick. Not only that but he sleeps in his office: the Freudian couch is a convertible.

"And the child. What about the child?"

A cold hand reached up and clutched my heart. "He's with his parents."

"Have you seen him?"

"Of course," I lied.

"You waste our time," Bread said, "and your money."

Kerner was disgusted with me because I was afraid to see Monty; that's why Lucinda was there. Bread said I saw everything in terms of rewards and punishments. Well, this was what I'd turned back into, the child I was before I knew Charlie. And he said I wasn't a true feminist because, career or no career, big mouth or not, I thought only in terms of pleasing men. But never mind my therapy. Who cares? The world is deathly tired of what happens on the analytic couch, all the sad stories are remarkably similar . . . but after a while I stopped crying.

One afternoon Adam lured me into his car—not difficult to do—closed the door, and started off. I protested that it was too soon, he must stop sending all the roses, and I insisted on returning the jewelry. Though I absolutely refused to go to the ball, a discreet dinner would not be taken amiss.

"Lord, you love to talk," he said. Then I saw that we were crossing the bridge.

"This isn't fair," I cried. "I would have gone."

"I thought you might need a little help. Some company." He put his hand on mine. "It's hard. You don't have to go if you don't want to, Fran."

The plastic plants in the lobby were just as dusty, and the orange halls still smelled of stale cigarettes and cooked cauliflower. But now the apartment was rigidly neat, and a strong smell of pine disinfectant replaced the smells of barbecued ribs and nail polish remover that I remembered.

There was a strong resemblance between Ellie and her mother. But what had been gentle in Ellie was abrasive in the mother, and Ellie's rather endearing, infuriating vagueness was congealed in Mrs. Marvin's solid irrationality. Her red lips were pursed, her blond hair pulled tightly back under a black plastic hair band, her eyes hostile. She wore red slacks and high heels, and she mentioned a time-share in Florida that was going to waste because of "all this." Mr. Marvin was watching television.

I knew it was going to be hard, that's why I'd avoided coming. But it was worse than I had ever dreamed. All the starch had gone out of him. He sat in his room, listlessly playing with some plastic toys. His eye was bandaged, and when we first came in he turned his head from time to time to look at a soundless TV that was turned on, presumably to keep him amused. His clothes and sneakers were too new and creased, and he had never been so clean in his life. His hair was wet and combed down.

When I spoke his name his head whipped around, he stared

at me, squinting the good eye and peering at me. His mouth was open. Then he mouthed the word: *Fan*. But no sound came out.

"Monty, you little bum." I went over and sat next to him. I put my arms around him and hugged him, pulling down the neck of his shirt in back, from habit, to take a look. The red marks were gone. He didn't have a fever or anything, but I sure didn't like the looks of him. "You know, I've missed you. What are you doing, hanging out over here?"

Kerner sat down on the other side, with a grunt. "If you'd stand up, the grownups wouldn't have to crawl around the floor to talk to you. Hey, Monty?" But Monty kept looking at me.

"So. Aren't I even going to get a hello?" I looked at Kerner. "What's the matter with him?"

"He doesn't talk."

I felt as though I'd turned inside out. "What?"

"That's right."

"Do you mean since . . ."

"You got it."

Oh, God. "Monty." I grabbed him by the shoulders. "Listen, it's me. Say my name." He only stared. "You know Fan. Remember how we used to play ball? And how I gave you baths . . . remember Baby the cat, disgusting old Baby? And Auntie Johanna?" Some auntie. "You know what, you can come and visit me, okay? We'll do all sorts of silly things." Again his mouth made that soundless *Fan*. "I'll make you a fried-egg sandwich, just the way you like. I'll read *The Little Engine That Could*. Okay, Monty? Okay?" I ended up shaking him, till Adam took my hands and moved them away.

Out in the hall I turned on Mrs. Marvin.

"Don't you ever take him out? Why isn't he at Mother Bumpy's?"

"You have a nerve, Mrs. Morse." Mrs. Marvin's cold green eyes hardened. "I raised two children, I don't need any advice from you. All he needs is to get away from all these terrible memories, back to Wilmington where he can lead a normal life."

"Wilmington. Wilmington? What do you mean?" I stared at Kerner, who shrugged.

"I've heard it's a possibility."

"Well, it's more than that, Dr. Kerner. Ellie can't manage this way, with two jobs and her school, and the two girls. My husband and I gave up our lives, but we can't stay here forever. This child needs stability."

"Stability. In Wilmington? You'll break his heart; he'll never say another word." My voice was getting louder. "If you raised two children, where were you when Ellie needed you?"

"I think I've heard enough from you. The nerve. The things I've heard about your household, you and your late husband—if you'll allow me. The drinking, the loose sex. What was going on the night the child was injured was inexcusable, you didn't deserve to be parents. And the beatings—that's why the child won't talk."

Around then, Kerner started shoving me toward the door. The worst of it was she was right. As we started to leave, me half in tears, Monty came running out of the bedroom, flung himself around my leg like a car boot, and wouldn't let go. It took ten dreadful, unforgettable minutes to get him off, and I left with a memory neither he nor I will ever forget: me turning my back and leaving while he screamed in Mrs. Marvin's grip.

"Fan! Fan! I want Fan!"

In the elevator, when I was as unguarded and inside out as a milkweed pod, Kerner put his arms around me and held me very tightly, then kissed me all the way down to the first floor. We immediately pretended that it was unimportant . . . just some basal response to the scene that had just taken place, a coming together to compensate for that terrible tearing apart . . . instead of the urgently important thing it was.

After that I didn't have a chance. God knows I protested. I kept telling Adam I'd be a terrible mother. Look at me: I was obsessed with my work, I was compulsively neat and clean, I was impatient, authoritarian, and perfectionistic. I was finding in my therapy that I was infantile and unconsciously hostile to men, which I would inevitably take out on a male child . . . and I'd be back on the vod within a week. Kerner didn't say much. There was nothing to say. I was arguing with myself. Then Ellie phoned me a couple of days after my visit to say that

Monty had virtually stopped eating. He kept asking for me. In fact I was all he talked about.

"I don't know, Fran. It's crazy. I didn't know he was so attached to you."

"Neither did I." But I know now that Monty picked me out a long time ago, maybe when Charlie began to hate him. Kids are uncanny in their perceptions: he knew I couldn't resist stray cats or homeless waifs with pigtails. I didn't hold out long. The kid was on a hunger strike. And with Monty there is no compromise.

For the first few days he was back he wouldn't let me put him down, making Baby uncharacteristically jealous. Since my arms didn't have the strength of those of a full-time mother, I could barely lift him. It was like being crippled. My good neighbors helped feed us—I couldn't have done it without Adam. Monty slept wedged against me as though he were part of my body. (And soon Adam too.) When he finally allowed me to put him down, he wouldn't let me out of his sight. He was suspicious of Angelina when she returned. Hadn't she left him once? Going back to work was painful, but I explained that I had battles to fight to make the world better for both of us.

He saw my face the first time I got a good look at his eye socket and started to cry, clinging to me harder. It was a fearsome sight. The eyes are entrances to the mind; but within this cavity there was no magic light, no dancing angels or any dark tunnel leading deep into the soul, only a dark cave of glistening pink flesh. And it was terrible when he told me that Daddy had taken his eye but was going to return it for Christmas—a desperate fiction of Mrs. Marvin's.

"He's not, Monty. He's gone."

"No. Gramma promised!"

"Gramma was wrong. I'm sorry, pal. No eye—but we'll get you a nice glass one."

He covered it with his hands as he had done that terrible night.

"Fan, I want to see on both sides."

I took him in my arms. "I'll help you, Monty. I'll do my damnedest."